the one who changed me

usa today bestselling author
aj alexander

dedication

*To Aliza, Angelina, Ann, Sade, Dylan, Posey, Xio, Leslie,
Preslaysa*

*For reminding me to believe in myself and to always write
stories from my heart.*

one
marissa

My eyes roam around the dimly lit bar as I try not to think of my latest conversation with my mother about why I couldn't be more like my sister, Sutton. Otherwise known as the perfect child.

Don't get me wrong, I love my sister, but there's just something about being compared to her daily that grates on my nerves. You'd think after all this time, my parents, particularly my mother, would stop constantly comparing us to each other, but apparently, I'm not that lucky. In my mother's eyes, Sutton does no wrong—well, unless she hasn't called her for a few weeks, or she's reminded that she hasn't stepped foot in our childhood home once since leaving five years ago.

I know what you're thinking, but I don't hate my sister. We used to be thick as thieves, before she left me and everyone else in Magnolia in her rearview mirror. The moment she graduated high school, she hightailed it out of town and hasn't come back once. It's hard to maintain a relationship with someone who would rather forget you existed than come home to visit. Unlike me, who went to college and came right back home.

No, I wasn't sucking up for brownie points. I love Magnolia. Sure, I left for college, but it was always my plan to come back to my hometown. I have a job I love, and I'm saving up to buy a beautiful two-story farmhouse with a welcoming, oversized front porch on the other side of town from my parents. I've been dreaming about buying and raising a family in that house since I was in my teens. I'd planned on owning it by now, and maybe also having a few kids, but then life happened. Even though things haven't turned out the way I planned, I'm determined to own that house. It's my dream house to raise a family whenever I choose to have one. Which, according to my mother, better be soon or my womb is going to shrivel up like a raisin. Yeah, moms exaggerate these things when they have grandbaby fever.

My mom doesn't seem to care that I'm happy and successful. Instead, she's constantly reminding me what Sutton has that I don't. The biggest difference between the two of us is that she has an insanely rich tool bag of a perfect fiancé. Ever since Sutton announced her engagement to Maxwell, never Max, it's all my parents want to talk about. Hell, I can't even get away from talking about her perfect life at work because my boss is obsessed with her, but that's a whole different issue.

And that's why I find myself sitting in a bar in downtown Chattanooga on this fine Friday evening. This isn't the closest city to Magnolia, but I don't want to take the chance of running into anyone I know because I doubt I'd make the best company. Right now, all I want is to be left alone to enjoy my couple of shots and then head over to my room at the hotel a few blocks down the road.

I've made it a rule since my epically public breakup in high school that I keep all my escapades as far away from Magnolia as possible. The last thing anyone wants is to run into one of their one-night stands in the middle of the grocery store, right?

"Is this seat taken?"

The corners of my mouth pull up into a sultry smile as I turn toward the owner of the voice, my eyes wandering down his body. The man is tall, just how I like them, with dark hair in a stylish cut. His muscular frame fills out his tightly fitted white T-shirt tucked into a pair of dark-colored jeans, and a leather jacket hangs open on his shoulders, giving me the perfect view of his washboard abs.

"Sure, but only if you buy me a drink," I respond, throwing back the shot I've been nursing for the last few minutes.

"Done," he responds with a smile before placing a black motorcycle helmet on the bar between us and taking a seat. "Can I get a scotch on the rocks and another shot for..." His voice trails off, his eyes locking with mine.

"Marissa," I tell him with an easy grin, appreciating the fine specimen of a man standing in front of me. "And you are?"

"Finn," he says with his unusually thick country twang, sending a shiver of need down my spine.

Shit. That country twang gets me every time, making me turn into a puddle of girlish goo on the floor.

"So, what brings a lady like you to a place like this?"

I barely resist the urge to roll my eyes. I've heard almost every pickup line there is, but this one is always a turnoff for me. There's just something about it that screams, *Red flag. Stay away.* Sending any hopes of us moving past anything more than a few drinks. Too bad. He was definitely my type, but you win some and you lose some, I guess.

Don't judge me. A woman has needs just like men do, and any woman that tells you that anything is better than the genuine article is lying. There's nothing wrong with having consensual sex with a hot guy you meet in a bar. One-night stands are the best. No one gets hurt that way. We both can scratch an itch before returning to our lives.

"Good booze and great music. What more could a lady ask for?" I respond, plastering a fake smile on my face, hoping that he gets the hint.

That isn't a lie, but it's also not the complete truth either. There's only one reason I drive hours to Chattanooga at least once a month to enjoy watered-down drinks: anonymity. Living in a small town kind of puts a damper on that. Everyone knows everything about you, especially if you grew up there. Couple that with the fact that I'm the chief deputy for the Magnolia County Sheriff's Department, and everyone in town knows me on sight. It makes it almost impossible to enjoy a night out on the town. This could have been any bar with any band playing popular nineties music and it would be the best place in the world. Mainly because it was as far away from Magnolia as I can get while still having to work the next day.

Magnolia is the type of town that everyone wants to live in. The quaint, small mountain town that you read about in romance novels or see come to life in Hallmark movies, but if you've lived there your entire life, you'd need a break now and then. Taking the two-hour-and-some-change drive to a major city every couple of weeks protects my sanity. Sometimes I can even be persuaded to find someone to spend some time with in the nearby hotel.

When I said there was only one reason for driving hours to have a drink, I lied. There's another, even more important, reason why getting out of Magnolia is a good idea. You know the saying *don't shit where you eat*? I take that to heart. I take any and all activities with the opposite sex to another town, far away from any prying eyes.

"Are you from around here?" He leans in closer; the scent of motor oil and leather fills my nostrils as I breathe in.

"No. Just passing through," I respond as the bartender places our drinks in front of us. I tilt my head back, downing my shot, relishing in the burning taste of tequila as it slides down my throat. Finn takes a sip of his drink, as well, before turning to me with a smirk.

"I don't believe you," he says, his eyes locked on mine.

I raise an eyebrow, intrigued. "Oh, really? And why is that?"

"Because you look like you have a story to tell. And not just any story, a juicy one. Come on, I can tell you're itching to tell someone. Why not tell me?" He leans in even closer, his breath hot against my skin as he speaks.

I can feel my pulse quickening as his words wash over me. He's right, I do have a story. It's literally on the tip of my tongue.

For some reason, I feel the need to spill my deepest, darkest secrets to a perfect stranger. I can see how it is going to play out, the images running through my mind. I'll tell him about how my parents want me to be just like my older sister. She has a great job, a house, and a fiancé that supposedly loves her more than life itself. And me, I'm jealous. I had that at one time. I was someone's everything, and then it went up in a puff of smoke.

Campbell Thomas was my first boyfriend, first love, first everything. We were inseparable. Spending nights under the stars talking about our future together: marriage, kids, the whole nine yards. Neither one of us had a care in the world, or so I believed. When he told me he'd been accepted to Tennessee State in Nashville, I thought everything was perfect. We'd head off to college together, graduate, move back home to Magnolia, and then finally start the family we'd talked about. I was with the boy I loved, and who I thought loved me desperately. What could go wrong?

A lot, apparently. I spent most of my junior year working odd jobs around town, trying to save up enough money for us to start our life together when we went away to college. But because of all the work I'd been doing, we had less and less time to spend together. As the school year ended, he became distant, not returning phone calls and canceling dates at the last minute. I thought he was planning on asking me to marry him—hell, everyone did. How the hell could I have been so wrong?

Instead of getting down on one knee and asking me to marry him, he broke up with me. He said we wanted different things out of life and that it'd be best to make a clean break now before it was too late. I was heartbroken, but what could I do? If he didn't want to be with me, there wasn't anything I could do about it. However, that was only the start.

On the first day of senior year, I was there, front and center, when Campbell dropped to one knee and proposed to Emmeline Harris. Everyone was shocked, none more so than me. Not only had my boyfriend of three years broken up with me, but he was now down on one knee, asking someone else to spend the rest of their life with him. It seems Emmeline and Campbell were soulmates. A fact they figured out over the summer while I was working on gluing the pieces of my broken heart back together.

My heart shattered to pieces that day. I believed that what we had meant something to him, but obviously, I was wrong. To make matters worse, he tried to convince me it just happened and had nothing to do with the reason he broke up with me. I wanted the white picket fence and a small-town life, the life we both grew up having, but he didn't. He wanted to get as far away from Magnolia as he could, unlike me. And it was those feelings and the need to escape that brought him and Emmeline closer together.

He told me she was there for him in a way I never could be. She was able to sympathize with his feelings of wanting to get as far away from Magnolia as he could and never come back. One thing led to another, and the feelings between them blossomed into something more, and he broke up with me. He promised he never cheated on me, and I believe him. But that doesn't negate the fact that Emmeline was having his baby. That's right, not only did he not waste any time jumping into bed with someone else, but he knocked her up almost immediately. When their parents found out, his dad practically forced him to propose to her, leaving me to deal with the fallout.

That was the day I decided I was done with relationships. I had pinned all my hopes and dreams on that relationship, and when it was over, I was left with nothing. It took me months to bring myself up out of the pit of despair I was in, but when I did, I knew I was stronger for having done it. I promised myself that no one person would have that much control over my happiness ever again. I knew then that I'd never allow myself to be so wrapped up in another person again. I had goals in life that I wanted to accomplish, and I refused to let anyone stand in the way of achieving them.

I went to Tennessee State and got my degree in criminal justice before coming back to Magnolia and joining the sheriff's department. It wasn't exactly how I planned to come back to my hometown, but I still had plans to live out my dreams. The plan just changed a little.

But that's not really what he was asking. This stranger doesn't want to know every thought and feeling I've ever had leading me to this moment with him in a bar. What he wants is in my pants, and I'm mostly okay with that. Most people only know the parts of me I allow them to see, never letting more than a few people close enough where they could hurt me. But the way this man is looking at me is as if he can see into my soul makes me want to spill everything, but I have a feeling that has more to do with the multiple shots of tequila I've had since getting here and not some cosmic connection between the two of us.

"Too bad you'll never find out," I whisper before placing my glass on the bar and signaling the bartender for another one.

His eyes widen in surprise, probably shocked by my response, before twinkling with mischief. "Oh, and here I thought you were going to make this easy."

"Anything worth having in life is never easy."

I can feel the tension crackling between us as I smile back at him. Alarm bells ring in my ears, warning me to run in the opposite direction, but I can't ignore the magnetic pull I feel toward him. He's dangerous for my heart. I can feel it in my soul. There's something about this man that has my mind screaming for me to run in the opposite direction, but my heart is screaming for me to stay. I just wish I knew which one was right.

I try to maintain my composure, but my heart is pounding in my chest and my palms are getting sweaty. I take a sip of my drink, hoping to calm my nerves.

He notices my unease and chuckles. "Indeed, it isn't," he says, his voice low and husky. "Good thing I'm always up for a challenge."

The moment the words leave his mouth, my eyes zero in on his pants, my cheeks heating instantly.

"If you wanted to know what I was packing, all you had to do was ask."

"Does this always work for you with the ladies?" I question, tilting my head to the side, trying to make sense of the man sitting in front of me.

At first, I had every intention of writing him off as just some guy, but now I'm intrigued. The only problem is, I'm not sure if that's a good thing or a bad thing.

"*Ladies* would imply multiple women. Right now, the only one I have eyes for is you."

Men like this are a dime a dozen. Gorgeous and exuding confidence, focused on getting between a girl's legs and nothing more. I could give him what he wants. It would be so easy to pay my tab and walk out the door with him to have a night of wild passion. But the little voice in the back of my head is telling me this man is dangerous. He doesn't look like a criminal or that he could even hurt a fly, but my senses are telling me to run in the other direction. Too bad I'm not really listening.

"You can't be fucking serious right now." I can't help but smile at his words and the confidence with which he's trying so desperately to keep my attention.

"Ah, there it is…" he whispers, a downright illegal smile spreading across his face.

I can't help but feel a flutter in my chest at the sight of his smile. It's dangerous how easily he can pull me in with just a few words and a flash of those pearly whites. But I'm not one to back down from a challenge, especially when it comes to men like him.

"There's what?" I ask, trying to keep my voice level despite the growing heat in my body.

He leans in closer, his eyes locking on mine. "A smile. I've been trying to get a real one out of you since I sat down."

"And why is that?"

"Because before I sat down, you looked like you had the weight of the world resting on your shoulders." He reaches forward, brushing his finger down my cheek. "The silly pickup lines were just a diversion to get your attention."

"And what makes you think you have my attention?"

He chuckles, the sound low and deep, sending shivers down my spine. "Because, darling, I can see it in your eyes. The way they light up every time I speak."

I roll my eyes, trying to hide the fact that he's not entirely wrong. "You're full of yourself, you know that?"

He leans in closer, his breath hot against my ear. "I'm just confident in what I want, and right now, that's you."

Before I can even register what's happening, he's kissing me. Our lips mold together in sync as if we've done this a million times. His tongue gently caresses my lips as he grips the back of my neck, pulling me tighter into his chest, eliciting a loud moan of pleasure from me. He plunges his tongue into my mouth as if he's trying to devour me whole. Fire burns in my veins as I wrap my arms around his neck, pulling him closer to my body. All these feelings are foreign to me, but I know in my heart that I want—no, I *need*—more.

"The things I want to do to you, Marissa," he growls before nipping lightly at my lip and standing up straight, taking me along with him. "I guess you win this round."

"I'd love to think of this as a win-win situation," I whisper softly as he brushes his thumb along my bottom lip, sending another shiver of need through my body.

First impressions be damned. I had no intention of giving this man the time of day. I was going to take my free drink, make a polite excuse, and then make my way back to my hotel room alone. But after that kiss, there's no way I'm letting this man out of my sight. It's just one night, right? What's the worst that could happen?

two
finn

I can't decide if I'm more hurt or offended that the girl I haven't stopped thinking about for the last five years may not remember me. It's a strange feeling—one that I'm not used to.

I can't blame her, if I'm being honest. We were in high school the last time we saw each other. I was the shy, geeky kid who couldn't have a simple conversation with my classmates about anything. Seriously, I'm surprised I even became friends with Marissa's older sister, Sutton. Maybe it was the fact that we spent more time in the library, hiding from the trauma of not being one of the cool kids in high school.

However, there is one word in that sentence that I want everyone to pay attention to: was. Going away to college was just what I needed. Well, that and a roommate that was determined to break me out of my shell freshman year. I transformed. I figured out what to do with my hair, and my long limbs are now filled out with muscles, making me a little more interesting to the ladies and giving me the boost of confidence I was lacking in my teens. Trust me, I'm still the same geeky kid at heart who prefers to spend his Friday nights at home reading instead of cruising for ladies.

"How does another drink sound?" I question, leaning back while signaling the bartender for another round.

"Yeah. A drink sounds good right about now."

She's flustered. It's written all over her face, the same as when we were kids. Her cheeks turn a delicious shade of pink as her eyes look anywhere but at me, but at least I have her attention. Something I've longed for since the first time I set eyes on her.

I remember it like it was yesterday. Her long, dark hair hung loosely around her shoulders, with streaks of red brought out by the halo of sunlight behind her head. She was wearing a pale-yellow top, covering her short, curvy frame, and a pair of dark blue jeans tucked into a pair of brown cowboy boots. A bright smile was plastered on her face as she stole my heart.

I had been friends with Sutton for a long time, but I knew Marissa as a person. We went through our awkward teenage years together, although she made it through the awkward stage a lot quicker than me. Growing up, Marissa used to tag along with us, going to the lake and watching movies, and she even went as far as studying with us. It wasn't odd for me to go to their house to hang out with Sutton, and the three of us would end up doing something together. To most people, it would've been a nuisance having their baby sister hang around with them all the time, but Sutton loved it, and it never bothered me one bit, especially after that day. I always knew Marissa was an amazing person inside and out, but in that moment, it was as if I was seeing her for the first time, and I was determined to make her mine. That is until I saw Campbell come strolling up behind her, throwing his arm over her shoulder, and kissing the top of her head, which reminded me she was completely out of my league.

Marissa was the girl everyone loved and wanted to be like. She was ridiculously gorgeous and had what could only be described as the perfect life. What could I possibly have offered a girl like her? Not that it mattered anyway, because Marissa had Campbell. Mr. Perfect. The boy all the girls dreamed of. Those two were a match made in heaven, but something must have happened.

"So, what brings you to the bar today?" Her sultry tone brings my mind back to the present as the bartender places our drinks on the bar in front of us.

Marissa's eyes lock with mine, staring deep into my soul, searching for something, and I let her. I have nothing to hide. For the first time since leaving Magnolia after graduation, I have her attention, and I'm not about to lose it now.

"I'm on my way home."

"To your wife and kids?" Her gaze flicks down toward my hand before quickly returning to my eyes, causing me to chuckle softly.

"What type of guys have you been running around

with?" I shake my head, lifting my left hand and wiggling my fingers. "No wife. No kids. Just hasn't really been in the cards for me."

The irony of her question isn't lost on me. I assumed, like everyone else in town, that Marissa and Campbell were well on their way to being married after graduation. It's one of the main reasons I went to college on the other side of the country. Of course, there were plenty of colleges right here in Tennessee or neighboring states, but I didn't want to be around to watch the girl I'd fallen madly in love with marry another man. When I left after graduation, those two seemed more in love than ever, never giving me or anyone else any inclination they wouldn't be tying the knot before heading off to college together.

But man, were we all fucking wrong.

I couldn't help but notice the lack of a ring on her left hand or even a tan line signifying there was once one in that place, causing a million questions to run through my mind. Each one sitting on the tip of my tongue, begging to be asked, but I know I shouldn't. However, maybe I can use this new knowledge to my advantage.

"A girl can't be too careful, can she?" She snickers as she lifts her shot off the bar in front of her, throwing it back with ease. "You look like someone who leaves a trail of broken hearts in his wake."

"Something like that..." I allow my voice to trail off, neither confirming nor denying her statement when the only broken heart after each of my relationships was mine.

I'm not a prude by any means. When I was in college, I may have taken the phrase *sowing your wild oats*, as they say, a little too seriously. My newfound popularity with the ladies went right to my head. I tried to find someone to replace Marissa. In my immature mind, I just needed to find someone to make me forget her. Instead, it only made it worse. I hooked up with girls and even dated a few of them seriously, but I could never allow myself to give my heart to someone besides Marissa. No one ever compared.

After what seemed like my millionth failed relationship, I decided that I'm destined to be alone. I've loved Marissa Torres since I was sixteen years old, and I was content to do so until the day I died. But now, by a chance of fate, I may not have to.

I used to spend hours imagining what it would feel like to have her arms wrapped around me, whispering into my ear how much she loved and cherished me. But at some point, it was time to come back to reality. So, instead of manning up and at least telling her how I felt, I kept quiet, trying to make my feelings as obvious as possible. I'd bring her flowers on her birthday, or just because. I made sure I always brought her favorite snacks when I came over for movie night and even went as far as to carry them around in my backpack on the rare occasion she was having a bad day. My mom always loved when my dad did small things like that, just letting her know he cared, so I assumed that was the best route to go especially because Campbell wasn't nearly as perceptive to her wants and needs. In retrospect, she could've taken that as me being a good friend, when in fact, it only made me even more obsessed with my best friend's little sister.

"What about you?" I ask, filling the silence.

"What about me, what?" she says, signaling the bartender for another shot.

"Any broken hearts in your wake?"

"Just my own," she mumbles, barely loud enough for me to hear, before flashing me a smile. "Nope. Single and completely free."

I couldn't help but notice the way her smile didn't quite reach her eyes. There was something in the way she held herself that hinted at a deeper pain festering beneath the surface. I want to push her, to know who broke her heart so terribly that it's written clearly across her face.

"He's an idiot," I asked, trying to keep my voice steady.

"Who?"

"Whoever put that sad look in your eyes."

She snorted, signaling the waiter for another shot. "You don't even know me, Finn."

"Maybe not, but that doesn't make him any less of an idiot." I lower my voice, angling my head so only she can hear me. "If you were mine, wild horses couldn't pull me away from you."

"But I belong to no one, Finn," she points out before reaching for her bag.

Shit. I need to slow down or she's going to walk out of this bar, and the spell will be broken. I finally have my chance with the girl of my dreams, and I'll be damned if I scare her away.

"Can I have a dance before you go?" I ask, pushing off the bar stool and reaching my hand toward her.

I don't want to seem desperate, but tonight could be my only chance for her to see me in a different light. To show her I'm not that shy, scrawny boy that pined after her in high school.

"One dance?" she questions, her eyebrows pulling down in thought.

I hold my breath, barely moving a muscle, as I wait for her to decide about our dance. I should let her leave and head back to the hotel, but I know in my heart that this moment will change everything.

For a moment, she looks like she's about to decline my offer, but then she nods slowly. "Sure, why not?" she says, her voice soft as she places her hand in mine.

An electric current shoots through me as I lead her toward the dance floor, spinning her around once before pulling her tightly to my chest. We sway to the sounds of the music playing in the background. I don't even know if we are moving to the beat, but right now, it doesn't matter because, for the first time in years, I feel at peace.

I hold her against me as I've imagined doing a million times over the years, burying my nose into the top of her head and inhaling her delicious scent: strawberries and sugar. My arms slide down her back, my hand sliding into the back pocket of her jeans as I pull her closer. A shiver runs through her body, letting me know that she's just as affected by me as I am by her.

"I thought we were dancing." She tries to pull away from me, but I tighten my grasp, pulling her body tightly against mine.

"We are dancing," I respond as I continue swaying from side to side. "Dancing really isn't my thing, but I can move to the beat."

"At least there's something you aren't good at."

I pause, pulling back slightly so I can look directly into her eyes. "I'm not perfect, Marissa. No one is, and if they tell you otherwise, we both know they're full of shit."

"Fair enough," she squeaks, her eyes looking anywhere but at me.

"No need to be nervous, Marissa. I may not be perfect, but there's something here between the two of us."

"D-does that l-line work on a-all the l-ladies?" she stammers, pulling her lip between her teeth for what seems like the millionth time.

I drop my mouth to her ear. "It's only a line if I don't mean it."

A shiver runs through her, and I have a feeling it has nothing to do with the temperature in the bar. I draw back, holding her gaze with mine as we continue swaying to the music. She places both of her hands on my chest, pushing me back slightly, but I only pull her closer.

"Every man says that until it comes time to follow through."

I'd do anything for Marissa, give her anything she desired. All she'd have to do was ask. Sort of. The one thing I refuse to do is let her go.

"You really shouldn't say things like that to someone you just met. Someone might get the wrong idea," she murmurs, her voice no louder than a whisper. Her face turns three different shades of red.

I need to put the brakes on my emotions or I'll scare her away. Marissa isn't like the usual girls I'd find in a bar, and I need to remember that. I'm not used to things working out how I plan, but I will try my hardest to ensure nothing damages my chance with her.

"And what idea might that be?"

"That you want something more than one night," she responds defensively.

"You and I both know that there's so much more between us than just one night, Marissa."

Maybe this isn't the best strategy, letting her know she means something to me. This is supposed to be a quick hookup, something to forget when the sun peeks over the horizon. Marissa has no idea that I want so much more from her, not yet, at least.

"I still can't figure out if I want to kiss you or slap you." Her body tenses in my arms.

"If I get a choice, I'd prefer another taste of those sweet lips, sugar." I chuckle softly, brushing my lips against her cheek. "Tastes just like sugar."

"Sugar? Have we started giving each other nick-names?" She snorts loudly before slapping her hand over her mouth, her eyes widening in surprise, causing me to laugh. I honestly can't remember the last time I smiled. Being an aerospace engineer doesn't leave much time for fun and games.

"This is fucking embarrassing."

"Nothing to be embarrassed about when being your-self. I find it endearing." She tries to pull back from me. When will this girl get it through her head that I'm not letting her go?

"Easy there, sugar. I won't hurt you."

"Not physically."

I get the feeling that Marissa's heart is a little more battered than I expected. It's going to take a lot more than some sweet words and a little flirting to get her to open up to me. Good thing I'm up for a challenge.

three

"Who hurt you so badly you can't trust a good thing when it's right in front of your face?"

I keep my head down, not wanting to answer his question. The truth is beyond pathetic. So pathetic that the last thing I want to remember is the day my life changed forever. It was years ago; I should be over it by now, but that little voice in the back of my head continues to remind me that I'm just not good enough. Especially for a man like Finn.

"Are you still here with me, sugar?"

Goodness, who knew such a simple word could turn my insides to liquid? Sugar. It's something to put in my coffee or to borrow from a neighbor. But when Finn says it, it takes on an entirely different meaning.

"Where else would I be?" My head pops up, and I plaster a big smile on my face. "You said you were headed home. Is it for a visit or for good?"

"What?" he questions, leaning forward so our noses are only a few inches apart.

"Are you going home for a visit or for good?" I blurt out the very first thing I could think of.

Finn inches closer, his lips brushing against my skin, causing my breath to hitch. "Oh, I'm not sure yet. The verdict is still out."

My heart rate quickens, and I can feel my cheeks flush. I need to keep my wits about me. The last thing I need to do is fall for a man with a gorgeous smile and a sexy country twang. Been there, done that, and had my heart shattered into a million pieces. I'm not too keen on a repeat performance, especially since I can't say I'm 100 percent over what happened.

For a moment, we just stand there, staring at each other as we sway slowly to the music. I can feel myself getting lost in his deep brown eyes, and I have to remind myself to snap out of it.

"Sounds ominous."

"Nothing as exotic as you're thinking. My mother called, so I came."

"Momma's boy, I see." I giggle, turning to head back to the bar.

Standing in the middle of the dance floor is probably safer, much safer. This man, with his smooth words and devilish grin, is playing a dangerous game. But I can't help feeling drawn in, curious about where this could lead if I give it the chance.

"Through and through." He threads his fingers through mine, pulling me forward. "I know she'd love you."

"Aren't you putting the cart before the horse? We just met. Do you expect me to just jump on the back of your Harley and ride off into the sunset?"

"How many hours is it from here to Vegas?" He huffs out a laugh as he steers me toward a darkened corner of the bar.

The hairs on the back of my neck tingle as we step into the shadows. I pull back, wanting to put as much space between the two of us as possible. I should know better than to let something like this happen. I'm a cop, goddamn it.

"You're not a serial killer, are you?"

"Do I look like a serial killer, sugar?"

I take a step back, but he matches every move I make with one of his own. I continue backward until I bump into the wall.

"What do you want from me?" I ask, trying to keep my voice level despite the growing heat in my body.

He leans in closer, his eyes locking on mine. "I want to explore every inch of you," he murmurs, his breath tickling my earlobe.

I shiver, both from the sensation and the intensity of his words. This man is dangerous, but I can't resist the pull he has on me. "Why are you looking at me like I'm something to eat?"

"Because you are." He groans before capturing my lips with his in a heated kiss and pushing my back against the wall, trapping me with his body.

He licks the seam of my lips, and I open for him. He

swipes his tongue into my mouth with a groan as I slide my hands over his shoulders, tugging on the short hairs at the base of his neck and pulling him closer to me.

My heart pounds inside my chest as he threads his fingers through my hair, tugging roughly on the strands to deepen the kiss. This is beyond anything I could ever have imagined. My soul is on fire, burning me from the inside out with need, desire, and lust. I need Finn like I need air. I've tried to ignore the magnetic pull I've felt towards him since he sat down on the bar stool beside me, afraid of being rejected, but now there's no going back.

"You're the sweetest thing I've ever tasted." He trails kisses down my neck, nipping and sucking at the sensitive skin as his hand snakes between our bodies. "This is your last chance, sugar. If we go any further, I'm not sure I'll be able to stop."

"I don't want you to stop," I moan.

"Hope you don't mind riding on the back of my bike," he responds before threading his fingers through mine and leading me out of the dark corner and toward the bar. Every noise in the room ramps up to about a thousand as I try to make sense of what's happening.

I can hear Finn murmuring something to someone before he pulls me in a different direction. Blistering wind smacks us both in the face as he opens the door and pulls me out behind him. It isn't until I feel him placing something on my head that his words register.

"Oh, no! There is no way in *hell* that I'm getting on the back of that thing with you."

"Why not? Don't you trust me?" He flashes me another smile, turning my brain to goo once again. I swear his smile is going to be the death of me, and he knows it.

"Doesn't matter if I trust you or not. I'm not getting on the back of that thing unless you make it worth my while."

I slap my hand across my mouth, realizing what I just said. Finn doesn't seem like the type of man to back down from a challenge, and I just laid one down.

"What do I win if I can get you on the back of this bike?" he questions, stepping into my personal space.

My breath hitches in my throat. I desperately want him to lean down and kiss me again, but my stubbornness wins out.

"It doesn't matter, because there is no way I'm getting on the back of that death trap." I tilt my chin up in defiance, realizing too late that I played right into his hands.

He leans down so our lips are just a hair's breadth away from each other. "Oh, we're just going to see about that," he whispers before capturing my mouth with his.

The kiss was electric, sending shivers down my spine. I can feel every inch of his body pressed against mine, and my hands instinctively run up his back, pulling him closer. His tongue traces my bottom lip, asking for entrance, and I eagerly grant it. The taste of him is addictive, and I never want this to end.

"You win this round," he growls before nipping

lightly at my lip and standing up straight, taking me along with him. "We'll walk."

"Just let me grab my bag and we can be on our way." He reaches past me and grips what seems to be a roll of clothes off the back of his bike.

"Everything you need is in there?" I question, unable to fathom how anyone could fit any amount of clothing in that small backpack.

"Yes. When you spend most of your time on the road, you learn how to pack light. Besides, I honestly don't know how long I'm going to be at my parents' place."

I nod, unable to find my voice, as he leads me down the road. I vaguely hear him say something about a room on the bottom floor, but I don't pay attention. I know I should listen, but my mind drifts back to his words from a few moments ago. I haven't given Finn any expectations for anything besides tonight. I know love isn't in the cards for me, but since meeting Finn, it seems my heart may have other plans.

His voice brings me back to the present. "We're here."

He pulls me through the door, slams it shut, and pushes me up against it. His hands are all over my body, exploring every inch of my curves. He grips the bottom of my shirt and pulls it over my head, leaving me in a white cotton bra.

Without hesitating, Finn smashes his lips against mine for a third time, pinning me to the door with his body. This kiss feels different from all the others, as if he's sharing a part of his soul with me and giving me a part of himself. A part he has never shared with another.

He continues to nip and suck along my neck before he pulls back, searching my eyes for something. I don't wait for him to find what he's looking for before leaning forward and brushing my lips against his, whispering, "Take me to bed before I change my mind."

four

finn

The words I've been longing to hear for years have finally reached my ears.

"Mine." I reach into the cup of her bra and pinch her left nipple as she hisses.

My other hand slides up her leg, hooking it around my hip. I shift my hips forward, grinding my cock into her.

"Are you wet for me, baby?" I ask as I slide my hand between our bodies, popping open the button of her jeans and slipping my hand into her panties. My fingers run along her slit before sinking two fingers into her and latching my lips onto her throat.

"Your pussy is hungry for me," I growl into her ear, finding that magic spot and curling my fingers. "So beautiful."

I pull my fingers from her and shove them into my mouth, licking them clean.

"Please," she begs, her eyes hooded with want.

Her eyes travel down my body, locking on my cock as

I unbuckle my pants and pull it out. Her pupils dilate, and she licks her lips, desire written all over her face.

"Do you want my cock, baby?

"Yes," she moans breathlessly.

I hoist her up by her ass cheeks and thrust into her core, both of us moaning. Her juices drip down my balls as I pump in and out of her at a punishing pace. Marissa bumps her head against the wall, meeting me thrust for thrust.

"I'm close, baby. I've wanted to be inside you all night. I don't know if can last much longer." I grit my teeth together as I try to hold off my impending release.

Marissa's eyes meet mine as she snakes her hand between our bodies and rubs her clit, slowly at first, before picking up the pace, her walls tightening around my shaft with each pass. My balls tighten as I feel my release approaching.

"Come for me, sugar." I lift her higher on the wall. "Give it to me. Give me everything."

My hips continue slapping against hers until she shouts my name and both of us tumble over the edge into oblivion. I slow my pace, pumping in and out of her as we come down from our high, not wanting to lose the connection we have finally made.

I lean forward so our foreheads are touching. "Was it everything you were expecting?"

"And then some."

She presses a gentle kiss on my lips, and we continue to stare into each other's eyes just as my cell phone rings.

"You aren't answering that," she says as I gently lower her legs to the ground.

"I have no intention of it." I lean forward, planting a kiss on her lips. "I'm not finished with you yet."

I give her ass a swat before she takes off running toward the bed in the center of the room, my ringing phone all but forgotten. I strip off my clothes as I follow close behind her, catching her just as she reaches the bed, and we both tumble onto it.

"Did you mean what you said?"

Her entire body stiffens as I shift our bodies on the bed, pulling her back to my front. My dick hardens as my hand slides down her stomach, tickling the hairs that cover her pussy before pinching her clit between my fingers.

"Every word. One night of mind-blowing orgasms."

I slide down her body, wrapping my lips around her clit and sucking it deep into my mouth.

"Are you sure we can't come to some type of understanding?" I say before biting down gently and sliding two of my fingers between her lips.

My mind is racing with possibilities of what my future with Marissa could be like if she'd only give us a chance. We grew up together, our parents are best friends, and we will both be in Magnolia for the foreseeable future. It would be as easy as breathing for the two of us to explore the connection between us, but the only problem is, she doesn't know any of that. To her, I'm just some random guy she met in a bar. A way to scratch an itch, but to me, tonight is so much more.

"Fuuuuck." The words are dragged from her lips as I find the magic button, her back bowing off the bed. "Do you really think this is the best time to have this conversation?"

"I want more than tonight, sugar." I look up the line of her body, our gazes locking. "Tell me you'll at least think about it?"

I shouldn't be pushing so hard, especially because she has no idea that we are headed to the same town in the morning, but I can tell by the look in her eyes that she's scared. Scared of what, I have no idea, but if I don't at least convince her to think about there being something more between us, then I could lose my chance.

"I can't," she whispers as a single tear trickles down her cheek "One night is all I can give."

"We'll see."

Unable to wait any longer, I pull my fingers from her pussy and climb up her body. Her legs part slightly, allowing me to enter her in one swift motion.

"Fuck me," she moans as she lifts her hips, and I slide deeper inside her.

I want to take my time this time and love her the way she deserves, but there's no going back now. Marissa has meant everything to me for years, and it's finally time to show her. I had every intention of keeping my libido in check, only wanting to have a few drinks with her before heading back to my room alone, but there was something about the sad look in her eyes once I sat down that drew me in. It was at that moment I knew I had to make her mine.

I pull out slowly before slamming back into her so hard that the headboard smacks against the wall, mixing with our moans of pleasure. Her legs tighten around my waist as her walls grip my cock harder.

"Are you ready to come? I want you to soak my cock." I growl, pulling her ear between my teeth as her walls tighten, sending a tingle of pleasure up my spine as my orgasm builds.

Her mouth pops open in response, her nails raking down my back as she tumbles over the edge. I raise her legs, throw both over my shoulders, and slide deeper into her channel.

"That's it, sweetheart. Milk my cum from my cock," I growl, pounding her petite body into the mattress.

Her walls tighten as she comes for the second time, making my body convulse. Ribbons of cum shoot from inside me as I find my release and collapse on top of her.

After a few moments, Marissa squirms from the pressure of my body on hers. I roll to the side, pulling her body flush against mine.

"This isn't a onetime thing. There's something between us, sugar. Something I'd love nothing more than to explore."

Her body stiffens before I plant a kiss on the back of her neck.

"Just think about it, okay?" I hold my breath, waiting for her to give in to the chemistry between us.

She spins around in my arms, her hand cupping my cheek. "We're both adults. Why can't this be a onetime thing? No one ever has to know." Her eyes flit across my face, searching for any signs of doubt on my face, but she won't find anything.

"This is more than one night, sugar," I respond with conviction, needing her to know that I have every intention of making her mine.

She opens her mouth to reply as I hear my phone ring again.

"I'd better answer that this time," I grumble, kissing her before climbing out of the bed. "I'm sure it's probably my mom wanting to know when I'm arriving in town."

"She's just worried about you. Anyone would be worried if they knew you were riding around on that death trap you call a motorcycle without a helmet."

"Helmets are required when operating a motorcycle in the state of Tennessee."

"If you had one, that is." Marissa sits up, resting on her elbows as her eyes widen in surprise, motioning toward the hotel room with her chin. "In our haste to find the nearest flat surface, you left it on the bar."

"No, I didn't. Besides, I'm sure the bartender would've held it as collateral until I came back to pay our tab."

"Oops." Marissa giggles before dropping back down

on the bed. "He must be losing his mind right about now. I wasn't drinking the cheap stuff."

"I got it covered, sugar." I chuckle, pulling on my boxers and heading toward the door.

"I better call her back before she sends the National Guard after me," I grumble, grabbing my pants off the ground and fishing out my cell phone. Taking a deep breath, I brace myself for my mother's wrath as I hit the redial button.

"Where are you?"

"At a hotel in Chattanooga," I respond, not feeling the need to give her any more information than necessary. "I checked the weather report before I left Birmingham, and it said something about rain rolling in. I decided to head to the next city and stop off the night. The last thing I wanted was to be stuck in a downpour."

I wink at Marissa, causing her to giggle softly. I know I shouldn't lie to my mother, but the alternative isn't really an option. Not only would my mother be beyond excited that I've finally gotten my chance with Marissa, but that would also involve me telling Marissa who I am, and something tells me Marissa would not take that information well. I need to convince her that we have a chance to be together outside the bedroom before letting her know about our past together.

"Good idea." My mom sighs loudly. "The last thing I want is for you to get into an accident because you were rushing home."

"Sorry I didn't call you, Momma. I didn't mean to worry you."

I should've known she was going to be worried about where I was. Marissa was right. She wasn't too fond of the idea when I told her I was riding my motorcycle all the way to Magnolia. I'm sure her mind was racing with horrible scenarios of what could've possibly happened to me.

"I know you hate me checking up on you, but I was worried, since I hadn't heard from you after you left Birmingham hours ago. I was expecting you'd be here by now."

I glance down at my watch, my eyes widening. It seems time flies when you're having fun.

"Shit. I'm sorry, Momma. I stopped at a bar to have a drink and relax. I completely lost track of time."

Only part of that is true; I stopped and grabbed a drink, but I found a very different way to relax.

"I guess I can forgive you, but only if you're here first thing in the morning."

"I promise. I'll be on my way as soon as I wake up."

"Be careful and drive safe. I know you've been riding that awful death machine, and I do nothing but worry."

"It's not a death machine, Mom." I chuckle, running my hands through my hair. My mom has given me a hard time ever since I purchased my Harley a few years ago.

"It is. Even your father agrees with me." I can hear her sniffle softly.

"I know. I'll call you in the morning and let you know when I'm leaving."

"I love you, Finn."

"I love you, Momma," I say with a smile before ending the call and turning toward the bed, expecting to find Marissa waiting patiently for me to come back for round two, but I find her fast asleep. Her arms are curled tightly around the spare pillow, and a soft smile is on her face.

"I guess round two will have to wait until morning." I chuckle before quickly stripping down to my boxers and climbing into bed. As I wrap my arms around Marissa and pull her close to me, my eyes close, and I release a contented sigh. It feels like I can breathe for the first time in years, and it's all because of Marissa sleeping peacefully in my arms.

five

I pull the door to the hotel room open slightly and slip through before releasing the breath I was holding. My eyes flick back to Finn's sleeping form, my body heating at the memory of the night we spent together before the cold light of day came peeking through the window.

"Sorry, Finn," I whisper before pulling the door shut and heading toward my hotel room. I'm not sure if it's a coincidence or another symbol of my horrible luck, but we're staying at the same hotel. Another sign from the universe that leaving the bar with Finn and allowing him to have his wicked way with me was a terrible idea.

What was I thinking?

That's it. I wasn't thinking at all. I was so wrapped up in my own thoughts and feelings that I forgot that sleeping with Finn wasn't an option. I wanted him the moment he sat down beside me at the bar. Getting hit on isn't anything out of the ordinary for me. It happens frequently when I come into the bar, but Finn was different. He had trouble written all over him. I should've let him buy me a few shots, made some small talk, and then headed back to my hotel room alone. Instead, I did the exact opposite and found myself beneath him in bed, unable to think past the way his lips felt against mine. Everything else became background noise.

Sound familiar?

This is the same thing that happened with Campbell. I was so wrapped up in the perfect plan I had set up for our future that I never noticed he was unhappy, which drove him right into the arms of someone else.

Everyone has told me a million times that he made the choice to leave me and marry Emmeline, but I should've noticed he was miserable. My desire to make the perfect life for us overrode everything else. Now the only thing I have to show for it is a broken heart and a small apartment above the spa on Main Street, located almost directly between the station and my parents' house.

Things could be different with Finn...

"No," I growl into the empty room as indescribable pain shoots through me.

I refuse to lead him down a road of misery. I'm broken.

But he said you're his.

"People say a lot of things in the throes of passion," I respond to the voice in the back of my mind as I grab my small overnight bag off the bed before heading right back out the door. I send up a silent prayer of thanks that I never unpacked, choosing to head directly to the bar instead of spending any time getting comfortable in my room.

I make quick work of checking out of the hotel room and climbing back into my car, pointing it toward Magnolia. I just need to get home and forget all about last night. Then things can go back to normal. I don't regret one moment of the time we shared last night. But one-night stands happen, and that's all this can be. Besides, I'll never see Finn again. He's headed home to see his family, and it's time for me to head back to real life. Being with me will bring him nothing but misery. Once I get home, last night will become nothing more than a fond memory.

Just as I'm getting into my car, my cell phone rings. I don't even need to pull out my phone to check who's calling, knowing there's only one person who would dare call me this early in the morning. I open the car door quickly, tossing my bag into the back seat before answering the call on the fourth ring.

"Did you enjoy your night?" Peyton asks.

Peyton was my roommate throughout college. It was rocky at first, which was understandable. We were two very opinionated females thrust into a 12X19 square-feet dorm room because we came from neighboring towns and the school believed it would help make our transition to college life easier. Well, it didn't, but after Peyton's high school sweetheart, Jules, dumped her, we discovered we had a lot more in common than we thought. The rest is history.

When I told her I was moving back to Magnolia after graduation, she was all too willing to join me. She wanted to be close enough to her family to visit for the holidays, or in case an emergency popped up, but far enough away that they couldn't come knocking on her door without calling first. I really should've thought about that before coming back here. If I had, I could very well have avoided this entire conversation.

"I take it by your silence that it was indeed a good night."

"The best." I laugh softly, a smile spreading across my face as I'm reminded once again of the night I spent with Finn and the way my body heats at the memory. "I'm pretty sure you aren't only calling me to ask about my night."

"Guilty as charged."

"What do you want, Peyton?" I question as I climb into the car, pointing it toward home.

"I'm hungry," she whines. "Could you pretty please stop at The Sugar Spot and get me something?"

The Sugar Spot is Peyton's favorite bakery in her hometown of Birch Cove, only twenty miles away from Magnolia and right on my way home. You'd think after starting her own bakery, she'd learn how to make her own version of the Tennessee Mountain Apple Stack Cake, but she swears it'd never taste the same. Whenever I'm coming anywhere near Birch Cove, Peyton always begs me to stop and grab a slice for her.

"I have a sneaking suspicion you convinced me to

head to Chattanooga just so I'd make a stop for you on my way home."

"Me?" she responds in mock horror. "I'd never do something so manipulative."

"Yes, you would," I deadpan, knowing Peyton would do anything humanly possible to get a slice of her favorite cake. "And you're lucky I love you and I'm hungry. I'll bring it by the shop on my way back into town."

"Thank you!" she squeals, giving me a mental picture of her jumping up and down, clapping her hands like a little girl. "Text when you get close, and I'll have your coffee ready for you because Lord knows you need it. You're cranky."

"Wouldn't you be if your demanding best friend called you at," I pause, glancing down at the digital clock on my dashboard, "seven-thirty in the morning to ask you to get her a baked good? You could probably make it yourself if you tried."

"It's not the same, Mari, and you know it!" she shouts before taking a deep breath. "Damn, I thought you'd be slightly more agreeable after getting laid. You got laid, didn't you?"

"Goodbye, Peyway."

"I fucking hate when you call me that. The least you can do is come up with a nickname that isn't the same as our favorite Asian fast-food restaurant in college," she grumbles, her irritation with the silly nickname I gave her one drunken night in college clear in her voice.

"I know," I respond before ending the call.

The last thing I want to do is have a conversation with Peyton about Finn. She'd want details and answers to questions that I don't know the answer to. Thankfully, I'll never have to find out because I'll never see him again.

Tennessee is a decent-sized state, and he could've been traveling anywhere. I never told him anything more than my first name. Marissa is a common enough first name, and I never told him where I lived. That's something I never do, especially with a random hookup. I'm not stupid. You never give out your personal information unless you want to end up in a body bag.

Why the fuck am I stressing about this? This was a one-night stand—an unbelievable one-night stand—but this was never meant to go beyond that.

Then why does it feel like my life will never be the same?

six

finn

"Mom, I just stopped to fill up my gas tank, and then I'm headed toward Magnolia. It shouldn't be more than a few hours until I get there." I throw back the last bit of my disgusting gas station coffee before tossing the cup into the trash can and throwing my leg over my bike.

"You should've been here by now," she snaps back, causing me to roll my eyes.

Leaving almost an hour later than I planned is the least of my concerns. I wasn't surprised to wake up in bed alone this morning, but it still stung when I rolled over and knew there was no chance of me going another round or two with Marissa.

I threw the sheets to the side, climbed out of the bed, and began searching. The room was small, but I'd hoped she was in the bathroom, taking a shower or even using the restroom, but deep down, I knew she wasn't there. She had slipped away while I was sleeping. The question is why.

"Ma, I'll be there as soon as possible. You don't need

another man in your life lying in a hospital bed." I wince as I realize what I said. My mother has dealt with it enough over the last month. The last thing she needs to do is deal with my smart-ass comments. "Momma..."

"Don't worry about it, sweetheart." Her voice drops to barely above a whisper. "I'm sorry, Finn. I'm just eager to get your father's appointment over with."

"It's okay, Momma," I respond, wishing that my mom didn't have to deal with any of this right now, let alone ever. "I promise I'll be home when you get back from his appointment. I'm getting a later start than I had planned."

"You really should have flown, as I suggested."

"Ma," I say her name in warning, starting up my bike to let her know I don't want to have this conversation again.

"All right. All right. Just please, take your time on the way here. You're right, I don't want to visit the hospital again for a long time. See you soon. Love you, sweetheart."

"Love you, too, Momma," I say before ending the call, shoving the phone into my pocket, and then pulling away from the gas pump.

When my mom called me, letting me know my father had had a stroke, it was as if all the air had been sucked out of the room. My dad is the strongest man I know. He would still run three times a week and go fishing on the weekends. Everything changed for me at that moment. For years, I've stayed away from Magnolia, wanting to protect myself from the pain of seeing Marissa and Campbell. My parents came to visit me, but I was so wrapped up in my own life that I didn't notice that I was missing out on time with them.

Now I'm on my way back home to help my mom take care of Pops and run Tallywackers for the foreseeable future. Although my dad is out of the woods, he still has a long road to recovery ahead of him. It could be months, years, or possibly never. There's no telling when my pops will be well enough to do anything on his own, let alone take care of our family business.

I always wondered what life would've been like if I hadn't gone away to college or if I returned home after graduation. I never dreamed of being an aerospace engineer. It kind of just fell into my lap. I've always been good with numbers, and my original plan was to come home and help my father run the business. But one of my professors noticed my abilities and pointed me in a new direction. Aside from having both of my parents back in Magnolia, there was nothing forcing me to come home. So, I took an internship with NASA, and the rest is history.

It seems the traffic gods are shining down on me because I make it back to Magnolia in record time. I drive down Main Street, taking in the sights of my hometown. It seems nothing has changed. Even after being away for years, everything looks the same.

I drive past the 365 Diner, nestled close to the center of town, near the fountain. Our small, local post office is a few blocks down, sitting right next to the bookshop, Twice Read Tales, where Sutton and I spent more time than anywhere else. As I continue down the street, there are a few businesses that have different names or have replaced old ones, but mostly, nothing has really changed. That's the one thing I can always count on in Magnolia. Nothing really changes. People come and go, moving on to the bigger city, but the look and feel of the town never changes.

I turn right and head toward my childhood home. It doesn't take too long before I'm pulling into the driveway. The outside looks exactly as it did the day I left for college, aside from for the wooden wheelchair ramp covering the front stairs for my father. He isn't paralyzed, thankfully, but he still doesn't have full use of his arm and leg on his left side. Other than that, my parents took the time to revamp the kitchen and add hardwood flooring throughout the living areas, new tile in the bathrooms and kitchen, and fresh paint on all the walls. My dad said it was a waste, but we both knew it would make my mother happy, so we made it happen.

"Home sweet home," I mumble to myself as I shut off the engine.

I never really thought about what it would be like when I pulled up in front of my parents' house for the first time in years. My mother would probably have come running out the door with my father hot on her heels, yelling at her to be careful on the stairs. She'd shush him before throwing her arms around my neck and giving me a big hug, telling me how much she missed me. Pops would come down the stairs, giving my hand a hard shake before telling me we were headed to the river for a fishing trip with his buddies this weekend. But not this time. This time, my mom is at the hospital with my dad, waiting to hear from the doctors about whether he's ever going to walk again.

I grip my helmet, pulling it off my head and placing it on my seat. "Everything is the same but so different." My hushed tones startle me as I reach up and rub the ache in my chest, willing it to disappear as I climb off my bike and head toward my parents' front door.

Taking the stairs two at a time, I grab the handle and turn, but it doesn't open. "What the hell?" I mumble before reaching for the potted plant sitting next to the door and lifting it to find the spare key for the front door.

I didn't think to bring my keys because my parents have never locked their front door. My mom always claimed that she had an open-door policy, but it also helped that they had the county sheriff on speed dial.

Having found the key, I slide it into the lock. Just as I'm pushing the door open, a police siren rings through my parents' house. I turn and scan the street, looking for approaching sheriff vehicles but see nothing.

"Where the hell is that noise coming from?" I question as I kick the door shut, noticing a large white box affixed to the wall in the entryway just above the thermostat controls.

My parents hate anything with too many bells and

whistles, so I'm surprised to find the control panel for a home security system that my mother seemed to have forgotten to warn me about. If I was a burglar, I'd be worried, but since everyone in town knows me, this should be easy to explain away. But first, I need to shut this damn alarm off.

I punch numbers into the keypad, trying desperately to stop the sound from ringing in my ears. I tried both my parents' birthdays, my birthday, and even their anniversary to shut off the alarm, but nothing worked. Somewhere in the back of my mind, I remember that someone from the alarm company sometimes calls, just in case the owner of the alarm cannot shut it off in a certain period of time. To ensure the police aren't called, each owner is given a password to notify the police that there's no threat to their homes or well-being. The only problem is I don't know what that code could even be.

"Can today get any worse?" I chuckle as I hear the house phone ringing in the kitchen.

seven

marissa

"What can I do for you, Dolores?" I grumble into the phone as I pull on my green Magnolia County Sheriff's Department polo shirt that shows off all my curves, as well as my tan cargo pants. Nothing fancy, but I love it. There's something about not having to choose what to wear to work every day that's liberating. "I'm not late, am I?"

I double-check my watch before grabbing my keys off my end table and shoving them into my pocket. I've been a part of the sheriff's department since I graduated from college, working my way up the food chain to become the chief deputy, much to my father's chagrin. It's not the most glamorous position, but it's rewarding. There's something about working to keep the people who helped you grow into a woman safe that gets to me.

"For once." She giggles before clearing her throat. "We got a call about an alarm going off at the Buckley house over on Maple. Someone attempted to input the security code a few times. The service asked us to send someone around to check it out."

"Why are you calling me?"

Dolores huffs. I can practically hear her eyes rolling through the phone. I know I should just listen to what she has to say, but it seems getting her riled up is my new favorite pastime. "Colt is at a meeting in Rose Hill, and you're about to start your shift."

Colt Butler is considered to be the catch of the century here in Magnolia. Born and raised in the town, comes from a good family, and is now the county sheriff. According to all the mothers in town, it's only a matter of time until someone's daughter snaps him up, and my mom was devastated when she realized it would not be me. His chiseled jawline with hair that has that just-got-out-of-bed look would make him any woman's fantasy, but Colt and I can't be anything more than friends.

He's more like an older brother to me than anything. We never really spent time together when I was younger, but we're so similar it's crazy. There's no way we can be anything more than friends. Especially because he's desperately in love with my engaged older sister. Now, if I can just convince him to sweep Sutton off her feet, it would make my life so much better. Colt would stop sulking around and taking out his jealousy on all of us at the station, and Sutton could move home and take all my parents' attention off me. Leaving me to continue living my carefree life without them breathing down my neck and asking me questions I don't know the answers to.

"And you want me to go check it out because my place is only a few blocks away?"

"Yes, please."

"Mark me as responding and call Colt to let him know. I'll swing by on my way to the station."

"Copy that," Delores responds as I quickly end the call and head out the door.

My family and I used to spend many a Sunday afternoon having dinner with the Buckleys. Sutton and their son were thick as thieves until they both hightailed it out of town after graduation. Last I heard, he'd become some hotshot at NASA and was too good to come back and visit his parents, much like my sister.

It doesn't take me long to find my way to the Buckleys' house and pull the car to a stop right behind a black Harley. "It's just a coincidence," I mumble to myself as I climb out of my SUV and draw my weapon, approaching the front door slowly and checking my surroundings for any sign of forced entry. No broken windows and the door is still fully intact.

"Must be a false alarm," I say to myself just as the front door swings open and my one-night stand comes strolling through, a devilish smile plastered across his face.

"Hey, gorgeous. Haven't seen you around here before."

My eyes widen in horror as I draw my weapon, pointing it toward the center of his chest. What the fuck is he doing here? Surely, he couldn't have found me that quickly. How would he have done that? He doesn't even know anything about me besides my first name. And I know for a fact that I never once mentioned where I live. Somewhere in my head, I hear my dad's voice, growling at me about sleeping with strangers. Fuck!

"Do you know the code? The noise is giving me a massive headache." A sly smile crosses his face.

"And that's my problem because…?"

"Well, you're the reason I didn't get much sleep last night." He winks at me before continuing. "You must be surprised to see me again after you snuck out of my room before the sun came up."

"It wasn't before the sun," I mumble as I try to focus on anything else besides the way his warm laughter fills the air, and my core tightens. Down, girl. I need to get my damn body under control. Not only has my one-night stand broken into someone's house, but somehow, he found me.

"Semantics." He makes his way down the steps, close enough to reach out and brush his fingers down my cheek. "Now, are you gonna help me with this alarm, sugar, or are we going to find the closest bed so I can give you a repeat performance of last night?"

"You seem a little full of yourself." My breathing picks up as I take a few steps back, wanting to put some space between the two of us.

"Maybe, but one thing is certain"—he leans in, tilting my chin upward—"I am going to kiss you."

"Who said I wanted you to?" I respond breathlessly, trying to wrench my chin free from his grasp.

I have two choices right now: I can bide my time and wait to see how this plays out, or I can holster my weapon and kick this asshole's ass. I'm decent at self-defense tactics, even with him being almost twice my size, but I don't want to take the chance that he can get a hold of my weapon.

"So, you don't want me to kiss you?" he questions as I slowly raise my weapon, pressing it to his chest, directly over his heart.

"Not at all. But what I really want to know is how you found me and why you broke into the Buckleys' house." I flash him a megawatt smile as I take a step back, and he raises his hands in surrender.

"Marissa? Why the heck do you have a gun pointed at my son's chest?" Finn and I jump apart, like we've been caught with our hands in a cookie jar.

"Your son?" I question, moving between Mrs. Buckley and my stalker. "I know what Finn looks like, and this is not my sister's skinny, pimple-faced best friend." My cheeks heat with embarrassment as I go over everything this man said to me last night.

He was coming home because of a family emergency. Mr. Buckley had a stroke about a month ago. He's out of the woods, but he has a few hurdles to get over before we can say for certain everything is back to normal. Mrs. Buckley told my mom at the church picnic last week that her son was moving back to help her take care of the bar.

But why didn't he tell me who he was? Finn Buckley watched me grow up. He had a front-row center seat to my awkward teenage phase. But he never showed any romantic interest in me before last night in the bar. So why the hell was he all too willing to get me into bed last night? What changed?

Before I can open my mouth to ask another question, Finn chimes in. "Can you please put down the gun and come inside? I'm sorry, Ma, but someone forgot to tell me you got an alarm system. I triggered the alarm when I came into the house."

"Oh, Lord above. I'm so sorry, sweetheart. The sheriff suggested we get an alarm system so it would be easier to alert the police or the paramedics if something happened to your father."

"Well, that was mighty nice of him, Ma." His eyes flick toward mine as he lowers his arms to his side. "Are we good now, sugar?"

The deep rumble of his voice wraps around me like a warm blanket. I should cuff him, take him to the station, and find some way to get him as far away from me as possible. But I highly doubt Finn's parents are going to press charges against their own son.

Finn winks at his mother. "Marissa and I were getting reacquainted with each other. This was all a misunderstanding. We haven't seen each other in years. It's only natural that she didn't recognize me."

I quickly holster my weapon as he takes a step forward, wrapping his around my shoulder. All the color drains from my face as I try to pull away from him, but he only pulls me tighter into his side.

The chemistry sparks between us for the second time as his mother eyes both of us skeptically. "I'm going to go inside and get us something to drink. Finn, can you please get your dad's chair out of the trunk and help him inside?"

"Sure thing, Ma. Right after Officer—"

"Deputy," I interrupt him, causing a bright smile to spread across his face.

"Deputy Flores and I finish our conversation."

"Make it quick. It's warm, and I don't want your father trying to get into the house himself. You know he's just as stubborn as a mule."

"That he is," he responds, brushing his lips against the top of my head, causing a shiver to run through my body. We both watch as his mother heads into the house. A few minutes later, the blaring alarm silences.

"Finally, I'm able to think." Finn groans softly.

I squirm from his grasp as I try to step away from him, but he grips my arm tightly.

Before I realize what's happening, his lips crash into mine once again. The fight for dominance has begun. He uses his free hand to pull my entire body flush against his. I gasp in surprise as he groans, sliding his tongue into my mouth before deepening the kiss. I give myself over to the pleasure, allowing my emotions to take over for a few moments before my brain catches up with what's happening, and I bite down hard on his lower lip. The metallic taste of his blood fills my mouth as he pulls away from me.

"You bit me!" His thumb brushes against his lip, checking for blood.

"Well, next time, you'll think before kissing someone without their permission," I growl, wiping my mouth with the back of my hand. "Was this just a big joke to you, Finn?"

This is what I needed. I needed to keep the walls around my heart firmly in place. Sleeping with Finn was a mistake, even more so because he wasn't some random guy I met at a bar. I didn't care about Finn Buckley. And I don't *want* to care about him either.

"There's nothing fun about the time we spent together, sugar."

"Stop calling me that."

He rolls his eyes at me, and I briefly imagine pulling out my gun and shooting him in the leg. I have probable cause; he broke into the Buckleys' house, after all. Well, not technically because he had a key, but I could always leave that and the fact that he's their son out of my report. Maybe if he apologizes for lying and being a complete asshole, I'll pretend this never happened, but based on the smug look on his face, I doubt that's going to happen.

"Now that you know who I am, what do you think my chances are of getting a repeat performance?"

"If you want a quick death, try kissing me again. Finn, I don't do repeat performances."

"And why's that?"

"Isn't that the point of a one-night stand? They're supposed to end after one night."

"Is that a hard-and-fast rule? Couldn't you make an exception for me?"

"No, but it doesn't matter because it can't happen again."

His finger wraps around a strand of my hair, sending a chill down my spine.

What in the hell is it about this man that causes my brain to take a back seat, allowing my emotions to be more in control? Whatever the reason is, I need it to stop —cold turkey. We may be in the same town, and our parents may be friends, but he's only in town to help with his father. Then he'll be on his way back to where he came from and far away from me.

"You should get to your father before he hurts himself." I motion my head toward Mr. Buckley, who has lost his patience waiting for his son and has climbed out of the car. Both of his arms are resting on top of the hood of the car, his shoulders rising and falling quickly as he tries to catch his breath.

"When can I see you again?"

"Never."

"It's a small town, sugar. I'm sure we are bound to run into each other once or twice."

"If you see me, please turn and go the other way."

"Now, I know your momma taught you better manners, Marissa. Ignoring someone isn't very neighborly."

"You know nothing about me, Finn. I haven't seen you since you graduated high school with my sister."

"I beg to differ. I know you, Marissa. Maybe not as well as someone who's been around Magnolia for the last five years, but I see you.

"Proving you wrong is going to be my new favorite hobby. You can argue with me all you want, but I like a challenge."

"If you are done with your mental sparring match, I'd love for my son to grab my chair. No need to fuss, but I can't make my way up the ramp and into the house myself." Mr. Buckley's voice breaks the spell between the two of us, and I jump backward. Instead of having a few feet between us, my face is only a few inches away from Finn's, and my hard nipples brush against his chest as my chest rises and falls quickly.

"Duty calls," Finn groans before planting a kiss on the top of my head.

My heart stutters at his words, and a nervous tension gathers in my stomach. I don't want to see him ever again, but I don't really have a choice in the matter. We live in a small town, where everyone takes care of each other. With Mr. Buckley being sick, I'm sure my family will be here plenty, trying to help where they can. The last thing I want to do is be alone with him right now, if ever.

"I have to head to the station and report for my shift. Let your parents know I'll call the alarm company and report this as a false alarm, but they might want to call them, as well."

"See you around, sugar."

I don't say another word as I turn on my heels and head directly for the car. Tears prick my eyes, but I refuse to let them fall as I climb into my SUV and head toward the station. Finn has affected me in a way no one else has for years. He can push all my buttons to where I can't help but fire back with a snarky retort. He brings out the worst in me. Some would call that passion. But me, I call it nothing but trouble.

eight
finn

It's been three weeks since I came back to Magnolia, and I haven't run into Marissa Flores once. It's not for lack of trying. I figured it would be easy to create a situation where I could accidentally run into her in town. There are only so many places she can hide from me, but it seems I underestimated how badly she wanted to avoid me.

I've been going back and forth to the doctors with my parents. We even scored an appointment with a specialist in Nashville. Pops's prognosis is good, but there's a long road to recovery ahead of him. I knew this before I even came home, but somewhere in the back of my mind, I assumed I'd be on my way back to my life in Texas before the end of the month.

Ma has been telling me it's fine for me to go, that she and Pops will be fine without me. Which I'm sure they will be, but if I'm being honest with myself, now that I'm back, and after having seen Marissa again, I don't want to go back to Texas. I didn't have a life there. I had a job, a nice apartment, and even a few buddies I could grab a few beers and watch the game with, but there was something missing. Apparently, that missing piece was Marissa.

"The usual?" Peyton asks from her spot behind the counter.

Not only is she the owner of this bakery, but she's my best chance at finding a way into Marissa's heart. Her red hair is piled on the top of her head, a few tendrils falling to frame her face, and her bright green eyes shine brightly as she hands an older couple a large box with two white bags resting delicately on top.

I nod in response to her question as I slide my card across the counter. Every day, like clockwork, I come to grab a coffee from My Soul to Bake, hoping to run into Marissa. This is her best friend's bakery, after all.

Set in a remodeled vintage gas station on the central corner of our little town, this place looks like it was taken straight out of a movie. It's been around since before I was born, but it didn't turn into the thriving hot spot that it is today until Peyton Atkins took over. She's turned this place into an award-winning pastry shop.

I should be ashamed of all the things I've been doing for a chance to catch a glimpse of Marissa around town. The biggest being hanging out in her best friend's bakery first thing in the morning every day.

After I got my dad settled in the house, and I apologized profusely to both for triggering the alarm system, my mom filled me in about everything that had changed in Magnolia since I left after graduation. Most of it was inconsequential. Mr. Jenkins passed away a few months ago and willed his beloved bookstore to his niece, but she has yet to step foot in town. There's a new real estate development company that has been buying up land all around the county, wanting to capitalize on our southern charm. And most importantly, Marissa's best friend from a neighboring town moved here and took over the old bakery.

Using that tidbit of information, I came up with a plan to see Marissa. I come to the bakery in the late morning and grab a cup of coffee before taking a seat at a table near the window, giving me the perfect view of anyone coming in and out of the stores along Main Street as well as an unobstructed view of the parking lot. It's pathetic, I know, but I'm slowly going out of my mind while waiting to run into her. I've even contemplated triggering the alarm again just to see if she'll respond.

"Stalking is illegal, you know." Peyton's voice brings me back to the present as she flashes me a smile and hands me back my card along with a receipt.

"I have to actually see her in order for it to be stalking, wouldn't you agree?"

Peyton discovered, quicker than I anticipated, that I was here because I was trying to accidentally bump into someone. She tried for days to get information out of me, but I refused until she managed to put two and two together. It might have also had something to do with her friend avoiding the place like the plague ever since I started waiting for her every morning.

"That's a plausible explanation, or you could ask someone who knows her for help."

It's not like I haven't thought about it before. If anyone in town could help me peel away the layers around Marissa's heart, it would be Peyton, but somehow, that seems like I'd be admitting defeat. I want her to want to be with me, to want to take the time to get to know me better. And at this point, it seems everyone in town knows my sad story.

"Who said I needed help?" I raise my eyebrow in question.

"Anyone with a set of eyes." She shakes her head. "I don't know if you've noticed, but Marissa is avoiding you."

"No, I had no idea," I respond sarcastically, causing her to giggle softly.

"Look, no need for the attitude. Lucky for you, I'm in a good mood." Peyton's eyes lock with mine as she motions for me to lean closer.

I lean forward, more than intrigued by the secrets she is prepared to share with me.

"You didn't hear it from me, but Marissa worked an overnight shift at the station last night and should be off around noon. She has no plans for the rest of the day besides having lunch with me." Peyton pretends to cough loudly, ensuring a few heads turn in the bakery. "But I think I'm sick and will need to cancel."

"Oh, you poor thing," I respond in mock horror, a

plan forming in my head. "I think I need to grab a few more coffees for the road."

"You got it, my friend." Peyton winks in my direction before grabbing a few cups off the counter and filling them with coffee and all the fixings. "I'm putting Colt and Dolores's names on their cups to make it easier for you, or you'd have two very pissed-off coffee drinkers."

"I owe you one."

"Yea, you do." She smiles up at me before getting back to work.

I've been trying to run into Marissa the old-fashioned way but never once thought of going to the station. Knowing she has no other plans for the day, thanks to a certain someone, it'll be that much harder for her to come up with an excuse as to why we can't at least have lunch.

"Good luck," Peyton says with a smile as she slides the cup carrier across the counter. "Remember, this conversation never happened. Seriously, never happened."

"My lips are sealed." I chuckle, making a show of locking my lips and throwing the key over my shoulder as I check my watch. "I think I might head over there now and see if maybe I can spring her early."

"It's a very strong possibility you could swing it. Nothing ever happens here in Magnolia. She's probably just sitting there, twiddling her thumbs and watching the seconds tick by on the clock."

"And you say that as if it's a bad thing."

"For the people who love and care about her, not in the slightest." Peyton flashes me a smile before she uses her hands to shoo me toward the door. "Now get out and go make our girl fall madly in love with you."

I give her a mock salute before turning on my heel and strolling out the door. I turn right and head down Main Street toward the station, choosing to walk the few blocks instead of hopping in my Pops's truck. I send up a silent prayer of thanks for having the forethought to borrow the truck instead of riding my motorcycle, allowing me to eliminate one more excuse Marissa could have for not going to lunch with me. I need to make sure I stack as many cards in my favor as possible before asking her out, although I'm not above fighting dirty.

"Hey, Finn," Dolores greets me as I walk in the door.

I flash her a smile as I set the cup of coffee with her name on it on the counter. "For you."

"Okay, what do you want, Mister?"

Dolores has lived here most of her life, but I don't know much about her. She keeps to herself mostly and is nice to everyone she meets—the perfect person to work the front desk at the sheriff's department.

"Why do I have to want something? Can't I bring a pretty lady a cup of coffee without ulterior motives?"

"You can if said pretty lady doesn't already know you only have eyes for one woman, who just so happens to be in her office."

"And who told you that?"

"I have eyes, Finn." Delores pulls the cup off the counter and takes a healthy pull. Her eyes drop closed as she savors the flavor before pinning me in place with her stare. "Or it could be the fact Marissa has been drinking a lot more office coffee than usual."

"I don't know what you're talking about," I respond, reaching back and rubbing the back of my neck.

Here I thought I was playing it cool, but it seems my feelings for Marissa are written across my face. No problem. This gives me one more person in my corner to help convince Marissa to give me a chance.

Dolores shakes her head. "Have it your way. I'm going to ask again. What do you want?"

"I honestly don't want anything. I was hoping to ask Marissa to have lunch with me, since hanging out and waiting for her to come into the bakery every day this week isn't working."

"Man, do you have it bad."

"Maybe I do, maybe I don't. But I was wondering what you think my chances are today?"

"Of getting Marissa to agree to go on a date with you?"

"Not a date, just a thank-you lunch," I respond quickly, motioning for her to continue speaking.

"Whatever you want to call it, I have a feeling the odds don't seem to be in your favor today." Dolores shakes her head before taking another pull from her cup. "I heard her talking to Colt today about wanting to cut out early because she has plans for lunch with Peyton."

"Oh, you don't say?" I question, wondering how Peyton is going to convince Marissa she's sick and not just trying to get out of their plans for this afternoon.

Although Peyton said she planned on being *too sick* to go out with her as an excuse to give me an opening to have lunch with Marissa, there is no guarantee Marissa is going to buy it or even agree to have lunch with me. I may just need some additional reinforcements in my back pocket.

"Maybe you could put in a good word for me. Help loosen her resolve a little, for when I do finally ask her out."

"I don't see that being a problem," Dolores responds cheerfully, just as Colt comes strolling around the corner.

"You better have brought me one, too," Colt says as he makes his way around the receptionist's desk, slapping me on the shoulder.

"Sorry, only one bribe per visit to the station." I wink at Dolores, causing her to giggle softly, her cheeks turning a light shade of pink. "Here you go." I grab the last cup from the carrier and hand it to him.

"Thanks," he responds, taking a healthy pull from the cup. "So, are you still trying to get a date with Marissa?"

"What makes you say that? I just want to apologize for the other day at my parents' house."

"So that's the excuse you're going with?" He takes another pull from his coffee before setting it down on the desk in front of him. "Whatever your reason, I know there is something more there."

I open my mouth to respond but close it quickly. Maybe Colt has a point, and besides, what's so wrong with everyone knowing how I feel about Marissa? I tried to keep it under wraps when we were younger and look where that landed me.

"See, I told you anyone with eyes already knows," Dolores chimes in.

"I'm the sheriff. It's my job to pay attention to how people interact with each other. The way you light up whenever her name is mentioned tells me everything I need to know. Now I'm just waiting for you to grow a pair and make a move."

"Fair enough." I reach over, clapping him on the back. "So, when are you going to grow a set and tell Sutton how *you* feel?"

I know all about the massive crush Colt had on Sutton Flores in high school. Hell, everyone in town did, besides Sutton, that is. She could never see herself clearly, choosing to believe that no one would ever be able to see past her plain looks, especially the captain of the football team.

"Touché." Colt chuckles as Marissa comes around the corner, freezing in place as she notices me standing there.

This woman is a vision, with wisps of her hair hanging loosely around her face from having escaped the bun sitting on top of her head. Her toned body is a thing of beauty as she practically glides toward me. Her luscious lips are the color of a blush rose, competing with her vibrant green eyes for my attention.

"What are you doing here?"

"I thought you said she was in a good mood," I

mumble to Dolores, causing her and Colt to laugh loudly.

"I never said whether she was in a good or a bad mood. Just that she had plans," Dolores responds, ducking her head slightly.

"And she's right here." Marissa rolls her eyes. "I am in a good mood. Just not in the mood to deal with you." She turns on her heels, heading back into her office as I quickly come to my senses.

"Not even a thank-you for coming to visit? What would your mama say about your manners?"

I lean against the counter, the perfect picture of ease, even though I'm anything but. Being this close to her awakens the demon I've kept trapped inside me for years, reminding me once again that Marissa Flores is the only woman for me, now and forever.

"I'm sure you'll tell her all about it during her weekly visits with your parents." She turns around, crossing her arms over her chest.

Not only were Sutton and I close, but so were our parents. They always try to find time to get together during the week, even more so now that Pops had his stroke. Who am I to pass up the chance to hang out with her parents? I'll do anything I can to weasel my way into Marissa's good graces, but sadly, it hasn't been helping.

"I know exactly how you can make me forget all about telling your momma how rude you were to me. Let's go to lunch, and all will be forgiven."

"Thank you for the offer, Finn. But I don't get off for

a few hours yet, and I already have plans to have lunch with Peyton today."

Just as he finishes her sentence, a phone rings in her pocket. Everyone but me reaches for their phone, trying to see who's being called.

"It's me," Marissa says before flipping her phone open and answering. "Hello."

Her eyes pull down in confusion as they flick toward me before quickly glancing away.

"You're up to something, aren't you?" Colt smirks in my direction.

"I have no idea what you mean."

Dolores shakes her head as we wait patiently for Marissa to hang up the phone.

"Anything serious?" I question, trying to stop myself from fist-pumping the air to signify my victory.

"Peyton's sick."

"She mentioned something about not feeling well when I was at the bakery before coming here. I hope it's not contagious."

"Why do I have a feeling you have something to do with this?" Marissa strolls toward me, poking her finger in my chest. "It doesn't matter. I'm still not going anywhere with you."

"Why not? I just want to take you to lunch and apologize for the problem I caused you when I first arrived back in town. Is that too much to ask?"

"Then take Colt. It was just as much a pain in the ass for him as it was for me," she responds coldly.

"No, it wasn't," Colt chimes in. "Just a ten-minute phone call to the alarm company."

"Marissa, please put the poor guy out of his misery and let him apologize properly," Dolores adds her two cents before winking in my direction.

"What do you say, sugar?"

"Didn't I tell you to stop calling me that?" she grumbles before sighing loudly. "You really don't need to thank me for doing my job."

"Yes, he does," Colt says before grabbing her by the wrist and pulling her toward me. "She'd love to go to lunch with you, Finn. And you can leave right now."

"What? I have a shift to finish."

"You know that any calls that come in over the next hour I can handle alone, right?"

She opens her mouth to respond, but Colt places his hand over her mouth. "And I promise to call you if anything comes up."

"I swear all of you are conspiring against me."

"Finn was desperate enough to come track you down at the station to have lunch with you. The least you can do is join him," Dolores says as she leans forward to rest her elbows on the desk.

Okay, maybe that's going a little too far. I'm not desperate, at least not *that* desperate. I would wait until the end of time for her to come to me, but I don't have to.

"I promise I won't bite—well, that is, unless you want me to."

"Not happening, Finn."

"Anything you say, sugar."

Colt laughs loudly, shaking his head at our antics before stepping behind her and shoving her toward the door. "I don't want to see you here until your shift on Sunday."

Hmm, it seems Marissa doesn't have any commitments for the next few days, giving me more than enough time to convince her to give us a chance. If we happen to find ourselves in bed for the second time, I won't complain, but that's not my intention. I want to show her I want more from her than amazing sex. I want everything.

"Let's go before I change my mind," Marissa grumbles before storming towards the door and walking through it.

"Good luck," Colt and Dolores say in unison.

"Thanks. I'm going to need it," I respond as I feel everything click into place.

nine
marissa

"We can take my pops's truck." Finn smiles as he places a hand on the small of my back, leading me toward the opposite side of the parking lot, away from my truck.

"No, thanks. I have to head home right after our lunch." I step away from him, putting some much-needed space between us.

Can't this guy take a hint? After holding him at gunpoint a few weeks ago in front of his parents' house, you'd think he would know I'm not interested in having any type of relationship with him. Although I know deep down that it's a load of bullshit.

I want Finn Buckley. I want him more than I've wanted anything in my life, but that scares the shit out of me. I'm a fucking mess, a basket case, someone broken almost beyond repair and not fit to be in any type of relationship. Being in a relationship with me will do nothing but cause us both a world of hurt. And I've been hurt enough by the opposite sex to last me a lifetime. I'm not about to put myself in that kind of situation again.

I've never been instantly attracted to a man the way I was to Finn. I have fun, then I say my goodbyes and never think of said fun again. The idea of possibly having something more with Finn is ridiculous. But when his lips pressed against mine that first night, all rational thought went out the window. I reach up and touch my lips, remembering his against mine. The way his body pressed against mine ignited a fire inside me I'd never felt before, even with Campbell.

"How about we walk?" He smiles down at me, shoving his hands into his pockets. "It's a nice day today, and it's only a few blocks from the diner."

"The benefits of living in a small town," I mumble softly before heading in that direction.

I don't look at him. I can't because I can't bear to see that hurt look on his face at my rejection. This isn't the first time I've pushed a guy away, and it won't be the last. I'm doing this for both our sakes, and after this lunch, I can go back to ignoring him. It won't be much longer until he gets the hint and finds someone else to turn his attention to. It's what I want.

Then why do I have this sick feeling in my belly at just the thought of him speaking to someone else?

"I've always missed being able to walk almost anywhere I need." The deep baritone in his voice soothes the ache in my heart as he steps beside me, bumping my shoulder. "It's just lunch, sugar. I'm not asking you to run off to Vegas and marry me, okay?"

"That's not what you were saying the other night at the bar."

"Blame it on the alcohol."

"Maybe we can blame the whole evening on the alcohol."

"No. I can never come to regret spending one moment with you, Marissa."

My head shoots up, locking eyes with his for the first time since we left the station. "You don't mean that."

"Lord, give me strength." He sighs, tipping his head up toward the sky. "We need to get some facts straight. First, I don't say things I don't mean. If I tell you I'd love nothing more than to throw you over my shoulder, carry you back to your apartment like a caveman and show you have much I want you to belong to me, I mean it."

I freeze, and my eyes widen in surprise as he takes a step closer to me, his scent enveloping me and drawing me closer to him. I would love nothing more than to give in to the urge to raise up on my toes and allow him to wrap me in his warm embrace and bury my nose in his chest.

"Second, I know you've been hurt. I have every intention of showing you I have more than just desire for you. I want everything."

"How do you know I've been hurt? I haven't seen you since you left town right after graduation." I try to act nonchalant about it, but I know deep in my soul he's right.

I never truly recovered from what Campbell did to me. I know there was nothing I could've done to stop him from finding someone else or even getting married in the future. But I've always wanted to know why. To know what I had done that made it so easy for him to give his heart to someone else. To give Emmeline the life he promised me.

In some respects, I wish he had cheated on me. Then everything that happened after our breakup would've made sense to me. I wouldn't have spent years going over every interaction or conversation we had over the last few months of our relationship trying to find the reason. We were together for years. Getting married was the next step, but he couldn't take that step with me.

"It's your eyes," Finn responds, cupping my cheek in this palm. "There's a soul-deep sadness in them that seems to be engrained into your soul. You can see it in the way you move, the way your smile doesn't always reach your eyes. I just want to be given a chance to show you how life could be, how happy you could be with me."

Fuck me. No one besides Peyton knows how deeply what happened with Campbell has affected me, but he deduced what happened just by looking into my eyes. His words have stripped me bare, showing the deepest parts of my soul to a stranger, and that's terrifying.

"Don't be scared, sugar." Finn leans forward, running his hand along my arm and threading his fingers through mine. "We will take it one step at a time."

"Okay." My breath hitches slightly as he leans forward and brushes his lips against mine.

I'm lost in his eyes as we stare at each other. The magnetic pull between us grows stronger as my gaze flicks back and forth between his lips and eyes.

"You're a dangerous creature, Finn." I groan as he steps away from me and turns in the diner's direction.

"So I've been told," Finn mumbles as we walk along the street, our hands clasped together in complete silence. Not the awkward silence some people experience on first dates, but a comfortable one. Just two people enjoying spending time together.

"Why didn't you tell me who you were in the bar that night?" I ask, causing Finn to stop dead in his tracks.

His brows pull down in confusion as he tries to think of the correct answer before he smiles at me. "Would it have made a difference?"

"Yes."

"Are you sure about that?"

"I definitely wouldn't have slept with you," I respond quickly, knowing in my heart that it's true.

The pull I feel between Finn and me is undeniable, but he's from Magnolia. Not to mention he's my parents' best friends' son and used to be joined at the hip with my older sister. Being with him brings complications into my life that I don't need right now.

"Damn, way to bruise a man's ego." Finn grips the back of his neck, chuckling softly.

"I didn't...I mean, it was...but you're only here for a sh-short time and—" Finn places his finger over my lips, stopping the stuttered words coming out of my mouth.

"You're thinking too hard about this, Marissa. I've known you since we were kids. Our parents are best friends, and I was best friends with your sister. How could I have possibly believed you didn't know who I was?"

"But—" I huff, dropping my eyes toward the ground. "You don't even remotely look like you did before."

How do I explain to him that I was so wrapped up in my head that I didn't even notice? But now that I know, I can see everything. Finn may look different, but he's still the same guy I secretly crushed on before I met Campbell. His eyes are still the same warm chocolate-brown color they've always been. His smile still makes my insides melt just a little when it's directed at me. His voice still wraps around me like a warm blanket, making me feel safe and protected.

"Okay, I'll admit, I realized pretty quickly that you may not have known who I was, and I should've said something, but let me ask you one thing," he pauses, pulling his hand from my grasp and lifting my chin, forcing me to look at him. "Do you regret it?"

"No," I respond reluctantly.

It's true. I don't regret the time we spent together. It was the first time in years that I felt something other than the simple urge to be with a member of the opposite sex. But the effect Finn is having on me is not something I want to think about right now.

"I can work with that," Finn responds before stepping toward me and leaning forward.

A shiver runs down my spine as our lips connect, his hand sliding down my arm before he winks at me and threads his fingers through mine again, continuing down the road toward the diner.

I peer at him from the corner of my eye, discreetly checking for any signs of distress on his face but finding none. He's the picture of ease with a soft smile on his face as we walk in silence. The exact opposite of me. On the outside, I hope I portray the picture of calm, cool, and collected, but inside, I'm a jumble of nerves, barely hanging on by a thread. I need to keep my wits about me when I'm around him. But that nagging voice in the back of my head can't get over the fact that he chose me.

"How's your sister doing?" He tugs softly on my arm to get my attention.

"She lives in Nashville and is engaged to a fucking tool bag named Maxwell, never Max." I scoff, having no desire to talk about my sister and her perfect life. I've had enough of those types of conversations with my mother.

"That's an odd name. Maxwell, never Max. What is he, a secret serial killer?" Finn responds, causing me to laugh loudly.

"No. Apparently, he hates when people shorten his name. He said it makes him sound like some inbred hick."

"He sounds like a joy to be around."

"Oh, he is. I don't have any idea what my sister sees in him. She says she loves him and that I'd understand him better if I got to know him, but neither one of them has stepped foot in Magnolia, and we can't seem to find the right time for my family to go visit them. Not that I have any desire to be in the city. It's a great place to visit, but Magnolia is where I call home."

"I couldn't agree more. Magnolia has always been home for me," he responds, pulling the door to the diner open.

"Then why did you stay away for so long?" I ask, instantly regretting it.

I don't want to give him the wrong idea. This is nothing more than a lunch to allow him to stop bugging me about going out with him, nothing more. However, there is a part of me that wonders why he's still in town. According to my mother, Mr. Buckley is doing much better and has even gone to see a specialist about his condition. He's already moving around easier than he was. I doubt Mrs. Buckley still needs Finn's help to take care of his dad. So why is he still here?

"That's for me to know and you to find out." He chuckles as I stride toward him and through the door.

The 365 Diner is exactly what you'd expect a small-town diner to look like. It has an old-fashioned feel to it, with vintage barstools and a cash-only policy to keep away as many tourists as possible. We don't get many, but they come through from time to time when they're passing between Nashville and Knoxville as Magnolia is perfectly positioned between both, making it an ideal stopping place when you're on a day trip.

"How can this place look exactly the same, yet

different at the same time?" Finn says before waving at Rachael to get her attention.

"As I live and breathe, look who the cat dragged in." Rachael comes to a stop in front of the two of us before winking at Finn. The hairs on the back of my neck raise instantly as I thread my arm through his and step closer to his side. "Haven't seen you at the coffee shop in a few days. I was beginning to miss that smiling face of yours."

My eyes narrow at Rachael, wanting nothing more than to rip her hair out for the way she's acting toward Finn right now. Can't she see we came in together? It's more than obvious that we're on a date. He's mine, and I'll claw her damn eyes out if she thinks for one minute, I'll be sharing him with anyone.

What the fuck? No, no, no! What the hell was I thinking? This is not a date. We're just two grown adults having lunch together. I have no claim on him. Hell, I'm not even sure if I like him.

Yeah, keep telling yourself that one.

"Easy, sugar. I only have eyes for you," he whispers in my ear before planting a kiss on the side of my head as Racheal grabs two menus and leads us to a booth.

My cheeks heat as I drop my head, not wanting to see the smug look on his face as I slide into the booth, immediately picking up the menu. I'd never admit it to Finn, but I spend more time here than at my apartment. I'm a horrible cook, and since I live on the other end of Main Street, it's so much easier to stop on my way home from the station than to go grocery shopping.

"What's good here?" he asks, raising an eyebrow at me.

"I'd have to say that you can't go wrong with a classic like chicken fried steak or meatloaf. Our patty melts are also to die for and are my favorite." She continues prattling on, the sound of her voice grating on my nerves with each passing second. I'm about to tell her to fuck off when a hand appears on the top of my menu, pulling it down just enough so Finn can see my face.

"What do you think I should get?" he asks, completely ignoring Rachael as she continues to rattle on, oblivious to the fact that all his attention is focused on me.

"Why are you asking me?"

"Because, to me, your opinion is the only one that matters."

My mouth drops open as my brain seems to short-circuit for a few moments. For the first time in years, I'm speechless. This is an odd feeling because I always have a snarky retort or sarcastic comment for someone, but right now, my mind is completely blank.

If this was anyone else, I would give him a hard time for trying so hard. That his poetic and flowery words are useless. That he's trying way too hard for another chance to get into my pants, but instead, they give me butterflies in my stomach. I can feel deep in my bones that he means everything he's saying to me with his heart and soul. And that is terrifying.

I clear my throat loudly, pointing at the first item I see on the menu and showing it to him.

"Is that what you want?"

I nod my head, my eyes pointed down at the table as I feel myself blushing at the weight of his stare on me.

"We'll both have a cobb salad and a couple of waters."

"Are you sure I can't interest you in one of our daily specials or even a slice of one of our homemade pies?" Rachael flashes him another brilliant smile, and I snap.

"He said we wanted salads and water. I have places to be and would love to eat my lunch before tomorrow."

With a nod, Rachael spins on her heels and heads back toward the front of the store.

"I never envisioned you as the jealous type, sugar."

"I'm not jealous," I growl. "You were flirting with her as if I wasn't even here. That's disrespectful, not to mention rude as fuck. If you'd rather have a date with Rachael, I'm sure she'd be more than willing to have a seat with you."

I slide to the end of the booth and push to my feet. I need to get out of here. Not only have I made a complete ass out of myself, but I also need to get a handle on these foreign emotions before I do something dumber than I already have.

"Sit down, Marissa." The commanding tone in his voice leaves no room for argument. It's as if my body has a mind of its own, and I immediately sit down and slide along the seat, stopping directly in front of him.

"When did being polite to someone become flirting? I

asked her what's good to eat here because I don't think I've stepped foot in this place since high school. The only woman I see or will ever see for the rest of my life is you."

I can feel the heat rising to my cheeks, and I try to will it away. What the hell is going on with me? I was adamant about not wanting to go to lunch with Finn before leaving the office, and now I'm getting jealous because he smiled at our waitress. I have no claim on Finn. He can smile or talk to whoever he wants, and there is nothing I can do about it.

"Now, do you want to tell me what that was all about?"

"No," I respond, turning my head toward the window as I notice Rachael approaching our table.

"I'm sorry, Marissa. I didn't realize the two of you were on a date. But can you blame me?" Her cheeks pink slightly as she places two cups of water down in front of us.

"I'm sorry, Rae. I'm just in a bad mood. It's been a stressful couple of days," I mumble as she smiles brightly before disappearing down to the other end of the diner, more than likely embarrassed by my actions and wanting to put as much space between us as possible.

"Are you sure this isn't a date?"

"Yes. This is two adults having lunch."

"If you say so." He chuckles, which has anger bubbling in my veins.

"I say so," I respond darkly, knowing that this is all it can be.

Finn reaches over, squeezing my hand lightly. "I'll prove you wrong, Marissa. I'll convince you to let those walls you've built around your heart fall and let me in."

I don't say a word. I can't, even if I wanted to. I've had these walls around me for so long I don't even know if I want to let them down.

"Okay," I respond, ducking my head as I pull my hand from beneath his.

"Trust me," he responds, winking at me in hopes of putting me at ease.

"I don't trust people easily."

"I can only imagine. But I'll try my damndest to make sure you know you can trust me. That I'll never hurt you. That I only ever want to see you smile."

My heart squeezes tightly in my chest. That sounds like a vow—more than a promise—to do all those things and more for me. But I refuse to get my hopes up. Someone once promised me the world but left me for someone else. It's quite possible that this is all a game to Finn. I mean, look at him. He could have any woman he wanted. He doesn't have to chase a girl; he probably has women lining up, just waiting to get a date with him. Right now, he's living for the chase, but the moment he catches me, he'll be gone.

"Your order should be up in a few moments." Racheal's voice brings me back to the present. "Do you need anything else while you wait?"

"No. Thanks, Rae." I force a smile on my face before turning my attention back to look out the window.

"What made you decide to join the sheriff's department?" Finn asks, moving on as if he didn't just drop the equivalent of an emotional time bomb in my lap a few moments ago.

"I've always wanted to come back and help the people of Magnolia. I'm a horrible cook, and the thought of replacing someone's insides makes me gag. So being a sheriff's officer was the closest thing I could think of." I smile softly as I reach for my glass and take a sip. "Besides, my dad is the best man I know. He spent his life serving this community, and it's an honor to carry on his legacy."

His body leans toward me. I'm not even sure if he's noticed, resting his arms on the table as if he is enthralled with whatever I'm saying.

"What about you? Why NASA?"

"Have you been keeping tabs on me?" The side of his lip pulls up in a delicious smirk.

"No, but your parents are both very proud of you. When you got the position there, your mom would tell anyone she met how proud of you she was." I shrug my shoulders, the pang of my parents' own disappointment weighing heavily on my heart.

"I was good with numbers." He chuckles, sliding out of the booth and coming to my side. He takes a seat, sliding across the seat until his leg is pressed right against mine. "I had planned to come back here and help Pops run Tallywackers, but one of my professors got me an internship there, and the rest is history."

"Ummm...Your s-seat is o-o-over there," I stutter as he places his hand on my knee, giving it a squeeze.

"That was entirely too far away," he whispers, resting his forehead against mine. "You smell good enough to eat."

A shiver runs down my spine as his nose runs along the shell of my ear before he inhales deeply.

"Who said I wasn't?" I respond before ducking my head slightly.

This is a bad idea. Flirting with him will lead to kissing, which will lead to sex, which will lead to things I don't even want to think about right now. I should push him away, not encourage him further.

A soft moan escapes my lips as he bites down on my earlobe, nibbling lightly, threading his fingers into my hair and angling my neck to the side, trailing light kisses down my neck.

"You have no idea all the filthy things I want to do to you right now. Too bad we are in a restaurant full of people," he whispers as my eyes flick up to see if anyone is watching before focusing back on his face.

"But I promised you I'd show you I wanted more than just sex from you, sugar."

"But what if that's all I can give you?"

Releasing my hair, Finn tugs my body towards him. "For now." He groans, brushing his lips against mine.

Unable to control the feelings swirling in my body, I lean forward, pressing my lips softly against his. Both of us moan as he grips the back of my neck, pulling me tighter into his body. He dominates our kiss, nipping and sucking my lip between his before thrusting his tongue into my mouth. I wrap my arms around his neck and pull him closer to me. Nothing but pure, unadulterated desire courses through my veins.

But as quickly as it starts, it's over, and we break apart with a gasp.

"Wow," I whisper softly, brushing my fingers across my lips.

"I second that." Finn chuckles softly before planting a kiss on my forehead and pulling away from me. "I better get back on my side of the table before I get carried away again."

"Yeah. That's a good idea." I unwrap my arms from around his neck, scooting away from him.

Holy fucking shit. I agreed to come to lunch with Finn to allow him to thank me for doing my job and to convince him he can chase me all he wants, but I won't be caught.

I've partially accomplished one of those things. The verdict is still out on the second.

ten

finn

"What are you doing here? Didn't you have a date with your dream girl?" Nolan shouts from behind the bar as he wipes down the countertop.

Nolan has been working at the bar since I went away to college. I had helped my dad at the bar every day after school, on holidays, and even on the weekends, so when I left for college, my mom and I hired Nolan. He had just moved to town and was looking for a job, and the rest was history.

It took a little while for the rest of the town to warm up to him, but his hardest sell was my dad. However, you'd never know that he had any reservations about Nolan. Now, he's part of the family. He was there for my dad when he needed him the most, and I'll never be able to repay him for the things he's done for my family.

"Why hasn't my father fired you yet?" I scoff, dropping onto the barstool in front of him.

Crashing and burning is not the best explanation for what happened between Marissa and me today. After our kiss, she closed in on herself. No more snarky comments or witty banter. It was in that moment, I realized I pushed her too hard. It was a risk for sure, and this time, it didn't pay off, but I'm not giving up. There's something there between Marissa and me. I just need to get her to open up to me long enough so I can see it.

"Did you crash and burn again, Boss Man?" Shelly giggles as she places a plate of chocolate cake in front of me.

Shelly has been the cook during the lunch rush ever since I came back to town after Pops's stroke. We've always had a small kitchen in the back just in case someone needed to rent out the place for an event, but Pops was adamant we didn't need to serve anything besides peanuts. He always claimed this was a bar, not a restaurant, but business had been slowing down as people moved out of town. We needed to figure out something to breathe some life back into the business. Adding a lunch and happy hour menu was the easiest option.

"What's this?" I slide the plate closer.

"Think of it as a new menu item," Shelly responds with a smile before leaning on the bar, waiting to hear my opinion on the cake. Too bad for her cake is the last thing on my mind right now.

"More like she wanted to give you some comfort food in case you crashed and burned with your lady love again."

"I don't know why I told either of you about my lady problems."

After a few beers one night after the bar closed, the two of them managed to pry some information out of me. Both had been wondering why I was still in town, since my father was doing so much better, and I needed some advice on what to do next.

"Because it was either us or your mother," Nolan responds before grabbing a glass from under the bar and filling it with my favorite beer. "You look like this might be more your speed."

"Sorry, Shelly." I wink at her before grabbing the glass and drinking almost half of it down at once.

"Damn. That bad, huh?" Shelly snickers as she slides the cake back toward her, grabs the fork, and shoves a large bite into her mouth. "Just means more for me."

Nolan bumps Shelly's shoulder, motioning with his head to the right. "Finn, since you're here, why don't we get started on the inventory count?"

"Can I bring my beer?" I respond, taking another healthy pull from the glass.

"You own the place." He chuckles before disappearing into the stock room behind the bar.

"Don't mind me. I'll just be sitting here, eating my cake all alone." Shelly stuffs another bite of cake into her mouth as I walk around the bar to follow Nolan. "Just try to talk a little louder so I can hear what's going on. A woman's opinion never hurt."

"I'll see what I can do." I refill my beer and head into the storeroom.

"Besides, Nolan is still hung up on the mayor's

daughter, Cora. He isn't the best person to ask for help with getting a girl's attention," Shelly chimes in, a devious smile creeping across her face.

"Shut it, Shelly. You know nothing about my relationship with Cora," Nolan hollers as he pops his head out of the back room.

"Or lack thereof. You aren't faring any better than me, my friend."

"Aren't you due for your daily stalking trip past the vet clinic? Can't miss your chance to get a glimpse of your lady love either," Shelly says as she checks her watch, and a devious smile creeps across her face.

Ever since Nolan came to town a few years ago, he's only had eyes for Cora. I don't know much about his past other than that he grew up in foster care, joined the military at eighteen, and somehow ended up here in Magnolia. Besides my family, Cora was really the only other person in town that didn't keep him at arm's length. Last time we chatted, he hadn't tried to make a move on her, claiming she deserves more than he can give her, but I can tell she is all he can think about.

I give Shelly a one-arm hug before ducking into the storeroom. Nolan is pretending to count the boxes of the new cider we got in from the Tennessee Cider Company a few days ago. I would consider Nolan to be one of my closest friends here in town and one of the few people that know the true depth of my feelings about Marissa.

"You counted that one already." I place my now-full glass on a box near the door before leaning against the door frame. "I have a feeling you wanted to talk about something more than my failed date with Marissa."

"I thought you said you didn't crash and burn," Nolan responds, not bothering to look up from the clipboard in his hand. But he stops counting.

Nolan may not want to be having this conversation, but I have a feeling he needs someone to talk to about what's going on in his head. Hell, we both do. If there is anyone in this town that knows what it's like to be in love with someone who doesn't know you even exist, it's me. The two of us can work together to find a solution to at least one of our problems.

"I didn't. Things just didn't go as I planned them."

"How is that any different from saying you crashed and burned?" Nolan drops the clipboard onto a nearby stack of boxes and takes a seat. His head drops into his hands as his shoulders roll forward.

"Because that phrase implies there's no chance of me having a second date."

"And there's a chance?"

"Oh, yes, there is. Even if she doesn't know it." I grab my beer from the box, striding toward Nolan and taking a seat on the box next to him. "Why don't you tell me what you really want to talk about?"

"Am I that obvious?" He chuckles humorously. "But we aren't talking about me. We're here to discuss you."

"There's nothing for me to discuss. Marissa has been hurt. It's written all over her face, and she won't open her heart easily. I need to give her space. Go slow and reassure her that I won't hurt her."

"I think you're completely full of shit." Nolan's head snaps up, his gaze locking with mine.

"As if you're one to talk. You won't even have a conversation with Cora because of your misguided feelings of not being good enough for her."

"Again, we aren't talking about me and my feelings for Cora."

"True, but I believe we both have the same problem. We need to build trust with our ladies. To show them it's safe to let their guards down and show us their souls. If we can get them to let their guards down, it should be smooth sailing after that."

"Easier said than done," he responds, slamming his fist on the box beside him. "At least your girl is in your league. Cora is in a whole different solar system. She'll never want anything to do with a guy like me."

"You never know unless you try," I say, slapping him hard on the back. "Don't be me, Nolan. I've spent years going through life, searching for a replacement for the girl I fell in love with in high school, but was too much of a pussy to let know how I felt."

"It could also have been the perfect boyfriend she was head over heels with."

Nolan isn't wrong. Seeing how happy and in love Marissa was with Campbell was a big reason I kept my feelings to myself, but it wasn't for noble reasons. I knew there was no way she'd return my feelings, so I kept them locked deep inside.

"Lucky for me, Campbell isn't in the picture any longer."

"For now," Nolan responds, pushing to his feet and grabbing the clipboard. He begins counting the boxes correctly this time, one after the other, before writing the tally on his list and beginning again.

"Are you going to explain that statement?"

"What's there to explain?"

"Do you have any idea what happened between her and Campbell?"

I pause because, if I'm being honest, I never cared. My ma always tried to keep me informed of what was going on in Magnolia, but I never really paid attention. If it had nothing to do with her or my father, I barely paid attention. If I had, it wouldn't have taken me this long to find my way back to Marissa. The moment I knew she and Campbell weren't married, I'd have come right back to town, hoping to have a chance with her.

"I didn't think so. Campbell dumped her a few months after you left for school."

"Okay—"

"I'm not finished yet." Nolan turns toward me. "He ended up married to Emmeline Baker and had a baby on the way six months later."

"Motherfucker," I swear, my anger bubbling to the surface. "I knew they had broken up, but I never knew all the details."

"Yeah, it was the only thing people in town could talk about for almost a year after it happened. The rumors and speculation didn't die down until she headed off to college."

"No wonder why she's so skittish about getting into another serious relationship."

Marissa must have had her guard up for years. The hurt in her eyes all makes sense now. I have a feeling I've been pushing her too hard, but for some reason, I can't help myself. Marissa being single and clearly into me was the last thing I expected to happen when I came back to Magnolia. But now that I see my opening, I'm going to take it. I'm going to make sure that Marissa knows how much she means to me.

eleven

marissa

"I'm about to head out. Do you need anything else before I go?" Dolores pops her head into my office, scanning the room for Lord knows what.

"What are you looking for?" I laugh loudly before pushing back from my desk slightly, resting my heels on the corner.

"Don't let Colt catch you doing that. He'll have your head." Dolores scoffs, coming the rest of the way into my office and shutting the door.

"Oh, this must really be serious if you're closing the door." I pull my feet off my desk, my eyes locked on Dolores as I try to figure out what her end game is here.

"Can you be serious for a minute, Marissa?" She flops down into the chair in front of my desk, running her hand through her shoulder-length blonde hair. "I wanted to know how you were doing, really."

"Why wouldn't I be okay?" I cross my arms over my chest. "Why does it feel like everyone around me knows something I don't?"

I wince slightly as I watch her shoulders roll forward,

as if she's closing in on herself. Dolores drops her chin to her chest and responds softly. "I di-didn't mean a-anything b-by it. I j-just wa-wanted to check on you. I'm sorry."

"No, I'm sorry." I sigh, pushing to my feet and strolling around my desk.

Everyone has been acting strange around me for the last few days. Everyone goes silent when I walk into a room, and I see people whispering as I walk by on Main Street. Usually shit like this wouldn't bother me, but for some reason, this has me on edge. I know if it was important, Colt or someone would tell me, but I hate not knowing, especially if it has to do with me.

"I'm fine." I give her a reassuring smile. "I promise."

"I know we aren't close, but I want you to know you can trust me, Marissa. I don't have many people in my life that I could call a friend, but I try my best to be there for the people I care about, and I care about you." She sighs as I take a seat next to her, wrapping my arm around her shoulder and giving her an awkward hug.

Now I'm even more worried than I was, but I push those feelings to the side. I can tell that Dolores was being sincere when she asked me if I was okay, not searching for gossip like I'm so used to happening.

Ever since mine and Campbell's epic breakup years ago, every time he comes back into town, the questions and whispers start all over again. People aren't being mali-cious, and I truly believe that deep down they are asking because they care, but I also know it's interesting. So, even though I know very little about Dolores, I believe she's being sincere.

"Maybe we can even be friends," she mumbles, shrugging my hand off her shoulder and standing.

"I'd really like that," I respond, and she flashes me one of her award-winning smiles.

That smile is the main reason Colt hired her. He claimed we needed someone at the front desk that would put people at ease when they walked through the door.

"Me, too," she responds. Her eyes scan my face, no doubt searching for any signs that I'm lying, but she won't find any. It's been a very weird couple of weeks. Discovering my one-night stand is none other than Finn Buckley. Something that, no matter how hard I try, I can't seem to forget.

I shake my head, hoping to clear the memories from that night out of my head. I don't want to think about the way his eyes scanned me from head to toe as if he was ready to devour me, body and soul, or how his voice sent a shiver of pleasure all the way through me when all he said was my name.

Nope, no thinking about it. It will only lead to wanting to spend another night with him, not that I don't already want to do just that, but it can't happen. There is no way that things will work out between Finn and me. Maybe before, well, everything, that girl who had an open heart would believe that love could fix anything. But I'm not that girl anymore.

"Fine. I'll take your word for it, but I want you to

know you can tell me if you're having a hard time. I won't tell anyone. I promise. Even if they ask." She smiles before turning on her heels and heading for the door.

"Thank you. I'm sorry I made you feel uncomfortable. It's been a weird week."

She giggles before pulling the door open. "Colt headed out before I came in here, so I turned the dispatch radio up so you can hear it in here."

"Thanks. Have a good night, Dolores, and I'll see you at church tomorrow," I respond as I hear Colt calling my name through the radio.

"I can grab that..." she trails off, glancing down at her watch quickly before turning back toward me.

"Nope. Have a good evening, Dolores. He's calling for me specifically, anyway." I stand and follow her out of my office. I wait for Dolores to make it out the door and climb into her car before grabbing the radio and answering Colt. "Good evening to you, too, Sheriff Grumpy Pants."

I started calling him that ridiculous name after I told him Sutton was getting married to that tool bag a few months ago. I know better than anyone how obsessed he is with my sister. I should leave him be, but after the stunt he pulled yesterday, I'm all too willing to rub salt in his wounds. I'm petty like that sometimes.

"How many times have I told you to stop calling me that?" he growls, causing me to laugh even louder, a huge smile plastered on my face.

"Probably a million, but you know I'm never going to

stop, not until you do something about the douchebag she plans to marry."

This isn't the first, and it definitely won't be the last, time I've made that statement. Colt is crazy about my sister. For him, Sutton is the one that got away. He keeps trying to be casual about it, but I see the pain in his eyes each time he asks how Sutton is doing. He gobbles up every detail, breaking his own heart in the process. I should put him out of his misery and stop answering his questions, but what's the fun in that?

Sutton isn't any better. The few times she has called me or my parents, our conversations always stray to her asking questions about Colt, although she manages to never directly ask if he's dating anyone. I give her the answers without provocation, much to her delight, because I know those two would be perfect for each other if they just got over themselves and took the plunge. Then she can move home, have babies, and all those things my parents keep pestering me about.

Just like you refuse to do with Finn. Shut up, brain. No one asked you. This isn't about me and my baggage from being dumped by the man I thought I'd spend the rest of my life with. This is about figuring out how to get Sutton and Colt together.

Yeah, she's engaged, but her fiancée is an asshole, and she deserves better. Sure, he's rich and all that nonsense, but that doesn't change the fact that she belongs with Colt, and we all know it. They just need a push in the right direction, and since I hardly ever talk to my sister, I push Colt. Maybe one of these days he will snap.

"Why is your sister sitting on the side of the road crying?" Colt growls over the line, bringing my mind back to the present.

"My sister? Sutton?" I question, wondering the same thing.

My sister hasn't been back to town in years, not even for holidays. She calls my parents weekly to check in and make sure that they are doing well, but besides that, nothing.

"Unless you have another sister I wasn't aware of." Colt is clearly losing his patience with me, but I don't know any more than he does at this point.

I was hoping for a quiet night of hiding in my office and pretending to work while I watch *Love Is Blind* episodes on my computer, but no. Apparently, the universe has other plans. Like it hasn't fucked with me enough over the last day or two.

Apparently, my sister is stuck on the side of the road somewhere in town. I haven't heard a peep from her since I got her wedding invitation in the mail about a week ago. I'm almost 100 percent sure my parents don't know she was planning on coming into town or they would've rolled out the red carpet.

Colt's voice coming through the radio brings me back to the present. "Marissa. I need to know what's going on."

"How the hell should I know, Colt? Here's a

thought. How about you ask her?" I snap, wanting answers just as much as he does.

My sister isn't a reckless person. She doesn't just show up somewhere without letting someone know ahead of time. Something must be wrong. If that asshole fiancé of hers did something to her, I'll kill him.

"I should bring her into the station for you to deal with," Colt growls.

"Are you going to cuff her?" I laugh loudly at the irony of the situation. Colt has been looking for the perfect opportunity to get my sister back in town. Maybe now he'll grow a pair and tell her how he feels. "I don't want to know about your kinky fantasies about my sister, Sheriff."

I've known for a while that Colt and Sutton should be together. Hell, I knew it when we were in high school, but those two were both too afraid of being hurt that neither said anything to the other. Maybe if I give them both a little push toward each other, they'll finally have the courage to say what needs to be said.

"If I had to guess, it must have something to do with the douche canoe she plans to marry," I grumble before sighing loudly. "Just talk to her, Colt. I'll bring a hand radio with me in case someone calls, and I'll figure out what she's doing back in town."

Colt rattles off their location and says he'll see me in a few minutes. I can barely contain my laughter. "This is the perfect opportunity to give those two a little shove in the right direction," I say to myself before grabbing a set of keys off the hook, getting into a SUV, and heading toward the outskirts of town. Colt must have been on his way back to the station when he ran into Sutton on the side of the road. But the question remains: What the fuck is she doing there?

It doesn't take long for me to reach the location Colt described. Colt's truck is pulled to the side of the road, his lights flashing to let oncoming traffic know they need to proceed carefully. Sitting precariously on the edge of the ditch is my sister's car, the door flung open wide.

"Did she have an accident?" I mumble to myself as I shift the vehicle into park and climb out. But instead of running toward my sister and Colt, I remain frozen in place, trying to make sense of the sight in front of me. Colt has his arms wrapped tightly around my sister, her head tucked under his chin, and her arms are wrapped tightly around his waist.

"Tell me everything," Colt demands as her eyes fly open in shock before hardening slightly.

"I don't think that's any of your business," Sutton mumbles nervously as I stride toward them, wanting to sort this out as quickly as possible.

"Hey, sis, you all right?" I eye the two of them skeptically as Colt releases Sutton, putting some space between them.

"Perfect." She plasters a fake smile on her face.

My head swivels back and forth between them, trying to make sense of what's going on but quickly decide to give up for now. Whatever happened between my sister and Colt before I got here isn't what's important. What's important is finding out what's going on with her. We may not be as close as we were when we were children, but above all, she's my sister.

"How about we go home and talk?" I ask Sutton, pinning Colt in place with a stare and letting him know he isn't invited.

"That sounds like a good idea," Sutton whispers as she strides toward me, one of her shoulders brushing against his slightly. She gasps slightly, her eyes widening as if she's been electrocuted before she schools her features. "It was nice seeing you," Sutton calls over her shoulder to Colt as I turn on my heels and follow her toward the SUV.

"I'll call a tow truck and have someone at the garage take a look at her car," Colt shouts toward us, his eyes still locked on Sutton as she climbs in, pulling the door shut behind her.

"Thanks, Sheriff." I wink at him before ducking back into the SUV and joining my sister.

"Buckle up, Sutton," I command as I put the vehicle in reverse, my eyes locked on Sutton the entire time.

She nods her head, only moving enough to put on her seat belt, but she never once looks away from him. Her eyes remain locked with his as we back up slightly, pulling around him and getting back onto the road. As we pass, I notice he hasn't moved a muscle. Standing there like a statue, his eyes locked on Sutton as we drive past, moving further into town.

"How interesting," I mumble to myself, making a right instead of a left to head toward our parents' house.

"What's so funny?" Sutton questions, her head snapping back to mine.

"Nothing." I smile, shaking my head, wondering how long it's going to take for these two to realize they're perfect for each other.

"Can I get a beer? Whatever you have on tap," someone asks, breaking me from my daydream.

"Coming right up. We have a nitro stout I've been dying to pour for someone." Nolan smirks in my direction, shaking his head at me for what seems like the millionth time today, before turning to fill the beer. "Here you go. Do you want to start a tab or cash out now?"

The customer says something to him before sliding his card across the bar and disappearing into the crowd.

"Tab it is," I say, grabbing the card and tucking it into a cup near the register.

We rarely hold credit cards for tabs, but I guess today we do. It wouldn't be the strangest thing that's happened today. Ever since I went out to lunch with Marissa the other day, I haven't been able to focus on anything else.

On the days I stay above the bar, I stay in bed until it's time to open, but that wasn't possible this morning. I tried for hours to get back to sleep, but it was next to impossible with the raging hard-on that came every time I closed my eyes. The image of Marissa laid out, naked and on display in bed, waiting for me to have my way with her, haunted me. Making me yearn for another night with her. I was hoping that spending time with her would ease my need, but it only made it worse. Now the only thing I can think about is what it feels like to sink between her milky thighs, the sound of her breathlessly moaning my name. I'm addicted. But I want more than sex from Marissa. I want everything. I just need to convince her to give me a chance.

"When are you going to get your head out of the clouds?" Nolan questions, knocking his shoulder into mine, motioning his head toward a woman standing at the end of the bar, waving us over. "That beauty has been trying to get your attention for the last few minutes."

"Marissa is here?" I stutter and spin around quickly. My eyes scan the bar, wanting to catch a glimpse of her before she disappears a second time.

"Oh, you've got it bad. Too bad for you, she won't give you the time of day." Nolan chuckles, grabbing my shoulder and pointing me in the direction of the woman standing at the end of the bar. "Her."

As soon as my eyes find the woman in question, her cheeks pink slightly before her head snaps in the other direction. I don't remember her name off the top of my head, but she's been in a lot recently. If I remember correctly, she came into town a few weeks ago for a bachelorette party with some friends. They were a good group of women, not too out of control, but Nolan and I had our hands full trying to get them into cabs and on their way home that night.

Ever since then, she seems to pop in once or twice a week during lunch. She always sits at the end of the bar, places the same order, and then leaves. She doesn't speak much, but that's not too unusual, but today is the first time she's gone out of her way to get my attention.

"Ah." A light bulb goes off in my head as I stride toward the register, typing in an order for a club sandwich, a glass of water, and a caramel apple cider from Tennessee Cider Company. "I'll go back and let Shelly know the order is up. Can you let her know her sandwich will be right out?"

I don't wait for him to respond before grabbing a glass from beneath the bar and filling it with water. "Take this to her while I grab her beer."

"She doesn't want me to bring her anything."

"What?"

"Finn, you can't be that dense, can you?"

"What the fuck are you talking about, Nolan?" I deadpan, eyeing him skeptically.

"She wants to talk to you. Not me or any other man in this bar. She's probably been coming in here for weeks, trying to work up the nerve to talk to you."

Nolan has been pushing me to talk to her, saying she'd be an easy hookup, but that's not what I'm looking for. I've never really been into one-night stands. I'm no saint by any means, but Marissa is everything I've ever wanted for my future and so much more. I'm not about to throw all that way for some random woman who came into my bar.

"I talk to her," I respond, running my free hand across the back of my neck.

Nolan crosses his arms over his chest. "Asking her if it's going to be cash or charge doesn't equal a conversation, Finn."

"Right," I grumble before heading toward the woman. It seems Marissa took more than my heart with her when she scurried out of the hotel room in Chattanooga like her ass was on fire.

With a shake of my head to clear my mind, I stride toward her, the glass of water gripped tightly in my hand. This woman is the exact opposite of Marissa. Her auburn hair hangs in loose waves; the tips brush against her shoulders as she turns towards me. Her eyes widen in surprise as I get closer before she jumps to her feet, knocking the bar stool backward with a thud.

"I'm s-so s-sorry," she stutters, bending down quickly to grab it and returning it to the upright position before taking a seat.

"No problem at all. It happens to the best of us." I smirk at her before placing her water down on the bar in front of her. "I already put in your lunch order. I'll bring your cider when your sandwich is ready."

I pause for a moment, waiting to see if she has any other requests before continuing. "If you need anything before your lunch is ready, give us a shout. One of us will come running."

"Thank you," she responds, her eye cast down toward the bar, allowing her hair to shield her face.

"You're welcome," I say with a smile before turning and heading toward the kitchen and letting Shelly know there's another order.

"That's it?" Nolan asks, stepping in my way as I try to head back toward the bar. "You didn't stay and talk to her? Try to get her number? Nothing?"

"No." I chuckle before slapping him on the shoulder. "If you want to talk to her so badly, be my guest."

"Okay, what gives?" Nolan asks. "Or did something happen with Marissa last night?"

"I don't know what you're talking about." I step around him, grabbing a rag to wipe the already-clean bar as he pulls it from my hands.

"Try that on someone who has no idea how much you love her." He grabs my wrist and pulls me toward the small storeroom behind the bar, ensuring no one can overhear us. "Finn, talk to me. Your head is in the clouds, and you're blowing off a perfectly willing female who clearly has the hots for you."

"Not every woman I'm nice to wants to get into my pants."

"True, but you're different today."

"I don't have time for this," I grumble, attempting to step around him. Still, he follows my movements, making it almost impossible to get around him. "I have a business to run, man. I can't sit back here with you and talk about our feelings.

I need to get my head on straight. It was just one night. The best one of my life, but that's beside the point. I can't force Marissa to give me a chance to win her heart or even to go on a date with me.

"You need to pull your head out of your ass, Finn. If you want her, go after her. Make Marissa see what an awesome guy you are, and she'd be a fool to turn you down or move on."

"It's not that simple, Nolan," I grumble, taking a seat on a pile of crates and dropping my head into my hands. "Something happened, but she said it can never happen again. No matter how much I want it to."

I omitted the fact that we slept together, and Marissa doesn't know how infatuated I am with her already. The chances of Nolan spilling his guts to her are slim, but I'm not willing to take any chances. The last thing I need her to think is that I went and blabbed about what happened between us. Not only will that ruin any chance I might have to be with her, but she'd also kick my ass.

"I never took you as a coward, Finn."

"I'm not."

"Then why are you sitting here with your tail between your legs and not fighting for your girl?"

"She isn't my girl."

"Not yet." Nolan disappears for a few minutes before shoving a cold beer in my face. "You need a drink."

"Did you pay for this?" I question, pulling it out of his hand and taking a long swig.

"Why should I? You own the place, but if it makes you feel better, take it out of my pay." He rolls his eyes, dropping beside me. "But because I work here, I wanted to let you know to stop being an asshole and get your shit together because Marissa is here."

I stand quickly, knocking the crate I was sitting on to the floor as he places his hand on the center of my chest. "Whoa, there. She isn't alone."

"So, Colt is with her. I know she had to work a shift at the station today. They probably came in to grab something to eat. What's the big deal?"

They come in here all the time, although not as often as I'd like, choosing to eat at the diner instead.

"Colt isn't with her."

I narrow my eyes in his direction, quickly losing my patience. I haven't laid eyes on her in days, which isn't unusual, but today it feels like an eternity. I asked her to give me a chance to get to know her, and she didn't respond. The waiting is killing me. I want to storm into the station and demand she give me a chance, but that wouldn't end the way I want it to. Marissa is as stubborn as a mule. Instead of choosing to give us a chance, she'd dig in her heels, and I'd be back to square one. And that I can't have. So, I wait, no matter how much my heart yearns to know if she will give us a chance.

"Get out of my way." I shove him to the side and go storming toward the front of the bar, eager to see Marissa.

As soon as I turn the corner, I freeze. Marissa is standing a few feet away, near the doorway, her eyes scanning the bar, searching the room for something before locking with mine. My eyes start at her feet and make their way up her long legs, which are covered in her Magnolia County Sheriff's Department uniform. Her hair is pulled into a messy bun sitting on the top of her head, with a few strands hanging loose, framing her face.

"I didn't know uniforms did it for you." Nolan's voice startles me back to the present. "Maybe if you ask nicely, she'll cuff you."

"You're an asshole," I chuckle, noticing who she came into the bar with. "As I live and breathe. Sutton Flores," I shout, not bothering to hide my excitement at seeing my high school best friend.

"Asshole," Sutton mumbles, barely loud enough for me to hear, before plastering a fake smile on her face. Her eyes lock with mine, widening in surprise. "Finn?"

"In the flesh." I smile as she strides toward me, reaching over the bar and pulling me in for a tight hug. "Oh my God, how have you been? I didn't even recognize you."

"I get that a lot." I chuckle, returning her hug before taking a step back. My eyes immediately focus on Marissa. "And I've been all right. How's the city treating you?"

"Not as well as I expected." She sniffles as the two of them slide onto the two empty bar stools in front of me.

I chance a glance at Marissa, wanting to know what

happened, but she's no help, only shrugging her shoulder before placing a comforting hand on her sister's back.

Instead of prying further, I quickly change the subject. "What can I getcha?"

"Bottle of Jack. One glass," Marissa answers without hesitation, pinning me in place with her stare. Her eyes focus on my lips as her tongue swipes across her top lip before pulling the bottom one between her teeth and nibbling on it.

I bite back a groan, dropping my hand beneath the bar and palming the bulge in my pants. My mouth waters as images of her gorgeous body, laid out before me, ready for me to feast upon her luscious skin, filter through my mind for the millionth time today.

"I don't have the patience for your crap today, Buckley," she responds, shaking her head slightly, trying to regain control of the situation, but now that I know she is barely hanging on, just like me, I have to see how far I can push her.

"Did someone get up on the wrong side of the bed?" I respond in a sing-song voice before leaning forward and whispering into her ear. "I'm sure we have time for a quickie in the backroom, but you'd have to be quiet."

Her gaze flicks to mine as if I've called her name, and she shifts on the stool, dropping her head downward and inhaling sharply. The spot over my heart aches at the thought of not being able to catch another glimpse of her. Her lips move for a few moments before leaning back, her entire face pinking as her hand moves directly toward her gun.

"I will fucking shoot you, Finn."

Fuck, why does that sound appealing right now? I give my cock one final squeeze before taking a step back and winking at her, the side of my mouth pulling up slightly. "Duty calls."

I don't spare her another glance as I stroll toward the other end of the bar to take care of a customer, fighting to look as if nothing unusual happened. I try desperately to remain focused on the customer, but I can't resist the urge to glance down the bar, making sure she's still sitting there.

"The way you feel about her is written all over your face," Nolan says as he places a beer in front of them with a roll of his eyes.

"Is it that obvious?" I respond, turning to add the drink to their tab while grabbing the bottle of Jack and one glass Marissa requested.

"Yes, it is. It's also obvious that what happened between you two wasn't one-sided either. You two could've set this place on fire when she walked in." He stares down, motioning toward Marissa.

"I know there's something there. I can feel it," I respond, raising the glass and rubbing the back of my hand against the spot over my heart. "Now, if I can just get her on board, my life will get so much easier."

"Try being charming. Ladies dig that." He winks as

he strides toward them, with me hot on his heels. As I get closer, I hear the tail end of their conversation.

"The same time I slept with Finn Buckley."

"You did what?" Sutton screeches as I place the bottle of Jack Daniels and a glass in front of them before heading back down the bar.

My cock hardens as the need to remind her of what it feels like to have a cock between her lower lips overwhelms me.

"It seems you might have a little problem." Nolan stifles his laugh with a cough, and I punch him hard in the stomach as the feeling of her eyes tracking my movement crawls up my spine.

"There's nothing little about it." I scoff before forcing thoughts of her out of my mind and heading into the back room to calm down.

I try to concentrate on anything other than how good it would feel to be balls deep inside Marissa right now. Hearing her scream my name in ecstasy, letting every motherfucker know who she belongs to, but it's not working. *Dead kittens, Grandma in a bikini... Nothing is working!* Unable to resist the urge any longer, I palm my cock through my jeans, groaning at the delicious pressure. Unbuttoning my jeans, I reach inside and pull out my cock. My pre-cum is already dripping down my shaft. I groan as I use it as a lubricant, pumping my hand up and down my shaft a few times, hoping to relieve some pressure.

It doesn't take long for images of Marissa, laid out on

the bed, her fingers sliding between her lower lips as she pumps in and out quickly, to flood my brain.

"I can't wait to be buried inside you," I whisper as if she can hear me, gripping my cock tighter.

"Can you feel me? How tight my pussy is, squeezing your cock as I ride you?"

I pump in time with the sounds of her moans echoing in my mind. She pumps her fingers in and out faster, lifting her hips to match each downward movement of my hand. My balls tighten as I'm nearing my release.

"Yes," I groan, trying to keep my voice down as my release vibrates through me. Hot white streams of cum shoot all over the floor as I squeeze the last remnants from my cock. Breathing heavily, I tuck myself back into my pants, zip up, and clean up my mess on the floor before collapsing onto the pile of crates, trying to make sense of what I just did.

I usually have better control over myself than this, but my obsession with Marissa is now out of control. And I'm powerless to stop it. Fuck, I feel like I'm teetering on the edge of madness, going out of my mind with the need to claim her. I want every part of her to belong to me. To be the only man she will ever think about for the rest of her life. The only way to ensure that happens is to show her how amazing we can be together. That I'd never hurt her but cherish her and treat her like a queen from now until eternity, if only she'd give me a chance.

Nolan was right. I'm not a coward. If Marissa doesn't

want to spend another night with me, I'll have to convince her. There's something between us, a soul-deep connection that we're powerless to control, but she's been hurt before. I need to prove to her I'm worthy of her love to ensure there's any chance of us spending more than just that one night together.

With a renewed sense of purpose, I stride out of the back room, nearly knocking Nolan over. "Where's the fire?" he questions before our eyes lock.

We stand there in silence for a few moments before a bright smile crosses his face. "Go get her, tiger."

I chuckle as I continue in their direction, once again catching the tail end of Sutton and Marissa's conversation.

"Was it good at least?" Sutton questions as my eyes instantly focus on Marissa.

I hold my breath, waiting for her to answer her sister's question. I can feel the strength of our connection deep in my soul, but it could all be in my head, the desire to have a shot at a relationship with Marissa after all these years overriding all my other senses.

"The best," she responds softly, a soft smile crossing her face. "Too bad I can't decide if I want to shoot him, arrest him, or fuck him again."

I release the breath I didn't know I was holding before stepping close to the pair. "I'm game. Just not in that order. There are laws against that type of thing."

"You're in so much trouble." Sutton giggles,

wobbling slightly on the chair before taking another healthy pull from her glass.

"Is everything okay here?" I question, noticing for the first time how unstable she is. My eyes flick toward the half-empty bottle of Jack Daniels sitting on the bar. Marissa seems to be the picture of sobriety, sitting upright on the bar stool, her eyes focused on her sister.

"No. Not at all." She hiccups, using the bar to turn her body toward me.

"And why's that?"

"Her fiancé cheated on her," Marissa chimes in from beside her before Sutton wails loudly.

"On my 800 thread-count sheets!"

"Is that the only thing you care about?" Marissa responds before shaking her head at Sutton. "Face it, you don't love him. Maybe you never did. You just loved the idea of being with him."

Sutton sinks in on herself, taking her sister's words to heart. Not wanting to let Sutton spiral, I speak up, trying to keep her mind on the conversation and not on the reminder of what has happened to her.

"I don't understand why you're so upset. He sounds like a piece of shit for cheating on you."

"You wouldn't understand, Finn. You think with the brain between your legs and not the one between your ears."

I chuckle humorously. "Trust me, if I thought with that brain all the time, I'd have your sister bent over the bar right now instead of helping you with your life problems."

"Finn!" They both shout at the same time before I break out into a fit of loud laughter.

"I really am tempted to shoot you," Marissa grumbles before shoving Sutton's glass toward me on the bar. "Finish this for her. She's done."

"I am not." She reaches for the glass as I grab it off the bar and throw back the last bit as I eye her skeptically. "One tiny sip won't hurt, Marissa. Besides, what Colt doesn't know won't hurt him."

"I'm on duty, Finn. The last thing people want to know is that I've been drinking while putting them in handcuffs."

I wink at Marissa, my eyes catching sight of Colt coming through the front door, his eyes scanning the room, no doubt in search of Sutton. "I've always had a thing for handcuffs."

"Oh, my God! Do you ever quit?" Sutton cackles loudly, as if she doesn't have a care in the world.

I don't know much about the woman Sutton has grown into, but my best friend loved deep. If she had any feelings for the man she planned on marrying, she'd be an inconsolable mess right now. Marissa is right. She more than likely liked the idea of him instead of being deeply in love with him, but who am I to talk? I have every intention of convincing her sister to fall madly in love with me and vow to never leave my side. It shouldn't be too hard, right?

"Not when it comes to your sister." I lean forward, resting my elbows on the bar. My eyes remain focused on Marissa the entire time. "Now that you're home, how about putting in a good word for me with this one? I need all the help I can get."

"I got your back!" Sutton shouts, no doubt meaning to say it loud enough for me to hear, "Finn's a good guy, sister. Besides, you already know he's good in bed. Why not go another round?"

"She said I'm good in bed?" I chime in, a sly smile crossing my face.

"I said no such thing," Marissa growls before slamming something onto the bar. "I need to get back to work."

"On the house. Consider it a welcome home present for little Ms. Sutton." I give her a mock salute before sliding her card back across the bar. "I'm sure I'll be seeing you ladies around."

I give Marissa one final look before striding down the bar, grabbing Colt's attention.

"What can I get for you?" I ask, already knowing what he's here for.

Sutton Flores is back in town and on the outs with her fiancé. It was only a matter of time before Colt came searching for her.

"I'm here to see Marissa." He rubs his hand across the back of his neck.

"Are you looking for Marissa or her sister?"

"Sutton's here?" His eyes widen in surprise before his head turns as if on a swivel, searching for his lady in love.

"At the other end of the bar, but be warned, Marissa gave her Jack Daniels in an attempt to find out why she was back in town. So, in short, she's drunk."

He doesn't say a word, just nods his head before turning on his heels and heading in their direction, but I call his name.

"Colt. Why would you come here searching for Marissa?" I question, wanting to know why, of all the places, he believed she'd be here.

"No reason in particular, just a lucky guess. But a word of advice: If you want her, go get her. You never know when some asshole might swoop in and steal her right from under your nose," he says with a smile before striding down the bar, his eyes laser-focused on Sutton.

I watch as the three exchange words before Colt bends down and throws Sutton over his shoulder and strides toward the door, catcalls and whistles following behind them. A gentle smile crosses my face at the thought of those two finally getting their chance at happiness. If they could find their way to each other after all these years, there's a chance the same could be said for Marissa and me. I have to take the first step. I can't expect fate to do all the work in this situation. It's time for me to get the ball rolling.

Now that I've decided, I scan the room for Marissa, glimpsing her the moment she steps out the door, and it swings closed behind her.

"Shit," I shout, hopping over the bar and chasing after her. "Marissa!"

Her entire body tenses as she turns toward me. Our eyes lock as a soft smile spreads across her face. She's just as gorgeous as ever—curves in all the right places, dark chocolate-colored hair I remember having wrapped tightly around my hand as I pounded into her from behind.

"I have a question for you." I lick my lips as I step toward her, tucking the few strands of her hair behind her ear. "Do you want to go out with me?"

"We went out to lunch the other day."

"You know exactly what I mean, sugar. I want to take you on a proper date."

She looks up at me, her eyes shining with an emotion I can't place, and I stop breathing. It's as if our entire future plays out before my eyes. The white picket fence, a stupid dog that I'll complain about owning but secretly be in love with, Marissa round with our child. Everything. I can see it all as if it's destined to happen.

"I told you before. I could only give you that one night, Finn," she whimpers.

Electricity sizzles between us as she leans toward me as if she's being pulled by an invisible string in my direction. I scan her face, trying to commit every detail to memory: the color of her eyes, the way a few strands of her hair fall into her face. But neither of us makes a move. It's as if we're in our own world, and nothing else exists but the two of us.

"But plans change," I grunt, brushing my thumb across her bottom lip as I lean forward, my eyes focused on hers. "I'm going to kiss you now."

The need to claim her lips is almost overwhelming as I lean forward and brush my lips against hers. Electricity zips through my body as an unknown force pulls us closer together.

"This is a bad idea," she mumbles against my mouth before nibbling on my bottom lip and running her tongue along it, begging for entrance.

"It's all I've ever wanted." I groan before gripping the back of her neck and crushing our lips together.

She gasps in surprise as I shove my tongue into her mouth, tasting her sweetness. Every nerve feels like it's on fire as a sense of completeness settles over me, something I've never felt for another person in my life. Something in the universe is telling me to hold on to this girl and never let her go.

Someone clears their throat loudly, causing us to break apart with a gasp.

"Sorry, but I need help changing out the keg," Nolan says sheepishly before turning and heading back into the bar.

"I can't do this, Finn," Marissa whispers softly, brushing her fingers along her lips. "I promised you one night. That's all I can give you right now."

"I know you can feel the pull between us, Marissa. I also know you're scared shitless, but so am I." I rest my forehead against hers and clench my eyes shut tightly.

Marissa only shakes her head before taking a step back and putting some much-needed distance between the two of us. "I have to go."

Every muscle in my body yearns to wrap her in my arms and never let her go, but I stop myself.

"Goodbye, Marissa."

"Goodbye, Finn," she whispers, something flashing in her eyes before she turns and hurries toward the sheriff's department SUV, climbs in, and peels out of the parking lot without a backward glance. Once the vehicle is out of sight, I head back inside the bar to help Nolan.

"I thought I was going to have to spray you two with the hose," Nolan says the minute I step into the bar, causing me to chuckle darkly.

"I wish, but I have a feeling I'd only scare her even more," I respond, striding past him toward the storeroom where the kegs are being kept.

Every cell in my body yearns to claim Marissa as my own. I need her in a way that I haven't needed anyone in years. But first, I have to convince her I'm worthy of the honor of calling her mine.

"**I**s it always so quiet around here?"

I jump slightly in my seat at the sound of Dolores's voice as she comes strolling through the front door.

"You mean besides my sister running out of gas on the side of the road when she was running away from her cheating fiancé?" I laugh, dropping my feet to the floor and getting them out of her way.

"That's what happened?" I nod my head, barely containing my laughter at the look on her face. "Damn, I miss everything good," she huffs as she strides around her desk, taking the seat next to me.

Thankfully, working the overnight shift last night wasn't as bad as I thought it would be, besides having to deal with my sister and Colt. I hid in my office for the rest of the evening after running out of Tallywackers with my tail between my legs. I wasn't ready to see Finn again so quickly, but if I'm being honest with myself, I don't regret it. It was nice catching up with my sister and watching her squirm as Colt finally made his move. My mother called a few times right after I got back from the bar, but I ignored her. I know I should probably answer, but I'm a terrible liar. I don't know how she does it, but whenever I even think about lying to her, she knows immediately. She always tries to sell me some nonsense about how moms know these things, but I'm really bad at it. Either way, I'm going to pay for not answering the phone, but that's future me's problem, especially after she finds out my sister is in town and I didn't tell her.

"What are you doing here so early?" I question as she stuffs her bag beneath the desk and begins turning on all her computers.

I have no idea what any of these monitors and computers do, but she does. Dolores runs this entire station like a well-oiled machine, making sure that Colt, Waylen, and I have everything we need. We'd be lost without her.

"Colt sent me a text last night, asking me to come and man the phones while you're at church today because he wasn't feeling well."

"Oh, yeah, he isn't feeling well at all. He has a case of the Suttons." I raise my eyebrows for full effect.

It takes a few minutes, but Dolores catches on. "Oh, my god! I'm so happy for them."

"Me, too." I laugh, watching her bounce around in her chair, clapping her hands in joy. "Let's just hope Colt seals the deal this time."

"I have faith in him. So, quiet night?"

"Same as always. You grew up in Magnolia. Nothing ever happens around here." I chuckle softly. "Sometimes we get calls to head to Birch Cove or Rose Hill, but nothing else, mostly."

Being a Magnolia County sheriff's deputy means we get calls from all over the county, but it's never anything eventful. The most that happens is we get a call to run some kids off Old Man Wynter's property for drinking and tipping over his cows. What can I say? We live in a small town surrounded by more small towns. Teenagers have to find creative ways to have fun.

"I don't know about you, but I hope that never changes."

"I second that. Nothing really changes around here. It's one of the main reasons I never want to leave."

Sure, there's always a chance of something dangerous happening, like anywhere else in the world, but mostly, we have nothing to worry about.

People move from the city, thinking that they want a quiet life, but soon realize that sometimes it's too quiet. I kind of feel sorry for those people. They move here from Nashville or Knoxville, expecting a Hallmark movie, and they get that, for the most part. But adjusting can be hard, especially when everyone in town knows your business. We all try to make their transition a little easier, but most of the time, they just end up moving back to wherever they came from. It takes a special person to love a town like Magnolia.

"What do you think happened to her fiancé?"

"I don't know, and I really don't care. He was a douchebag of epic proportions, and I'm glad she came to her senses before she married him."

"Yes, the rumor around town was that he didn't even come to ask your father's permission to marry her."

"Yeah, my dad was pissed."

Sutton had to do a lot of damage control after telling my parents she was getting engaged. I know it's the twenty-first century, but my dad is old-fashioned. He wanted to meet the man his daughter was planning on marrying, to get to know him better than just what she told him.

Just as Dolores is opening her mouth to say something else, I notice a very expensive Mercedes, which I only know because of the hood ornament resting precariously on the tan hood, pulling into the parking spot directly in front of the door. The two-tone car sticks out like a sore thumb against the view of Magnolia behind it.

"Do you think someone is lost?" Dolores questions from beside me as I push to my feet, striding toward the door.

"I have no idea, but either way, I have to go out there and find out what they want."

"Can't we just wait for them to come inside?" Dolores questions, leaning to the side and attempting to get a glimpse at the newcomer.

"We could, but I'd rather be safe than sorry. I don't know who or what is in that car or what they want. Be ready to call in backup if things go wrong."

Dolores nods her head as I inch slowly toward the door. "Make sure to lock this behind me," I say over my shoulder as I unclip the top strap of my holster, resting my hand on my weapon, ready to draw it if needed. I wait for her to scurry around the counter before I step out the door, and I hear it locking quickly behind me. Once I'm sure she's had enough time to get back to her desk, I approach the vehicle just as the door swings open and the last person I expected to see climbs out.

I've only seen my sister's fiancé in pictures, but I've never had the displeasure of meeting him in person. Sutton never offered to bring him home to meet us, and my parents and I never could figure out the right time to go and visit her in the city. I wouldn't say we hated him, but he was definitely not our favorite person for keeping Sutton away from home, or at least that's how my parents felt. I, for one, know the truth. Sutton didn't want to take a chance at running into Colt. A fact that's 100 percent obvious after what happened at the bar last night. The only question is, why the hell is Maxwell here? Did she call him and break things off with him, or did he come after her?

"Can I help you, sir?" I bite out, trying not to sneer at him in disgust.

He isn't a bad-looking man. His dark-colored hair and piercing green eyes remind me of another man in my life, but I shake those thoughts free. I need to focus all my attention on Maxwell and why he's here, while also making sure he doesn't find out where my sister is. Well, not until I'm ready to tell him.

"Where can I find the Floreses' home?" he snaps, checking his watch. "I'm kind of in a hurry, but my fiancé is missing. She isn't answering her phone or my texts."

"Missing, you say?" I scoff. "Hold that thought."

I turn on my heels and knock on the door, waiting patiently for it to open. Dolores pokes her head out, her eyes scanning her surroundings before landing on Maxwell standing a few feet away from me.

"Is that?" she questions, her eyes widening in surprise.

"Sure is." I smile as she begins to giggle softly. "Can you call Colt and let him know I need to talk to my sister?"

"Your sister?" Maxwell's eyes roam down my body before flicking toward my face. "I don't see a family resemblance at all."

"Yes, we get that a lot, *Max*." I roll my eyes before pulling my phone out of my pocket and shooting off a text to Sutton.

"Oh, I wish I was a fly on the wall when you tell them her fiancé is here and wants to speak with her. Max doesn't seem too happy with her."

"The name is Maxwell." He scoffs. "And I'm standing right here."

"We know." I flash him a fake smile before turning my attention back to Dolores. "Make sure to call his cell and the house phone."

She nods her head at me before disappearing back into the station. I unlock my phone and dial Sutton's number just to be thorough. When she doesn't answer, I hang up and dial again.

The last thing I want to do is walk in on the two of them doing the deed because that would be very awkward, especially because I have every intention of bringing her soon-to-be ex-fiancé there with me.

After dialing Sutton's number a third and fourth time with no response, I give up and shoot off a text to Colt. I can call him once I have Sutton's car to let him know we're on our way, because I have a feeling she might need to make a quick getaway. "I have to swing by the garage to grab Sutton's car, but then you can follow me to where she's staying."

"Why doesn't she have her car with her?"

I don't bother responding to his asinine question as I dial the number to Empire Auto Garage, waiting patiently for Jackson to pick up the phone. "Let me just make a call to the auto garage, and then if you don't mind giving me a ride over, I can take you to Sutton."

"Fine, but I don't want your boots in the car. Getting mud and grime out of the carpets is expensive."

"You know what? How about I just ask them to bring the car here?" I say through clenched teeth before spinning on my heels and heading a few feet away as Jackson answers the phone.

"Empire Auto Garage, Jax speaking."

"Jax, it's Marissa. I need my sister's car; please tell me

it's done," I plead through the phone, causing him to chuckle.

"Yeah, it's done. Just need to fill the gas tank. Tell her to be more careful next time or it could cause very expensive damage to the engine."

"Will do, but I need one more favor. Can you drive it over to the station?"

"And be late for church? No."

"You won't be late. I'll have Dolores drive you back to the garage as soon as you get here." I sigh, eyeing Maxwell standing by his car.

"What'd going on—" he begins, but I immediately cut him off, not wanting to be late for service myself.

"Not now, Jax."

"Fine. I can take a hint; I'll be there in a couple of minutes." I quickly shove my phone into my pocket before coming to a stop in front of Dolores.

"What's going on out here?" she questions, her eyes flicking between me and my sister's douchebag soon-to-be ex-fiancé.

"You know how you asked what happened with Sutton's fiancé?" She nods her head. "Well, I guess she forgot to make a phone call."

"I don't know how she was planning on marrying him instead of being with Colt," Her eyes narrow as she tilts her head to the side, examining the man. "Where the hell did your sister find this clown?"

"I've been asking myself the same question for years."

I chuckle, clipping my weapon back into the holster. "But one thing I know, he better not make me late for church," I mumble, sending up a silent prayer of thanks for one more distraction because I needed something to focus on besides Finn Buckley.

fourteen
marissa

"Your lunch is here," Dolores sings as she comes strolling into my office, a bright smile plastered on her face.

"I really wish he'd stop doing this," I mumble, clearing off a spot on my desk and pulling out a set of plastic silverware.

"And deprive me of the chance to give you a hard time about making this man beg for your attention? Now, why would he do that?"

"You are obviously team Finn all the way."

"So is almost every other woman in this town, Marissa." Dolores giggles as she closes the door behind her. "If you don't snatch him up soon, someone else will, and where will that leave you?"

"Happy," I respond, knowing damn well I'm lying through my teeth.

It's been almost a month since my non-date with Finn, and by some miracle, I've mostly avoided him. We've seen each other around town in passing, giving a friendly wave or making small talk, but nothing further than that. Sure, we see each other in church on Sunday, but I've been sticking close to my parents. It seems childish, but they make a good buffer. Besides, they are show-up-early-and-leave-last type of people, giving me the perfect excuse to keep my contact with Finn to a minimum.

I've been reinforcing the walls around my heart. Pushing all my emotions and feelings for Finn deep inside, hoping for them to fade away or for him to lose interest, whichever comes first. I thought things were going well until two weeks ago when the meals started arriving.

It seems someone ratted me out and gave Finn my schedule here at the station. So, every shift, I receive a meal from 365 Diner or even the fancy restaurant at the country club, along with a note.

"What does the note say today?" Dolores asks, placing the take-out box from the diner in front of me and handing me a small envelope with my name on it before taking a seat.

"Probably something cheesy again," I scoff, but my heart flutters slightly in my chest.

Finn isn't playing fair. Most men would beg for another roll in the hay, my phone number, or even naked pictures. Trust me, it's true. But Finn does nothing but send me sweet messages. I'm surprised he hasn't even asked for my phone number, although I have a sneaking suspicion Dolores would gladly give it to him if he asked.

"Stop complaining. I know deep down you are swooning over every note he sends."

"Why do you say that?" I lean back in my chair, crossing my arms over my chest.

"Because you keep them all in your top desk drawer." Dolores giggles, nodding her head toward the left side of my desk.

"I like the photos," I grumble, popping open the take-out box, exposing one of my favorite meals: fried green tomatoes.

"I don't believe you at all." Dolores opens her Tupperware container, holding her lunch, and places it on the desk between us. "Oh, your favorite."

"I wonder how he figured that out."

"I have no idea." Dolores's eyes twinkle with mirth as she digs into her lunch. "Now, open the card. I've been waiting all day to find out what today's note says."

"All right. All right." My heart melts as I read the message inside the card before slipping it closed and sliding it toward Dolores.

The front of the card has a picture of a beautiful Tennessee sunset over the mountains with the message, *Almost as beautiful as your smile*, scrawled on the inside.

Gah! Could he be any more perfect? I expected him to send me pictures of himself shirtless after a run or when he got out of the shower, but no. He's been sending me pictures of things that remind him of me. He even had the nerve to send me a picture of him and the most adorable golden retriever puppy I've ever seen. Who the hell told him I've always wanted a golden retriever puppy? It's not fair in the slightest. It's as if he discovered it's not about what is on the outside. I already like that part of him, but he wants to make sure I know the type of man he is underneath.

I'm brought back to the present by Dolores squealing. "Finn is the sweetest man in the world. I swear he is setting the standard for any man I date in the future."

"What do you mean?"

Her cheeks are pink as she slides the card back toward me. "I'm sure you can tell I have little experience with men, Marissa. I read more romance stories than I experience in real life."

"That's because men are pigs," I retort. "The right guy is out there for you, Dolores. I just know it."

Dolores reminds me a lot of my sister when we were growing up. Her black-rimmed glasses are always resting on the bridge of her nose, and her blonde hair is always pulled back in a ponytail. When she isn't here at the station, I always see her with her nose stuck in a book. I can't tell you how many times I've pulled her back from the curb or steered her body from bumping into something or someone on the street. She doesn't wear flashy clothes, always choosing to try to blend into her surroundings. The only colorful item I've ever seen her wear is a pale pink, threadbare sweater that she's had for years.

She hasn't had the best life. Both of her parents passed away when we were seventeen, and she had to drop out of high school to get a job and take care of her younger brother and sister. She did everything for them, working multiple jobs to ensure they had everything they needed. People in town would try and help when they could, but she never complained to anyone. Once her brother and sister graduated from high school, they couldn't get out of town quickly enough, and we haven't seen them much since. I know they call her every once in a while, but I have a feeling it's to ask for something.

"Maybe. Maybe not. Not everyone can get a fairy tale ending like your sister and Colt."

"Tell me about. Only Sutton would break off her engagement with Max to get engaged to Colt the same day."

Colt didn't waste any time getting Sutton to agree to move back to Magnolia and marry him after she broke things off with Max. There were rumors going around that she was pregnant or secretly cheating with Colt, but I've squashed them. What happened between those two and how quickly things progressed might not make any sense to anyone, but I'm glad that my sister and Colt found their way to each other.

"You make it sound as if she was the one in the wrong." Dolores huffs, crossing her arms, "I happen to think its romantic."

"That's not how I mean it and you know it. I've been their biggest cheerleader for years. My sister and Colt were meant to be together, end of story."

"And you and Finn aren't? You shouldn't keep Finn

hanging for too long. Either tell him you aren't interested or give him a shot at your heart."

I have a feeling that Dolores is speaking more from experience than anything. Even with working two jobs to support her siblings, I remember seeing her around town with Wyatt, the old mayor's son. They were polar opposites, but there were rumors that those two were more than friends. But after graduation, Wyatt joined the military, and no one has seen him since.

"Are you talking about Wyatt?"

Tears instantly collect in her eyes as she winces as if I smacked her. She immediately drops her head to her chest, hiding her face, but I saw it. The pain of heartbreak was written all over her face.

"Wyatt and I were good friends in high school, but nothing more. Besides, I haven't heard anything from him since graduation."

"Yea, he didn't even come back to town for his grandfather's funeral."

Dolores doesn't say a word, only nods her head as she pushes her fork around inside her Tupperware container. Most people would continue picking at her wounds until they found out all the details, but I pull back. I know what it's like for your heartbreak to be the source of town gossip.

We both sit there in silence. I eat my lunch while Dolores continues to shove hers around in the container. She takes a few bites before giving up completely and begins packing it up.

"What do you plan to do about Finn?" Dolores questions, her voice barely above a whisper as she places the last container into her bag.

"Nothing. I figure eventually, he'll tire of sending me lunch and not getting a response from me, and then things can go back to normal."

"You keep telling yourself that." She rolls her eyes and pushes to her feet. "Is that what you want?"

No. Yes. I don't know. A part of me wants Finn to lose interest, to leave me alone and let things go back to normal. But an even bigger part of me wants him to keep pushing, to keep picking away at the walls around my heart, and that part is terrified. I need to hold out a little longer until he finds someone better. Someone that can give him her whole heart the way he deserves because mine is broken. Battered. Damaged beyond repair.

Someone knocks on the door to my office, interrupting my thoughts.

"Don't think I forgot you haven't answered my question." Dolores giggles as she heads for the door.

"I wouldn't expect anything less," I respond as she pulls open the door, and Colt comes strolling in.

"Good afternoon, ladies. How have you been?" The words drip from his lips like honey.

"Good. What do you want?"

"Why do I have to want something?" His eyes shift to Dolores as she slightly shakes her head no before sliding out the door.

"You don't, but based on the way Dolores just went

slinking out the door, I have a feeling you're about to tell me something I'm not going to like."

Colt reaches up to rub the back of his neck, his eyes moving around the room and looking anywhere but at me.

"Come on, spit it out," I growl, wanting to know what's going on.

"We're getting a recruit next week. I'm going to need you to work all weekend to get him trained before the mayor's gala next week."

"You were right. I don't like that."

I haven't had a full weekend off in almost a month. I mean, we are a small department, with only three deputies, but Waylen and Aurora got married a few weeks ago and are leaving on their honeymoon tomorrow, which leaves Colt and me as the only two deputies at the station until they get back in two weeks.

"I'll give you a full week's vacation when he gets back. You don't even have to take your phone. Consider it a thank-you for all the time you've put in at the station."

"You know it's my job." I groan but know exactly how I want to use my time.

Peyton has been bugging me to go camping at Watauga Lake for a girls' weekend. I'm not the outdoorsy type, but Peyton loves the place. She keeps going on and on about how immersing ourselves in nature is cleansing for the soul or something. She has had the whole thing planned out since a couple came through town on their way home to Nashville after spending the weekend there.

But heading out of town for a few hours has a certain appeal right now, especially as I'm trying really hard to avoid a certain someone.

"But I want a week of vacation and every weekend off for a month when I get back. The new guy can cover for me."

"Done," Colt responds without a second thought.

"That was too easy. What else do you have to tell me?"

Just as Colt opens his mouth to respond, my phone vibrates across the desk.

"I'll leave you to your phone call. He'll be here Wednesday of next week." Colt gives me a salute before turning on his heels and heading out the door as I answer the phone.

"Hello." The smile disappears from my face the moment I hear the voice on the other end of the phone. I've been ducking calls from my mother for weeks, sending her to voicemail or downright ignoring her calls. I see her in church on Sundays, but duck out as soon as possible, avoiding any chance of me spilling the beans about what's going on with me and Finn. I knew I'd have to talk to her eventually, but I couldn't risk her asking me over for dinner or to visit the Buckleys with them. That would throw a very large monkey wrench into my plans for continuing to ignore Finn and not wanting to talk about it with anyone, especially my mother.

"Hello, Mother. To what do I owe this pleasure?" I try to keep the sarcasm out of my voice but fail miserably.

"Why have you been ignoring my phone calls?"

"I've been really busy at work. We have a recruit reporting for duty soon, and I need to get all the training material and everything together for them to start next week. And with Waylen on leave for his honeymoon, we've been swamped."

I'm a horrible liar, have been ever since I was a kid. That's why I went with something that was as close to the truth as possible. There is a recruit coming who I have to train, and we have indeed been swamped since Waylen got married. She just doesn't have to know that all these changes in plans only happened two minutes ago instead of the two weeks I've been ignoring her.

"Save it. You've been ignoring me because you didn't want me to find out that Finn Buckley has been sending you secret notes and lunches for the last two weeks."

Damn. Busted.

"No, Momma. R-really—" I stammer before she cuts me off.

"Save it for someone who doesn't know you. How do you think he knew that fried green tomatoes are your favorite? But that's not why I'm calling. Your father and I would love for you to come over for dinner tonight. I'm making chicken and dumplings."

"You play dirty, Momma."

"I have to if I want to see my daughter for more than a few hours at church." She laughs loudly. "I already talked to Dolores, and she said you get off at five today. I expect you to come right to the house. Dinner is at five-thirty."

"See you then. Love you, Momma."

"Love you, too, sweetheart," she responds as I hang up the phone.

"Sorry!" Dolores pops her head back into the room as if nothing happened. That's one of the many things I like about her; she rolls with the punches. "She promised muffins for the weekend shift next week if I told her."

"I understand. She's also making me some chicken and dumplings."

"I don't think I could convince you to bring me some, could I?"

"You think right. Only one bribe per transaction. Now, get back to work." I chuckle as she flashes me a bright smile and disappears, pulling my door shut behind her.

I work for the next few hours, focusing on getting the last bit of my paperwork done before diving into organizing the training material for next week. I have plenty of time, but I hate waiting till the last minute. You never know when life is going to throw you a curve ball. Thankfully, I manage to get most of it organized, but when I log in to our personnel server, I can't seem to find any information on the recruit coming next week.

"That's strange," I mumble to myself before logging out of the system for the night and heading out of the office.

"Enjoy dinner at your mom's place tonight," Dolores says as I head toward her desk from my office.

"I'll try. She probably wants to give me a hard time, wanting to know when I'm going to settle down and give her grandbabies."

"Ha. Has she not met you?" She laughs loudly. "She has a better chance of getting grandbabies from Sutton than you."

"I know! That's what I keep telling her," I respond before stopping in front of her desk. "I tried to get the paperwork set up for the recruit coming next week and couldn't find it. Can you remember to ask Colt to put his information in when he gets a moment?"

"No problem. He's on a phone call with an officer from Birch Cove right now, and he's off tomorrow, but I'll write myself a note so I don't forget to ask."

"Thanks, Dolores." I wave goodbye to her before heading out the door to my SUV.

It doesn't take long for me to make my way to my parents' house on the other side of town. My parents have lived in the same house all my life—a few streets over from the Buckleys, in a charming ranch-style home that sits on nearly an acre of property in a cul-de-sac and has a huge backyard.

"Here goes nothing," I mumble to myself as I pull into the driveway and shut off my SUV.

This dinner with my parents is going to go one of two ways: Either my mom is going to nitpick at me for every little thing until I end up storming out of the house, or she wants to tell me something and isn't sure how I'm going to react.

I love my parents, and I know they love me, but sometimes, my mom doesn't do the best job at showing it. It's one of the many downfalls of being the youngest child. People say that being the youngest child means your parents go easier on you and spoil you rotten, but those people are probably older siblings. Sure, I got away with murder when it came to my dad, but my mom was a different story. She was a little lenient with me when I was younger, but now, it seems as if I'm constantly living in my sister's shadow. My mother is constantly comparing the two of us, wanting to know why I don't have X, Y, or Z like my sister. Most people would just ignore their phone calls, only dealing with those nagging family members when it's unavoidable, but it's almost impossible for me. My parents know where I work, all my friends, and have a key to my apartment.

"Hello, sweetheart," my mother says as I walk into the house, closing the door behind me.

"Hey, Momma." I give her a kiss on the cheek as she walks past me into the dining room. I turn to the right and see the table set to perfection.

"Are you expecting company?" I question, heading past the dining room to the kitchen and grabbing a bowl off the counter before heading back the way I came.

My mother has always had a thing for the whole family eating at the dinner table like all the TV sitcom families did. We'd talk about our days and tell jokes, but never at the dining room table. That table was reserved for holidays and when guests come over. The fact we're having dinner in there is a sign that something is wrong.

I come around the corner, carrying a bowl of salad, and place it in the center of the table before moving around it and giving my dad a kiss on the cheek. "Hey, Dad."

"Hey, sweetie." My dad grabs my hands, giving them a tight squeeze.

"Is this a special occasion?" I question, taking a seat beside my father.

My mother seems a little frazzled, which is unusual for her. Her face is makeup free, and there are little tendrils of her silver hair flying loosely in her face. There's something wrong. My mom always looks her best, both inside and outside of the house. She was the perfect southern belle growing up, never leaving the house without her hair done perfectly—not a hair out of place—and wearing tasteful makeup. Whatever that means. She tried to push those ideals on my sister and me, but we weren't having it. Although Sutton took some of her teachings to heart, going to school to become a fashion designer and launching her own clothing brand. For her to be serving dinner in the fancy dining room, on a random Wednesday evening, and serving her famous chicken and dumplings... Something is very wrong.

"No, dear. I just felt like sitting in the dining room today. The kitchen table is wobbly, and your father hasn't had time to fix it. Now, grab your father's hand so we can say grace before the chicken and dumplings get cold."

I follow my mother's instructions and grab my dad's hand, bowing my head as he says a blessing over the food. As soon as he finishes his prayer, they both dig in. My mother even takes the time to make me a plate. Okay, this just got very weird.

"Ma. Dad. Someone, please tell me what's going on. You're freaking me out."

"Is that how you went to work today?" my mother questions, her eyes scanning my body before shifting back to my eyes. "You should put on a little makeup or something."

"What's the point? The only people I see at work are Colt and Dolores." I narrow my eyes at my mother, wondering what she's up to. "What do you know that I don't?"

"Nothing. I was just talking to Dolores, and you did say that you had someone new coming to the station in the next week."

"I'm not trying to impress the recruit, Mother. I'm there to work, not score a date."

"Who says you can't do both? I mean, you couldn't be bothered with Colt, but you never know. This guy could be the one."

"Of course, Ma. I forgot that the only way to validate my life is to have a man." I roll my eyes. "Can I at least finish my dinner before you tell me what a disappointment I am?"

"You aren't a disappointment, honey. Your mother just wants you to be happy," my father says, placing his hand over mine and giving it a hard squeeze.

My dad is the exact opposite of my mother, giving me love and affection in spades. He was firm with both me and my sister, but he also encouraged us to follow our dreams and become the best version of ourselves. As you can imagine, that made for a lot of interesting conversations in my house, but somehow, we made it work. I know what you're thinking. Both of my parents loved us and each other, but they are the definition of opposites attract.

I scoff under my breath before reaching toward the center of the table and grabbing a freshly baked roll. That's one bonus of living close to your parents, home-cooked meals whenever you want to deal with the lecture.

"I know…" My voice trails off as I take a large bite of my roll, pushing my chair back from the table and standing. "I'm just in a bad mood today."

"Where do you think you're going?"

"To the restroom. Is that all right with you?" I snap, not even bothering to wait for her response. I know I'm going to get an earful about respecting my parents and manners when I sit back down to the table, but I need a break from her criticism for a few minutes.

I brace my arms on either side of the vanity and gaze at my reflection in the mirror. My once-bright green eyes are dulled with some emotion I don't want to think about right this moment. I thought I was above all this, especially after all these years, but it seems with everything else going on in my life, I have to be confronted with mommy issues.

"I really could use a haircut," I mumble at my reflection as I grab my long chocolate-brown hair and toss it into a messy bun at the top of my head. Not the proper hairstyle, according to my mother, but I'm off work, and the last thing I want to do is deal with my hair right now.

My mother has been picking at me my whole life. It's her way of letting me know she cares. I know it's odd, but she's complete shit at expressing her feelings. So instead of telling me I did a good job when getting an A on my project in school, she wanted to know why I didn't get an A-plus. Being constantly reminded that I'm not good enough is taking its toll once again. I thought I was past all of this. That I no longer cared what my mother had to say about me, but I guess not.

"Why do I let her do this to me every time?" I say into the empty bathroom, already knowing the answer to my question. "But there is definitely something up."

I usually make it at least an hour before my mother picks at me. But she immediately went to her usual defenses when I asked what was going on. That is an even bigger tell that there has to be something wrong.

After taking a few cleansing breaths, I swing open the bathroom door and head back to the table. My parents have their heads bent toward each other, whispering softly as I enter the room. I open my mouth to say something, but my mom notices me and pulls back, sitting up ramrod straight in her chair. "Let's eat before the food gets cold," she says louder than necessary before shoving a large forkful of food into her mouth.

"Why are you two acting so weird?" I question, pulling out my chair and taking a seat.

"We aren't being weird, sweetheart." My dad smiles before reaching across the table and giving my hand a squeeze.

"I'm not taking another bite until one of you tells me what's going on." I pull my hand from beneath his, crossing my arms over my chest. My parents are on edge, and I want to know why.

"Why does there have to be something going on?"

"Ma, you made my favorite dinner, with homemade rolls, and I'll put money on the fact that there's a peach cobbler."

"I wasn't busy this afternoon after we went to visit Charlotte and Mason, and I decided to make your favorite dinner. You've been so busy that we haven't spent much time together—"

"We need to just tell her." My father places his hand over my mother's, their eyes locking on one another while having a silent conversation.

I wait there patiently for one of them to talk when my mother sighs loudly. "Ma, you're making me nervous." My voice shakes slightly as my heart tries to beat out of my chest. "Lay it on me."

"Campbell has moved back into town."

I gasp in shock, not being able to make sense of what

my mother is telling me. Sure, he's come back for holidays and special occasions over the last few years, but his mom always gave mine a heads-up, giving me more than enough opportunity to steer clear of anywhere he might be.

"How did you find this out?"

"Charlotte and I saw Peggy this afternoon in town. She was so excited to tell both of us that her baby was coming home for good with her favorite grandbaby."

"He's her only grandbaby, darling."

"Yes, I know, but I wanted to give her all the information." Ma pats Dad's hand before turning her attention back to me. "She also went on and on about how Emmeline cheated on him, leaving him to raise that little boy all on his own."

My shoulders instantly sag at the mention of my ex-boyfriend. Campbell and I were together almost all the way through high school. The couple that everyone wanted to be like. It's only natural that I'd have some feelings about him being back in town. But right now, I don't know what those are.

I haven't heard from Campbell or seen him since graduation, and apparently, now he's back in town for good. I can't avoid him or make sure that I'm on shift the weekend he's in town. I'm going to have to find some way to deal with him being around, but today isn't that day. Right now, I want to stuff my head in the sand and pretend none of this is happening.

"According to Peggy, Campbell is back in town,

trying to create a good life for himself and his son. Right now, he needs the support of his family and friends, and so does his son."

"Mm-hmm," I respond, barely paying attention to what she's saying.

This is not what I was expecting them to tell me. Maybe a declaration that Sutton was pregnant, or they were moving to Tahiti because of the warmer climates. Not that my ex was back in town. Maybe moving to the city isn't such a bad idea after all.

"Apparently, that hussy disappeared with her Pilates instructor almost a year ago and left Campbell and that poor, sweet boy all alone. Campbell tried to make a go of it in the city, but with his son starting school this year, he needed some help. Being a single parent is hard enough. He's going to need his family now."

My mom pauses for a few moments before digging back into her dinner. "Well, now that we've gotten that out of the way, let's enjoy the rest of our dinner."

Both of my parents continue their meal as if the bomb they dropped on me didn't change the direction of my life forever. Maybe I'm being a little dramatic, but now I have to figure out a way to avoid Campbell while also maintaining my stance of keeping Finn at arm's length. Yeah, nothing too hard at all.

fifteen

marissa

inner continued with no more surprises. My mom made enough to feed an army, which means I will have more than enough food to eat for the foreseeable future.

"Maybe you and Campbell will run into each other around town. I'm sure he could use a friend right now." My mom eyes me over the top of the tote bag she's packing with all the leftovers.

"I'm probably the last person Campbell wants to see right now, Ma," I grumble, wondering what exactly she's thinking. "Heck, I'm not even sure I want to see him."

"Why's that? I know he hurt you deeply when you broke up, but you two were also close friends before you started dating. And right now, I have a feeling friends is what he needs."

"We'll see," I answer noncommittally.

If I'm being honest, I don't know if I'm ready to see Campbell, let alone be his friend, but my momma has a point. We were friends before we started dating. There's nothing saying we can't be friends again at some point in the future.

"That is, unless you're worried Finn is going to get jealous about the two of you being close." It seems like my mom is more fixated on what's going on with Finn and me than I would've liked. It's more than obvious that she's up to no good.

"I know what you're trying to do, but there's nothing going on with Finn and me." I smile at her as I push back from the table, heading directly for my dad.

"Yet," she whispers as I plant a kiss on the top of my dad's head. "You never know how things are going to turn out."

"I love you both very much and know how much you love me, too. How about you two get one daughter married off before you push me into a relationship?"

"I call it careful nudging." My mom smiles as I lean down and kiss her cheek, picking up the bag off the table. "There's enough food there for you to have lunch and dinner for a few days. Oh, I also added pie for you and some muffins for the boys and Dolores."

"Oh, muffins!" I laugh as I head for the door, wanting to do anything but head home and be alone with my thoughts.

As I climb into my SUV, I try to imagine what my life would have been like if things with Campbell had turned out differently. My heart broke that day, but I know that what happened between us was for the best. I would have given anything to be the woman he wanted, the woman that was meant for the future we had painted for us, but sometimes, things don't work out the way we want them to. He wouldn't have his little one, and I... Well, who knows where I'd be, but that's all in the past now. Sometimes the past is best left in the past.

"Fuck! I need to get out of here," I mumble to myself before throwing the car in reverse.

I could probably head to Nashville for the night, but that's way too involved. Taking the hour and some change drive to Nashville won't take too long, especially on a workday in the early evening, but then I'd have to get a room. And rooms require some planning, not to mention I have to work tomorrow.

I drum my fingers on the steering wheel, letting my brain wander and find something for me to do. The entire town probably knows that Campbell is back in town by now. Their nosy asses will be on the lookout for any signs that his return has affected me. It has. I'm just not sure how yet. And they don't need to know any of that. Right now, I need to collect my thoughts.

I definitely can't go home. My mom will call to see how I'm doing and ask me a million questions. She's up to something. I'd bet my next paycheck that she and Ms. Peggy both are. Ms. Peggy wasn't happy with the way things went down with Campbell and me. She was team Marissa all the way and would be as delighted, if not more, as my mother for the two of us to get back together. If it were up to them, Campbell and I would be planning our wedding before the end of the year.

With going home being out of the question, that doesn't leave very many options. I drive around aimlessly for Lord knows how long. Just as I'm about to give up and go home, the sign for Tallywackers comes into view. It's not my favorite place to hang out, but beggars can't be choosers. It's a bar. I can get tequila. It's happy hour, so I can just about guarantee there are plenty of people there ready to drown their sorrows. The perfect place to hang out and shut off my brain for a few hours.

But there's only one problem. There's a high probability that Finn will be there. His father owns the bar, after all. I'm supposed to be avoiding him, so showing up at his father's place of business, wanting to drown my sorrows, isn't the best idea.

Just as I'm about to give up and head back toward my apartment, I have a bright idea: I'll call. It's so juvenile, but it might just work. I can call and ask for Finn. When they tell me he isn't there, I'll know it's safe to go there and blow off some steam.

Having made up my mind, I pull over on the side of the road and dial the number for Tallywackers. I only have to wait a few seconds for someone to answer.

"Hello, Marissa." The sounds of the music playing loudly in the background make it almost impossible to decipher who answered the phone.

"Hello?" I pull the phone away from my ear before

saying the first thing on my mind. "How the hell do you know who's on the phone?"

"Caller ID," the unknown voice chuckles. "It's Nolan, by the way, and I know why you're calling, and he isn't here. He isn't set to be here until tomorrow night, so it's safe to come get a drink. I'd need one, too, if I found out my ex was back in town."

"How did you know that? I just found out a few hours ago."

"Ms. Thompson has been telling anyone she can that he's bringing her grandbaby home for good. The rest was just a logical guess. I'm sure your parents sat you down to tell you. Am I wrong?"

"No. I just wish everyone wasn't making such a big deal out of it. We broke up a long time ago."

"That's not any of my business, Marissa. But if you'd rather talk to me about a certain bar owner's son, I'm all ears."

"No thanks, but I will take that drink since said bar owner's son is nowhere in sight, right?"

"Would I lie to you?"

"The verdict is still out, but I'll be there in a few minutes," I respond quickly before ending the call and pointing my car in the bar's direction. I know I should be embarrassed that Nolan figured out that I'm avoiding Finn and that he knows Campbell is back in town, but things could be so much worse.

I pull into a spot near the entrance to Tallywackers. The parking lot is relatively empty, as you'd expect for a small-town bar in the middle of the week. There are a few cars sprinkled around the parking lot, but none that I can place, thankfully. The last thing I want is to have to explain to anyone, especially my mother, why I headed here instead of home after she told me about Campbell.

Yea, I'm a grown-ass adult and can drink when I want. However, that will lead to questions about what's going on between Finn and me. Which will lead to questions about Campbell and me. Which will lead to having a conversation I'm not the least bit ready for right now.

I turn around in my seat, feeling around for my gym bag on the floor. I'm the last person you'd see in a gym, but I keep a change of clothes in my SUV for just this occasion. People wouldn't give me too hard of a time for being in a bar on a Wednesday night, but there's something about getting completely obliterated while in uniform that seems very unprofessional. Not only does it go against several rules of professional conduct from the county, but if people have to worry about whether I'm drinking on the job, I'd lose their trust. Yes, I've known almost all these people my entire life. They should know my character better than anyone else, but there is nothing logical about how people feel. Once trust is broken, it's hard to repair. Trust me, I know that better than most, and I don't want to take that chance.

"Finally." I sigh, grabbing the gym bag and climbing out.

I make it through the door and to the bathroom with no one noticing before quickly changing, stuffing my uniform into my bag, and heading back to my SUV. With that taken care of, I slam my door shut, lock it, and head for the entrance.

Tallywackers has been in Magnolia since before my parents were married, and it still looks the same. Housed in an old brothel, it lives up to its name, hosting burlesque and drag shows whenever possible. It's a place to see and be seen in Magnolia, making it the last place I want to walk into right now. I'll have a few drinks to waste some time and make it home in time to catch my shows. What's the worst that could happen?

My eyes scan the bar before landing on Finn behind it. Motherfucker. I need to get out of here, but as soon as I turn to leave, I run smack dab into something hard.

"Ouch." My hand flies to my nose as I take a step back and come eye-to-eye with Nolan. "You lied to me."

I eye him skeptically, taking a step away from him. Nolan and I don't know each other well, but he's worked here since before I graduated. His shaggy blonde hair is hanging slightly over his right eye as he looks me up and down like he's sizing me up. "No, I didn't. Finn literally walked in a few seconds after I hung up the phone."

"But you said he wouldn't be here until the weekend."

"Okay, that was a lie, but you need to stop avoiding the man. He's driving all of us insane. Please put us out of our misery."

"I really need a damn drink." I sigh, my eyes flicking to Finn standing behind the bar.

"Yeah, I can only imagine," Nolan responds. "Look, stay and have a few drinks and then head home."

"Sounds like a plan." I smile at him before turning and heading toward the other end of the bar, but Nolan grabs my shoulder, pulling me backward and pointing me toward Finn.

"You'll have to talk to him sooner or later. Might as well get it over with."

Nolan is right. I can't keep avoiding Finn forever. I just need to thank him for all the meals and sweet notes he's been sending me but tell him I'm not interested. I can do that. No problem. I've turned letting men down gently into a professional sport.

"No more dawdling. He's seen you, so you might as well head over there," Nolan whispers in my ear before shoving me toward the bar.

"What can I get for you, darlin'?"

I grin at Finn, who is standing behind the bar as I slid onto a barstool, not bothering to stop my eyes from roaming down his body as if I'm seeing him for the first time all over again.

It seems silly, but I haven't been able to stop thinking about how Sutton swore up and down that Finn had some kind of crush on me. That he brought my favorite snacks and always seemed to have exactly what I wanted just lying around. I never used to give it a second thought at the time. Sure, he was cute, but he never gave me a second glance, especially when Campbell was around.

But now I'm starting to think she might have been on to something.

"Darlin'? What happened to *sugar*?"

"Nothing. I just wanted to try a different one, see how I liked it."

"And how is that working for you?"

"Not my favorite. I think I'll stick with *sugar*. Every pretty girl needs a pretty name."

"How about my name, Finn? That's what most people use."

Finn flashes me a smile, leaning his arms on the bar. My breath hitches as our gazes meet. His chocolate-colored eyes sparkle with the same need that's burning like fire in my veins. Electricity sizzles between us as I lean forward, my body being pulled toward him by an invisible force. But neither of us makes a move. I inhale deeply. His scent goes directly to my lady bits. The perfect aphrodisiac for my sex-starved brain. That must be the reason for my reaction. Isn't it?

"Can I get a scotch on the rocks?" someone says from somewhere in the bar, causing us to jump away from each other.

Finn shakes his head before knocking on the bar. "I should go take care of my customer."

"Yeah. I'll have a double shot of tequila. And keep them coming. Thanks." I pull my bottom lip between my teeth before dropping my head downward.

What the fuck was that?

I'm supposed to be letting him down easily. Maybe

have a couple of drinks to calm my brain after hearing about Campbell being back in town, and Finn Buckley is the last thing I need right now. He's the worst kind of trouble. I'm all about having a good time, but Finn Buckley is off-limits. I just hope my libido has gotten the memo before I get too much alcohol into my system because right now, Finn Buckley is what's on the menu.

"Can I get you another one?" I ask, leaning toward Marissa with a practiced grin.

I'm not one to brag, but I've been told I have a panty-dropping smile. A smile that gets me almost any woman I want—well, except the one I've been in love with since before I graduated high school: Marissa Flores.

Marissa has been avoiding me for the last month. I expected it after Nolan told me what happened between her and Campbell, but I'm still beyond frustrated. With each passing day, it becomes harder and harder to be patient. To wait for the right time to make my move. I was reaching the end of my rope when she came strolling into my bar with Sutton almost a month ago.

Before then, I was surprised I hadn't seen her around. I figured she was avoiding me for the most part, but there are only so many things someone can do in Magnolia. She is a gorgeous woman in her twenties. Bars are their natural habitat. Almost every member of her graduating class comes strolling in here on Friday and Saturday nights, but never Marissa. I'm assuming this is the reason

I ran into her in a bar so far away from Magnolia. She likes her privacy. Hell, I can't blame her.

Marissa has been here for hours, drinking and shooting the shit with me. We talked about everything except Campbell. I'm dying to know if they've run into each other since he's gotten back in town. My mom barely made it in the door before she was telling me about her run-in with Campbell's mom. There's no doubt the town gossip hotline will be in full swing by tomorrow about how Emmeline cheated on him, leaving him to raise that little boy all on his own.

"Hit me." She gives me an easy grin, drinking down the last bit of liquid in her glass and sliding it toward me, across the bar.

"You got it," I respond through clenched teeth.

My dick has been hard since the moment she came into the bar hours ago. The light shining through the door casts an angelic glow around her entire body. Her curvy frame was on display for every man to see, her sun-kissed skin encased in a pair of tight blue jeans and a tight, white, almost-invisible shirt. I bite back a groan, dropping my hand beneath the bar and palming the bulge in my pants.

I told myself that I'd take things slowly, but Marissa is making it almost impossible to think of anything besides what her skin tastes like. Hell, I can't go more than a few minutes without thinking of her or finding something that reminds me of her. She's like a drug, and I'm her willing addict. The color of the leaves on the flowers filling my mother's garden reminds me of her eyes. The rich, dark color of the beer sitting in the glass on the bar reminds me of her hair. I've never been the type of person who enjoys sweets, but I've eaten more strawberries in the last few weeks than I have in my entire life, attempting to remember the taste of her skin on my lips. And now here she is, sitting at my bar.

"Can I get that drink?" Her breath hitches as our gazes meet again, and her eyes sparkle with the same need that's burning like fire in my veins.

Fuck. I give my cock one final squeeze before pouring her another shot of tequila and filling a glass of water, placing it on the bar in front of her. "You should really start drinking water, too. We don't want you getting dehydrated," I mumble before sending up a silent prayer that I don't blow my load right here as she places her lips on the edge of the glass. Marissa never once breaks eye contact as she drinks the liquid down and flashes me a sultry smile.

"That's a good idea, Finn," she practically purrs before grabbing her shot and tossing it back. "But I have to prefer tequila." My eyes focus on her lips as her tongue runs slowly across them before she winks in my direction.

"No more tequila until you drink some water," I command, refilling her glass and pouring her another shot. "Don't let anyone catch you with this. I'd never serve it this way to anyone else."

"What? A glass of water?" She leans down slowly,

wrapping her lips around the edge of the glass and taking another long sip.

"No. With a shot of tequila as a chaser."

"I promise I won't tell. It'll be our little secret."

Is she flirting with me?

I chuckle softly as her eyes snap up to mine as she takes another long pull from her water glass before grabbing the shot and tossing it back. A delicious shade of pink runs down her neck, disappearing into the top of her shirt and leaving me to wonder how far the color goes. I lean forward, taking a few strands of my hair between my fingers. Her breathing picks up as I bring them toward my nose and inhale deeply.

"You smell delicious," I groan softly, rubbing the hair between my fingers.

"Can I get whatever dark beer you have on tap?" Someone smacks the bar loudly, breaking me from my trance.

"No problem," I grumble before releasing her hair and turning to fill the customer's order.

I turn my attention to pouring a good beer, trying to focus on anything other than what almost happened. Moments like these have to mean something, right? Something about tonight is different, and I can't place it. I haven't been able to get her to give me the time of day since I took her to lunch weeks ago. I figured it was nerves about letting someone close, but if that was the case, she wouldn't be here. Couple that with the information about Campbell being back in town, and I have a feeling she's here to forget. She wants to forget all about what happened in the past with Campbell, about him being back in town, and she plans on using me to do it.

It's times like these, when it's just the two of us, that I know in my heart there's something between us. As if she woke up this morning and knew that I was her soulmate. The time we wasted on other people was worth it because it led to the two of us finally finding each other.

When the hell did I grow a vagina? That won't happen. This is real life, and I'm not a chick flick in the making. Life doesn't work like that. Marissa is locked up tighter than Alcatraz. It's going to take more than some innocent flirting to convince her that we belong together. But the question is, how do I break down those walls? I've tried giving her space. I've tried letting her know how I feel about her, but nothing is working.

But the way she looks at me tells me that there's a chance this will turn into something more. I just need to plant the seed in her mind and hope that one day I'll mean as much to Marissa as she does to me. That I'll be her everything.

"How fucking long does it take to pour a beer?" the customer growls from behind me as I slam the glass on the bar forcefully, making the liquid slosh on the bar top and over both our hands.

"Here you go, sir," I say with my best customer-service smile plastered on my face. "Do you want to start a tab or cash out now?"

"Tab. I seem to have found a reason to hang out a

little longer than planned," he growls, his attention completely focused on Marissa's shirt as he holds his credit card out toward me.

"If you're looking for some company, my friends and I are more than willing to oblige."

My fists ball at my sides as I fight to maintain control. Not only will I lose a customer when I break his nose for speaking to Marissa like that, but she'll hand me my ass if I step in. Marissa is more than capable of taking care of herself. She's always has been able to. Not to mention, if things got out of control here, I'd be calling her, not the other way around. She'd kick my ass and then call Colt on herself.

"No, thank you." She plasters on a fake smile as she turns toward him.

"Move along," I growl, grabbing the card from the guy's hand before swiping it quickly through the machine and handing it back to him.

Thankfully, the guy doesn't cause any trouble and leaves.

"What would I have done if you weren't here?" Marissa asks as I will my eyes to bore holes into the back of the guy's head as he moves toward a table full of other guys like him, more than likely some tool bags from out of town.

"Knocked his ass out." I chuckle, raising my eyebrow and daring her to contradict me.

"You're probably right," she responds as her eyes flash

toward the table of idiots across the room. "Guys like that don't scare me."

"Then what scares you, sugar?"

"Right at this moment, the realization that I'll never be the person I was before this moment. That once I walk out of this bar, nothing will be the same." She drops her chin to her chest, running her finger along the rim of her glass.

"I see the real you, Marissa. The lonely woman with walls around her heart, too afraid to let someone love her. It's okay to be scared. I'll give you some time, but at some point, you will be mine."

"I'm afraid of that, too," she whispers, but I pretend I didn't hear her.

The next few hours pass quickly as the bar fills, which is not unusual for any night here in Magnolia. Remember? Small town. There's only one other option for something to do in town for those awake after nine p.m.: cow tipping. And that activity is reserved for people who legally can't step foot into Tallywackers. I check on Marissa frequently, making sure she always has a drink in her hand, occasionally forgoing the shots and giving her a glass of water instead, much to her dismay. I also make a habit of scaring away anyone who tries to sit down within a few feet of her, and she scowled at me every time. I know it's probably insulting because she can take care of herself, but I'm hoping she finds it endearing that I want to protect her from the bad guys, or at least that I can.

"Are you ever going to make a move?" Nolan slides

up beside me, punching my shoulder lightly. "You've been complaining that she's been avoiding you, and I deliver her to you on a silver platter."

I grunt in response as he shoves more beer mugs into the fridge below the bar. *I thought he had left hours ago.* It seems my obsession with Marissa has gotten a little out of hand.

"If you don't hurry, you're going to be too late." Nolan motions his head toward the group of guys approaching Marissa.

I stiffen, ready to step in if needed, but as usual, she has it all under control. After a few moments, they sulk away with their tails between their legs, in search of a new victim.

"One of these days, she won't tell them no. Then what are you going to do?"

"The same thing I've done all these years." I flash him a menacing look as Marissa turns toward me, a soft smile on her face as she wiggles her fingers in my direction. "Now, get back to work."

"You got it, boss." Nolan gives me a mock salute before heading down the bar to grab a customer's order.

"Can I get one more for the road?" Marissa places her empty glass in front of me, her cheeks pink from the alcohol.

"I think you've had more than enough." I shake my head, knowing full well I don't have to worry about her drinking and driving. I mean, she's a sheriff's officer, and drunk driving is against the law.

"But you were taking so long. A girl needs attention." She winks at me before pushing to her feet, lifting her glass as she leans forward across the bar, and wiggling it in front of my face.

"Water for you." Marissa pokes out her bottom lip at my decree. "How are you getting home?"

"You." She smiles brightly. "I didn't expect someone else to be paying for my drinks all night."

I grip the lip of the bar tightly, remembering all the assholes that have been revolving around her all night.

"I'm not wasted, but I don't think I should drive." She flops down onto the stool behind her, almost missing it completely. "I'll never hear the end of it if I end up in the drunk tank."

"I doubt that would be very becoming for an officer of the law," I mumble as I wipe down the bar and take an inventory of what I need to pull from the back to restock for tomorrow.

I glimpse Marissa out of the corner of my eye, rolling her fingers around the rim of her glass. Her apple bottom and long legs are hidden from view below the bar, but the only thing I can think of right now is what she would look like naked, sprawled out for me to devour.

Images of our almost-kiss from earlier filter into my mind. The way her hair felt wrapped around my fingers and the scent of her hair as I buried my nose in it, a floral scent like a warm spring day. My cock hardens at the memory of her hard nipples poking through her shirt as I pulled her toward me, wishing the bar wasn't between us.

"Anything else you need?" Nolan brings my mind back to the present. "It's almost closing time, anyway."

Closing time? My eyes flick up to the clock, noticing that it is, in fact, almost ten. Yeah, I know that's usually when the party gets started in most places, but here, everyone needs to be home in time to make sure they can make it work on time the following day, even on a Friday. We close earlier on Saturday night because no one is allowed to miss church service, regardless of how bad their hangover might be.

No one wants to be known as the person who was out too late drinking the night before and couldn't make it to service. It might be bad for business, but it's damn near a public service for a few of the men in town. It keeps them out of trouble with their wives and the Lord and gets me more customers earlier in the day.

"No. You can head out. If I need anything else, I'll make Marissa help."

Marissa sticks her tongue out in my direction before spinning around to face the bar. "I'm not paying my tab."

I bite back a moan at the sight of her entire back exposed as she turns. The need to run my fingers along her spine before tasting her soft flesh is driving me mad.

"Yeah, put her to work." Nolan waves as his eyes shift down before flicking back to mine.

"What?" I question, unable to fathom what would cause him to react that way as he motions downward. I follow the path of his hand and notice my rather obvious bulge straining against the fabric of my jeans, begging for release.

"Shit." I step closer to the bar, biting back a groan as my bulge rubs against the lip of the bar. I clear my throat, searching for anything to help this awkward situation. "I'll see you on Monday. You're scheduled to work tomorrow night."

Nolan winks in my direction before spinning on his heels and heading toward the back room.

Marissa turns toward me. "What was that about?"

I wave her question away. "Nothing important. Want to call it?"

"Can I get on the bar?" Marissa asks, pulling off her boots and dropping them to the floor beside her.

"Do I have a choice in the matter?" I hold my hands out and grasp her hand, supporting her weight as she climbs up on top of the bar.

"No, but I like to give you the illusion of power."

Marissa places two fingers in her mouth and whistles loudly, getting everyone in the bar's attention. "Last call, ladies and gents. Please tip your bartender!" she shouts just as someone plays "Closing Time" by Semisonic on the jukebox in the corner.

Patrons begin to filter toward the bar to cash out. Thankfully, most of the crowd left a few hours ago, and only a few stragglers remain.

My eyes focus on Marissa, her hips swaying back and forth, giving me my own private show and another excuse to take not-so-secret glances at her lithe form. She travels down the bar, playing air guitar and an imaginary keyboard while mouthing all the words along with the song. Some patrons join her show, singing into her imaginary microphone. Her excitement exudes from every pore in her body, making it damn near impossible not to smile.

"I'd love to be going home with that piece of ass," a gruff man growls as he places his now-empty glass on the bar.

"Well, good thing you aren't," I retort, turning to the register and swiping his card.

When I spin back around, my eyes widen, mesmerized by Marissa's ass as she sways into a squat before making her way back up. Her eyes close as she raises her hands in the air and tilts her head toward the ceiling, letting the music overtake her body.

Without taking my eyes off Marissa, I drop the man's card and receipt onto the bar top. I don't know if he signed his check, took his card, or dropped dead on the floor. I'm completely mesmerized by Marissa as she continues swaying to the music.

"Take a picture. It lasts longer." She giggles as she points toward the front door. "Everyone's gone."

I duck my head in embarrassment as I walk around the bar and head toward the door. "Get your shit together, Finn. Marissa isn't the first woman you've flirted with, although she will be your last," I mumble to the door as I flip the lock before grabbing my dick through my pants and trying to relieve some of the pressure.

I take a deep breath, thinking of everything from my parents going at it right on the bar in front of me to my eighty-nine-year-old grandfather wearing a Speedo. After a few minutes of those disturbing images filtering through my mind, I feel comfortable walking around the room.

"Lord, give me strength," I mumble as another song plays.

I send up a silent prayer before heading back behind the bar without sparing a glance at her. If I do, I'll be trapped under her spell for a second time. Now that I can focus, I manage the remaining side work in no time.

"Shut that thing off, Marissa. It's time to go. I need to close up," I say, not bothering to look at her for fear of losing my concentration.

I've tried to count out the register three times, but every time I catch sight of her, my brain short circuits and I have to start over.

"One more song," she whines.

"One more song. That's it. And then home for you."

Having finished my count, I shove a large stack of money into the bank deposit bag for drop-off and shut the drawer. Marissa flashes me a bright smile and a mock salute before she continues her dancing. "Shit!" she screeches, her body tipping sideways.

Without thinking, I launch myself forward to catch her. Using the momentum of her body, I spin around and pin her to the back of the bar.

"You need to be more careful," I chastise her, only now noticing the situation I've put myself in.

My body is almost flush against hers, pressing her against the back bar. My desire awakens for the second time tonight.

"Finn," she whispers, molding her body to mine as she wraps her arms around my neck.

Her eyes never leave mine as she presses her lips gently to mine.

Pleasure shoots through my veins as I wrap my hand around her waist, pulling her closer. I pull back, looking directly into her eyes, searching for permission before crushing my lips to hers again. She gasps in shock as I slide my tongue into her mouth, massaging it with mine. She sighs softly, melting into my arms, as she surrenders to me, giving me the only thing I've wanted for the last four years.

We break apart, gasping for air, and I take a step back. "I'm sorry. I shouldn't have done..."

"Don't you fucking dare," Marissa growls, pulling my head down to meet her lips again.

I clench my lips tight, not wanting to give in to my desire for a second time.

"Are you sure about this?" I whisper as she nibbles along my bottom lip and pulls it between her lips.

"No," she groans as she leans back, indecision swirling in her eyes as her hand slides between us, gripping my shaft tightly through my jeans. "But I have a feeling I'll regret it for the rest of my life if I don't do this."

I watch her closely, searching for any signs that she might regret what had just happened. Her chest rises and falls quickly as she drops her head on my shoulder. I don't move a muscle as I lean my head back and send up a silent prayer for strength as her other hand slides down my chest, pinching my nipple. Hard.

"Please, Finn." She straddles my leg, grinding her pussy down on my knee as she rocks back and forth. My resolve crumbles.

I've never been able to deny her anything, and I don't plan to start now. My need to bury my cock deep inside her is quickly becoming uncontrollable.

"I just want to forget everything. For one night, I want to be the center of a man's universe," she purrs, popping the button of my jeans open and lowering the zipper. "One night of indescribable pleasure, and then we go back to normal."

"Are you sure this isn't the alcohol talking?" I growl, hanging on to my last bit of control.

"I'm not drunk, Finn." Marissa sinks to her knees in front of me. My eyes zero in on her hands as she pulls out my cock, her thumb brushing against the tip. "I know what I'm doing, and I want this. I want you."

"I don't have any condoms." I watch in awe as she licks her lips in anticipation before sliding my cock between her lips.

"I'm on the pill," she responds before sliding my cock deep into her mouth, gagging slightly before sliding it almost all the way out. "Have any other excuse?"

A part of me knows that nothing about this situation is a good idea. Marissa has never shown an interest in me. If I'm being honest with myself, I doubt she ever noticed me before right now. And now that she's horny and has beer goggles on, I look like the best option. But my lower half has wanted Marissa since I first laid eyes on her. I wanted to be her rock. The man to give her everything she's ever wanted and so much more. And now she's asking me for another one-night stand.

A wave of pleasure rolls through my body, my head dropping back to my shoulders, as her lips sink back down around my cock. Marissa moans loudly around me as I thread my fingers into her hair.

This is a bad idea, but this will probably be my only chance to show Marissa how things could be between us. She says that I can only have her for one night, but there's no way I'll be able to let her go after this. She's mine.

"If you're going to suck my cock, baby, you'd better do it properly," I growl, shoving my cock down her throat in one motion.

She gags loudly before easing her head back slightly and thrusting forward. The tip of my cock slams against the back of her throat.

"You want me to fuck your mouth?"

She moans her answer around my cock, sending vibrations of pleasure up my spine.

"Your wish is my command."

I set a relentless pace, her mouth taking everything I have to give. My cock disappears between her lips as my balls tighten.

But the only place I want to come tonight is balls-deep inside Marissa, feeling her walls spasming around me.

I tug tightly on her hair, pulling her head back. My cock slips out of her mouth as a line of drool dribbles down her chin.

"I wasn't done," she smirks.

Streaks of mascara run down her cheeks, and trails of drool flow down her chin, yet she's never looked more beautiful. Grasping her hand, I pull her up and capture her lips as soon as they're within reach.

"I need a taste," I say against her lips, and she quickly shimmies out of her jeans, kicking them to the side before plastering her body against mine. I plant a searing kiss on her lips before shoving my hands under her arms and lifting her onto the bar. "Lean back."

Marissa quickly follows my instructions, spreading her legs wide for me. I run my hands up her thighs, kneading her flesh and brushing the tips of my fingers against her pussy before repeating the process again and again.

"Finn..." She squirms in place. "Stop teasing me."

"Like you've been doing to me all night?" My thumb brushes against her clit, and her back arches off the bar top. "I've been thinking about bending you over this bar all night. Ripping every stitch of clothing off your body and having my wicked way with you."

"Less talking and more doing."

I chuckle softly as I lower to my knees, replacing my thumb with my tongue and pulling her clit into my mouth, along with her panties. "I've never tasted anything like you in my life."

Marissa leans up on her elbows, locking eyes with me as she massages her tits through her shirt. Unable to wait any longer, I grip the waistband of her panties and pull, ripping them from her body. Her entire body trembles as I give her lower lips one long lick before shoving two fingers into her pussy.

"Yes," she hisses, lowering her hands to the edge of the bar and rocking her hips, fucking herself on my fingers.

"That's it, baby. Take what you need." I fist my cock, pumping in time with her movements as her walls spasm around my fingers.

"Oh, I'm so close." Marissa picks up the pace, rocking back and forth faster as my fingers disappear inside her.

When I sense she's almost to the edge, I pull my fingers out and stand.

"What the fuck!" Marissa screeches as she tries to sit up, but I use my arm to push her back, holding her in place.

"The only place you're going to come is on my cock," I say before sucking my fingers into my mouth and licking them clean.

I line myself up, brushing the tip of my cock against her hardened nub. "This is your last chance, Marissa. You can tell me no. I'll help you get dressed, and we can go our separate ways."

I hold still, waiting for some sign that this is what she really wants. She's been drinking, but she has her wits about her. Marissa can tell me no, and although it would pain me, I'd do exactly what I said.

"I want you," she responds, reaching between us and sliding my cock between her folds.

I shift backward before sheathing myself deep inside her. "So fucking tight."

Her walls clench around my cock as I try to ease all the way out before thrusting forward once again. I pick up the pace, using the bar for leverage, and pull my body forward, thrusting deep inside.

"Fuck, your pussy is perfect," I mumble into her neck as I pull the sensitive skin behind her ear between my teeth.

"It's never been..." Marissa wraps her arms around my neck, pulling me into her chest. Marissa gasps loudly as I hit her G-spot with the tip of my cock.

"I know," I respond, knowing exactly what she's trying to tell me.

I've wanted Marissa for years, and now that she has finally given me the chance to have her, there's no turning back. Bitterness and sorrow swirl through my body, not knowing what will come in tomorrow's morning light. She promised me one night, and by some chance, I managed to convince her that we are so much more than a one-night stand. That I will love her until my dying day because I've dreamt of calling her mine for all these years. Now I just need to convince her of that fact.

"I'm close." I clench my jaw, needing her to come before I tumble over the edge. "Can you come for me, sugar?"

She nods, lifting her legs and wrapping them around my waist. I reach between our bodies, pressing down on her clit and rubbing tight, small circles.

"I'm gonna come," she pants, digging her nails into my shirt and raking them down my back.

She screams, her voice echoing off the walls of my bar as I lift her legs over my shoulders and pump faster. Swirls of color blur my vision as I thrust forward, burying my cock deep inside her as I come loudly, moaning her name.

I lower her legs to the sides as I slide out of her with a groan and reach for a bar towel to wipe her clean. I throw it to the floor, not wanting my employees to clean up my mess, and tuck myself back into my pants.

"What are you doing?" I raise my eyebrow in question as I watch Marissa slide off the bar and head away from me.

"I said—"

I stride toward her. "You didn't think I was finished with you yet, did you?"

She's going to do everything she can to put a stop to this, to walk away from me in the morning and pretend this never happened, just like that night in Chattanooga. But I won't let that happen a second time. I couldn't then, and I sure as hell can't now. Marissa needs to understand that now that I've had a taste of what things could be like between us, I won't ever be able to go back.

seventeen

marissa

"Why the fuck is it so bright in here?" I grumble, throwing my arm over my face.

I've never been a morning person, but I've gotten used to getting up before the sun since I started working at the sheriff's department. But being awake at the crack of dawn after drinking enough tequila to last a lifetime isn't my favorite. It's one reason I try not to drink unless I have a longer shift on Fridays. This way I can recover from my hangover in peace and sleep the day away.

I try to roll over and bury my nose in my pillow, hoping to fall back to sleep, when memories of last night filter through my mind. The way Finn made my body sing for him in a way no one else has before.

He lived up to his promise and then some, giving me pleasure beyond my wildest imagination, repeatedly, until we both passed out from exhaustion. Too bad it was only meant to be a onetime thing. I wouldn't have minded one more round before heading to work.

"No sense crying over spilled milk," I mumble to

myself before throwing off the covers and climbing out of bed before heading directly for the bathroom.

I brace my arms on either side of the sink, and my eyes widen in surprise at the slightly purple marks covering my skin. Lifting my arms overhead to pull my hair up, I feel the pull of the muscles in my back, reminding me how he made me arch in pleasure.

"Fuck." I groan, my head shifting from side to side, taking in the marks covering my skin.

It's as if he wanted to mark me, needing to show everyone I encounter that I belong to him, just like a caveman. Usually, that type of behavior is a complete turnoff for me, but instead of being disgusted, I'm turned on. These marks might come in handy if I run into Campbell at some point.

"This was a mistake. It never should've happened the first time, let alone a second time. I need to forget about last night and move on."

This situation is nothing new to me. I go out on the weekend to blow off some steam and have some fun. Nothing more, nothing less. It's sex. One night of fun and then things go back to normal. But this time was different. Finn is different. I'm not expecting him to profess his undying love to me—hell, we barely know each other. We spent two amazing nights together, and now I can't seem to get him out of my system. He's the only thing I can think about most days and the last thing I think about before I go to bed. Hell, I don't want to admit it, but I was glad when I saw him at Tallywackers last night. I knew that he'd never mention anything about Campbell and treat me the same as always, like I was the center of his universe.

I turn around to head back out of the bathroom and notice a note taped to the doorframe.

Your clothes are hanging on the back of the door for you.

I'll have breakfast waiting when you come down.

-Finn

He has no intention of making this easy for me, does he? I had planned on getting out of here as quickly as possible and heading directly to the station. The last thing I want to do is have an awkward morning-after conversation, and I certainly don't want to have that conversation with Finn.

But it's nice to have someone care for me like this. I've always been made to feel like I was second best. First by my mother and then with what happened with Campbell. I was beginning to feel like I didn't deserve to be someone's everything. I know my parents love me, and I think Campbell loved me at one point, but that never stopped me from feeling like I wasn't good enough, even if it wasn't intentional on their part. I shake my head, not wanting my mind to wander too far from reality. The situation is simple. Just because we slept together doesn't automatically mean we're going to be together forever.

I reach behind the door and grab my clothes, pulling them on quickly before scurrying past his discarded clothes and heading down the long hallway to the front of his apartment. Although he failed to give me the tour last night, I found Finn rather quickly, sitting at the kitchen table while drinking a cup of coffee.

His eyes flick toward mine, and a bright smile spreads across his face. "Breakfast is served."

"Do you live here?" I question, taking in the small kitchen and dining room.

Nothing is really decorated, making it the perfect bachelor pad for Finn to bring someone for some privacy after a long night at the bar. Jealousy shoots through my veins at the thought of Finn spending time with anyone else, but that's fucking ridiculous. This is only meant to be one night. Who he spends his time with has nothing to do with me.

"No. I'm still trying to figure out what's going on with my dad, so most of my stuff is still in Texas. This is a small apartment above the bar that I crash in sometimes after a long night."

That's right. Finn isn't staying. He's only temporarily in Magnolia until his father is moving around easier, and then he'll be on his way back to his real life and forget all about me. I need to remember that because if I'm not careful, I could lose my heart a second time, and this time, I'm not sure I'll recover.

Finn pushes back from the table and stands to his full height, giving me the perfect opportunity to take in the sight in front of me. A pair of gray sweatpants hang at his waist, showing off his abs. I lick my lips at the sight of the deep V disappearing into his pants, wanting nothing more than to step over and nibble my way down his body before taking his cock into my mouth for a second time.

"Please, have a seat," he says, motioning with his hand toward the chair a few inches in front of me as we lock eyes.

Get a fucking grip, Marissa! I had an itch, and I scratched it with Finn a few times, but just because he's giving me some attention doesn't mean I'm falling in love with him. Falling in love is for losers. The last time I let someone into my heart, it ended badly. The last thing I want is to allow that to happen again, especially with someone who grew up in Magnolia. I'm not addicted to how he makes me feel after spending just one night with him. After mind-blowing sex, it's only natural.

Keep telling yourself that.

Shaking the unwanted thought out of my mind, I stride toward the table, trying desperately to figure out how to get my damn libido under control. I just need to make an excuse to grab one of those delicious muffins in the center of the table and get to work. Then I can try to figure out what the hell is going on with me. Those are the priorities.

I grab the back of the chair, attempting to pull it out, but Finn has other plans. Wrapping his arms around my waist, he pulls me toward him, spinning me around in the process and crushing his lips to mine. His cock grinds into my belly as I slide my hands over his shoulders and into his hair.

"Finn," I moan as he devours my mouth, nibbling and sucking on my bottom lip until they open for him, giving in to our desire. I get lost in the sensation of his lips and hands touching me as he lifts my leg, wrapping it around his waist and thrusting his cock against me.

"I really need to..." My voice trails off as we break apart with a gasp.

"Eat. Breakfast is the most important meal of the day." He punctuates every phrase by thrusting his length against me, rocking back and forth, causing it to slide across my clit.

"I can't," I moan, pulling him closer to me.

"You can," he breathes as he nibbles down my neck before capturing my ear between his lips, rubbing the lobe between my teeth. "I changed my mind. I want your pussy for breakfast."

Finn wastes no time lifting me in his arms and striding into the other room, laying me gently on the couch. His eyes roam down my body, setting my skin on fire as he drops to his knees. He leans forward, brushing his lips against mine before gripping the hem of my shirt and exposing my skin.

"I've never tasted anything as delicious as your skin in my life." He groans, planting kisses along my stomach before popping open the button on my pants. "Lift."

I follow his commands, lifting my hips and allowing him to pull everything off before depositing them on the floor with my shirt. His eyes flick up to mine as he spreads my knees wide enough for his shoulders to fit and kisses the inside of my legs before slowly licking my pussy from back to front. He sucks my clit deep into his mouth, and my back arches.

"Fuck!" I scream before biting my lip, willing myself to keep my voice down.

"No, I want to hear you scream," he says as he continues lapping at my juices. "I want every mother-fucker to know who you belong to."

He slides two fingers between my folds as he continues to nibble at my clit.

"I need you to scream my name, sugar. Scream so loud the walls shake."

My hips come down, riding his fingers as I climb toward my release.

"Yes, yes, yes," I chant repeatedly as stars suddenly flash through my eyes as he adds another finger. My body jerks, and I go over the edge. Liquid sprays from my pussy, all over the bed and his face, but he continues to suck, not letting go of my swollen clit and drawing out my pleasure further.

"Finn!" I scream loudly, gripping the fabric of the couch tightly and holding on for fear I will float away. He continues pumping his fingers in and out as I come down, my entire body melting into the couch.

"Fucking delicious." He grunts as he lifts his head,

wiping my cum from his face. A mixture of pride and devotion swirls in his eyes as he leans forward and takes my mouth in a punishing kiss.

This kiss is so different from every other kiss we've shared. His desire is clear, but there's something else. A possessiveness that wasn't there before. I thought that what happened last night was a spur-of-the-moment decision. A chance meeting where two consenting adults wanted to have some fun, but not this time. I have a feeling our nights together meant more to Finn than I expected, and that scares the hell out of me.

We break apart with a grasp, and Finn smiles, pushing to his feet and reaching his hand toward me. "How about that breakfast I promised?"

This man is seriously bad for my health. After a few nights in bed with him, I have hearts in my eyes, and I'm dreaming about spending forever in his arms.

"No can do. I need to head to the station, and I'm sure you have something to do at the bar. Shipments to process, you know, things like that." I duck my head, not wanting to meet his eyes as I grab my pants from the ground and slide them back into place.

"You don't have to be at the station for a few hours, I bet. Besides, I can't send you off to work on an empty stomach."

"I never made you any promises, Finn." I stare straight into his eyes.

Something passes across his face but disappears

instantly. "I don't know what you expected of me, but whatever it is, I can't give it to you."

He reaches out, gripping my hand tightly in his. "I understand that this wasn't planned by either of us. I'm not asking you to marry me tomorrow. I just want a chance to get to know you better."

Wait. What? But I can't do this.

"You already know me, Finn. We've lived in the same town all our lives. You were best friends with my sister. Hell, our parents go to the same church, for goodness' sake."

"Everyone goes to the same church, Marissa. There's only one in town," he whispers, brushing his lips gently against mine.

Ugh, this is one of the main reasons I keep my escapades out of town. Now I have to see him all over town and risk the chance of having to explain what happened between us to my mother, of all people. The best thing to do is to make sure this never happens again and that things go back to the way they were before I ever met Finn in that bar in Chattanooga.

"That's beside the point," I mumble, bending down and grabbing my shirt before sliding it over my head. "I'm glad you understand, and we're on the same page. We need to chalk this up to having too much to drink, and things can go back to normal." I cough slightly, trying to regain my composure.

"I was stone-cold sober, sugar," he says as my eyes

drop to the bulge in his pants that is growing larger. "Are you sure I can't interest you in one more round? I'd love to take you from behind on the stairs again."

My core clenches tightly at the memories of being on my hands and knees, ass up in the air, as Finn pounded roughly into me.

"No, that's okay," I squeak out as my legs clench together, and I try desperately not to fidget in place. "I need to get going. Colt will be on my ass if I'm late to relieve him."

"Have it your way. Let me have your phone." My body moves on autopilot, reaching into my pocket and handing him my phone. He hits a few buttons before I hear a soft chime from nearby. "Now you can't ignore me anymore." He flashes me another wicked smile before wrapping his arms around me and pulling me toward him. "If you don't stop looking at me like that, you won't make it to work."

He takes a step back and winks at me before striding out of the room toward the door. "Come on, I'll walk you to your car."

I bite down hard on my bottom lip to stop the moan bubbling in my throat from escaping. I clench my eyes shut as my chin drops to my chest. "Lord, give me strength."

"You coming?" he shouts from the other room, and I scurry after him toward the door.

I need space and time to think and get my libido back

in check because if things keep going the way they are now, I'll be in very real danger of losing my heart for a second time.

eighteen
marissa

"Look what the cat dragged in." I jump as I turn to see Peyton sitting at my kitchen table, sipping coffee. I was hoping to avoid this conversation for a few days, or at least until after I'd had a few hours of sleep.

"Is there any chance this could wait till I get more sleep?" I ask, as if I don't already know her answer.

"You're kidding, right?" She slips off the barstool. "I brought coffee and cinnamon buns. Besides, your mom said you were acting strange after she told you about Campbell. She asked me to stop by this morning to check on you. You go shower. I'll wait."

"I'm regretting ever introducing you to my mother. But if you must know, I had sex," I tell her, smiling sweetly, and pull out the chair across from her. "Are the cinnamon buns in that bag because I'm starving?"

I'd be lying if I said my heart doesn't flutter with just a hint of his smile or the idea that I could wake up next to him every morning, wrapped in his arms, feeling safe and protected from the outside world. But I can't get ahead of things. I need to take things one step at a time.

"Wait... how is that news? You have a lot of sex, so much that I get jealous. So please explain to me how this is big news."

I love my best friend, but sometimes I forget how direct she can be. If she wants to know something, she asks. No matter where we may be or who else is around. She wants to know immediately, but this is one secret I plan on keeping for as long as humanly possible.

"Fair enough, but I had sex with someone who I may want for more than one night." I slide my thumb into my mouth and begin nibbling on the tip.

"Now I'm intrigued. Not only did you have mind-blowing sex last night, but you're trying to keep it from me. Unless you went for another round with the mystery man from your weekend in Chattanooga over a month ago." Peyton snatches her cup of coffee off the table and takes a healthy pull.

I refused to share any information with her about the amazing night Finn and I spent together in Chattanooga, but not for lack of trying. She begged and pleaded with me for days, but when she realized I wasn't going to budge, she let it slide. However, I have a feeling it was more so because she was more intrigued by Finn's sudden interest in me. Not that it was really all that sudden. I know I have to tell her at some point, but right now, I want to keep it to myself. I have no idea how things are going to play out with him, and the last thing I need is someone else meddling in my business. My mother does that enough to last a lifetime.

"Now the more important question is, why are you here and not still in bed with that hot hunk of man meat?"

"Because I have to be at the station by noon to start my shift." I glance at my watch and notice it's only a little after eight a.m. "If we would've gone another round, I don't think we'd have come up for air before dinnertime."

Once again, all rational thought exits my brain, replaced by a random thought of Finn. *This shit is really getting old.* It was fucking sex. I mean, I love sex as much as the next person. It's a basic human need. I'm not ashamed of that fact, but there was something about having sex with Finn that I can't get out of my mind. It's like I've become dickmatized or something.

"Okay, it's official. I hate you," Peyton huffs, placing her coffee back on the table and leaning back in the chair.

"You aren't allowed to hate me. It's in the best friend rules," I respond, grabbing the second cup of coffee off the table to take a sip. The warm liquid travels down my throat as I hum in pleasure. "But could you at least tell me why you're feeling so hostile towards me this morning?"

"Here you are, having mind-blowing, amazing sex with a man that can melt your icy heart, and I killed my vibrator yesterday. You're one lucky bitch."

"I wouldn't go that far. He'll tire of me soon, just like—"

"Don't you dare bring up that asshole of an ex

during this conversation," she growls, pushing back from the table and dragging her chair beside me. "I don't want to hear that nonsense coming out of your mouth again. He's back in town. So what? He no longer controls your life. Don't let him continue to have this power over you."

"What would I do without you?" I wrap my arm around her shoulder, pulling her to my side.

Peyton Atkins is my opposite, but I wouldn't trade her for the world. At first glance, you'd never believe the two of us were like sisters, but we complete each other. I trust her with my life, my deepest secrets, but I'm still hesitant to tell her this one.

"You'd live." Peyton plants a sloppy kiss on my cheek before reaching into her bag and handing me a box with one of her infamous cinnamon rolls in it. "With that out of the way, tell me more about the man that put that smile on your face, or I'm going to tell your mom what you were really doing last night."

"First off, I'm not the one who lied to her. You did. Second, I have to know what you told her first."

"I told her that you got drunk at Tallywackers, your phone died, and I brought you home with me. And we both know she likes me better. It'd be your fault I had to tell her the lie in the first place."

"You're probably right."

It's not a complete lie either way. There's a pretty good chance that Peyton would've been at the bar last night. My mom doesn't need to know that she doesn't go out during the week because she opens the bakery every morning at 5:00 a.m. But this could be risky.

"Thanks for the heads-up. I wouldn't put it past my mom to ask me just to make sure our stories line up."

"This isn't her first rodeo. Since you have to go to the station, she may even ask Dolores or Colt, too." Peyton giggles, taking a healthy pull from her coffee cup. "But I'm your best friend. It's my job to lie for you when it's deemed necessary."

It's probably not the best idea, but this is what Peyton signed up for when she agreed to be my best friend. I never have to ask her permission to put her into my lie. Either one of us just knows that we need to cover each other's ass the moment anyone brings up questions. And then we immediately report what was said to the other to make sure the story is believable. As long as you can get others to believe the lie, there's hope that everything will blow over quickly.

"Now, tell me what happened, or you're gonna have some explaining to do."

"You'll be in trouble, too, because you lied to her."

"I'll just tell her you made me do it."

Fuck, she has me there. Do I want to get into this with her right now? No, but if I don't tell her something, she won't let it go. She's like a shark who smells blood in the water. She won't rest until she gets the information she's searching for.

"I'm waiting," she huffs.

I don't want to tell her any specifics about Finn. I

can't stop the shiver that runs through my body. Last night with Finn was nothing more than sex. An itch I needed to scratch. There was nothing special about the way it felt when he touched me. Like I was cherished and, dare I say, loved. Nope, nothing at all. I'm not going to even think about how he took care of me this morning instead of rushing me out the door. He was just being nice. I'm sure he reacts that way to all the women he sleeps with.

Not about to go there again.

I take a deep breath, willing my emotions to go back to being locked behind the wall I built around my heart years ago. I'm well acquainted with how men make you believe that you are their everything and how quickly they can change their minds. This thing with Finn can never be anything more than sex, especially if I'm reacting to him like this.

"Hello... Earth to Marissa?" Peyton waves her hand in front of my face to get my attention. "Bless it. That dreamy look on your face says it all."

"It was no one special. I just picked up someone at the bar, and my phone died. I was upset when I left my parents' house last night, so my mom just wanted to make sure I was all right."

Finn's smoldering green eyes immediately pop back into my mind. That was fun while it lasted. I managed not to think about what Finn did to my body for a whole ten minutes while we were having this conversation, but now, images of the wickedly delicious things he did come flooding back to me. Moisture pools between my legs as I remember what it felt like to have his muscular arms wrapped around me as he pounded into my pussy from behind or what it would felt like as the soft stubble on his face rubbed against the inside of my legs while he fucked my lower lips with his tongue.

What in God's name is happening to me?

"Just some random hookup doesn't put that kind of smile on your face. I call bullshit. I want to know details about Mr. Perfect."

"He isn't perfect, not by a long shot."

"Maybe not, but he's pretty close to it if he has your attention enough that you don't want to tell me about him. Give me details."

I pop open the lid; the smell of sugar and cinnamon causes my stomach to growl loudly.

"I really hate repeating myself," Peyton huffs, grabbing the box with the delicious cinnamon bun away from me. "I'm holding this hostage until you answer some of my questions. The main one being, who is this mystery man that thawed my best friend's heart?"

"Someone who lives in Magnolia," I respond, not giving her any further information.

"Wait, is it Campbell? I told you not to bring him up in this conversation, so you might have taken me too literally. It better not be that asshole! Not that I wouldn't support you getting back together if you wanted to, but you better make him grovel first. He owes you that much." Peyton continues rapidly firing questions at me, not giving me a moment to answer before finally stopping completely. "Sorry. You can answer now."

"The way you shift between moods never ceases to amaze me." I giggle, shoving the last bit of pastry into my mouth before washing it down with coffee.

"I'm not telling you who it was. Yes, you know them. No, it wasn't Campbell. We aren't ever getting back together."

Peyton is silent for a few minutes before huffing loudly. "You better have a damn good reason for not telling me, Mari. You held out on me last time, but something tells me this guy is different. If it was horrible, I highly doubt you'd have that smile on your face, so what gives?" she questions, eying me skeptically for a few minutes.

"Are you kidding me!" I shriek, jumping to my feet as I pace back and forth. "It was the best sex I've ever had. And yes, before you ask, even better than when I was with Campbell."

Campbell and I were each other's first, which made it a lot easier to figure out what we both liked and didn't like. The first few times were uneventful, but after some practice... let's just say there is some truth behind the saying *scream myself hoarse*.

"Damn, girl." She whistles softly. "Are you going back for more?"

"I'd love nothing more, but I don't do seconds or relationships."

My supposedly dead cell phone rings in my pocket, but I ignore it.

"You need to get that? Could it be the hottie from last night asking for another round?" She laughs, finishing her coffee and tossing it into the trash can a few feet away from the table.

"No, it's probably my mother," I respond, checking my watch. "Do you need to go? Everyone should be heading into the bakery soon for their coffee before heading in to work for the day."

"Nah, I have a few more minutes to kill. Besides, I just baked some fresh cookies before I came here. I gave Katie instructions to offer free samples in case I don't get back in time." Her voice trails off as my phone rings again. "How many times has she called you already?"

"More than I'd like to admit, but I've ignored everyone but you. We both know what she's going to say. A lecture about being more responsible with my phone while also wanting to make sure I'm okay after they dropped the bomb on me that Campbell was back in town."

"If he comes anywhere near you, tell him to go fuck himself. His cheating on you should've been a pretty good indicator that he isn't relationship material. Once a cheater, always a cheater."

"He never cheated on me, Peyton. I don't know how many times I have to tell you that."

"I still think the timeline is too much of a coincidence," Peyton grumbles.

This isn't the first time I've tried to convince Peyton that Campbell never cheated on me. To her, he's the worst kind of man. The kind that left me brokenhearted.

"He didn't cheat on me or Emmeline. My mom told me she's the one who cheated on him and ran off."

"Yeah, that's some bullshit. Leaving your husband is one thing, but abandoning your child... I could never."

"Yeah, I can't even imagine what he's going through right now. No matter what he's done to me, no one deserves to be treated like that." I sigh loudly before pushing to my feet. "From what my mom says, he never saw it coming. He seems like he's been a good husband and father. Did everything he was supposed to do, but it didn't matter. Now he's back living with his parents and raising their son alone."

"I still don't like him."

"You don't even know him, Peyton. I've forgiven him for what he did to me, and now it's time for both of us to let it go."

"I don't know..." Her voice trails off, causing me to chuckle.

"At least don't be mean to him for no reason."

"What if I have a reason?"

"Then you can do whatever you want. Be as big of a bitch as you want, but he has to give you a reason."

"I can live with that. I'll try to be nice, but I make no promises."

"That's all I can ask from you."

"Now, about your mystery man..." I groan in

response. "Come on! You always tell me the details so I can live vicariously through you."

"There really is nothing to tell."

"Besides the mind-blowing sex."

"Are you going to let me tell this story or what?"

"Sorry. Shutting up now." She makes a big show of locking her lips and throwing away the key before folding her hands on the top of the table.

I wait a few moments to make sure she doesn't have anything else to say before continuing. "I actually met him in Chattanooga last month." She opens her mouth, and I place my hand over it, silencing her. "No, he didn't stalk me. But he knows me. Apparently, he grew up here and was on his way back for a visit with his parents. He won't be in town much longer."

"Oh, my god! Are you planning on leaving me? I can't move right now. Business is booming, and I'm finally making some money, but maybe in a few years I can figure it out."

"Girl, pump your breaks." I shake my head. "He's leaving town, not me. No matter how mind-blowing the sex is."

"I call bullshit. If it was just sex, you wouldn't be telling me about it."

"You were sitting in my apartment when I walked in the door. Did I have any other choice but to tell you?"

"No, probably not. But still. I never hear about your sexcapades other than when you're leaving town and when you will be back. But this one is different. I have to pry even the tiniest bit of information out of you. Usually, you offer it up freely. Now spill, Marissa.

I take a deep breath and tell her everything that's happened over the last few weeks. How I met the most gorgeous man I've ever seen in my life and how we ended up running into each other right here in Magnolia. I told her about that first night with Finn, about my feelings about Campbell being back in town, and I go into detail about how the idea of letting Finn in scares the shit out of me. I leave out some key details, Finn's name specifically, and that something about him just calls to me. As if he's the missing piece in my life I came here searching for. Something that I never once felt in all the years since Campbell and I split. If I'm being honest, these growing feelings for Finn are beginning to run deeper than anything I ever felt for Campbell.

"You're in so much trouble."

"Tell me something I don't know. I don't know if I can survive heartbreak like that again. It's better if I keep him at arm's length. He'll tire of me, eventually."

"Next time I hear you talking badly about yourself, I'm going to smack the shit out of you," she growls, slapping me hard on the shoulder. "You're an amazing woman, and any man would be lucky to have you on their arm."

"Maybe. But Peyton, I can't be in love."

"But you said something about him calls to you." I nod my head. "You need to at least see where this can lead."

"Maybe."

"No maybe, missy!" Peyton pushes back from the chair, grabbing our trash and shoving it into the container. "If this mystery man asks you out, you're going to say yes. You are going to tell your brain to fuck off and listen to your heart for the first time in years. And then you're going to come home and call me immediately and tell me all about it."

"Really? I'm going to do all that?"

"Yes, or you will face my wrath."

"Fine. If he asks again, I'll agree to a date. I could go out with him and hate everything about him."

"Sure. Or he can be that someone you've been looking for," she responds quickly before wrapping her arms around my shoulders and giving me a quick squeeze. "Now that that's settled, I need to head back to the bakery, and you need to shower. You smell like sex."

"Love you, Peyton."

"Love you, too." She giggles as she strolls out the door, closing it tightly behind her.

I glance at the clock on the wall and see I have a few hours before I need to head to the station. Pushing to my feet, I shuffle toward my bedroom, heading directly for the bed. Not even bothering to remove my shoes, I plop down but leave my feet hanging off the end of the bed. I want nothing more than to fall asleep and dream about how things could be with Finn.

I remember the way he looked at me with hunger in his eyes, as if I was his last meal. His chiseled chin, his full head of dark, perfectly tousled hair, from just getting out of bed. The way it felt to have his full lips pressed against mine.

My core tightens for the second time today, and I'm powerless to stop the feelings running through me. Electricity shoots down my spine as I pop the button of my jeans and slide my hand into my panties, rubbing my clit with my finger.

Pulling my lip into my mouth, I imagine him lifting me in the air and setting me on the counter in the bar, then scooting me to the edge and burying his nose in my neck.

"You smell fucking delicious," he groans, licking up the side of my neck before pulling my earlobe between his teeth. "I could fuck you right here in the bar again. Anyone could come in and see us."

I slide two fingers between my folds, spreading my legs wider as I insert them and drag them across my G-spot.

"Fuck me, please," I whimper as I imagine him dropping to his knees and burying his nose between my lower lips before replacing my fingers with his tongue.

I moan loudly before his hand flies up to my mouth. "You need to be quiet, sugar. I refuse to let anyone else hear your sweet little moans," he growls before plunging his tongue back inside me.

My back arches off the bar as he continues to fuck my pussy, my walls tightening around him.

"You're so tight, baby. I can't wait to sink my cock

between your pussy lips and have you milk it dry," he whispers before biting down on the inside of my thigh. I check over my shoulder to ensure we don't have any company.

I slide my fingers in and out of my pussy, wetness dripping down my hand with each thrust. My hips lift off the bed as I chase my release.

"Please. Please. Please," I beg as I continue to fuck myself with my fingers.

My other hand slides up my body, pinching my pebbled nipple between my fingers. A mixture of pleasure and pain shoots through my body, and my core tightens.

"Come for me, sugar. I want to taste your juices on my lips for the rest of my life," he whispers as I imagine his eyes locking with mine as I come. My mouth opens wide in a silent scream.

"Fuck." I moan as the final shockwaves of pleasure shoot through my body, but I'm still left feeling empty because that wasn't even close to the real thing.

I hiss, yanking my fingers from between my legs just as my cell phone rings in my pocket. I roll over to the side, reaching into my pocket for my phone quickly and pulling it to my ear.

"Hello?" I ask tentatively, wondering who would call me this early in the morning.

"OMG, Marissa! Did I wake you? I'm so sorry!" Dolores's voice filters through the phone, and I smile.

"Hey, Dolores. And no worries. I was just waking up," I say, throwing my legs over the side of the bed and sitting up. "What can I do for you?"

"I hate to bother you, but do you think you could come in early today? Colt got a call about a decent size accident on the 40 and could use some backup."

Pulling the phone away from my ear, I check the time before responding. "Sure. I need to hop in the shower and can be there in thirty minutes."

I can hear Dolores mumbling to someone before she comes back. "Colt says he'll pick you up."

"No problem. I'll be ready," I respond before ending the call and flopping back onto the bed.

Apparently, there is no rest for the wicked, at least not today.

nineteen
finn

It's been four days since Marissa and I fell back into bed with each other. I expected her to slink into her shell, needing to be coaxed back out, but the exact opposite happened. It's as if she finally stopped fighting the pull between us. *Fighting* probably isn't the best word for it. I think a better word would be *accepted*. She's accepted that I'm not going anywhere. I won't lose interest suddenly or stop calling. I'm in it for the long haul.

As if on cue, the alarm on my phone sounds, letting me know it's time to send Marissa her daily text messages. I've been sending her messages every day since I weaseled her number out of her, and today is the day I'm finally going to ask her to go out with me.

Hey, sugar. Did you have a chance to each lunch yet today?

SUGAR

Yes, but I'm going to have to work out more regularly if you keep sending me slices of that delicious chocolate cake.

I make a mental note to thank Shelly. It's kind of embarrassing, but I can't cook, and the takeout bills were getting to be expensive, so I enlisted Shelly's help. Between my mom and Mrs. Flores, I've been able to get a good idea of what Marissa's favorite foods were. Although Mrs. Flores stopped being as helpful once she discovered Campbell was back in town.

At first, I was hurt by her change of heart, but it makes sense. Marissa wasn't the only one that planned for her to spend the rest of her life with Campbell. It only makes sense that her mother would be team Campbell, but I just have to work a little of my magic and win her heart.

> I'll **stop sending** it if you really want me to.

SUGAR

> J/K. I may agree to a date if you promise to bring me an entire cake.

> Done. I'll pick you up at the station after your shift. What time do you get off?

Shit. It's so easy for me to banter back and forth with Marissa, but that was not the way I wanted to ask her on a date. I had plans of sending her flowers and maybe asking Peyton for help to make it perfect for her. I wanted it to be special, not a spur-of-the-moment ask while texting back and forth during work.

SUGAR

> Sure. I get off at seven, but I need to head home to change. Can I meet you at Tallywackers at 7:30?

Sure. I can't wait, sugar.

"Hell yeah!" I pump my fist into the air, causing the few patrons in the bar to shift their attention to me. I should be embarrassed by my outburst, but this is a step in the right direction. It's taken weeks, but I've finally convinced Marissa to go on a real date with me. Sure, I took her to lunch, but that wasn't a date. It was lunch, a lunch that I had to fight tooth and nail to convince her to agree to go. This is a real date. I asked, and she said yes. I have no idea who or what convinced her to give us a chance, but I won't look a gift horse in the mouth.

"Shit, what do I do?" I whisper to myself as I panic. I was so focused on setting up a date with Marissa that I hadn't put any thought into where we would go or what we would do.

I can't go with the usual dinner and a movie, and I sure as hell can't bring her back to the apartment over the bar or we'll end up back in bed together. Not that I'd complain, but Marissa needs to know that I want more than an amazing fuck.

"I'm going to need some help."

"Help with what?" Shelly chimes in on cue, appearing right next to me. "I've been calling you for like five minutes, Finn. What has you so deep in thought?"

If anyone knows how to find the key to a woman's

heart, it's Shelly. I want to move things further along with Marissa. To take her on dates and be seen in public with our friends. This cloak and dagger shit is taking its toll on me. I want to be with her, to be the one she comes home to after a long day of work. The person she shares her burdens with when she's having a rough time. At the moment, I'm nothing but her fuckboy, ready to obey her every command. When did I become so pathetic?

"I need to come up with the perfect date to take Marissa on. Tonight."

"Damn, you couldn't give a girl some warning?" she grumbles, leaning against the back bar.

"Hey, you got as much time as I did. I saw an opening, and I took it. Lucky for me, she said yes." I wrap my arm around her shoulder, pulling her to my side and kissing the top of her head. "I have you and your chocolate cake to thank for it, too."

"It's gonna cost you."

I roll my eyes at her response. Shelly would give me the shirt off her back if I needed it, but she would also make sure I remembered for the rest of my life that one time she helped me. Who am I kidding? I'd probably do the same thing to both Nolan and her.

"Can't you just help me out of the kindness of your heart?"

"You know me better than that."

"I do," I respond, already prepared for this turn of events. "You can have the next two weekends off."

"I'm listening."

"Don't push it, Shelly. I need help, but I could always just ask my mom."

"An entire weekend?"

"Yup." I pop the letter P at the end of the word. I knew that I'd get her to do just about anything for me if I promised her time away from this place.

"Make it a month and you got a deal."

"Okay, but you need to create some premade items that Nolan and I can heat in the oven to serve during lunch.

"Oh, and I need you to make me another one of your chocolate cakes to give to Marissa tonight. It was a condition of her agreeing to go on a date for me."

"Of course, you need one of those." She sighs, checking her watch to make sure she has enough time. "Okay, I can do that. Do we have a deal?" She holds out her hand for me to shake, and I don't hesitate, clutching it in my hand and giving her a firm handshake.

"A picnic," she responds immediately.

"You don't need any time to think about it?"

"Nope. Nolan and I have had a list of ideas written on a piece of paper in the kitchen for almost two weeks for just this occasion. Let's face it, Bossman, you're a smooth talker but not much else." She sighs loudly, waiting patiently for me to give her a hard time.

But I don't. "Where's a good place to take someone for a picnic?"

I remain silent, waiting for her to give me an answer. I know I haven't been on a date in a while, so I admit I'm a little rusty. I've taken women on dates before, but it's been years, and not one of them meant anything to me. I was going through the motions, attempting to forget Marissa, but it got me nowhere. I always found a way to turn women away before they could get too close because I was never drawn to them. But with Marissa, she's always been different. So different that it terrifies me.

"It should be somewhere special. Somewhere that you feel is the perfect place to tell Marissa how you feel because I know you. Now that she's given you an opening, you're going to go full throttle."

"The Meyers Farmhouse," I suggest, after taking a few minutes to think. "Sutton, Marissa, and I always went there to watch the stars and catch fireflies when it was warmer out."

"Perfect," she responds quickly before wrapping her arms around my waist and giving me a tight squeeze. "What time are you going?"

"She's meeting me here at 7:30."

"Perfect. You'll be able to eat while watching the sunset, and the skies should be clear tonight. Stargazing is very romantic."

"Thank you so much, Shelly. I owe you one."

"Yeah, you do. Now, let me get back to work so I can make sure you have a fabulous picnic dinner to eat, along with Marissa's chocolate cake."

"Oh, no, we can't forget the cake." I chuckle as she unwraps her arms from around my waist before turning on her heels and heading back into the kitchen.

"Someone seems happy," Nolan says, slapping me hard on the back.

"Fuck yeah. I finally snagged a date with my girl." I smile, checking my watch for the time.

There are only a few more hours until it's time to meet my girl.

Yeah, my girl. Two words I never thought I'd say to describe Marissa Flores. Marissa is mine in almost every way possible. Now I just have to sell her on the idea. Feeling like a schoolboy getting ready for his first date, I head toward the back of the bar and up the stairs to my temporary apartment.

twenty
marissa

"How's my favorite deputy doing today?" Peyton chirps as she enters my office at the station, carrying a large tray of cookies. "Please tell me those aren't for me." I groan, rubbing my overly full stomach.

Finn has been sending me lunch and notes every day during my shifts, but now he sends me texts. And I have to admit, he's slowly wearing me down. I've started looking forward to his text messages and notes. I long to hear his voice right before I go to sleep at night. I want to give him my heart to trust that he'll take it and cherish it from now until eternity, but something is holding me back.

That annoying voice in the back of my head is telling me to remain on guard, that he isn't staying, just like everyone else in my life. Their longing to leave Magnolia is stronger than their feelings for you.

"They aren't for you," Peyton deadpans, bringing me back to the present. "So why did you text me *911* a few minutes before dinner time, when I'm the busiest?"

"I need you."

"Oookay… I love to be needed, but I need some more specifics."

"I need your help," I say sarcastically as I push back from my desk and stroll toward her.

"Aww. Are you missing a certain someone?" She grips the top of the chair and braces herself before slowly lowering the tray of cookies onto my desk.

"I thought those weren't for me."

"They aren't, but there's no way I can continue to hold this tray while I work on prying the reason for your emergency text message out of you."

"I'm not that bad."

"Yes, you are. Now, tell me what's going on." Peyton leans back in the chair, crossing her arms.

"I agreed to go on a date with my friend, and I'm panicking. I don't want to take the chance that I'll text him and cancel, so I need someone to sit here and babysit me."

"Well, yay! I'm so glad you finally took the plunge, but there's no reason for you to be freaking out."

"There are plenty of reasons to be freaking out. Least of all, I haven't been on a real date since I was with Campbell. What if I forget what I'm doing or if I suck at it or… I don't know… Anything else that could make things go epically wrong?" I respond, glancing out the window.

"Hold on, let me savor this moment." She smirks. "I've never seen you this frazzled, ever. This man might be the one, based on how you're acting. When are you going to put me out of my misery and tell me your mystery man's name? If I knew who he was, it would be a lot easier for me to help."

My body tenses with anticipation at the mere mention of his name. My cheeks heat from embarrassment as I quickly stand and head for the opposite side of the room.

"So you can stalk him until he breaks up with me?" I fidget with my hands, nervously glancing at the door.

"That was one time!" she shouts before slamming her hands over her mouth, causing me to laugh loudly. "And I saved you from a lot of heartache. He was dating three other girls at the same time."

She huffs, reminding me of the one and only time I've tried to date since Campbell broke up with me. The captain of the football team asked me to go to the movies, and I agreed, but Peyton's spidey senses were tingling. She went to our meeting spot two hours before we were supposed to meet and waited. She caught my date with another girl, and they looked like they were more than friends. Peyton texted me a picture of them making out in front of the theater, and I immediately texted him to tell him to fuck all the way off.

"Is that what you're afraid of? Do you think you're going to get played?" She tilts her head to the side, eyeing me inquisitively. "Or is there something else going on?"

"Nothing is going on. I'm just nervous is all."

I've been resisting his charms for a while now, but after our last night together, I don't know how much more I can handle. Although my mind is made up that I want nothing to do with him, my body has other plans.

I spent almost every night since then, lying awake at night, moisture pooling between my legs, as all the images of the dirty things he did to me that night filter through my mind. I imagine what it would feel like to have his muscular arms wrapped around me as he pounds into my pussy from behind, claiming me as his once again. Or what it would feel like as his beard rubs against the inside of my legs while he fucks my lower lips with his tongue.

I spend most nights fighting those images, convincing myself that there is nothing between Finn and me, but my body knows better. It won't let me have a moment of peace until I bring myself endless pleasure, calling out his name.

"Where is your phone?" Peyton pushes to her feet and strolls around the desk, opening and closing every door she can reach.

"Calm down, girlie. It's right here," I respond, pulling it out of my pocket and showing it to her.

"Thank you." She snatches it from my hands and tucks it into her shirt, right between her tits. "There. I'll keep it safe."

"You know I have no problem going down there to get it, right?

"I know, but the fear of someone walking in and catching you with your hand down my bra will probably outweigh the need for your phone."

"Touché." I chuckle before grabbing my computer

screen and spinning it toward her. The screen is covered with different outfits I found by googling the phrase *first date outfits*.

"Wow, some of these look a little too fancy for any place in Magnolia. Do you know where you're going?"

"No."

"I need that information before I can advise you on what to wear."

My brows pull down in thought, trying to figure out the best way to get that information.

"Call him." Peyton giggles, flicking the center of my forehead right between my eyebrows. "I can see the smoke coming out of your ears as we speak."

"I don't know. I just finished texting him a few minutes ago."

"Call him."

"Maybe he's busy at work."

"Call him."

"But—I—what?"

"Marissa, I swear on everything holy that if you don't call him, I'll do it for you. And we both know you won't like that one bit."

"You don't even know who he is."

"Then I call every number in your contacts until someone knows who I'm talking about." *Fuck*. I always knew Peyton was stubborn, but this is a whole new level. I should've known when I told her I was thinking about canceling my date. It's the reason I asked her to come here in the first place. A request I'm regretting at this very moment.

"Fine. I'll call him."

"Don't you need your phone?"

"No, I have his number memorized." My cheeks heat as I pick up my desk phone and dial Tallywackers. I let the phone ring a few times, waiting for someone to answer.

"Hello."

"Hello," I respond, waiting for whoever is on the other line to read the caller ID.

"Can I help you?"

Oh, no. Did the caller ID not work because I was calling from the station? My eyes flick toward Peyton and notice the sly smile on her face.

"Aren't you going to ask for him?"

"Uhhh..."

"Hey, Marissa, what can I do for you today?" Finn's deep voice filters through the line, and my shoulders instantly relax.

I'm not ashamed of what's going on between Finn and me, but I want to keep it quiet for a little while. At least until I know that he isn't going to shatter my heart into a million pieces. I promised myself I would never give a man so much power over how I live my life, and here I am, afraid of my best friend finding out who I'm going on a date with.

"Hey. I just wanted to know where we were going on our date. I'm trying to figure out what to wear."

"You don't have to wear anything if I get a vote."

Finn's gravelly voice sends a shiver down my spine. "But you can dress casually. We aren't doing anything fancy."

"I can hear you!" Peyton shouts, causing my cheeks to heat in embarrassment.

"Shut it, you," I growl at her.

"No need to be so rude," Finn responds.

"I wasn't talking to you."

"To who? Me? I thought you were on the phone with your mystery man, who sounds gorgeous, by the way."

"Why thank you, Peyton." Finn raises his voice slightly, probably to ensure she can hear him.

"Oooh, he knows my name. That narrows down the list considerably."

"Will you both shut it for two seconds so I can ask my question?" I huff, pulling the phone away from my ear and covering it with my other hand.

"This is not helping. I'm freaking out here, Peyway. Can you please just sit there quietly and let me find out where we are going tonight?"

"Fine. Take away all my fun," Peyton huffs, crossing her arms and poking out her bottom lip.

"Thank you." I flash her a smile before bringing the phone back to my ear. "Now, as I was saying. Are you going to tell me what we're doing?"

"No, it's a surprise."

"I hate surprises."

"I know." He chuckles softly before ending the call.

"He's good." Peyton giggles, causing my cheeks to heat even further.

"Shut up." I spin in my chair to face the wall, not wanting to see the smug look on Peyton's face. "He said to dress casually."

"Okay, that helps. Now, let's find you an outfit."

We spend the rest of my shift searching for the perfect outfit before Peyton makes a beeline back to my apartment to grab everything I need to get ready. She does my hair and forces me to use the shower in the locker room to take a shower and shave my legs. I smell just like a field of strawberries once I'm finished, and I head out of the station with a pat on the butt and well wishes from both Dolores and Peyton.

I arrive at the bar quickly, pulling into a spot near the back stairs leading down from the apartment above the bar. Just as I'm locking my car, I notice Finn strolling out the back door. His hair is damp from a recent shower. He's wearing an almost-new button-up shirt with the sleeves rolled to the elbows and dark jeans fitted perfectly to his muscular legs.

"Didn't your mama teach you not to stare?" He chuckles as he comes to a stop a few inches away from me.

I drop my head to my chest. Nothing like ogling a man to make things awkward. To maintain some of my dignity, I ramble off all the ideas I came up with of what we might do tonight, trying to look anywhere but at him.

Finn steps into my line of sight, causing me to stop my rambling and look into his eyes. "Good evening, sugar." Finn stalks toward me. "I've been looking forward to seeing you all day. I missed you."

My breath catches in my throat as I straighten my back, unwilling to give in. "It's only been four days. How could you possibly have missed me that much?"

I back up slightly, eager to get away from him.

"Spending a minute away from you is torture. I want your face to be the first thing I see in the morning and the last thing I see when I close my eyes at night." He continues to stalk toward me with passion in his eyes.

"You can't mean that," I whisper as I back closer to my car, needing to put some more space between us.

Finn's hand cups the side of my face, and I lean into it, relishing the feel of his calloused fingers as they caress my skin.

"I promised you I'd never lie to you, sugar. I meant every word," he murmurs.

"What if everything goes to shit?" I breathe.

"What if it doesn't?" he whispers into my ear, sending a shiver down my spine.

I push slightly on his chest, trying to get him to release me. But he pulls me closer, brushing his lips against mine. Unable to control the feelings swirling in my body, I lean forward, pressing my lips softly against his. Both of us moan as he pushes me backward, pressing my body into the hood of my SUV, and devours my mouth. He dominates our kiss, nipping and sucking my lip between his before thrusting his tongue into my mouth.

I wrap my arms around his neck and pull him closer to me. Nothing but pure, unadulterated desire courses through my veins. Without warning, he grips my ass, pulling my pants tightly against my swollen nub as he lifts me off my feet and sits me on the hood, pressing his swollen cock against the seam of my pants.

"Do you feel that? How much I want you? Need you?" he growls.

I wrap my legs around his waist, and he thrusts his cock into me, sending shockwaves of pleasure through my entire body as the seam of his jeans grinds into my drenched center.

"More, more, more," I chant as I use my arms to glide my pussy up and down his shaft.

Suddenly, the door to the bar swings open, and we both freeze.

"Get a room!" someone shouts as they pass by.

I bury my head in his chest, and his smell envelops me. He smells like the air after a spring rain, exactly the way I remember. A fresh, clean smell that has forever been associated with him.

"I better get you inside. I don't want to give the whole town a show," Finn says, giving me a small peck on the lips and lowering me back to the ground.

"I'm sorry." I hang my head in shame as I step to the side. "I don't know what came over me."

Distance. Distance is what I need right now. And a chance to clear my head. If I'm not careful, I could lose myself in him, forgetting about everything besides Finn.

Maybe he's what you've always wanted.

No. I shake that thought out of my head. I've never

believed in fate or any of that nonsense, but maybe Mr. Buckley's stroke happened for a reason. Maybe fate was at work, ensuring that Finn and I would find our way to each other. Is that even possible?

"I wouldn't mind something coming over you again, but first, let's go inside so I can grab everything we need." Finn runs the tips of his fingers down my arm before grasping my hand, bringing me back to the present.

Shocked by the intimacy of the moment, I pull my hand free from his grasp.

"This isn't a good idea," I say once again, trying to ensure my heart stays intact when things go south between the two of us. I step around him and head for the door.

He reaches out and grasps my hand. "I just want to spend time with you. We can worry about everything else later."

The vulnerability in his voice is enough to bring another piece of the walls around my heart tumbling down. I barely survived when Campbell left me all those years ago, but one thing I'm sure of, I won't survive Finn leaving me.

I sigh as I take his hand, not wanting to resist any longer. "Okay."

twenty-one

finn

It takes about ten minutes for me to gather everything I need for our date. Shelly worked a miracle and created the perfect picnic dinner, complete with her famous chocolate cake. I thought Marissa was going to kiss Shelly when she presented her with a cake of her own, making her promise not to share even one piece with me.

"Where are you taking me?" Marissa asks, her head swiveling back and forth, trying to figure out where we're going.

"I told you it was a surprise."

"And I told you I hate surprises," she grumbles, crossing her arms and bringing all my attention back to her nipples poking through the fabric of her shirt. Looks like our little rendezvous in the parking lot affected her just as much as me. I can't say I regret kissing her. In fact, the only thing I regret is that we got interrupted.

The moment Marissa stepped out of her SUV, I knew that keeping my hands off her would be almost impossible. A painted-on pair of jeans and an oversized shirt. The skin of her right shoulder calls to me as the tips of her hair brush against it, taunting me, begging me to thread my fingers through it and pull her head back, taking her mouth once again and claiming it as my own.

"I thought you were taking me to dinner," Marissa questions, with confusion written on her face.

"No. I said we would go on a date. You assumed it would be something boring, like dinner." I smirk as I turn left onto my street. "We're going to my favorite place."

"Your parents' house?"

I chuckle darkly. "You aren't wrong. I love my parents' house, but this is a special place for me."

The old farmhouse sits on the edge of town, tucked back away from the main road, making it the perfect place to have some alone time with my girl. It sits on 6.5 acres of land with fruit trees, grapes, and a barn. Based on the pictures of the inside, I can tell there's a root cellar that could easily be turned into a wine cellar instead and a huge gourmet kitchen with a gas range and coffee bar.

"I'm going to own this place someday," Marissa whispers in awe as I pull down the driveway, coming to a stop right in front of the house. "I've been dreaming about buying and raising a family in that house since I was in my teens. I'd planned on owning it by now, and maybe also having a few kids, but ...Well, you know what happened."

"It seems we have more in common than I thought."

"What do you mean?"

"I also have always wanted to live in this house once I graduated from college. I had it all planned out. I would work with my father and save every penny I earned in order to put a down payment on it. I know my parents never took me seriously, but it was fun planning for the future. Imagining what my future family would look like."

"Are you like me and it looks nothing like you had planned?"

"I always imagined living in this house with you." She gasps in surprise as I reach over and squeeze her hand before opening my door, stepping out, and jogging around to open hers.

"Milady." I bow, making a sweeping motion toward the front of the house.

The two-story plantation-style porch wraps around the entire house. Oversized windows cover most of the front side of the house, each framed with black farmhouse shutters and an array of bright-colored flowers below them, welcoming visitors.

Her mouth drops in shock as the trees around the house light all at once as the sun drops behind the horizon. "I remember how we used to sit outside in the backyard of your parents' house when we were younger and count the stars. I figured what better way to make tonight special than to make my favorite house light up like stars while I have a picnic with my favorite girl."

"What are you talking about?" Marissa says in wonder as she looks around the front yard of her dreams.

"I may not have known this was the house you wanted to raise a family in, but I remember almost everything you ever said to me, sugar." I step closer, drawn to her like a moth to a flame. "But I can't take credit for everything. I had a little help."

"Shelly?"

I nod my head. "Nolan helped, too. I owe them both big time for the work they put in, helping me get ready for tonight." I bury my nose in her hair, and the smell of strawberries overloads my senses. "I just wanted to do something special for you. Something that you'd remember and share with our children when they're older."

"Don't you think you're getting a little ahead of yourself?"

"Maybe, but you and I are a done deal." I wink before threading my fingers through hers and pulling her back toward the truck. "Now, let's grab the blanket and picnic basket from the back and dig in. Shelly worked all afternoon to make us this feast."

She gives me a bright smile before reaching into the bed of the truck and grabbing the blanket. "Is there an extra piece of cake in there?"

"You have an entire one back at the bar."

"But that one's mine, and she said I didn't have to share. Also, that's at the bar and not here."

"True. That's why there's a piece in the basket. For each of us."

"I can't wait to see what else she packed for us," she

says in excitement, bouncing back and forth on the balls of her feet.

"Whatever you say, sugar." I chuckle softly, pulling the basket out of the bed of the truck and heading towards a flat spot under the twinkle lights.

Marissa doesn't waste any time laying out the blanket on the ground and digging into the basket of food Shelly made for us. Instead of acting on my desire to have her pinned beneath me, I focus on getting to know more about her.

In between mouthfuls, Marissa asks me every question she can think of to avoid having to talk about whatever this is between us. She tells me her favorite color is phlox, which I wasn't aware was an actual color. It's a specific color purple that can only be found in flowers. The color is named after the pink and purple in some of those flowers. She's always seen herself as a mother, wanting four children, preferably two of each, so they have built-in playmates.

The more we talk and spend time together, the more she lets her guard down, letting me see the real her she's kept hidden from the world. I don't know if she notices or not, but I won't take this gift for granted.

My eyes lock on her lips as she brings a wine glass to them and takes a healthy sip before licking her lips clean. My cock hardens as images of her lips wrapped around it as I pump my hips, thrusting deeper down her throat, swirl through my mind.

I watch as she takes another sip, and the muscles in

her neck tighten as she swallows the liquid down her throat, wishing it was my cum dripping down it as I blow my load and she takes it all, not wanting to waste a drop.

I know it might be too soon, but right here, with the lights twinkling in the trees around my future home, I realize that I'm completely head over heels in love with Marissa Flores.

The need to touch her suddenly overwhelms me, and I pull her into my lap, wrapping my arms around her. She fidgets, trying to escape my grasp, but I pull her tighter to my chest. After a few moments, she relaxes into my embrace. We sit there in complete silence for a few moments, her hand grasped tightly in my shirt as I rock her back and forth.

"Thank you," she whispers, pulling back slightly and tilting her chin up to look me in the eye.

"For what?"

"For making me feel special. For fighting for whatever this is between us. For...well, everything."

I sigh as I tuck a piece of hair behind her ear. "Silly girl, when are you going to realize that I'd do anything for you?" I whisper before kissing her gently.

My heart races—no, gallops—in my chest as emotions swirl through my mind. Yearning to feel the softness of her skin against my calloused fingers as I make her mine, ruining her for any other man who dares to lay his hands on her.

"Are you ready to stop running from me?" I groan as

she pushes gently on my chest, and I fall back onto the blanket.

She swings her legs over mine before lowering herself, straddling my lap.

The fear finally takes hold of my heart, making it feel as if I'm unable to breathe. I know in my heart that Marissa is meant to be mine, but will that love be enough to heal the damage done to her heart? To soothe the darkness in her soul that at times seems too much to bear?

I swipe my thumb across her cheek, her skin feeling like silk beneath my calloused fingers. I stare into her eyes, committing this moment to memory. "Tell me you can feel it, the connection between us."

"Yes," she whispers as she grips the tiny black hairs at the base of my neck, pulling me closer to her. Our lips brush gently against each other, and I groan.

I rest my head against hers, closing my eyes tightly as I fight for control. My mind and body are at war with each other as the magnitude of her words sinks in. A possessiveness unlike any other rages through my mind as the desire to claim her, mark her as my own, becomes almost overwhelming.

"I want to make you scream," I whisper, nibbling my way down her neck.

She groans softly, threading her fingers through my hair and arching her back.

"Tell me what you want, sugar."

"You to love me."

"Sugar, that's the easy part." Unable to resist her

allure any longer, I lean forward and capture her lips with mine before leaning back slightly. "Marissa, I love you. I have loved you since we were teenagers. You belonged to someone else then, and I was content to spend the rest of my life alone, loving you from a distance, but I need you to understand, sugar. You're it for me."

twenty-two

We stare at each other for a moment, my mind and my heart battling for what to do next. The words are on the tip of my tongue, but they won't come out. They can't.

Before I can decide what my next move will be, his lips are on mine. My arms wrap around his neck, pulling him closer to me. His body presses against mine, and the muscular ridges of his chest cause my nipples to become impossibly hard as they rub against him. All logical thought is abandoned as my body takes control.

Finn's fingertips dig into my skin, holding me against him like he's afraid I'll push him away. He doesn't know that I can't. Not this time. I'm no longer able to resist the pull we have had toward each other since the day he sat down next to me at that bar in Chattanooga.

A part of me is already head over heels in love with Finn Buckley. Or at least, I think I am. I thought I was in love with Campbell in high school, but the way I feel about Finn right now, in this moment, is beyond anything I could imagine. But what does any of that mean? My home is here in Magnolia. I have a life here, a family, and Finn is only here temporarily. How can I ask him to give up everything to be with me, to move back to his hometown and run his father's bar? Sure, that was enough for him at eighteen, but now he's seen the world and experienced life. Will that be enough for him? Will I be enough for him?

"Stop thinking so much," Finn whispers as he takes my ear into his mouth, biting down gently. "Just feel, Marissa."

Electricity pulses in my veins, turning into a burning need as one of his hands slips beneath my shirt. His calloused fingers brush against my nipples as he wraps his hand around my breast and squeezes. The heat of his palm against my skin brings a moan from my mouth.

"Sugar, I need you." The rough grumble of his voice caresses my skin, making goose bumps pebble on my flesh. "Let me love you," he whispers against my lips before pressing them against mine more forcefully.

"Finn," I moan, clinging to my last thread of control. My eyes lock with his as he trembles. The need he has for me is so damn clear in his face.

Finn pulls his hand from under my shirt and quickly spins me around in his lap, nipping my exposed shoulder with his teeth. I throw my head back, resting it on his shoulder, as his hand snakes up my body and grips my breast hard through my shirt again. I can barely control my breathing as he releases my breast, and his hand slides down my body, popping the button on the top of my jeans.

"Please," I beg as his finger brushes against the hairs covering my clit. I rock back, pressing the globes of my ass into his cock as he glides it between my cheeks.

He hisses loudly as he pinches my clit between his thick fingers, his beard tickling the exposed skin of my shoulder.

"Tell me what you want," he demands.

"You. Just you."

I moan loudly as he inserts one finger inside me, gently pulling it out before slowly sliding it back in. My eyes roll into the back of my head as I teeter on the edge of an explosive orgasm, embarrassingly fast. I whimper softly as heat crawls up my neck.

I can feel our hearts pounding in unison as if they have finally found each other again after all these years.

My chest rises and falls quickly as his other hand grips my breast through my shirt, manipulating my body like his own personal plaything. He leans forward, and my fingers dig into the blanket, anchoring myself as he presses his body flush against mine. The heel of his palm grinds down hard on my clit, causing my legs to tremble. My hips ride his hand like it's an Olympic sport, both desperate to come and aching for him to be inside me.

"That's it. Take what's yours." His breath fans against my ear before the sharp sting of his teeth on my neck pushes me over the edge into oblivion.

White, blinding euphoria explodes behind my eyes,

and a strangled cry echoes through the trees, letting everyone know what just happened between us.

"*Fuuuck*." Finn drags out the word, slipping his hand out of my pants.

My body collapses, only being held up by my arms, and my knees weaken in the aftermath of my world exploding.

"Hmmm," Finn hums behind me. "You're fucking delicious."

Gripping my hair, he turns my head and takes my mouth in an aggressive kiss, the salty tang I now taste informing me he sucked my cum off his fingers. As I turn in his arms, his hands grip my ass to pull me up against him. I wrap my legs around him and kiss him back, just as possessively. I use his grip on my ass to grind against the rigid outline of his cock and growl into his mouth.

Finn smacks my ass hard, his lips leaving mine to lean our foreheads together. "This will be fast, but I'll make up for it."

I suck on my lower lip and drop my feet to the ground as Finn spins me around, quickly shoving my face into the plush blanket. My hand flails, searching for something to hold on to. I need something to keep me grounded.

Air caresses my skin as he yanks my jeans down to my knees, kneeing my legs apart slightly. He drops to a squat behind me, his lips trailing kisses over my exposed ass.

"I never thought a thong could be sexy, but on you, it fucking is." He slides the small scrap of fabric to the side, exposing my pussy, and a warm lick has my breath catching in my throat. "Fucking perfect."

The rustle of his jeans being opened gives me a mere few seconds to prepare before the thick head of his dick is pushing against me.

"Oh, shit," I whine as he stretches me.

Finn keeps moving forward until his hips rest against my ass. His fingers grip my hips, digging into my skin, surely leaving bruises, holding still for only a few moments before pulling out slowly and slamming back inside me.

His hips snap against me, pounding into me like a rutting animal. This is a claiming, a desperation, a break in sanity, and I love it. I need him just as much as he needs me.

"You're so fucking perfect," he grinds out, his thrusts becoming more erratic, losing the smooth glide he had.

My mind can no longer process words, only actions. I'm overstimulated, yet not stimulated enough. The arousal racing through my body is climbing towards an impossible end. Higher and higher, clenching so hard around the intrusion that's controlling every aspect of my life in this moment.

"Fuck!" Finn roars, slamming into me only twice more before stilling, his seed spilling deep inside of me.

He's panting, his muscles twitching from the strain as he slows his pace, pumping in and out of me to draw out my orgasm. Tiny aftershocks course through my body as he rolls to the side and slides out of me with a groan. I lay my head gently on his chest as he pulls the covers up and over us. My lungs can't pull in enough air. I can barely hear anything over the sound of my heart pounding in my ears, but I am acutely aware of him. I hiss when he pulls back, his softening cock dragging against my sensitive flesh. He pulls my panties back over my pussy and tugs my jeans back up my legs, kissing my skin as he does.

"I've been waiting my entire life for you," he whispers into the darkness, letting me know exactly how much I mean to him. "I'm never letting you go." Finn plants a kiss on my forehead before dropping his head back onto the blanket and shutting his eyes.

There are a million things I should say that he needs to know, but I can't. Fuck. Fuck. I should never have allowed this to happen, to let him this close to my heart. He's leaving. He's going to leave me here again with a broken heart, just like Campbell did.

Right now, at the moment, I can see it all. See what life could be like if he stayed here with me. I know what he's said. He's shown me how much he cares for me, cherishes me, and loves me, but how do I know he won't just leave me?

My whole body shakes uncontrollably in his arms. "Sugar, are you okay?"

I scramble out of his arms, wanting to get away from him. From the pain running through my body at the mere idea of him no longer being a part of my life.

"I can't do this. I can't. Hurts. It hurts too much." I

gasp for air, trying to make sense of everything going on around me.

Finn reaches for me, but I flinch away from him. My head shakes back and forth as I drop my chin to my chest, not wanting to see the look of hurt in his eyes that I know is there. What more do I want from him? How else can he prove to me he loves me, that I'm enough for him?

"Marissa?" His voice is a rasp, disbelief filling it. Along with something else... Fuck. Hurting Finn is the last thing I wanted to happen, but I'm going to go with it. Pushing him away is what is best for me, for him. Then why does it feel as if my soul is fracturing? Something deep inside me is crying out in agony at the thought of losing him forever.

"Oh, God, what am I doing?" I press the palms of my hands to my eyes, welcoming the pain, needing it to tether me to the here and now.

"Sugar, talk to me. Tell me what's going on."

I shake my head back and forth as another sob bubbles up from my throat. Each breath feels like pure agony as shivers rack my entire body. "Make it stop. Please, make it stop."

"I'm here, sugar. Shh... let it all out," Finn whispers as he gathers me in his arms, lifting me in the air. We're moving. I don't know where we are going, but the pain is dissipating. Seeping away as if Finn is pulling it from my body.

My mind is screaming at me to push him away. Tell him I'm fine and to take me home. That I can never see him again, but my heart continues to scream in agony as I grip his shirt in my hand, burying my face in his neck as I breathe him in. His arms tighten around me as I hear the clicking sound of something opening.

His arms tighten around me as he pulls me into his lap. "Breathe with me, sugar."

I follow his instructions and try to draw breaths into my tight lungs. Slowly, it becomes easier to breathe. The tightness in my chest dissipates, but my heart still cries out in agony at what could happen next. He knows. He now knows how broken and damaged I am. This is why I don't do relationships. Why I'm unable to give him that last piece of me he so desperately wants. *Don't leave me. Please, don't leave me.*

"I'm not going anywhere." His chest rumbles as I freeze, completely unaware that I was saying anything aloud. But it doesn't matter. Because no matter how much I need him right now, I don't know if can have him.

"Promise," I whisper, and my eyes drift shut as the weight of the last few hours come crashing down on me.

I feel Finn's lips brush against my forehead before he whispers in my ear. "I promise, sugar."

As I drift off, I hope that when I wake up in the morning, everything will be as it should be and that I didn't set myself up for heartbreak once again.

The sound of birds chirping in the morning sun awakens me, and I bolt straight up in the bed, the remnants of my nightmare still circling in my mind. The soft light from the sunrise fills the sky as I look around, noticing that I'm lying in the bed of Finn's truck. It's then that I realize it wasn't a nightmare. That Finn gave me the perfect night, baring his soul to me, and I lost it.

I turn my head to the right, noticing Finn lying peacefully beside me. The blanket he brought for our picnic is draped over both of our legs, and the sunlight shines down on his tan skin, giving it a warm glow. Unable to resist, I run the tips of my fingers down the planes of his chest, taking my time to trace each of his ab muscles as they flex beneath my fingers.

Finn groans softly, and I pull my hand back.

Way to molest the man in his sleep, I chastise myself before lying down and snuggling into his side, my back to his front, pulling the blanket over both of us, wanting to enjoy the last few moments of happiness. Finn throws his muscular arm over my waist, pulling me tighter into his chest. My core tightens as his cock hardens between my ass cheeks.

"What time is it?" I mumble, slowly beginning to drift off a second time.

"The sun is up, so probably around six." He nuzzles into my neck before planting a kiss just below my ear.

I bolt up straight a second time, but not from a nightmare. "Fuck!" I grab the blanket and pull it off him before sliding toward the edge of the truck bed. "I have to go."

"What's the hurry, sugar?" he grumbles, reaching for me a second time, but I smack his hand.

"I'm going to be late for work!" Finn's eyes widen in horror as he moves. We both hop out of the bed of the truck and scramble toward the front. Thankfully, Finn cleaned up our picnic while I was passed out last night, and we could leave right away. We drive back to town in silence, both of us lost in thought. I'd love to believe that he won't remember what happened last night, but that'd be wishful thinking. I know at some point we'll have to talk about what happened, and I'll have to explain to him why I reacted that way, but not now. Now I need to get my SUV and head home to shower. Colt is going to be so pissed I'm late. Maybe I can go to my parents' house. My mom always has muffins, and those will be the perfect thing to placate Colt with.

"Of course, I'm late on the day the new recruit I'm training is coming in."

"I doubt Colt will mind. You've been working your ass off to get ready." I jump slightly at the sound of his voice, having been lost in thought the entire ride back to Tallywackers.

Finn pulls into a spot near my SUV and climbs out, rushing over to my side to open the door. "Thanks for the ride," I mumble, keeping my head down as I try to slide past him, but it's no use.

Finn grips my chin, forcing me to look at him. "Don't think I forgot what happened last night, Marissa. I meant everything I said to you. I'm not going anywhere."

"You say that now..." My voice cracks slightly, my sense of self-preservation telling me I need to end this.

That I need to hurt him before he hurts me, though I know deep down it's already too late. "We want different things."

"That's bullshit and you know it, Marissa. I think you're scared. Scared of the feelings we have for each other, but instead of letting me help you work through them, you're shutting me out."

Searing pain flows through my entire body as waves of agony pull me under. I'm just praying that I can hold on for just a little longer until the pain subsides. I yearn for numbness to cut me off from all these feelings that I'm so desperate to forget.

"I care about you, Finn. But—" I begin before he cuts me off. I wrap my arms around my waist, attempting to hold myself together.

"Don't you dare fucking finish that sentence, Marissa."

My head snaps up, locking eyes with his, and I see the soul-crushing hurt in his eyes and have no doubt that I'm the one that put it there. The weight of what's happening threatens to crush my soul.

I feel his strong arms wrap around me. "Everything will be okay." He buries his nose in my hair, but instead of calming me, it ignites a rage inside me.

"Things will never be okay again!" I scream, pushing out of his embrace. "This is all your fault." I pound my fists into his chest repeatedly. "You made me love you. You made me want things that I never would've dreamed of having before I met you. I was content with being alone, with letting some of my dreams for the future fade away into the darkness."

My hands fall to the side, dropping my head to his chest.

"And now it's all over."

"It doesn't have to be over, sugar." He pulls me forward, wrapping his arms around me again. "I love you."

He plants a kiss on each of my eyelids, the tip of my nose, and my cheeks.

"I've loved you since the moment I laid eyes on you."

A gut-wrenching sob escapes me as I bury my face in his neck. Snot and tears collect on his skin as I try to regain control of my emotions.

"Let me love you," he chokes out, brushing his lips against mine a few times before pressing them to mine.

I moan softly, nibbling on his bottom lip, and he immediately opens to me, his tongue sweeping through my mouth. I tug on the short hairs at the base of his neck, pulling him tightly to my body. I want to get as close to him as possible. To crawl into his skin and brand my name on his soul for all eternity.

"But you're leaving, Finn. You don't belong here, stuck in Magnolia with the rest of us."

twenty-three

finn

I thread my fingers through Marissa's hair, tugging her head back and exposing her neck to me.

"I'm never letting you go." I nibble down one side of her neck before making my way back up the other side. "You can't leave me."

Tears spring to my eyes as I bury my nose in her neck, clinging to her body like it's an anchor holding both of us together.

"I have to go," she croaks, trying to wiggle out of my grasp, but I tighten my hold.

Bitterness courses through my veins that fate could be so cruel. That it'd allow this angel to light up my entire world before ripping her away from me and plunging me back into darkness.

"No, you don't." I lean back, cupping her cheeks in my palms. "I'll follow you to the ends of the Earth, Marissa." I kiss the tip of her nose. "No one is going to keep us apart."

"But you have your life in Texas. My life is here in Magnolia. I love this town and the people in it. Sure, I went away to college, but the plan was always to come back here and put down roots. Magnolia has always and will always be my home." She nuzzles her cheek against my palm, clenching her eyes shut. "I won't ask you to give up everything you've accomplished for me."

"You're everything to me, Marissa. None of that means anything to me if you aren't here to share it with me."

Marissa covers her mouth with both hands, her head swinging back and forth as she tries to process everything I've just dropped into her lap. Everything else fades into the background as she backs away from me, slamming her back into the door of her SUV before sliding to the ground. My eyes lock on her as I search her face for any answer. Any sign that she loves me even a fraction of how much I love her.

But the only thing I see is fear.

"Okay." I take a step back from her, my arms dropping to the side. "I'm going to head inside."

"It's for the best," she sobs, her entire body trembling.

I back away toward the door. I want to push her harder, to make her understand what she means to me, but I can't sit here and watch her crumble in on herself, knowing it's my fault. She needs space to process everything that I've said to her and decide if being with me is enough. I need Marissa to understand that I'd do anything for her, give her everything that I am, and all she has to do is give me her heart in return.

I chuckle humorlessly as I continue backing away from her. "I love you more than life, but you need to decide if that's enough."

She reaches toward me, tears streaming down her face. I want nothing more than to run to her, scoop her into my arms, and promise never to make her feel this type of pain again, but I can't. I need to know that she's in this with me, that this all-consuming love I feel for her is bigger than family, than our jobs, than anything.

I stride toward her, unable to resist the pull I feel in case this is the last time I set eyes on her. "I'll love you always."

I plant a kiss on the top of her head before turning on my heels and striding toward the entrance of the bar. I don't stop as I fling the front door to my place open and stride through it.

I don't know where I can go to escape the pain that radiates through my body. I should've stayed, explained to her that I had already started the process of selling everything I own in Texas, that the only thing in life I need is her, and helped her decide. It would've been the easier choice, but if I did that, in the back of my mind, I'd always wonder if she really chose me or if I'd talked her into it.

I know from the few conversations we've had about her parents that family means the world to her, and the thought of disappointing them weighs heavily on the choices she's made in life.

She went to a state university instead of going across

the country like everyone else our age. It was probably to lessen the financial load on her parents. I always believed she joined the sheriff's department because of her dad, wanting him to be proud of her for following in the family legacy, but I was completely wrong.

Marissa is still in Magnolia because she loves it here, because Magnolia is part of who she is as a person, and she can't imagine starting a family and growing old anywhere else. She wants to be in Magnolia because this place is where she's happiest, but what she doesn't understand is that she is the reason for my happiness.

I'm not blowing smoke up her ass when I say I just need her to be happy. I want her to choose to marry me because she wants to. Marissa agreeing to be my wife *would* make me happy beyond my wildest dreams, but she has to want that happiness with me, as well.

Maybe I was delusional to believe that Marissa was over her relationship with Campbell. He's back in town and in the process of getting divorced. Maybe this is her way of letting me down easily instead of telling me the truth, that she really wants to have another shot at the life she planned for herself.

I take a seat at the bar, not bothering to turn on a light, just taking time to think about what my life could be like without Marissa in it. It's only been a few minutes, but it feels like an eternity. Everything feels flat and lifeless now that things with the two of us are so up in the air. As far as I'm concerned, this isn't the end between the two of us, but how things proceed is up to Marissa.

I've been telling her repeatedly that I'd do anything to be with her, and I mean it. I've already resigned my position with NASA, started planning on getting all my stuff shipped here, and have been checking into real estate here in Magnolia. But I didn't tell her any of this. I didn't want to frighten her way, but maybe that wasn't the right thing to do.

She kept repeating that I was leaving, that I wouldn't be satisfied with living in Magnolia for the rest of my life, but how could she doubt me? I've told her repeatedly how I felt about her, that I would do anything if it meant I could call her mine, and that wasn't enough.

"Looks like things didn't go very well since you're here so early in the morning." Nolan chuckles as he flicks on the lights.

I hiss, slamming my eyes shut while I wait for them to adjust. I can hear him walk past me, dropping his keys onto the top of the bar before grabbing a glass and slamming it on the counter.

"Coffee?" he questions.

I chuckle darkly, slowly opening my eyes. "I need something stronger than coffee at the moment."

He gives me a sympathetic smile. "I have just the thing."

He reaches under the bar, pulling out a bottle of our best single malt whiskey and two glasses.

"You hate whiskey." I reach my hand toward him, gripping one glass in my hand and waiting for him to pour me a healthy amount.

Without hesitation, I throw the glass back, drinking down all its contents before holding my glass out for another.

"I think I can make an exception this time." Nolan pours me another glass before filling his and placing the bottle on the table beside me. "What happened?"

He places a hand on my shoulder, giving it a small squeeze before striding toward the chair across from me and taking a seat.

"I told her I loved her. That I wanted to spend the rest of my life with her." My voice scratches against my throat from all the emotions clogging it.

"What did she say?"

I shake my head, unable to form the words. My heart feels like it's been ripped out of my chest, and it's only been a short amount of time. I won't survive if Marissa pulls away from me again, or worse. Images of her and Campbell laughing happily fill my mind, but I banish them immediately.

"She didn't say anything." I take a large gulp from my glass, welcoming the burn as it slides down my throat and warms me from the inside out. "She had a panic attack and then told me to kick rocks."

"Did she really say that, or are you being dramatic?"

"I'm not being dramatic, but she never said those specific words either."

"Well, that's a good sign, but what made you think that?"

"The fact that she had a panic attack at the mention

of being with me. I've told her in a million different ways that I care about her, that I'm willing to take things as slow as she needs. The only thing I asked for in return was her heart."

"She didn't say *anything* to you? Give you a reason for why she suddenly didn't want to see you anymore?"

His questions made me pause, thinking back to exactly what Marissa said when she shattered my heart into a million pieces.

"You never thought about that, did you? You were so focused on your pain that you didn't listen to what she was saying, you ass." Nolan takes a sip from his glass, his eyes locked with mine as shame fills me.

"I heard exactly what she said. She said that she cared about me." I finish my second glass and pour another one, hoping to dull the pain, if only for a little while. "That my life would be better without her in it. She's just scared of getting hurt again, but I've told her a million times that I would never do that to her."

"But actions speak louder than words."

I slam my glass down on the bar top, the amber liquid splashing on my hands. "I wish I could make it all go away. Her pain. Her fear. I'd give her anything she asked of me in a heartbeat. But she doesn't or is too afraid to trust me."

"But have you honestly given her a reason to trust you?" Nolan takes another sip from her glass as I lean forward, barely missing his chin with my fist. "Calm down, man. I know you. I know your feelings for Marissa are the real deal, but does she? You've been back in her life for a few months. She had her heart very publicly broken, and I have a feeling that she never truly healed from that."

"Tell me something I don't know, asshole," I growl, throwing back the last of the whiskey in the glass and pouring another one.

"But what proof does she have that you aren't full of shit?" Nolan takes another step away from me as I lunge forward. "The next time you swing at me, I'm going to hit back. Now sit the fuck down and listen."

"Remind me again why I haven't fired you yet?" I growl, plopping back down on the stool.

He completely ignores my question and continues. "Marissa knows nothing about the man you are today. She knows the boy who left town the moment he could, just like her sister and just like the man she planned to marry."

"But that's not why I left."

"You and I both know that, but does she? She only knows what you tell her, but she's learned not to place all her trust in someone's words."

I pause, listening to what he's saying for the first time since he came into the bar. Marissa and Sutton were thick as thieves. I'd even go as far as to say they were more like best friends than sisters until Sutton left for college. From what Marissa has told me, she's hardly talked to her sister since she left town. Sutton never even came home for a visit before breaking things off with the cheater and getting engaged to Colt.

Campbell is a slightly different story. Not only did he break her heart and every promise that he made to her while they were together, but he almost immediately married another woman and moved away. Giving someone else the life she always imagined she'd have with him.

"Fuck," I huff, my shoulder sagging.

"You get it now, don't you?" he questions, grabbing the bottle and my empty glass. "Actions speak louder than words."

"I'm an idiot. She thinks I'm going to leave, so she doesn't want to give me her heart. Not because she's afraid that I'll break it, but that I'll toss her to the side like everyone else in her life has, besides her parents."

"Now you're using your brain." Nolan slaps me on the shoulder, placing a glass of water on the bar in front of me. "She needs to see that you mean everything you say. Show her you're serious about starting a relationship with her."

"Keeping all my plans for the future was a mistake." I drop my head into my hands, and regret and sorrow wash over me. "What the fuck do I do now?"

"Show her."

It's like a light bulb goes on in my head as the perfect plan forms in my mind. I check my watch, noticing that it is only slightly after eight a.m.—too early to get too much done, but I can get started.

"I have to go." I jump off the barstool, stumbling slightly.

"No, you need to chill the hell out for a minute. You just drank your weight in whiskey."

"But I need to go back to Texas, call the realtor, and—"

"You need to go upstairs, take a shower, and drink some more water," Nolan interrupts me, coming around the bar and wrapping my arm over his shoulder.

"But I can't waste any more time! I need to make sure Marissa doesn't slink back into her shell."

"She won't go back into her shell in the next few days. All she needs is a little push in the right direction." Nolan grunts as he practically drags me toward the stairs leading to the spare apartment. "I'll call your mom while you pack and shower. I'm sure she'll have no problem getting you a ticket on the next flight to Texas and calling the realtor to ask her to meet you at your place to sign the contracts."

"I need to speak to someone about buying the Meyers Farmhouse on the edge of town, too."

I know I'm being selfish, but if I really love Marissa as much as I say, I need to show her. I need to make sure she understands that she is it for me, using both my words and actions. I don't expect her to fall into my arms and agree to spend the rest of her life with me, but I need her to understand that is where my mind is headed. All she needs to do is spread her wings, take a leap of faith, and trust that I'll be right there to catch her if she falls.

"The man must know what he wants." Nolan chuckles as I shake my head, pushing away from him and wobbling slightly. All the whiskey I drank has gone straight to my head.

"Go grab a shower. Shelly will be here in a few hours. I'm sure she'll have no problem taking you to the airport."

I chuckle before wrapping my arm around his shoulder and pulling him to my side. "Thank you."

"You can thank me with a raise."

twenty-four
marissa

I don't know how I make it into my SUV and all the way back to my apartment without getting into an accident. My emotions keep fluctuating between soul-crushing sobs and numbness. I keep waiting for Finn to reappear, but he doesn't. What started out as an amazing morning with the promise of a happy ending has come crashing to the ground. Finn left me standing there in front of the bar to pick up the pieces of my broken heart, and I deserved it.

I wanted to push him away before he could hurt me, and it worked, but now I'm an empty husk of the person I was before Finn came back into my life. I thought my feelings for Campbell were the epitome of love, but they're nothing compared to what I felt—no, feel—for Finn Buckley.

"I can't believe this happened." Tears pour down my face as I trudge up the stairs to my apartment, close the door tight behind me, and slide to the floor. "I just want the pain to stop." I bury my face in my hands and sob, trying to make sense of the last few hours of my life.

Everything was perfect. I was wrapped in Finn's arms, feeling safe. Loved. Protected. And in blissful ignorance of the pain I was about to cause the two of us. If I learned one thing from all of this, it's that denying my feelings for Finn would never have been possible. I was setting myself up for failure. If I really didn't want to feel this type of pain, I would've stayed as far away from him as possible, but my heart had found its other half.

"I should've known this would happen," I whisper, pushing off the floor and padding toward the bathroom.

I tried to be careful and protect my heart from Finn, but he broke down all my defenses, worming his way into my heart and becoming a part of me. A part that will remain broken until the day I die. He promised to give me everything I ever wanted, but I was too afraid to take that leap of faith. But I knew in my heart I couldn't let him give up everything he's worked for. He's worked too hard and been through too much to have to start all over again. Especially for someone like me.

I'm nothing special, I repeat in my mind as I turn on the water to the shower.

"If I don't get in the shower soon, I know Colt will be banging on my door, demanding a reason for why I'm so late," I mutter to myself as steam fills the small room.

The water warms up after a few minutes, and I climb in. I usually take my time in the shower, but after oversleeping and my emotional meltdown with Finn at Tallywackers this morning, I don't have that kind of time.

After taking care of my morning routine, I dress in a Magnolia County Sheriff's Department uniform and throw my hair up in a messy bun on the top of my head. I can feel another sob of pain bubbling up in my chest, threatening to escape from my mouth as I walk back into the kitchen, noticing a travel container with muffins sitting on the counter. I stride toward them, plucking a note off the top.

Take these to the station to welcome your new recruit. My muffins will make a great first impression

-Mom

I've never been so thankful for my mother's meddling. This is the prefect distraction for my lateness and will keep everyone focused on something other than my red, puffy eyes from crying.

Finn chose me over everyone else, and he wanted me to do the same, but I said nothing. I'm lost in my own battle between following my heart and listening to the voice in the back of my head telling me he's just like everyone else. I know in my heart that Finn would do anything to make me happy, but is he willing to give up everything he's worked for to move back here with me? Am I selfish enough to ask him to do that?

I move on autopilot, grabbing the tray of muffins off the table, along with my keys, and head down to my SUV.

Somehow, I point my SUV toward the station a few blocks away from my place. It only takes a few minutes before I'm pulling into the parking lot, noticing Campbell's old pickup truck parked in the visitors' spot.

I'd know that truck anywhere. We spent so many nights talking about our future in the truck bed, dreaming about what life would be like when we finally graduated from high school. For some reason, he didn't take it with him when he left, but his dad kept it under a tarp in their driveway, taking it for routine maintenance and driving it around every once in a while just to keep it in tip-top shape.

"Shit," I drop my forehead to my steering wheel and try to breathe through the swirls of anger and pain coursing through my body. "There's no way this can be happening to me. Maybe he's just here to file a police report."

I list a million different reasons in my mind for his truck being parked in front of the station, but deep down, I know why he's here. I remember his mom saying that Campbell had been working as a police officer since graduation. His irregular schedule must have been one of the main reasons he needed to come back to Magnolia. It makes perfect sense that he'd want to get a job here, but man, do I really hope I'm wrong.

I was aware the recruit was showing up at the station this morning, but no one mentioned to me it was going to be Campbell. Colt knows better than anyone how devastated I was when Campbell and Emmeline got married. Would Colt just spring this on me with no warning?

"I don't fucking need this today," I grumble as I climb out, leaving everything inside my SUV and storming toward the door.

I would love nothing more than to run into the station and give Campbell a piece of my mind. To let loose the rage bubbling to the surface, blaming him for everything that has happened between Finn and me, but I know deep down it's not his fault. He broke my heart into a million pieces, but the fear I feel is all my own.

"Before you get your ass on your shoulders, I wanted to tell you he'd be here." Dolores holds her hands up in surrender as I come storming toward her.

My mom's prodding about my looks last week makes even more sense. She always wants me to look my best, but she must have known I was going to run into Campbell at the station at some point.

"Let me guess, my mother advised against it," I grumble under my breath as Colt comes strolling out of his office, the picture of ease.

"Do we have a problem? Besides you being late, that is," Colt questions, his eyebrows pulling down in concern.

"Sorry I'm late," I huff. "But you should've warned me."

"Would it have made a difference?"

Would it? Honestly, I don't know. A million different feelings are flowing through my mind at this moment, the strongest being betrayal. I would expect my mom to be scheming to push Campbell and me together, hoping the sparks would fly again, but not Colt. He knows better than anyone what it's like to see the person you love in the arms of someone else. I noticed the way he lost just a little more of his heart each time he asked me about Sutton. Torn between wanting to know how she was doing and what was going on in her life and the need to forget about her so he could heal the broken pieces of his heart. It worked out for him, in the end, since they're engaged now, but that just isn't in the cards for me. If there was one person I thought would understand, it was Colt, but I guess I was wrong.

"No. Not really, but why did you hire him anyway?"

"Because he's a damn good officer, and we need the help. I know nothing really happens around here, but we're burning the candle at both ends since Waylen's been on vacation."

I nod my head, swallowing down the lump of emotion in my throat. "You should have said something, given me time to process it." My head swivels back and forth, searching for Campbell.

"Time to process? Marissa, you'd have thrown a fit and then sworn you wouldn't train him or even quit."

"I never would've quit. I love this job," I respond, glimpsing Campbell's dark hair as he rounds the corner.

"Hello, Marissa." Campbell smiles brightly at me. "Long time no see."

My eyes snap toward him, realizing that he hasn't changed one bit since the last time we saw each other, besides the addition of some tattoos. The same broad shoulders fill out a T-shirt that looks as if it was painted onto his body, and he has muscular arms with a colorful sleeve of tattoos running down the right side. I would expect myself to feel something now that he's back in my life after all these years, but there's nothing. No heartache, anger, resentment, nothing. All the anger I felt toward him a few minutes ago practically evaporated into thin air. Well, maybe I'm still a little pissed off that no one gave me a heads-up he was going to be here, but that's not on him.

"Hello, Campbell." I reach my hand out toward him as a peace offering.

I don't have any romantic feelings toward Campbell and haven't for years, but his being back in town is going to be very awkward. My biggest concern is Finn. He must know Campbell is back in town, but does he know that he's going to be working here with me at the station? A million and one questions are floating through my mind, trying to make sense of the jumble of feelings about Finn, and now I have to add this shit with Campbell on top of it. Fuck, I really need a vacation.

I shove all my feelings into the deepest parts of my soul and lock them up tight. I can deal with them later. Right now, I need to do my job. Campbell and I will be working together, me being his boss. I need to find a way to maintain a good working relationship with him. And that isn't possible while I'm trying to sort through my feelings for Finn.

It's been years since he shattered my heart into a million pieces, but I'm completely over it, or at least that's what I'm going to tell myself. I may not have any romantic feelings for Campbell, but the hurt at being tossed aside for Emmeline comes rushing back to the surface. Reminding me yet again of why I can't continue my relationship, or whatever we are going to call it, with Finn. Now we can both go on with our lives—him in Texas and me here in Magnolia.

"Now, with that out of the way, I don't want any issues out of you two." Colt throws his arms around my shoulder, pulling me in for an awkward hug. "Marissa is the chief deputy here. She'll make sure you have everything you need and will answer your questions."

"If you just head into the locker room, there is a uniform and everything you'll need for today. Go and get changed. I'll meet you in the training room in a few minutes," I say, a forced smile on my face.

Campbell nods before heading directly for the locker room, probably as excited to have that awkward moment over as I am. I watch him carefully, waiting for the door to close shut behind him before turning my attention toward Colt.

"I'll only be here for half of the day," I say, deadpan, daring him to say something different.

The last thing I want to do is spend the day trying to

figure out how to hold a discussion with my ex-everything and how to get over Finn.

"There are a million different ways you two could've let me know about Campbell, but you never did. Besides, you promised me a vacation."

"You're scheduled for an overnight shift today," Dolores chimes in as I glare in her direction.

"Yeah, about that. I have an emergency I need to take care of, so I won't be able to stay my entire shift."

Colt and I stare at each other for a few moments before he sighs loudly. "Are you angry? I couldn't turn him away because he broke your heart."

"I'm not angry that you hired him, Colt. I'm angry because you two kept the information from me." Dolores opens her mouth to respond, but I hold my hand up to silence her. "You should have told me. Not my parents. Me."

"Sorry, Marissa. We just weren't sure how you'd react," Dolores responds softly. "It won't happen again."

"I know it won't because I don't have any other exes for Colt to hire."

"You're working my overnight shift tomorrow. No complaints. Then you can start your vacation," Colt responds before turning and heading toward his office.

"Of course." I giggle before turning on my heels and heading back to my car.

I open the door and grab everything, leaving the muffins, 'cause I'm petty like that, and head back inside.

"Your mom said she sent muffins." Dolores peers at

me over the receptionist's desk, no doubt searching for the container my mom promised.

"She did, but traitors don't get Momma's muffins."

"I said I was sorry," she mumbles, ducking her head in embarrassment as I rest my forearms on the ledge above her desk.

"Yeah, you're so sorry that you immediately called my mother when my back was turned talking to Colt and Campbell."

"I didn't," she responds but quickly changes her mind. "Okay, maybe I did, but she asked me to call her the moment you saw Campbell. She said she was worried about how you would react."

I bet she was.

"And what did you tell her?" I raise my eyebrow in question, ready to call my mother and do damage control if I need to. The last thing I want my mother to think is there's still a chance of us getting back together.

"I told her there was no way you were getting back together."

"Good answer." I smile before tossing my key on the desk in front of her. "There's a container on the front seat of my car, but make Colt sweat it out for a few hours before you let him have one."

"You've got a deal." She smiles before scurrying out the front door.

Now that I've seen Campbell and gotten our initial awkward interaction out of the way, things should quiet down. Sure, my mom is going to want a play-by-play of each moment of the day, but I'll do everything in my power to avoid it.

The door to the locker room opens and Campbell comes strolling out.

"Here goes nothing," I mumble, taking a deep breath and heading toward the training room to prepare everything for his first day.

twenty-five

finn

"I was worried I wouldn't be able to make this happen in time," I mumble as I look around my new home. The home I want to share with the woman I plan on spending the rest of my life with, if I haven't completely fucked things up, that is.

I've been running full throttle since my plane landed in Texas a little over a week ago. Between selling my condo, finding a shipping company to cart all my belongings to Magnolia, buying the Meyers Farmhouse, and getting the renovations started, I've barely had enough time to sleep. Since my condo was practically sold before I arrived, that was the easiest part of this whole endeavor, but I managed to get things wrapped up quickly and hopped on the first flight back to Tennessee last night, wanting to get back to my girl as soon as possible.

"Sometimes things work out exactly how we planned," my mom responds as she walks into the living room. "This place was a little worse for wear after being empty for so long, but with the help of Connor and

Vance, you spruced it up and made it look as good as new."

"Almost. There's still a lot to be done."

I scan the room, trying to imagine what it would be like to create a home for Marissa and me between these walls. She said that she's always dreamed of raising a family in this house, and I plan on helping her make that dream come true. But I wonder if that dream could now also include me.

"Stop thinking so hard, sweetheart, and show me the rest of the house," Mom says with excitement, grabbing my hand and pulling me into the kitchen.

Since this is a farmhouse, I went with a classic farmhouse-style kitchen with large upper and lower cabinets and walnut-stained butcher block countertops, and a large island in the center of the room for the family to gather around.

This is one of the few places I splurged. Although neither Marissa nor I are the best at cooking, I remember how growing up we would all spend most of our time hanging out in the kitchen, watching our mothers bake or make dinner during the holidays. I wanted to make this space something more than just a place for eating and cooking. I wanted a place for the family to gather. The heart of the home.

Warm light fills the room as Mom pulls me toward the renovated sunroom. I had the contractors turn it into an outdoor living space, complete with comfortable seating and a small dining area. It's the perfect place to entertain friends and family on a cool summer day or just to spend a lazy Sunday afternoon, snuggling with a good book.

"I thought you wanted a tour of the house? It seems you know exactly where you're going."

"Okay, you caught me." She smiles. "I wanted to be the first to test out the porch swing."

"By all means." I smile at my mother, pushing the door open as she steps outside.

"It was a little difficult to find the same wood to match the rest of the house, but we managed." Connor, one of my contractors, smiles as he comes up the steps under the small overhang. "There should be just enough space under here to fit a few more chairs and still be able to stay out of the elements, no matter what the weather is."

Connor Bennet is from another small town near the Alabama-Tennessee border named Tyson Creek, about a four-hour drive from here. It took a lot of convincing to get him to get all this work done in such a short amount of time, but it seems money speaks volumes, and thankfully, I had plenty of it. You can get anything done quickly for the right price.

I'm not rich by any means, but I never really saw the sense of spending money on frivolous things. I had a place to sleep, my motorcycle, and a very lucrative job. After a few very smart investments, I created a decent nest egg for myself. The money wasn't doing anything but sitting in the bank, accruing interest. I spent a pretty penny on this house and the renovations, but all of it will be worth it if I can convince Marissa to take a chance on us.

"Thanks, Connor." I stride toward him, reaching out my hand. "I couldn't have done any of this without your help."

Connor grasps my hand in his, giving it a firm handshake. "The pleasure was all ours. Lucky for you, my business partner, Vance, and I know a thing or two about renovating old houses. We just finished up his a few months ago."

"I'll definitely be contacting your company to help finish up the work, if things go well. I'm sure Marissa has a million plans for this place."

"Don't be so pessimistic, dear. Things are going to go great," my mom chimes in from her spot on the porch swing. "You bought her a house, and not just any house, her dream house. How can she say no?"

"I think you and my business partner have more in common than you think. He brought his girl's dream house, too. He's just waiting for her to come home and see it."

"How's that going for him?" I question, not sure I'm ready to hear the answer.

I rub the spot over my chest at the thought of Marissa never coming back to me, the space between us growing larger with each passing day. I imagined picking up the phone and calling her a million times over the last week or so, explaining to her I was coming back for her, but I needed to see this through. Words can only get me so far. I need to show her with my actions that I am serious about the two of us. A grand gesture to let her know I am all in. This house is just the start of my plan, but I have one other trick up my sleeve.

"The verdict is still out," Connor responds solemnly as I hear the back door slide open. "Oh, speak of the devil. Finn, meet my business partner, Vance."

Vance slaps me hard on the back, his booming voice causing my mom to jump slightly in her spot on the swing. "You've got a great place here, Finn. There are still a few things that need to be done before it's exactly how you envisioned, but we made a list just in case you want to go with another company closer to home."

"He's already said he'd contact us once the missus sees the place."

"Good man. You never want to make too many decisions on your own without consulting the lady of the house." Vance winks at my mom, causing her to giggle.

"If I was only a few years younger..."

"Momma!" I say in mock horror as everyone laughs loudly.

"If there isn't anything else, we're going to get going for the day," Connor says with a smile as he pulls a piece of paper out of the folder he's holding. "This is the list of repairs Vance was talking about. Is there anything else on this list you might want us to tackle before the big reveal?"

I grab the paper and flip it open, wanting to make sure there is nothing pressing on it. Most of the stuff I knew already needed to be done, but most of it is cosmetic work that will make the house more visitors ready in the coming weeks, but I notice one thing missing from the list.

"Can we refinish the floors? They're looking a little worse for the wear," I ask as I hand the list back to him.

The two men share a look before Vance strides toward the door. "Let's take a look, but I doubt it will be a problem."

Connor, Vance, Ma, and I stroll back into the house, coming to a stop just outside of the kitchen where the hardwood begins. I had originally wanted to save the hardwood in the kitchen, but it was beyond repair in a few spots, and Connor wasn't able to find the correct wood to match. Instead, we went with a luxury vinyl plank tile that was a rich mahogany color and blended well with the original flooring in the house.

Vance squats down and runs his hand across the floor before standing to his full height. "I don't see that being a problem, but you will have to give us another week to get them refinished and stained to match the LVP in the kitchen."

I groan internally at the mention of going another week without having Marissa in my arms.

"Or we could probably get it done in a few days if we

had to," Vance chimes in, causing Connor to chuckle. "We can have everything wrapped up and ready for the big reveal on Saturday."

Four days. Only four more days until I lay it all on the line and let Marissa know I'm in this for the long haul. I can live with that.

"I don't want to put you guys out, but I'd really appreciate it."

Vance and Connor share a look before he smiles at me. "What's a few more days away from home? I just need to make a few calls and make sure my daughter is taken care of."

"Jade is her name, right?" my ma questions as we make our way toward the front of the house.

"That's right. She's been staying with some friends of ours while we are here working."

Connor's face lights up as he speaks of his daughter. I don't know his entire story, but my mom has spent plenty of time here with all the workers coming in and out of the house doing work, and she's gotten to know them all. Connor's wife died when Jade was born, leaving him to raise her all alone. I believe he said she is fifteen now and an amazing dancer.

"Bring her with you next time. I'll spoil her rotten." Ma smiles at Connor before her attention shifts toward me. "I can't wait to have some grandbabies of my own soon."

"I think Mrs. Buckley is trying to tell you something." Vance chuckles, slapping me hard on the back.

"I'm working on it, Ma," I respond, rubbing my hand across the back of my neck before opening the front door. "Just let me know the final total, and I'll have a check ready for you once the work is complete on Saturday."

I reach my hand out to both men, giving them each a firm handshake as they head through the door. "Here's our card. Just call the office or my cell if you have questions."

I take the card from his outstretched hand with a smile. "Thank you both again for getting everything finished so quickly. It really means a lot to me."

"To all of us." My mom smiles brightly, pulling both men in for a tight squeeze.

"It was our pleasure." Vance smiles down at my ma. "But if you ever decide you need a younger man, give me a call." He winks at her before turning on his heels and heading toward their truck.

"Remind me never to leave her alone with him again," I say to Connor.

"He's harmless." He smiles, following behind Vance and climbing into the driver's side of the truck. My mom and I stand on the porch as we watch them turn around and head back down the long drive toward the main road.

"Does she know I'm back in town yet?"

"Not yet, but news travels." My mom wraps her arms around my waist, laying her head on my bicep. "We can keep it secret for a few more days. I'll have a chat with Roberta and let her know to make sure Marissa is at church service on Sunday."

"Will she get suspicious?"

"Probably. I'm sure she already knows something's up because I've been avoiding her and Peggy like the plague this week, but no matter. Everything is going to work out, sweetheart. Have faith."

"Easier said than done." I chuckle nervously. "I just wish I knew if any of this was going to work."

"Do you love her?"

"What kind of question is that, Ma?" I recoil, barely keeping my temper in check. "Would I be doing all of this if I didn't? Marissa is the air I breathe, and I honestly don't know how I'm going to live if this doesn't work."

Ma shakes her head as she turns toward me. "Why are men always so dramatic?"

"I'm not being dramatic, Ma. I'm serious."

"Oh. I know you are, sweetheart. I just wanted to make sure before I gave you this."

My eyebrows pull down in confusion as my mom reaches into her pocket and pulls out a small black box, flipping open the top. Resting inside is a sterling silver ring, with a sparkling array of round diamonds that form a cushion-shaped center design.

"What's this?" I grasp the box in my hand before plucking the delicate ring from it, holding it between my fingers, and raising it into the air. Tiny rainbows glisten around me as the light catches on the diamonds.

"It's my original engagement ring," Ma responds, barely above a whisper. "When your father and I got married, we didn't have much. He had just gotten out of the military, and he had sunk his entire savings into the bar. I told him I didn't need anything special, but he insisted on buying me that ring. He said that I needed to have something to show the world that he had promised to spend the rest of his life with me."

My mom turns and strolls toward the railing that runs along the outside of the porch, resting her hand gently on it as she looks off into the distance. "He eventually bought me the bigger ring I have now, but I couldn't part with this one. The symbol of the original promise he made to spend the rest of his life loving me."

"Why are you giving it to me?" I whisper, not wanting to break the spell my ma is weaving as she tells her story.

"Because you're our son. And now you need it to make the same promise to Marissa."

"But she wasn't even ready to tell me she loved me when I left. I doubt she's ready to go down to the courthouse and get married." I place the ring gently back into the box, slamming the lid shut before holding it out to my mom.

I hear everything my mom is saying, but there is still this nagging voice in the back of my head that wants to rage against the idea of this ring. Warning me that if I push too far, I could lose Marissa forever, but I still need to show her how much she means to me. This house is a step in the right direction. Will this ring bring me one step closer to showing her I'm never leaving her again? I could easily take the ring from my mother and give it to

Marissa, but I'm afraid. Afraid of it putting the last nail in the coffin and sending her running away from me forever.

"Probably not, but don't think of this as an engagement ring. Think of it as a symbol of your promise to spend the rest of your life loving her, just as your father did when he gave it to me all those years ago." My mom pushes the ring toward me before wrapping her arms around my waist and hugging me tightly. "Just think about it, Finn. You already bought her a house. What harm can a promise ring be now?"

She releases her hold on my waist before turning her cheek toward me. "Now, give me a kiss. I need to get home to your father; he has a physical therapy appointment today. The last one if things go well."

"Tell Pops I said hello," I say before leaning down and planting a kiss on her cheek. "And thank you."

Ma gives me a knowing smile before giving my cheek a few pats. "You're welcome, my sweet boy. And don't think I forgot about those grandbabies."

"Oh, I won't." I chuckle as she makes her way down the stairs and to her car.

As I watch her car make its way down the driveway, I try to imagine what it will be like to see Marissa again for the first time since I left. My heart broke the night I left Magnolia without a word, but I knew Marissa needed time to think about how she felt about me and if she was willing to give us a real chance. I told her how much I loved her, and I plan on loving her for the rest of my life. I know staying here and fighting for our love would have been easier, but she needed to make that decision on her own.

"Now it's my turn to take a leap of faith," I mumble, thrusting the black box into my pocket and heading back inside.

twenty-six

marissa

"Can this week get any weirder?" I mumble as I prop my feet up on the edge of my desk, leaning back slightly in my chair, and put my hands behind my head.

I've spent the last two weeks training Campbell, which wasn't nearly as bad as I thought it was going to be. He and I have history. There's no denying it. I'm pretty sure Colt and Dolores expected me to throw a fit and demand they fire him, but what happened between Campbell and me is in the past. Does it still sting a little that he made a fool out of me in high school? Of course, it does, but I don't hold it against him.

Things are going to be awkward for a while, especially with everyone wanting to see how we're going to act around each other, but after a few days, they'll find some other gossip to pay attention to. Hopefully, it's not about Finn and my... Hell, I still haven't been able to think about what happened between Finn and me. Did we break up? Were we even together in the first place? It seems I keep coming up with more questions than answers as more time passes.

My skin flushes as memories of the last night we spent together play through my mind on a movie reel. It's awakened a need for him that is both overwhelming and frightening all at once. I've never connected with another man in the way I connect with him, and I probably never will. After a few days, I realized I made a mistake and that I had to find a way to explain my reservations to Finn, but instead of picking up the phone like a normal person, I headed to Tallywackers, hoping to catch him. But when I got there, the place was slammed. Shelly told me that Finn had headed back to Texas, and my heart shattered. Now, just thinking about him feels like the entire world is crashing down around me. I want to rage against anything and anyone standing in my way, but I know this one is on me. I fooled myself into believing Finn would understand how I feel, but I was wrong.

I believed that this time would be different. I thought that he wouldn't leave me for something better. That even if he had to go back to Texas, he'd still include me in his life.

I've run every different scenario in my head. That it was last minute. Maybe he got called back to NASA for some super-secret project. Maybe that is why he didn't call. I mean, how could he explain having to leave without giving some details? But none of those possibilities stop the soul-deep ache in my heart from festering when I'm alone, slowly consuming me until there isn't anything left but pain.

My only saving grace has been training Campbell and the fact that Colt spends less time at work now that he and Sutton are together. I'm happy for them, really, but I can't stand seeing the smile on their faces, knowing I'll never have that again.

"It's not like it matters to Finn, anyway," I whisper to myself, the pain of what happened the last time we saw each other still fresh.

No matter what the reason, Finn still decided to leave without a word. He could have texted me from the airport or, hell, even sent an email. But instead, once again, someone I care about has left me without a word, and I'm left wondering if he ever cared for me in the first place.

"You all right, Marissa?" Campbell asks skeptically as he pokes his head into my office. His eyebrows are pulled down in concern.

"Of course. Why wouldn't I be?" I mumble, not wanting to have this conversation with him. Hell, I don't want to have this conversation with anyone at all because I don't think my heart could take it. "What can I do for you?"

"I just wanted to talk to you for a few minutes."

I know that tone of voice, and I don't like it at all. *Please, someone, shoot me now.*

"Sure," I respond when I really mean *no fucking way.*

I don't want to have this conversation with him right

now. I wanted to have time to prepare, to get my emotions and mind in sync before taking a trip down memory lane. There's no way he's missed the tension in the station every time he walks into a room, or the way people clam up when he's around. It's only natural that he wants to get things out in the open sooner rather than later, but I really don't want to. At least not until I have a few days to process. He owes me that much, right?

"We need to talk."

"About?" I pull my feet off my desk and sit up, trying to keep the panic bubbling to the surface from breaking free.

"Don't play dumb with me, Rissa."

"First, don't call me that. You lost the right to call me anything besides my legal name the moment you proposed to Emmeline in front of the entire senior class," I snap back, instantly regretting it.

Reminding Campbell about how badly he hurt me won't solve anything. Yeah, his actions turned me into the woman I am today, but not everything is completely his fault. I told him everything that happened was water under the bridge, and I meant that, but he doesn't know me anymore. We haven't seen or spoken to each other since graduation. The familiarity we used to share is gone.

If I don't get control of my emotions, he's going to start thinking I still have feelings for him when I don't. But how do you explain to someone, who was once your everything, that it's his fault you're the way you are? He's the reason I can't open myself up to Finn, that I have probably lost the only person besides him that I've ever loved. That my life didn't turn out how I wanted it to because of his selfishness. That I'm content with how my life has turned out, but I can't feel any sort of happiness because it all seems pointless without Finn by my side.

"Yeah, and look where that got me," Campbell snaps back.

There's a snide remark on the tip of my tongue, but I swallow it down the moment our eyes lock. The pain of what happened between him and Emmeline is written all over his face. Their marriage may have ruined all my hopes and dreams for the future, but there isn't a doubt in my mind that Campbell loved her with his entire heart and soul, or he wouldn't have married her. He wouldn't have slept with her if he didn't, no matter what anyone said. Even though things didn't work out between the two of us, I know what he's feeling right now. Hell, it's probably a million times worse because they were married and had a child together.

Back then, our biggest concern was what we were going to do on a Friday night: go to the drive-in or cow tipping. There was a time when Campbell meant everything to me. He was the sun, moon, and stars all wrapped into one, but at some point, he decided I wasn't enough.

I've mended my broken heart the best I could, but I never really knew why. Yeah, he gave me a list of reasons why he was breaking up with me, but then, only a few months later, he was with someone else, married, and had a son on the way. And here I am, still that devastated little girl who no longer had the life she dreamed of.

"Sorry. That was a long time ago. I shouldn't be bringing up the past, especially with what happened between the two of you."

It's been years since Campbell and I broke up, but right now, the hurt still feels as fresh as the day he walked out of my house for the last time. These feelings for Finn are even more confusing. He's managed to weasel his way into my heart, wanting something I thought he understood we could never have. I told him that I couldn't give him any more than one night, but one night turned into two and then so much more. Now I wish that I could take it all back. If I had known that being with Finn would lead to some of the best moments of my life, I'd have run in the opposite direction. Now I'm sitting here, questioning every rule I've put into place to protect my heart.

"I deserve it. We both know that, but that's not why I came here." Campbell sighs, pulling out a chair from in front of my desk and taking a seat. "I never apologized for the way things turned out. I want to explain why I did things how I did."

"People talk, Campbell. I got the basics. You broke up with me and immediately ran to Emmeline, got engaged, and then knocked her up." I lean forward, resting my arms on my desk, locking eyes with him. "You're a decent guy. Things may not have worked out between us, but I know you loved her."

Campbell's shoulders drop in relief as a hesitant smile crosses his face. "I know I should be glad that you understand what happened, but I'm even more confused than I was before I walked in here."

I cock my head to the side, trying to make heads or tails of what he's saying. If I'm being 100 percent honest with myself, I haven't always felt that way about what happened between Campbell and me, but as I grew up, the hurt faded, and some things became clearer about the situation.

"What's there to be confused about, Campbell? It's been years since it all went down. We're adults now, with responsibilities and years of broken hearts in our rearview mirror." I smile brightly before reaching forward and giving his hand a squeeze. "I'd be lying if I said it didn't hurt. I thought we were going to get married and spend the rest of our lives together, but I grew up.

"But I've always wondered what happened between us," I mumble, turning my chair around and staring out the window. That pain of what happened feels just as fresh as if it happened all those years ago. But this time, the man who broke my heart was Finn, not Campbell.

"How did we go from planning our future together to you married to another woman with a kid on the way in a matter of months?"

Campbell sighs loudly, his footsteps echoing in the quiet room as he comes around my desk. He drops into a squatting position, grabbing both my hands in his. "Honestly, nothing happened between us. You had all these plans for your life. Plans that, as time moved forward, weren't in line with mine. You love Magnolia. You love being able to see your family whenever you want, even if they get on your nerves." He drops his head, his shoulders shaking as he laughs softly.

"I'm glad this is funny to you, Campbell." I try to snatch my hands away from him, but he tightens his grip.

"It's not funny to me at all, Marissa. But there were times in our relationship that it felt like you loved Magnolia more than me."

"That's insane."

"I know that now that I've grown up, but at the time, you had plans for the future. Plans that you laid out and set for both of us. At first, I just wanted to make you happy, but deep down, I knew that living the rest of my life in Magnolia wouldn't be enough for me. I wanted to see and experience the world."

"I could've done that with you." I pull back, looking him directly in the eyes. "I'd have done anything for you, Campbell."

"I know that now, but at the time..." His voice trails off as he pushes to his feet, placing both his hands on my shoulders. "I was a coward. I didn't want to ask you to give up on your dreams because of me."

Campbell stares at me, his eyes full of regret, begging for my forgiveness. Forgiveness that, before this moment, I thought I'd already given, but somewhere, buried deep in my heart, was the devastated seventeen-year-old girl who had her heart broken.

"I forgive you," I say, tears pooling in my eyes as a bright smile spreads across my face, and his shoulders sag in relief.

"I didn't know I needed to hear you say that until right now." He smiles brightly, dropping his arms and taking a step back, putting some space between us. "So, are you going to give Finn a chance, or what?"

"How do you know about that?"

"Our mothers are all friends, Ris-Marissa. They gossip even worse now than they did when we were younger."

"That's just peachy," I respond, swiping at the tears that are dangerously close to slipping free. "I really wish my mother would stop gossiping about things she doesn't understand. But if you must know, Finn left me without so much as a goodbye text. I guess spending the rest of his life in Magnolia wasn't appealing to him either."

"I have a feeling that you may not know everything." He smiles, grabbing my hand and pulling me toward him. My face smashes into his chest as I relax into his arms. "I know you, Marissa. He scared you, so you pushed him away."

"I did not." I pull back, scowling up at him, which causes him to chuckle softly.

"Yes, you did. You did the same thing when we started dating. And I'm sure you've done it to every other man you've dated since then."

"There haven't been many."

"I rest my case," Campbell mumbles, taking a step

backward and resting his hands on my shoulders. "A little birdy told me that Finn is over the moon for you. Just give him a chance. You never know, he might be the one."

"Maybe."

I need to be honest with myself. I'm in love with Finn Buckley. I may not be ready to jump into a relationship with Finn, but the feelings are there. Maybe they've always been there, growing into something beautiful, perfect, and beyond anything I could ever imagine. I wasn't searching for forever when he sat down on the barstool beside me, but it seems it may have fallen into my lap. Finn has made me feel things again that I don't know how to explain, things I never imagined feeling for another man again.

"I love him."

I shake that thought out of my mind. This isn't the first time I've fallen in love, but my head is telling me it won't last. But I've never felt this type of pull toward another man before. Usually, it's one night and then we part ways, but with Finn, it feels different. The thought of never feeling his fingers caress my skin or the way he literally takes my breath away when he walks into a room is terrifying. I don't know if I can give him what he's asking for, but for the first time, I want to try. My heart wants to open up, even if only a little, to see how things between us progress. But I'm terrified of getting my heart broken a second time because this time, I don't know if I'll be able to recover.

"Don't tell me. Tell him."

I really need to stop saying these things out loud.

"Okay, enough with the touchy-feely moments. I'm starving."

He stares at me for a few moments before his arms drop from my shoulder and takes a step away from me. "So, we're good?" His hand motions between the two of us.

"We're good. Whether you keep this job has nothing to do with me, Campbell. Colt is the county sheriff and calls all the shots. My job is to make sure you make us look good around town."

"I've been a cop since we graduated high school. I think I know a thing or two about wearing a uniform."

"Maybe so, but it's different when you're surrounded by the people you grew up with. You can't imagine how hard it is to get respect from the woman who changed your diapers."

We both laugh loudly, the sound filling the room, and I check my watch before pushing back from my desk. "Not that I don't love this trip down memory lane, but I need to head out of here for the day."

"You're not running away from me, are you?" His eyebrow raises in question as he stands, motioning for me to walk in front of him toward the door.

"Don't flatter yourself," I scoff, not wanting him to know how much his reappearance in my life has affected me. "I have plans with my best friend. You'll soon learn that nothing happens here in Magnolia, so there is no need for us to be here all the time. If you need anything, Colt is here, or I'm just a phone call away."

"This is going to take some getting used to." He sighs. "Did you want to grab some lunch before you head out with your friend? You can invite them along if you want."

I'm sure after everyone in town stops gossiping about what happened between us or forcing us together, we can be friends, but that is not happening right now.

"Maybe next time. If you ever meet my friend, Peyton, you'll know why."

"I look forward to it. Anyone you would consider your best friend is worth knowing."

"I'm going to tell her you said that." I chuckle softly.

"Just keep it in mind. My social calendar is completely free, besides hanging out with a five-year-old every day."

"You could have worse company." I smile and wave at Dolores as he opens the front door, letting me step through first. "How is your little one doing? I'm sorry, but I'm completely drawing a blank on her name."

"His name." He chuckles. "Ashton is doing great, all things considered. He starts kindergarten next week."

"Ah, I'm sure you will be neck deep in single moms in no time." I giggle softly, walking toward my car, and pause when I hear Campbell call my name.

"Does it get any easier?"

"What?"

"Dealing with the anger and pain of what she...?" He

runs his hand through his thick locks before pinning me in place with his stare.

"Some days are harder than others, but someday, you'll find someone that makes you believe that it's worth taking a leap of faith and trying again." I giggle nervously.

"One can only hope..." Campbell's voice trails off, then he sighs. "Okay, I won't keep you any longer than I need to. Enjoy your night."

"Thank you for the talk, Campbell. I really mean that."

"Anytime." He smiles before nodding his head and turning to head back into the station.

twenty-seven

"**I**s it going to get easier?" I mumble into my empty office as the sun filters in through the window.

I attempt to get up but immediately fall back into my chair as I wait for the room to stop spinning. Lunch with Peyton turned into dinner. Dinner turned into drinks. Drinks turned into full-blown wasted as I cried my eyes out over the boy who left me. Pathetic, right? I mean, I knew this was going to happen. I tried to prepare my heart for this very outcome, but it still hurts worse than anything I could imagine. I spend my nights lying awake, not wanting to close my eyes because I'll be transported back to that night. The night my life changed forever.

I tried to pretend that nothing had happened for the last few weeks, that my world wasn't slowly crumbling around me, but I'm sure everyone noticed. I know for a fact that my mother has. She even commented the other day at dinner about my obsessive need to check my phone. And she isn't wrong. I couldn't even focus on the briefing Colt was giving the other day because I was afraid I'd miss a call or text from Finn.

The feeling is 100 percent irrational because he hasn't called me once since he snuck out of town after our last night together. I know what you're thinking. Sure, I could text him, but what could I say to him that didn't sound pathetic? I find myself pulling up his number so many times, trying to find the words to explain how I was feeling, but I never make the call. I keep telling myself that if he wanted me, he would've stayed. But that still doesn't stop me from spending most of the day checking my phone, waiting to hear something, anything, from Finn.

Speaking of phone calls, my phone buzzes along the top of my desk a few times before I can grab it to check the caller ID, hoping it's Finn, but it's my mother.

"Hey, Momma. Do you need me to grab the donuts for Sunday school when I'm on my way over for service?"

"That's exactly why I'm calling, sweetheart. But I don't want you and Campbell to be late."

"How the heck did you know Campbell was even here?"

"His mother, dear," she responds nonchalantly.

"Of course, that's how you found out," I respond, checking my watch for the time. If we get moving in the next half hour, we can easily grab them. "It won't be a problem. I can just text Peyton and let her know when we are on the way. She'll have Katie run them out to the SUV for me."

"That's so sweet of her."

We sit in silence for a few minutes. I learned a long time ago that she has to be the one to end the call, not me. The last thing I want is a lecture about my manners and respecting elders.

"Momma, is there anything else?"

"Yes."

I wait a few minutes for her to say more, but she doesn't speak. My heart picks up as I begin to panic. Campbell is already back in town. Sutton is more than likely snuggled in bed with my boss—her new fiancé. So, there is only one other thing my mom wants to tell me.

"Finn is back in town."

I gasp softly, rubbing the spot on my chest over my heart. Just the mention of his name sends my world into another tailspin. I want to find him and give him a piece of my mind. Demand an explanation for why he disappeared after I laid my heart on the line. I fooled myself into believing that he meant every word he promised about never leaving me, but I was wrong.

"Oh," I respond as my mind spins, trying to make sense of what's happening.

Unimaginable pain shoots through my body at the idea of seeing Finn again, but I need to be stronger to keep my heart safe. We may live in a small town, but I can avoid him. Maybe. I collapse to the floor as the frayed edges of my heart rip open for the second time today.

"Sweetheart. Are you there?"

"I'm here, Momma." Tears pool in my eyes as all the

emotions I've been trying desperately to keep in check come bubbling to the surface. "I just don't know what to do."

"Oh, honey." Her voice softens as the last remnants of my control disappear.

My heart constricts in my chest as the expectations of everyone come crashing down around me. I gasp for air as sadness unlike anything I've ever felt overtakes me.

"I love him so much." Tears pour down my cheeks as the weight of my feelings hit me.

I clutch the phone tightly, biting down on my hand, hoping to quiet the sobs bubbling from my throat. My heart feels as if it's breaking in two. I want nothing more than to rush out of the station and beg Finn to bind us together in every way possible, but this is the real world. If he wanted me, he would have fought for me, or at least picked up the phone to explain why he was leaving Magnolia. But he made his choice. Sure, Finn is back in town, but for long? My mom didn't say anything about home moving here permanently. Nothing has changed. No matter how I feel about him, I have responsibilities here in Magnolia. My family is here. I've put down roots. I'm not about to uproot my entire life and go running to someone who may very well want nothing to do with me.

Searing pain flows through my entire body as waves of agony pull me under. I'm just praying that I can hold on for just a little longer until the pain subsides. I yearn for numbness to cut me off from all these feelings that I'm so desperate to forget.

"Make it stop," I whine, wrapping my arms around my waist and attempting to hold myself together. "I just want the pain to stop."

"I wish I could." She pauses, and a pregnant silence remains on the line before she breaks it.

"Are you going to be okay, or do your father and I need to come down to the station?"

Just the idea of them coming here makes me giggle. "No need. I'll be all right. I just need to get my emotions back under control."

"I have a feeling that's your problem, sweetheart. You keep your feelings bottled up and hidden away from the people you care about."

"Like you?"

"Yes, like me." She laughs softly. "It takes courage to tell someone how you feel, no matter if you've known them for a week or a few years. But you can't expect someone to know what you're feeling. You have to show them."

"I don't know what to do." Fresh tears run down my cheeks as I pull my knees into my chest and rest my back along the lower cabinets of the island. "Finn is everything I could have ever wanted in a man. He's so smart. He works for NASA and could be with anyone in the world, but for some reason, he chose me."

A smile creeps across my face as I continue to tell my mother all the wonderful things I've learned about Finn over the short time we've spent together, wanting her to know everything there is to know about the man who owns my heart.

"I could've told you that. Finn has been in love with you since you were children, but he was always too afraid to say anything."

"You knew and didn't tell me?"

My heart constricts at her words. Sutton always told me that he had a thing for me, but I blew her off, believing that if he had feelings for me, he would've said something to me. But back then, I couldn't see anything past my feelings for Campbell.

"It wasn't my place. You were so in love with Campbell, but then he broke your heart. After that you hid your heart away from everyone, even your father and me."

"Campbell hurt me."

"I know, but not every man will. You understand that, right?" she asks.

I nod, forgetting that she can't see me, but she continues.

"You love Finn, right? And he treats you well?"

"Like I hung the moon." My hand grips the phone tightly as I fight to keep control of my emotions. "He's everything."

Large, hiccupping breaths cause my body to tremble.

"Then what's the problem?"

I freeze, not knowing exactly how to answer her question. It's true that I'm irrevocably in love with Finn Buckley. Tears stream down my face as I gasp for breath. "But he left me. He didn't call, text, or even send a smoke signal. I had to find out from someone else. And now he's back and still hasn't said a word. I pretty sure he wants nothing to do with me."

"Do you know that for sure?" She laughs, "Or better yet do you know why he left in the first place?"

"Do you?"

"It's not my place to say anything, but I always knew Finn would be back. And before you say anything, it's not because of his parents. It's because of you." My mom chokes up. "All I've ever wanted is for you and your sister to be happy. To get married and have children of your own and raise them to be strong and amazing people just like you."

Unable to speak, I nod as tears continuously stream down my face while I try to regain my composure.

"But what do *you* want, Marissa?"

"What?"

"What do *you* want with your life, sweetheart? All your father and I want is for you to be happy. Even if you have to leave Magnolia to do it."

Laughter bubbles from my throat. "I want to spend the rest of my fucking life with Finn."

"Language, young lady."

"Sorry, Momma."

She's quiet for a few moments. "Don't let it happen again. And you're paying for our breakfast along with the donuts. I already told Peyton to expect you."

"Yes, Momma." I smile. "Love you."

"Love you, too, sweetheart," she responds before

hanging up the phone, causing me to chuckle softly as I shoot a text off to Peyton, telling her I'll take care of their breakfast and the donuts after church before I hear a knock on my office door, and it opens slowly.

I swipe at my face before grabbing a small pocket mirror out of my desk to ensure all evidence of my tears is wiped from my face as Campbell walks in.

"Umm... is everything okay?"

"I'm fine. What do you want?" I snap, wanting to be alone so I can process my conversation with my mother.

"I thought we were being nice to each other now?" He raises his hands in surrender.

"Who said that? I know it wasn't me."

"Touché..." His voice trails off. "Dolores told me to come talk to you about something."

I have a feeling I know exactly where this is going. I'm sure everyone in town knows that Finn is back in town, but the last thing I want to do is talk about it. Especially with Campbell. It's awkward and, frankly, no one's business.

"Not you, too." I groan, wanting the ground to open and swallow me whole. "I know he's back in town, and no, I don't want to talk about it."

"What? I mean, I'm glad Finn has come back safely, but Dolores told me to ask you about the girl who works at the bakery on Main." My eyes snap to him, widening in surprise. "She seems like she hates me for some reason, and I'd remember if I met someone like *her* before."

I gasp loudly before slapping my hand over my

mouth. *This can't be happening. Can it?* This has to be an episode from *The Twilight Zone*. There is no way that Campbell has a thing for my best friend. I mean, there's nothing inherently wrong with Campbell as a human being, but Peyton hates his guts on principle. Campbell broke my heart. End of story. She won't give a shit that we have a tentative truce or that he apologized for what happened all those years ago.

"Peyton Atkins."

"Anything else you want to tell me?" He raises his eyebrow in question.

"She's my best friend, and you're on your own. Good Luck with that." I giggle softly, knowing that Campbell has his work cut out for him with this one.

"Ah, it makes sense now." He shakes his head slightly before dropping down in the chair in front of my desk. "Are you going to church this morning?"

"Like I have a choice." We both chuckle softly before falling into an awkward silence.

Campbell stares at me for a few moments, his head tilted to the side as if he's trying to solve a math equation. "So, you're okay with me dating your best friend?"

"Oh, you're that sure of yourself, are you?" I lean back in my chair, not once taking my eyes off him. "Shift change is in about an hour. You can have your first shot at talking to her when we pick up the donuts for Sunday school."

Campbell doesn't say a word but nods his head before pushing to his feet and striding out the door, pulling it shut behind him just as my cell phone rings on my desk.

"Speak of the devil," I grumble to myself as I check the screen and see Peyton's name.

"My mom already called and told me. No, I have no idea what the fuck I'm going to do," I say without waiting for her to say hello. I know… manners and all, but I don't want to be having this conversation in the first place. I might as well get it over with as quickly as possible.

"You're going to go to church service today with your head held high and make him regret the day he broke your heart."

I moped around for days after I discovered Finn had gone back to Texas. Thankfully, Colt had given me a week of vacation, so I was able to wallow in my sadness. After two days of ignoring her phone calls, Peyton broke into my apartment, demanding answers. After making sure I got my spare key back, I told her everything. Being my best friend, she knew part of what happened, but I always kept back Finn's name, not wanting to deal with the sympathetic looks and phone calls that I knew would come whenever he came back to town. And I was right.

"I'm fine, Peyway. Really, I am."

"No, you aren't," she deadpans. "If I didn't know I had a rush of people on their way here before service, I'd be on my way to you."

"You don't need to do that," I whisper.

Even I can hear the quiver in my voice, so I can guarantee she can. I'm terrified that everyone knows about what happened by now, and the moment I walk into church service, everyone will be staring at me, ready to watch me crumble for the second time in my life. I know it's irrational to feel this way, but that does make me want to make an excuse and not go to service at all, but then he wins. Magnolia is my home just as much as his.

"Yes, I do," she chastises me. "I mean, you could always ask Campbell to pretend to be your boyfriend. Nothing like the thought of you back with your ex to have him begging on his knees."

"That's not gonna happen. Besides, he seems to have set his sights on someone else." I giggle softly, wanting to tell her all about his and my conversation from a few minutes ago, but I refrain.

"I wonder who the unlucky victim is."

"Hmmm..." I respond, not really answering her question.

There are exactly two things that Peyton will never tolerate. Cheaters and lying. She can't stand it. There is no way in hell I'm going to lie to her about who he has his sights on. It won't end well for me.

"You know who it is, don't you?"

"Yes." I smile, knowing that her not knowing who he's interested in is driving her nuts.

Peyton hates to admit it, but she is just as bad as everyone else in Magnolia. She wants to know everything going on in town, thriving on the drama to keep her occupied, but she doesn't spread it. She enjoys the show and basking in the fact she's in the know. Yes, I know it makes absolutely no sense, but we have to find some way to entertain ourselves.

"Are you going to tell me?" she deadpans, all the warmth from a few minutes ago seeping from her voice.

"Nope," I respond, popping the P for effect.

I meant what I told Campbell. I'm not doing a damn thing to stop them from being together, but I'm also not doing anything to help the situation either. Watching these two battle it out is going to be so much fun.

"You're no fun," she responds before sighing loudly. "But can I say one more thing before I go back to hating his guts and burning his likeness in effigy?"

"Sure." I chuckle, the tightness in my chest loosening slightly.

I'm not the angry eighteen-year-old girl whose heart was broken into a million pieces for the whole town to witness. I swore that I would never find myself in this situation again, chasing after a man and begging him to stay with me, but still, I've found myself in the same situation again. Except, this time, I poured my heart out to him and made him promise that he'd love me and never leave, but he broke his word and then left without as much as a goodbye text message.

I knew that Finn would be back in town at some point. Although his dad is doing much better, even up and walking around on his own, he has a long road ahead of him. Nolan and Shelly are doing an amazing job running Tallywackers in his absence, but at some point,

Finn would have to come back to ensure things keep running smoothly.

"Did you ever tell Finn how you felt?"

"Not in any certain words, but I tried to show him."

"Do or do not. There is no try."

"What are you, fucking Yoda now?" I giggle softly, trying to dismiss her words, but I know she's right.

I've been telling Finn from the moment I figured out who he was that there was no chance that we could be together. That, at some point, he would tire of me and go back to his life in Texas, but I never once told him how I felt.

"I'm not Yoda, but the words aren't any less true." Peyton sighs, pausing for a few moments to collect her thoughts. "Hear me out before you jump down my throat. Maybe he left to tie up loose ends in Texas before coming back here. To be with you."

"It's possible," I respond, hope fluttering in my stomach. "But why hasn't he called?"

"'Cause he's a male and doesn't think things through completely most of the time. There are several plausible reasons why he never called. I would ask if you called him, but we both know why you never picked up the phone."

"And why is that?"

"You would say it was because of work. You've been working yourself to the bone. You probably figured that if you could keep your mind busy, you wouldn't have time to think about what happened or deal with the pain of losing him," she responds. "But my guess is the real reason you didn't call him is because of your broken heart."

I want to snark back at her. Tell her she's wrong, but I can't because she's right.

"I can tell by your silence that I hit the nail on the head. Just let me say one more thing before I go back to planning ways to kill Finn in his sleep."

"Always so violent. However, you said that before. This would be a bonus thing that I never agreed to."

"So, arrest me. Can I say it or not?"

"Okay," I choke out, barely able to form words past the emotions clogging my throat.

"If you love him, tell him. He needs to know what he's missing out on, the woman that would have loved him until the end of time if only she'd pull her head out of her ass and stop pushing him away."

"I did—"

"Before you tell me you didn't push him away, let me remind you that I'm your best friend and know you better than you know yourself."

"Okay, fine. I pushed him away, but he still should've at least said goodbye."

The idea of giving voice to my feelings is terrifying. If I tell him, there's no going back. There's the chance that things won't work out or that he'd resent me for allowing him to give up his dreams to come back to our hometown. But the flip side of that is hope. When I think about a future with Finn, my heart feels light, as if the weight of the world has been lifted off my shoulders. If I can figure out a way to get my heart and mind on the same page, I'll be headed in the right direction, although that's a lot easier said than done.

"I'm not going to say he did the right thing either, but two wrongs don't make a right."

"You're right." I sigh as look toward the ceiling, wishing that none of this ever happened. No, that's not true. I wouldn't trade any of the time I spent with Finn for the world, but I would trade the pain. "This is a lot to think about."

"Okay, I said I was done, but did you ever think of going with him? I'd miss you, but you can be a police officer anywhere. Your family loves you, but I doubt your parents or sister would fault you for following your heart."

"I never thought about it. Having children and raising them in Magnolia has always been my dream." I use the same regurgitated answer I've been giving everyone since I came home from college.

"You came home, took care of your family, and joined the county sheriff's department, just like your dad. Heck, you even convinced me to move here with you. If you ask me, that's pretty badass."

Images of what my life would be like with someone who loves me with all their heart flood through my mind. Nights spent on the porch of the old farmhouse we both love, rocking in the rocking chairs and telling each other about our days. I can see it all laid out in front of me, and I yearn for it with my entire being. I've wanted that picture for most of my life, but it wasn't until this moment that I realized I have something else that I cherish more than anything. More than the house or the picture-perfect life.

"Dreams can change," I mumble to myself as tears pool in my eyes.

"They can," she agrees. "Just because this isn't what you envisioned your life being at this point, doesn't mean it wasn't meant to be."

I never expected Finn to come into my life and awaken the part of myself that I've kept hidden and locked away for all these years. Finn has been waiting for me to invite him into my life completely since the day I held him at gunpoint in his parents' front yard, and I need to give him an answer.

"What if I'm too late?" I ask the one question that has been filtering through my mind during this entire conversation.

Once again, Finn left me. He didn't bother to include me in any decision. What if that was his way of telling me he was done? That he no longer wants to be the only one fighting for whatever this is between us.

"Then he's an idiot," Peyton responds without hesitation.

"Thank you," I whisper to my friend, wishing she was here with me so I could give her a big hug.

If it wasn't for her making me open up about everything that was going on since I saw Finn again for the first time, I never would've admitted to myself how much he has changed my life for the better. How much I need him.

"Anytime. Just promise to name your firstborn after me, and we can call it even."

"You got it," I respond before checking my watch and swearing softly. "Is there a chance I can convince you to bring the donuts my mom wanted me to pick up for Sunday school to the church? We won't make it to the bakery in time and not be late for service."

"Oh, we can't have that, can we." Peyton giggles. "No problem. Don't forget to think about what I said."

"I won't," I respond before hanging up the phone, just as I hear a loud knock on the door.

"I was just coming to let you know our shift is over. But no one is here to relieve us," Campbell says, poking his head through the door.

"Yeah, we usually just lock up the station during church service, and then Waylen will be here later. Right now, we are what Colt likes to call being on call." I stride past him into the reception area and grab two handheld walkie-talkies, handing him one and grabbing a set of keys from the pegboard. "The county dispatch center will call us on these if anything big happens, but pretty much everyone in the surrounding area is headed to church."

"God forbid someone misses service." He grabs the walkie-talkie from my outstretched hand and clips it to his belt. "Well, I'll be heading out, then."

"Oh, no, you don't. Your girl is bringing donuts for Sunday school to the church."

"My girl, huh?" He raises his eyebrow at me as he pulls the door open and motions for me to head out before him.

"Well, at least you think she is." I laugh loudly before unlocking one of our SUVs and climbing in. "I'm driving."

"Yes, ma'am." He gives me a mock salute before opening the passenger side door and climbing in next to me. "Don't forget, you promised to help me talk to *my girl*."

"That I did." I smile brightly at him before continuing. "You know what? I'm kind of glad you're back here."

"Could've fooled me." He turns his puppy dog eyes on me.

"Fine, I'm lying a little, but seriously. Your being back in town and having a little crush on my best friend, who completely hates your guts because you broke up with me, is going to be interesting."

"I aim to please." He chuckles as I turn the ignition and pull out of the parking lot to head to the church.

"You don't need to be so smug about it."

twenty-eight

marissa

"So, everything is fine. Your mom is fine. Your dad is fine. Your sister is fine." Peyton steps up to the SUV as I shut it off and swing the door open.

I wait patiently as she takes a step back, allowing me to slide out of the car while scowling at something over my shoulder.

"Campbell Taylor, this is Peyton Atkins. She's my best friend and owns the bakery on Main Street."

"A pleasure to meet you." His voice drops a few octaves, a newfound seductive purr in his voice.

Peyton doesn't say a word. Her cheeks are a bright shade of pink, and her eyes widen in surprise. She stands motionless, not even uttering a word.

"Earth to Peyton." I chuckle, waving my hand in front of her face, but she doesn't move a muscle. "I think you may have short-circuited her brain."

"That may be a first for me," Campbell responds sarcastically, walking around the car and grabbing the boxes of donuts from Peyton's hands. He smirks at her before leaning forward and planting a kiss on her forehead. "I'll take these inside for you. See you later, Peyton."

"See you," she mumbles, an embarrassed and confused look on her face.

I have no idea what came over my friend, but it seems that Campbell might not have to work as hard to get into her good graces as I originally thought. The only question is if that's a good thing or a bad thing.

Peyton shakes her head before striding in the opposite direction.

"You know the front of the church is that way, right?" I question as I catch up to her, threading my arm through hers. "But what I really want to know is why you were waiting for me to arrive at the church."

I nervously twiddle with the edges of her shirt, waiting impatiently for her to answer. "The most stressful thing I have to deal with today is the possibility of running into Finn."

"Maybe you should brace yourself." All my muscles lock up as I freeze, unable to take another step. The hairs on the back of my neck stand up straight as a sense of impending doom overcomes me.

"If this is a joke, it's not a funny one, Peyton." I chuckle as I take a seat on the first bench I see. "Come on and tell me what's really wrong. I can take it. Just rip it off like a Band-Aid and tell me."

I grip her arm so tight that my knuckles start to turn white from the pressure.

"I saw Finn inside."

That small phrase feels like a punch in the gut as I buckle over and rest my arms on my knees.

"Sitting in the same pew as your parents."

"Of course, you did." I groan, dropping my head into my hands.

Of all the things I thought Peyton was going to tell me, that wasn't one of them.

I knew that Finn was back in town. I knew I'd have to deal with that eventually, but not a few hours after I was told. I need time to prepare what I'm going to say to him. To figure out the perfect way to tell him how I feel about him in hopes that he cares about me as much as he did all those weeks ago.

"Does he look happy?" I question, wanting to know everything about his life since he left town a few weeks ago.

"He looks good, but the light he once had in his eyes has dimmed." Peyton drops her head onto my shoulder.

"Did he say how long he was staying in town?" I mumble, laying my head on top of hers.

"He didn't say anything to me. Just smirked in my direction before taking a seat next to his mother. I was going to talk to him but figured any good friend would come out here and warn you. I didn't want you to be blindsided when you came into church."

A sense of longing fills me as I take a deep breath, letting my eyes slide shut for a few seconds as I try to calm myself.

"Mari," Peyton whispers, but I refuse to open my eyes. If I keep them shut, maybe, just maybe, I can pretend that this isn't happening. "He's right there."

I jump out of the seat, almost knocking Peyton to the ground as I catch a glimpse of Finn standing in front of me. My chest aches with the longing that I've felt since the last time I saw him. It's only been a few weeks, but it feels more like an eternity. He looks almost exactly the same as he did that day. His hair is damp from a recent shower, and he's wearing a royal blue button-up shirt with the sleeves rolled to the elbows and dark jeans fitted perfectly to his muscular legs.

"I have to go," Peyton says as she scrambles toward the open doors of the church.

I should follow her, but I'm frozen in place, unable to tear myself away from him. "Hi," I say, loud enough for him to hear.

The last thing I want to do is dig into all the hurt from the last few weeks, but I need to say something. I just need to figure out some way to make it past this awkward phase of trying to figure out what happened between us and how we are going to move forward. But I have no idea what to say. No matter what has happened between us, Finn just got back into town. He probably has a million things he needs to be doing, but instead, he's standing out here, watching me.

"Hi." His gravelly voice caresses my skin, pulling me closer to him.

I lift my foot to take a step forward, but I halt my

movements. If I go to him now, nothing will change. I won't ask him all the questions that have been running through my mind for the last two weeks. I won't tell him how scared I am of committing to him, of giving him my heart fully. But most importantly, I won't tell him how much I love him.

"How have you been?" I question, my hand clenched tightly by my side.

I want to know every bit of information he's willing to give me about our time apart. I'm sure I could get bits and pieces of information from either of our parents during our weekly lunch after church service, but I want him to tell me everything.

"Fine," he responds, reaching up and rubbing the back of his neck.

"Can I get at least *something* more than one-word answers from you?"

"Yes," he responds as his cheeks pink in embarrassment. "I'm sorry. This is a lot harder than I imagined it would be."

I smirk, and he takes a step toward me. To my surprise, I take a step back, bumping into the bench. Tears begin collecting in my eyes, but I quickly bat them away.

"Do you want to get some coffee and catch up?" he questions, not bothering to hide the longing in his voice.

"I don't think that's such a good idea," I whisper as I stride past him. "I really need to get inside before service starts. My momma hates it when I'm late."

Our shoulders brush slightly, and an electric current runs up my arm and directly to my heart, igniting the love I feel for him all over again. It's been weeks since we've seen each other, but in some way, it feels like he never left.

"Please wait." I freeze as he grips my arm softly, running his fingers down it before pressing something into my hand. "Just read it. Not now, but later, after service. I promise I'll explain everything to you after you read it. I just need you to trust me for a little longer."

"Trust you?" I whimper. "I trusted you before and you left me."

"I always planned on coming back, sugar." The sound of my nickname causes my heart to melt a little bit more. My body is still as he releases my arm and heads in the direction of the church without a second glance. "You're it for me, sugar. That hasn't changed," he whispers into the wind as I turn and follow behind him.

My eyes follow him as he passes into the main area in front of the church, filled with all the townspeople waiting for service to start. I try to keep him in my sights, but I lose him. Instead of standing there, searching frantically for some sign that he hasn't disappeared again, I continue toward the stairs and head through the front door.

What in God's name just happened?

One moment, I was laughing at the silly way Peyton reacted to Campbell, then the next thing I know, Finn is there, begging me to give him a chance to explain why he left me without another word. I thought I had more time to come up with what I was going to say to Finn the first time I saw him, but when Peyton told me he was inside, my mind went blank. I wanted to run and hide away in my apartment until I could process everything that happened and come up with the perfect thing to say, but that wasn't in the cards for me. The moment I saw Finn, I was tongue-tied, and any hope of protecting my heart went out the window. Instead of being angry, all I wanted to do was run to him. Wrap my arms and legs around his body and beg him to never leave me again.

"Soo…" Peyton nudges my shoulder the moment I step into the church, and we make our way further into the sanctuary, searching for my parents. "How'd it go?"

Almost everyone in town is scattered around the interior of the church. Wooden pews line each side of the long heart pine floor aisle. Colorful stained glass windowpanes line the outer walls on each side of the room, letting soft light fill the sanctuary.

"That good, huh?" she asks, trying to fill the uncomfortable silence.

My eyes scan the room before I catch sight of my mom, waving her hand in the air with eyebrows pulled down in concern before our eyes lock. With a sigh, I tug on Peyton's arm, pulling her toward where my parents are seated. When we get a few steps away from them, my dad slides from the pew, with my mother following quickly behind him.

"I was worried you two were going to be late." My

momma wraps her arms around my shoulders and gives me a warm hug before doing the same to Peyton.

"We'd never be late for service, Auntie Roberta," Peyton responds with a smile before giving me a wink over my mother's shoulder.

"Suck-up," I mouth toward her before stepping into the pew and freezing in my tracks.

This can't be fucking happening. I completely forgot about Peyton's warning from earlier until right now. Sitting on the other end of the pew are none other than Finn's parents, Charlotte and Mason Buckley. Peyton warned me that Finn was sitting near my parents, but not that his parents were here, as well. But what's more surprising is the fact that Finn isn't there.

"Hello, Marissa." Ms. Charlotte flashes me a bright smile as I take a seat beside her, leaning over as she wraps her arms around me. "Did you see him?" Her eyes flash over my shoulder toward the door.

"I did."

"Are you going to give him a chance to explain?"

I freeze in place, not entirely sure how to answer that question. I'm sitting in the middle of a church on Sunday morning, so lying is kind of out of the question right now, but *I don't know* doesn't seem like a good enough answer for her either. I doubt Ms. Charlotte would want to know I did, in fact, see her son, but it was only for a few minutes before he shoved a piece of paper in my hand, promising to explain why he hadn't contacted me for two weeks.

But he should be here in a few minutes.

Yeah, probably not the best idea to tell her that.

"How are you feeling today, Mr. Buckley?" Peyton chimes in as she squeezes my shoulder gently and takes her seat beside me. "I heard from Auntie Roberta that they cut back on your physical therapy visits."

My cheeks heat as I drop my chin to my chest and clench my eyes tightly shut, hoping the ground will open and swallow me whole. This is exactly what I wanted to avoid. The questions and sympathetic looks from people. And having to sit next to his parents and mine while listening to Sunday morning service, pretending that I'm not completely head over heels in love with their son but have no idea whether or not he feels the same. Sure, he's told me repeatedly that he cared about me. Promising to never leave me and to give me space, but he lied. He left me at the first sign of trouble.

"Oh, good morning to you, too, Peyton. I didn't see you there." Ms. Charlotte's sweet voice brings me back to the present, but I refuse to look at her.

"Good morning, ma'am," Peyton responds cheerfully.

"Are you looking for me?"

Fuck. I know that voice. The deep baritone that sends a tingle of need through my entire body and instantly transports me back to a few minutes ago. I will myself to keep my eyes down and focused on the floor, but I can feel his gaze on me, burning into me as he wills me to look in his direction, and I can't resist.

I lift my head, my eyes locking with his. I must admit, Finn is gorgeous. My skin feels as if it's on fire as he stares at me, something moving through his eyes as he watches me for a few moments before his mother's voice breaks the spell.

"There's my boy." Ms. Charlotte pushes to her feet, opening her arms and quickly pulling Finn into a tight embrace.

His eyes drift shut, and a soft smile blooms on his face as he wraps his arms around his mother before pulling back slightly and planting a kiss on her forehead. "You saw me a few minutes ago, Momma. I just had to run and grab something from the car." His eyes flick towards mine for a moment before returning to his mother.

Most men my age would scoff at the unwanted attention from their parents, especially their mothers, but Finn seems different. Just by the look on his face, I can tell he's soaking this right up, wanting to be near his mother just as much as she wants to be near him. It should be a turnoff, causing the warning bells to alarm in my mind, but it has the opposite effect. My insides are melting. There is nothing more heartwarming than seeing a man love his mother. Not in the mommy issues kind of way, but a genuine love and adoration for the woman that gave him life kind of way.

"I know, honey."

"You don't have to worry about me so much anymore, Ma." His eyes flick to mine quickly, causing my cheeks to heat even further.

Ms. Charlotte opens her mouth to respond just as the organ begins playing, signaling the start of service. I turn my head to the front, trying desperately to focus on the minister as he welcomes all of us to service.

"I forgot to give you this," Peyton whispers before dropping a maroon cup with her bakery logo in front of my face.

"Where did that come from?" I wrap both of my hands around the cup before running my nose across the opening, breathing in the rich aroma of my life juice. "Did you hide it inside your oversized bag or something?"

"It's called a messenger bag. This isn't a video game, Mari. Your jokes about my hobbies are getting old, friend." Peyton rolls her eyes at my mention of her secret before plucking the cup from my hands.

"Aww, don't be such a sourpuss. You know I love you," I whine, grabbing the cup from her hands and taking a healthy sip. The warm liquid slides down my throat, causing me to moan softly. Suddenly, someone coughs loudly, causing Peyton to giggle.

"What did I miss?"

"If you don't want Finn to attack you in the middle of church, I'd suggest you stop moaning like that."

My cheeks are set ablaze for what seems like the millionth time today as I turn my head slightly, peeking at the end of the pew where I assume Finn is seated. His eyes are focused directly on me, now black as onyx as they travel down my body. I pull my bottom lip between my teeth to stop the moan bubbling in my throat from escaping. He was supposed to be nothing more than a one-night stand, but I can't stop the way my skin tingles in need.

"Your secret admirer came to the shop and specifically ordered it for you." Peyton nudges my shoulder, interrupting my internal musings.

"You saw him?"

"No, Katie helped him. I had no idea he was even going to be here until I saw him sitting with his parents." Peyton looks from left to right before leaning closer to my ear. "He made her promise that I wouldn't tell you where it came from."

"He did..." I catch myself from saying another word and smile at her. "Well played, my friend."

"You can't blame a girl for trying," Peyton huffs softly before dropping her head to my shoulder. "Now, pay attention before Auntie Roberta gives us both an earful for not paying attention during service."

"What did he say to you outside of the church?" Peyton mumbles, and I hand her the paper I shoved into my pocket earlier. She fumbles with the paper, trying to open it, but I grasp her hand. I doubt there's anything private on that note, but a part of me doesn't want to know what it says.

"There's something going on between you two. Don't let your fear stop you from finding happiness."

I nod my head before shoving the piece of paper back into my pocket and turning my attention toward the front of the sanctuary. My body moves on autopilot.

Having grown up going to church every Sunday and on holidays, I can sing all the hymns and recite the required passages in my sleep, something I'm very thankful for at this moment because I can't focus on anything but Finn.

I have no idea how much longer the service lasted. It could've been hours or only a matter of minutes, but as soon as it ends, I need to read this note and find Finn. Grabbing Peyton's hand, I pull her toward the end of the pew.

"Where are you two off to in such a hurry?" my mom questions, her eyebrow raised. "The Taylors and the Buckleys are coming over for lunch this afternoon."

Of course, they are. I want to have time in private with Finn to read his note and maybe give him a chance to explain, but that won't happen with both our families around. Not to mention Campbell's family.

"Don't worry, Auntie Roberta. I just need to get Marissa to sign the receipt for breakfast this morning before I forget. We'll be right over after I get the bakery closed for the day. I'll even bring some of your favorite cookies."

The promise of cookies seems to appease my mother. "Oh, that would be great." She smiles brightly at the two of us before threading her arm through my father's. "We'll see you two at the house. Lunch is at two."

With a wave of her hand, she pulls my father into the crowd and disappears from sight.

I glance at my watch and sigh in relief. "Great. Just enough time to make it home and take a shower. I'd get a nap if someone wasn't dragging me off to the bakery. I really wanted to talk to Finn before lunch."

"Of course, you're going to talk to him, and we aren't going to the bakery. I had to come up with something in order to keep your mom off your back," Peyton whispers softly, leading me by the arm toward the door. "Take all the time you need. Just keep me in the loop. I'll keep your mom busy long enough for you to have a private conversation."

"I love you, Peyway," I choke out as we find the door, and I pull my arm free.

"I love you, too. Now, let's get you to your SUV so you can have a moment to read your message." Better to get it over sooner rather than later, but the moment I step out the door, I notice Campbell's mom waving at me. She has a bright smile plastered on her face and her hand wrapped tightly around a mini Campbell.

"Oh, Marissa. I was hoping to see you before we headed to your parents' house for lunch."

"More like corner you," Peyton mumbles as I elbow her in the side and plaster a smile on my face.

"How have you been doing, Ms. Peggy?"

"Don't be so formal with me. We were practically family at one time." She throws her arm around my shoulder, pulling me in for a tight hug. "Besides, I'm making your favorite for lunch today, chicken and dumplings."

Lunch and dinner after church service are a big deal in my family, hell in the entire town of Magnolia. A way for all of us to show off our cooking prowess and fill our stomachs at the same time. My mom, Ms. Peggy, and Ms. Charlotte always cook enough food to feed an army, ensuring Peyton and I have more than enough leftovers for lunch the following day.

"I'll call you whatever you want for some of your chicken and dumplings," I respond with a smile, causing her and Peyton to laugh loudly.

Campbell's mom and I always had a great relationship. It was rocky at first because we are two very opinionated women, but once she discovered I wasn't there to steal her baby boy, things changed.

"But you know as well as I do that my mom would have a fit if she heard me calling you by your first name. You'd do the same to Campbell if he did, as well." I check my watch as I scan the crowd for Finn. Usually, I'm all for small talk after service, especially with Ms. Peggy, but right now, I want to get to my SUV.

"She's right, Mamaw. You love to yell at Daddy for speakin' like he ain't got no trainin'," a tiny voice says from beside her.

"You mean home training, darling. And yes, we always need to be on our best behavior and use our manners."

My eyes shift downward, noticing a tiny hand wrapped in hers. I assume the tiny replica of her son standing beside her must be little Ashton.

Ashton is the spitting image of his father. A head full of dark brown hair, hanging like a mop around his head that on anyone else would look ridiculous. He has hazel eyes and rosy cheeks as he gives me a tentative smile before ducking behind his grandmother.

"And you must be Ashton." I bend down to his height and hold out my hand. He looks up at his grandmother for approval before reaching out and taking mine, giving it a small shake.

"It's nice to meet you, ma'am," he responds before quickly pulling his hand away from me.

"Please don't call me that. *Ma'am* is my mom. You can call me Marissa." Ms. Peggy clears her throat loudly. "I mean *Ms.* Marissa. We don't want you getting in trouble for not acting like you have home training." I give him a wink for good measure, causing him to giggle.

"It's nice to meet you, Ms. Marissa."

"Marissa and your daddy work at the station together, Ashie Pie." Ms. Peggy smiles down warmly at him as someone new catches my eye.

My eyes widen in surprise as I watch Campbell and Finn striding toward us, their heads thrown back in laughter as Finn pats him on the back. My eyes narrow, wondering when these two became so chummy but chalk it up to coincidence. Either way, this can't lead to anything good for me. That's one thing I'm sure of.

"Those two seriously look like the stuff wet dreams are made of," Peyton mumbles beside me, both of our eyes focused on the two gorgeous men coming directly for us.

Both are probably a foot taller than me with that just-got-out-of-bed look that comes so effortlessly for men. They're both deep in conversation about Lord knows what, which gives me the perfect opportunity to ogle them both. Although, no matter how hard I try to resist, my attention is drawn back to Finn.

"There's my little man!" Campbell shouts as he comes bounding toward us, quickly wrapping his muscular arms around his little boy and lifting him into the air.

"Daddy!" Ashton squeals in glee before throwing his arms around his father's shoulders. "Is it true that you and Ms. Marissa work at the police station together?"

"It's a sheriff's department, buddy. But yes. She's teaching me the ropes," Campbell responds before pressing a kiss to the top of his mother's head.

"So cool." Ashton looks at me as if I hung the moon, causing me to blush.

"Miss me?" Finn whispers in my ear, causing me to jump slightly. His gravelly voice sends a shiver down my spine as my cheeks heat in embarrassment.

"Don't be an ass," Peyton snaps, pushing him back slightly and stepping between us. "Or did you forget that you left her without so much as a *screw you* a few weeks ago? How dare you think you can come back here and act like nothing has happened."

"What does it mean when you call someone an ass?" Ashton's tiny head cocks to the side. "Mamaw said that if you say that word, you'd get your mouth washed out with soap. I never say it, but she did. Does that mean you're going to wash her mouth out with soap, Daddy?"

"Shoot me now," I mumble, causing Finn to laugh loudly.

Campbell sighs as Ms. Peggy ducks her head in embarrassment. "I'll explain it when you're older, Ash."

"You always say that," Ashton grumbles before turning his attention to me. "Will you tell me, please?" He gives me a very practiced puppy dog look, but I raise my hands in surrender.

"Oh, don't look at me, little man. If your daddy wants you to know, he'll tell you."

"She's right. Now, who wants to grab some ice cream before we head to the Floreses' house for lunch?"

"Yes!" Ashton shouts, pumping his tiny fist in the air as Campbell lowers him to the ground. "Mamaw, let's hurry before Daddy changes his mind." He immediately grabs Ms. Peggy's hand, attempting to tug her toward the parking lot.

"I guess that's my cue. I'll see you kids at the Floreses' in a little while."

"See you later, Ms. Peggy," we respond in unison as she turns on her heels and allows little Ashton to drag her toward the car, leaving the three of us alone.

My mind races to find a viable excuse to disappear to my SUV, but Peyton beats me to it. "Slipping her a note isn't very original, Finn."

"It's okay, Peyton." My head drops down to my chest, tears pooling in my eyes. I need to stay strong, to keep these emotions locked tightly in the recesses of my soul until I can get somewhere private. "He said he wants to apologize."

"I don't care." Peyton crosses her arms over her chest, locked in a staring contest with Finn. "Some things aren't fixed so easily with an apology."

"I know," he responds, his eyes sparkling with an emotion I refuse to name as they meet mine. "I need to tell her that leaving was the hardest thing I've ever done, but I needed to. I should have explained. Made sure she understood that I was coming back for her. That I'd never leave her."

"But you still left."

"I'm sorry, sugar," Finn responds before pulling me towards him.

I bury my nose in his chest and inhale deeply, overcome with his smell, which causes me to snuggle deeper into his chest, wrapping my arms around his waist as a sense of feeling safe and protected washes over me, as if Finn and I are the only two people in the world.

Wait, what?

I step out of his arms, putting distance between us once again. Hurt flashes in Finn's eyes before he drops his arms, shoving them into his pocket. "Please give me a chance to explain. If you still want me gone, I'll leave you alone. But I'm not leaving. I'll be waiting for you." He leans forward and plants a kiss on my forehead. "See you later, Marissa."

"See you," I mumble, even more confused by his

words than I was before. Finn smirks as I stride in the opposite direction, needing to put some distance between Finn and me.

"You know your SUV is that way, right?" Peyton questions as she catches up to me, threading her arm through mine.

"Yes, I know," I respond, trying to focus on anything else but the warring emotions in my heart. We walk in silence for a few minutes before I speak again. "What in the actual fuck just happened?"

"Your guess is as good as mine. But one thing I'm certain of is that man loves you."

"I wouldn't be so sure of that."

"I would stake my life and bakery on it," she says seriously. "I have a feeling he came to service today to make sure you knew he was back in town and to deliver that message to you."

"I'm so confused, Peyton. A part of me wants to tell him to fuck off and never speak to me again, and another part wants to beg him to stay."

"Yeah, love will do that to you." Peyton sighs. "But have you ever thought that you could have both?"

"Cuss him out and tell him how desperately I'm in love with him?"

"Yup." Peyton pops the P, similar to how I did to her earlier. "You can be angry at him for leaving, but that doesn't change the fact that you love each other."

"Why do you say he loves me, too?"

"It's written all over his face. Trust me, I know a thing

or two about being in love." Her mouth pulls up at the corner as she wraps her arm around my shoulder, pulling me into her side.

My entire body sags into her as I'm reminded of similar times. The two of us against the world. We were content to be each other's support, a shoulder to cry on, and a hetero life mate. That was all before I saw Finn again.

As if on cue, my stomach rumbles loudly, and we both laugh loudly. "Sorry, I'm keeping you from lunch. I know how much you love Momma's fried chicken."

"I've been dreaming about Auntie Roberta's fried chicken ever since church let out. I wouldn't mind having some leftovers for tomorrow."

"You know as well as I do my mom loves feeding people."

"All you have to do is bat your long eyelashes, and she'll give you anything you want. Hell, I'm sure she'll even cook it for you." We both giggle before stopping in front of another bench and taking a seat.

"Are you going to read the note?"

"Yes. No. I don't know. Ummm..." My voice trails off, not knowing the right way to answer that question. "Well, what about you? I thought you hated Campbell's guts, but your reaction to him earlier would say otherwise."

"He's hot and has a sexy-ass voice, but that's it."

I stop and turn toward my best friend. "That's it?" I question. My eyes lock with hers, searching for any hint that she might be lying, but she refuses to look at me. A telltale sign that she's lying through her teeth. "I'll let you off the hook this time, but just think about it. There's no rule that says you aren't allowed to date him. I gave you my permission, after all."

"Sure. I'll get right on that, right after you tell Finn how much you love him and y'all live happily ever after."

"We're not talking about me."

"Oh, yes, we were before you quickly changed the subject." Peyton threads her arm through mine again as we continue walking. "You need to at least read the note he gave you and hear what he has to say."

"You don't understand. There is no way I can survive if he leaves me again," I grumble, a single tear sliding down my cheek.

"Then you just have to make sure he stays." Peyton wraps her hand around mine and gives it a squeeze. "I know you're scared of being hurt. But you'll never learn to fly if you don't leap. You are the most loving person I know. You have a huge heart and so much love to give."

I open my mouth to respond but snap it shut. I'm not entirely sure what's going to happen between Finn and me, but the one thing I know is that I need to read that note.

twenty-nine
marissa

"How's my favorite sheriff's officer doing today?" my mom chirps as soon as we walk in the door, strolling past on her way to the dining room table with a huge plate piled high with fried chicken.

Peyton and I took our time coming back to my parents' house. We didn't talk, just walked around in silence, giving me time to think about everything that my momma and Peyton have said to me about Finn. No one expects to fall in love at first sight. This isn't a fairytale where the prince swoops in and gives the princess the life she always imagined. This is real life, where I have people counting on me, too. I have responsibilities to fulfill to my parents, to the townspeople of Magnolia, and to myself. But somewhere down the line, all those things became shackles, holding me here instead of being the dreams I was striving toward.

It wasn't until Finn left me two weeks ago that I realized that no matter how much I love Magnolia, dreams can change. I love Finn. I honestly don't care where we live, as long as we're together. We can be here, in Houston, or in Boise, Idaho. If we're together, that's what matters most to me. But how can I ask him to give up his life and take a chance on our love?

He's spent every day marking my heart, branding my skin, wanting to show everyone who I belong to. This type of caveman behavior should be a turnoff, but knowing he wants me in such a primal way leaves me wanting more. I haven't said the words, but I need to make my feelings for him known.

"I'm doing great," Campbell responds as he reaches for a piece of chicken.

"Where did you even come from?" I question as he pushes by me, pressing a kiss to the side of my ma's head.

"The kitchen," he responds quickly as my mom smacks his hand while somehow managing to keep the large plate balanced in her hand.

"I wasn't talking to you, Campbell," she snaps. "I know you haven't been over in years, but you know the rules."

"Yes, ma'am," he mumbles. "No one eats until everyone arrives."

"That's right." She turns her face slightly, baring her cheek to Campbell. "Now, go and wash your hands. Your parents and the Buckleys should be here any minute."

"She told you." I giggle as Campbell leans down to plant a kiss on her cheek before heading toward the bathroom.

"Do you know where your sister is? She and Colt weren't at service this morning, and I'm worried."

"I have no idea, Momma. I haven't talked to her or Colt in a couple of days. I bet she wanted to sleep in."

"Oh, that girl. I'm going to put this plate down and then give her a call. Those two have had enough time alone together. It's time for them to get back into the swing of things."

"I couldn't agree more, Momma." I stifle a giggle as I reach into my pocket and shoot off a warning text to my sister. Either way, she's going to get a good scolding from Mom for missing service. Serves her right.

"Make sure you go help Peyton finish setting the table after you wash your hands, as well."

"Yes, Momma," I respond before heading down the hall toward the bathroom. I wait patiently for Campbell to finish before sliding inside and washing my hands quickly.

Once I'm finished, I head back down the hall and head right into the dining room to find Peyton. Her eyebrows are pulled down in concentration as she moves around the large oak table sitting in the center of the room, with light gray tufted dining room chairs surrounding it. Her mouth is moving as she counts the place settings before she lets out a frustrated shriek, causing me to laugh loudly.

"Laugh it up. I've been trying to make everyone fit at this table since I came inside, but no matter how hard I try, I can't make everyone fit."

"That's because this is the grown-up table." I motion my head toward the buffet table on the opposite wall piled with food. "Behind the buffet table is a large folding table. That's where we will all sit."

"You seriously have a kids' table still?" She eyes me skeptically.

"We will always have a kids' table," I respond before striding toward the buffet. "Now, help me move this so we can finish setting the tables. My mom said everyone should be here soon."

Peyton and I work together to move the buffet, careful not to send the food tumbling to the floor, and slide the table from behind it. Now that there are enough chairs for everyone, we finish in no time. Peyton takes a seat at the table, pulling out her phone.

"We should probably go make sure my mom doesn't need any more help."

Her grip tightens around her phone slightly before she flashes me a fake smile.

"You go ahead. I'll be here catching up on some emails. Just holler if you need my help."

"Are you hiding from Campbell?" I question, glancing quickly into the other room.

She opens her mouth to comment, but I raise my hand.

"It's okay. Your secret is safe with me. However, just putting it out there that Campbell is a decent guy. You should give him a chance. One date. That's all he's asking for," I respond, glancing into the other room once again.

This time, Peyton catches me.

"Finn isn't here. I checked around the kitchen before I came in here." She smirks. "When are you going to read the note he gave you?"

My body tenses with anticipation at the mere mention of his name. My cheeks heat in embarrassment as I quickly stand and head for the opposite side of the room.

"What happened to chicks before dicks?" I fidget with my hands, nervously glancing toward the kitchen.

"I always have your back, Marissa, and you know it. But sometimes you need a shove in the right direction. This is one of those times."

Now that I've made up my mind to tell Finn how I feel, my nerves are going haywire. I've barely been able to resist his charms when he's near me. What happens when I want to demand answers for his behavior? Who knows what will happen if we are alone in a room together again? Although my mind is made up, I know I'm not ready for him to get down on one knee and propose or anything, but getting married in the future isn't off the table either. He said I was it for him. I need to ensure he knows he's it for me, too.

"No need to be nervous. Go to your room and read the note. Then you can decide what to do next." She tilts her head to the side, eyeing me inquisitively.

"Maybe I don't want to know what it says."

"Excuse me?" Peyton responds, confusion written on her face. "Have we entered the twilight zone or something? You've been moping around for weeks, wondering why he left and when he was coming back. And now you don't want to hear his explanation? What changed?"

"Nothing and everything."

"You aren't making sense."

"I know." I sigh, heading toward her and taking a seat in the chair next to her at the table. "I always thought that Campbell left because I wasn't enough for him. That there was something wrong with me that drove him into Emmeline's arms."

"And I've told you a million times that wasn't the case. The best-case scenario is that he was thinking with the brain between his legs instead of the one between his ears, and that's why Emmeline ended up with your ring on her finger."

"Don't be like that, Peyton. I'm being serious. We talked, really talked, about what happened to us. Until that moment, I didn't know that I was still searching for a reason that things ended the way they did between us. Wondering if there was something wrong with me that made him change his mind so suddenly."

"And what does that have to do with you and Finn?" she huffs, crossing her arms over her chest.

"Peyton." I put a little more force into my words, and she raises her hands in surrender. "Finn loves me. I didn't drive him away. He left because he needed to. Because there was something he had to do in order for him to be ready to commit to me completely."

"Duh. Took you long enough to figure that out. I blame the cheating asshole for that."

"Campbell never cheated on me. Whatever happened after we broke up had nothing to do with our relationship ending. I fell in love with Finn after we spent a few amazing nights together. Why couldn't the same happen with the two of them?"

"You finally admitted it out loud." She gasps, tears collecting in her eyes. "I feel like my little bird is finally ready to leave the nest."

"You're so dramatic." I shake my head at her. "Maybe it's time for you to leave the nest, too. I know the perfect guy."

"No way, Marissa. He broke your heart."

"We haven't been together in years. He is a part of my past, but he can be a part of your future. All you need to do is give him a chance."

"I'm scared. What if he..." Her voice breaks. "I lost everything when Jules broke up with me. You know what I went through. There are pieces of me missing that I can never get back. What if he doesn't understand? What if I tell him and he doesn't want me anymore?"

Peyton has secrets. Secrets that she has only shared with me, and I plan on keeping it that way. Peyton lost more than just her heart when her boyfriend cheated on her, leaving her to deal with his selfish choices on her own. And she fought to keep her head above water, barely surviving each day before beginning the battle again.

"Then I'll kill him and hide the body." I wrap my arm

around her shoulder, pulling her into my side. "I doubt very much that Campbell will react that way, but if he does, he never deserved you in the first place."

There's a loud knock on the front door, causing us to jump slightly. I push back from the table to get the door, but Campbell comes striding down the hallway. He gives me a playful wink before he swings the door open, and everyone files into the house.

"You're right." Peyton raises her voice slightly over the buzz of voices around the entryway. "But I'm not doing it alone. If I'm opening myself up to heartbreak, you are, too."

The noise level rises exponentially as Ms. Charlotte slides into the room, carrying two large casserole dishes in her hands. "Where do you want these?"

"The buffet table." I motion with my hands, not once letting go of Peyton as she tries to get a handle on her emotions. "Just clear some space. If you need any spoons or anything, they're in the center drawer."

My eyes search the room, looking for any sign of Finn but come up empty.

"Did you mean what you said?" I whisper into Peyton's ear.

"What?" She sits up, her eyes locking on mine.

"If I read Finn's note, you'll go out with Campbell."

"I don't know..." Her voice trails off as a hint of fear flashes in her eyes.

But fuck that. I'm not about to let my friend close herself off to love no more than I want to go back to the way I was before spending the night with Finn. I'm scared shitless to read this letter, to know his real reason for leaving me, but if I want things to move forward with us, then I have to take the next step.

"No more games, Peyton. We both need to take a chance on something more than a quick fuck from a random stranger," I growl before planting a kiss on her forehead and pushing to my feet. "It's time to take a leap of faith."

"Do you know where I can find Finn, Ms. Charlotte?" I say loud enough for everyone in the entryway to hear.

Suddenly, everyone in the room stops talking at the same time. The silence in the room is deafening as I stand my ground.

"I always knew you two would end up together. Your mother swore you and Campbell would get back together the moment he came back to town, but I knew it," Ms. Charlotte says as she throws a wink in my direction.

"Could you imagine what their babies would look like?" someone whispers, causing my cheeks to heat as Peyton nods her head in agreement, causing me to roll my eyes.

"Right, because we've all been taking too long to give you grandbabies," I respond, hoping to gain control of the situation again.

"You're not getting any younger, my dear. Next thing you know, you'll be sitting in a big, old house with nothing but cats to keep you company," my mom says as she comes strolling into the room, carrying a large platter of rolls.

"Ms. Charlotte?" I say just a little louder in hopes that she'll answer my question.

"It's the truth. Peggy has been parading Ashton around town, gloating to all of us how amazing it is to have a tiny version of her son," my mom huffs, placing the platter in the center of the table before turning toward Finn's mom. "Are you going to answer her, Charlotte? Lunch is ready."

I wait on pins and needles as she thinks about her answer, making a show by rubbing her fingers along her chin before responding. "Did you read his note? Everything you need to know is in there. Or at least, that's what he told me."

"Thank goodness. Now it's time for us to eat. I don't know about you, but I'm starving." Campbell smirks as he strolls into the room, his hand wrapped tightly around little Ashton's.

"Now it's your turn." I bump Peyton's shoulder with mine as her eyes follow Campbell through the room before he takes a seat directly across from her. "Maybe after lunch." She ducks her head, allowing her hair to fall forward, covering her face.

"Coward," I mumble, completely overwhelmed by everything that took place in the last few minutes. "Sorry, Momma. I'm going to have to miss lunch today."

"It's okay, sweetheart. I understand. But just know,

I'll be expecting those grandbabies sooner rather than later."

"No problem, Momma." I giggle before rising to my feet and heading upstairs to my childhood bedroom.

I'd love to have a few minutes to process what just happened, but I need to read Finn's note before I can do anything else. Lunch is now in full swing downstairs. The sounds of plates being passed as everyone makes small talk about their plans for the week and the latest gossip filter up the stairs. But I don't hear most of it. My mind is still reeling from what I'm about to do.

I take a seat on the edge of my bed, pulling the note out of my pocket. My hands shake as I open it. *What the fuck is this?* I flip the paper over a few times, searching for more of a message, but the paper is empty except for one phrase. "*Home is where the heart is,*" I whisper into the room, trying to make sense of his creepy message.

What does that even mean? My parents' house? His parents' house? Tallywackers? All of these places could be considered home for either of us, but I have a feeling this isn't what he's talking about.

"Of course, he's going to make me work for it." I shake my head, the irony not lost on me. I've made him work for every piece of my heart. Slowly breaking down the walls around my heart, drawing me gently out of my shell. He started slowly, sending me text messages, lunch on the days I had work, and the most adorable notes.

He wanted to make sure that everyone important to me knew his intentions. He even went as far as to ask my momma things about me that I wasn't ready to share, but I still resisted the pull I felt toward him, allowing my fear of being rejected to rule my decisions.

I used to believe that going on a date with Finn could finally convince him we weren't compatible outside of the bedroom and that there can be nothing else between us. Then neither of us would have to wonder what could have been. But instead, it was the exact opposite.

But where is he?

I flop back onto my bed and stare at the ceiling, running every conversation we've ever had through my head before it hits me. *Home.* The only place where we both envision spending the rest of our lives together. The old farmhouse.

"Time to make all my dreams come true," I say into the empty room before pushing off the bed and heading into the bathroom.

I shower quickly, shaving and buffing all the important areas before giving my hair a fluff and getting dressed. I slide the note he gave me into my pocket before doing one final check in the mirror, then I head for the door.

I rush out of my room and down the stairs, praying that everyone is still in the dining room enjoying their lunch. I don't have time for small talk.

"Please don't let me miss him," I pray into the hallway as I inch closer to the front door before coming to a screeching halt. Peyton and I walked here. I have no idea where my SUV is or how the hell I'm going to get out of here. My parents' car is blocked in the driveway. I could walk, but how long is he really going to wait for me to get there?

My heart pounds in my chest, blood rushing through my ears. My vision blurs as if I'm viewing the world through another lens. I'm panicking. I know it, and I'm powerless to stop my mind from running through all the ways things could go wrong if I don't get to Finn as quickly as possible.

Just as I'm about to spiral further, I feel someone brush against my arm, gripping it tightly and bringing my mind back to the present. I take a deep breath in, my eyes focusing on Ms. Charlotte standing in front of me.

"I was worried I was going to have to come upstairs and drag you to that house," Ms. Charlotte scolds as she places a set of keys in my hand. "Take my car."

"Thank you. For everything," I tell her, wrapping my arms around her.

"Don't hurt him, or you'll have to deal with me."

"I won't." I quickly release her and rush out the front door and hop into her waiting vehicle.

The drive seems as if it takes forever, but it probably doesn't take longer than a few minutes before the twinkling lights in the trees come into view, shining brightly against the Cumberland Mountains skyline.

I barely get the car into park before I'm climbing out and running toward the house.

Tears blur my vision as I rush toward the front door,

wanting nothing more than to see Finn again and tell him how much I love him.

I come to a dead stop a few feet from the front door to catch my breath, my hands shaking as I reach for the door. Suddenly, it swings open, and I see Finn. A bright smile spreads across my face, eyes locked on him and taking in his every feature. His dark hair is tousled perfectly and swaying in the breeze, and my hand itches to run through it.

"You're here," I whisper, coming to a stop a few steps away from him.

A mixture of fear and joy fills me as I worry I'm too late. His eyes snap to mine, scanning down my body before a blinding smile spreads across his face as he drops a set of keys from his hand.

"Welcome home."

"You bought it," I say reverently as I stare into the house.

"Of course, I did. This is the house where we planned to grow old." His arm snakes around my waist as he pulls me into the house, kicking the door shut. "It was worse off than I thought, but I managed to hire a contractor to do some basic work to bring it into this century. It's still a work in progress, but I couldn't make all the decisions without your input."

"How did you manage to get all of this done in two weeks?" Tears trickle down my face as I say the first thing that comes to mind.

"Lots of money." He chuckles, burying his nose in my neck and inhaling deeply.

"I messed up, sugar. I was so worried about scaring you away that I made it worse. I knew from the first moment I saw you again after all those years that I wanted to spend the rest of my life with you."

"But you never once called me or even said goodbye. I thought you were never coming back."

"Oh, you silly woman. I never intended to go back to Texas permanently. I had to sell my place and ship some bigger items to Magnolia, but that was it. My home is where you are."

"Can we have a do-over?" I ask as he plants gentle kisses up my neck before pulling my ear between his teeth and biting down softly.

"A do-over?"

"Yes. I know I messed up and pushed you away, but I was scared of being hurt again. I didn't trust you to catch me if I fell or to love me, flaws and all. But I realized something while you were away."

"What's that?"

"I've lived in Magnolia my whole life, searching for the happiness that I lost when I had my heart broken in high school, but I always knew there was something missing." I wrap my arms around his neck. "You."

I hold my breath, waiting for him to reject me like I imagined he would. But instead, he pulls me tightly into his chest, pressing a gentle kiss to the top of my head.

"It feels like I've been waiting my entire life for you to say that," he says as he lowers me to the ground and reaches into his pocket. My hand flies up to my mouth as I notice the black box he's pulling out of his pocket.

"Breathe, sugar." He chuckles as I release the breath I didn't even know I was holding. "This isn't a wedding ring."

"Don't you want to marry me?"

"More than anything in this world, but you said it yourself: You don't trust me." He places his finger to my mouth before I can say a word. "You're getting there, but you don't completely trust me, and I understand that. This ring is a symbol of the promise I'm about to make to you. I promise to love you until the day I die. To do everything in my power to make you happy. To be the person you can come to when you're having problems. And I promise to be the rock that keeps you grounded."

Lifting my chin, he leans down and brushes his lips against mine, and I moan in response. "Do you accept this promise?"

"Yes," I whisper, leaning into his palm as he caresses the side of my face.

We both smile before he lifts me off the ground, molding his lips to mine. This kiss is everything. All our pain and love wrapped together in one.

"I'm so sorry, Finn."

He growls before biting my lip. "There is nothing for you to apologize for, my love."

Then he captures my lips again in a searing kiss.

We had an unconventional beginning, but somehow, we found our way to each other. Finn and I will go through our ups and downs as we try to find our footing with each other once again, but there is one thing I know for certain: Sometimes, love is all you need.

epilogue
finn
two years later

"Welcome to My Soul to Bake!" A young girl flashes me a bright smile as I walk into the best bakery in town. I mean, it's also the only one, but people come from three towns over just to get their sweet fix.

I give the girl a curt nod before focusing all my attention on Peyton, who is standing behind the counter, helping a customer.

"Maybe this wasn't such a good idea," I mumble to myself, my nerves getting the best of me, but the only way to make this happen is with Peyton's help.

I wouldn't say Peyton and I are friends, but she at least tolerates me. Although it didn't take much to get Marissa to forgive me for leaving without a goodbye, Peyton was another story completely. But I think I'm starting to win her over since I make her friend ridiculously happy, but man, that girl can hold a mean grudge.

"Thank you, hun," the woman standing in front of me says softly before turning and placing her order on the counter beside her and reaching into her purse.

"You know your money's no good here. Besides, I'll just make Marissa pay for everything."

Marissa. Just the mention of her name causes my heart to swell to twice its size. Even after two years, I still want to pinch myself to ensure that my life with Marissa isn't just a dream. We've had our ups and downs, just like any other couple, but I wouldn't trade it for anything in the world. We go on dates and spend lazy Sundays snuggled on the porch swing on our front porch. The promise I made to her in front of our home still rings true. I've spent every day trying to show her with my actions that she's the most important person in my life as she slowly opened her heart to me, allowing me to get behind her walls. But there is only one more thing I want to give her to make my life complete: my last name. And I'm prepared to do anything I can to make that happen. Marissa has been leery about taking the next step in our relationship, which is understandable, but I think my girl needs a little push in the right direction. I just hope it doesn't completely blow up in my face.

"Good morning, Finn. Today's the big day?" Ms. Roberta flashes me a bright smile as Peyton narrows her eyes in my direction.

"Big day for what? What the heck is going on?"

"Don't worry, dear. I'm sure Finn will explain everything." Ms. Roberta raises her cheek in my direction. "I'll see you two at the church in a few."

"The church? Why are you going to the church? It's not even Sunday." Peyton's head swivels back and forth, trying to make sense of Ms. Roberta's cryptic words, but it's no use.

"I'll see you soon." I lean down, planting a soft kiss on Ms. Roberta's upturned cheek before wrapping my arms around her tiny frame and bringing her in for a hug. "Thanks for everything, Ms. Roberta."

"None of that, Finn. Call me Mom," she responds as she grabs her order off the counter, smiling softly at me.

"Okay, now I'm really confused," Peyton chimes in from her place behind the counter. "You really need to explain to me what's going on or I'm calling Marissa."

"Oh, calling out the big guns this time," I respond quickly, chuckling softly. "Finish up what you're doing, Peyton, and meet me at the table in the corner. I'll explain everything."

"Thanks so much for coming in, Auntie Roberta," Peyton tells her with a smile before her eyes flick to mine. "I'll grab Alicia from the back to take over the register, and I'll be right over."

I nod my head, turning on my heels and heading toward a quiet table in the corner. Once I take a seat, my hand slides into my pocket, grasping the promise ring I stole off Marissa's nightstand yesterday afternoon before she left for work. She even went as far as to call her mother, sister, and best friend to see if, by some miracle, she had left it at their house, with no luck. She was devastated, thinking that she had lost it somewhere, but what she doesn't know can't hurt her. It might hurt me, but I'm hoping when I get down on one knee and ask her to marry me, she'll completely forget that I took it.

I asked Marissa's parents for her hand, made sure that Colt could spare her at the station for a few days, and had Sutton and Ms. Roberta pick out the perfect dress for her, but I still have one more person to help ensure my plan goes off without a hitch. I should've told Peyton weeks ago when I started planning to hold a secret wedding for my girl at the church in town, but not only is she the closest person to my girl, but she can't keep a secret to save her soul.

I don't sit there for long before Peyton takes a seat in front of me. "What the fuck is going on, Finn Buckley?"

"I need you to keep an open mind and not say anything until I finish talking. Can you do that?"

"I make no promises. Now, talk," she deadpans, leaning back in her chair and crossing her arms over her chest.

"I guess that's the best I can ask for." I chuckle lightly. "You remember the promise ring I gave Marissa, right? I want to..." My voice trails off, wondering if springing this on Peyton at the last minute was the best idea.

"Ask her to marry you, and you need my help to plan it?" Her eyes sparkle with mischief. "I've been waiting for you to grow a set and make an honest woman out of her, but that doesn't explain why you're going to the church."

"Yeah, but there's more." My shoulders tense as my eyes lock with hers. This could go exceptionally well or horribly wrong, but either way, I'm going to be married to her best friend before the end of today. Finding my resolve, I decide to just rip off the Band-Aid and tell her. "Marissa and I are getting married in two hours at the church, and I need you to come with me so I can tell her, and you can be there to help her get ready 'cause I assumed you'd be her maid of honor."

Peyton's eyes widen in surprise as her mouth opens and closes.

"I see you're at a loss for words. That doesn't happen very often."

"This isn't a joking matter, Finn," Peyton deadpans, tears welling in her eyes.

Fuck. This is not how I had expected this to go. Sure, I knew she'd be sad that I didn't include her in the planning, but I didn't plan on her being this upset. I can't stand it when women cry. It breaks my heart. And it's even worse when I know deep down that I'm the cause of her tears.

"Come on, Peyway. Don't cry."

"Don't fucking call me that. Only Marissa can get away with calling me that." Peyton wails as she drops her head in her hand. Muffled sobs reach my ears as I push to my feet, coming to her side of the table.

"I didn't mean to not include you in the planning, but you can't keep a secret to save your soul." I drop to one knee, awkwardly running my hand along her back as patrons turn in our direction. "Please stop crying, Peyton."

"I'm not crying because I'm mad." She sniffs, grabbing a few napkins from the dispenser and blowing her nose loudly. "I'm so fucking excited for the two of you!" she shouts, throwing her arms around my neck, causing me to lose my balance.

"Thanks, Peyton. I was worried there for a minute." My shoulders sag in relief as I place Peyton back into her chair and push to my feet. "So, you in?"

"Am I in? Are you kidding me? Let's go!" Peyton squeals in delight as a large hand covers her mouth.

"I take it you told her?" Campbell smiles down at Peyton as she tilts her head upward and scowls at him.

Everyone in town has been taking bets on when these two will pull their heads out of their asses and give each other a chance. The love-hate relationship they have with each other seems to be more for show than anything because anyone can see the chemistry between them. I know Campbell just got divorced, but he does nothing to hide the way he feels about Peyton. I just hope she'll find it in her heart to give him a chance. He isn't my favorite person in the world, but everyone deserves a chance to be happy with the person they love.

"Yes. But she hasn't said yes to being Marissa's maid of honor yet," I respond, shaking my head at their antics.

"I'd say by the noises coming out of her mouth that she agrees...." His voice trails off as he pulls his hand away from Peyton's mouth, a look of disgust on his face. "Did you just lick me? What are we, five?"

"I couldn't answer him with my mouth clamped shut." She sticks her tongue out at him before turning her attention toward me. "Yes, I'll be her maid of honor. It would be my pleasure. But don't think you're off the hook for not telling me sooner," Peyton growls before pushing past Campbell and heading back behind the counter.

"Good." I smile before turning my attention toward Campbell. "What are you even doing here? Didn't you work with Marissa last night?"

"I did. I dropped her at the church and told her I was coming to get coffee," he responds, his eyes focused on Peyton as she pours one cup of black coffee and fills the other two with way too much cream and sugar before adding coffee.

"Good thinking." I grab the first cup off the counter and take a sip.

"Damn. You want some coffee with your cream and sugar?" Campbell chuckles, leaning against the counter.

"Don't knock the coffee or you don't get any," Peyton snaps before holding her hand out for my credit card.

"Fair enough," he responds as he reaches for one of the remaining cups on the counter. "But I like mine black."

Peyton slaps him hard on the hand. "Well, since these aren't for you, I don't have to worry about it."

"And I'm not paying for your coffee." I chuckle, reaching into my back pocket, pulling out my wallet, and grabbing my card before placing it in her hand.

"But you don't need any more sweetness, Peyton.

You're sweet enough as is." He winks at her as she pours another cup of black coffee and hands it to him.

"Flattery will get you everywhere." She giggles before turning her attention to the girl who welcomed me in earlier. "Katie, can you ring this asshole up? I need to get to the church and get my bestie married."

"Ouch." Campbell grips at his chest, stumbling backward slightly. "And things were going so well."

"In your dreams, Campbell," Peyton responds before quickly stepping around the counter and heading for the door.

"She'll let her guard down around you, eventually."

"Remember, Rome wasn't built overnight, you know. I'll win Peyton over to my side in no time. Besides, I have a secret weapon."

"And what's that?"

"An adorable seven-year-old son that no one can say no to, not even me."

"Man, do you have it bad," I mumble loud enough for Campbell to hear, causing him to chuckle.

"Never claimed I didn't." He claps me hard on the back before motioning toward the door with his head. "You better get going, man, before she ruins everything. I'll see you in a few hours."

I give him a mock salute before rushing out the door after Peyton. I catch up to her quickly, and we walk in silence for a few moments, enjoying the warm breeze and smell of fresh flowers blooming in the town square before she breaks the silence.

"And I know how to keep a secret. I didn't tell you…" Peyton steps in front of me, blocking my path.

"Tell me what?" I groan as I try to move around her, but it's no use.

I won't lie. It stings a little that she knows something that Marissa isn't telling me, but if she is keeping a secret, it's for a good reason.

"Nothing, it's a secret." Peyton huffs before turning on her heels and heading the rest of the way down the path toward the church. "Why did you want to get married all of a sudden, anyway?" Peyton asks, not bothering to look at me.

"Because I can't imagine waking up tomorrow morning and not having her there."

"But you don't have to get married to do that. You live together. You own a house. What is a piece of paper going to do to change that?"

I open and close my mouth a few times, trying to find the right words to explain my need for Marissa to have my last name and not sound like a possessive asshole, but I can't.

"I want her to have my last name. I want her to wear my ring on her finger."

"She already has a ring from you."

"Thanks for pointing out the obvious," I respond, downing the last of my coffee and chucking it into a nearby trash can. "But this time, it's different. When I gave her this ring the first time, it was me making a promise to her. Now I want it to symbolize our promise to each other," I respond, answering her as honestly as I can right now.

When I gave Marissa that ring, I promised to never leave her, but when I put this ring on her finger later today, I want it to mean something more. I want it to show the world that we have promised to love and cherish each other for the rest of our lives. I know it won't change anything in our relationship, but there's something about her having my last name that seems more solid. Something that will bind us together in every way possible, in both life and death.

"Okay, that's romantic as hell." Peyton sighs loudly. "I was a little worried about her and you two getting back together after what happened, but you've made her whole again."

"I will spend every day for the rest of my life striving to be the man she deserves," I mumble softly.

"You've put a sparkle in my friend's eye I've never seen before. The way she brightens when you walk into a room or at the mere mention of your name..."

Peyton steps in front of me, cocking her said to the side. "I was worried that would never happen for her."

We stare at each other in silence. Her eyes fill with sadness before it quickly disappears. Peyton always seems to be so happy and positive, going out of her way to make the people around her smile, but there's always been pain lurking behind her bright smile. She's been through a lot in her life, but she deserves to be happy just as much as anyone.

"It will happen for you, too," I respond, throwing my arm over her shoulder and pulling her to my side for a one-armed hug.

"If you break her heart, I'll kill you." She steps out of my embrace and stabs her finger into my chest. "And I can promise they'll never find your body. I don't binge-watch true crime documentaries for the fun of it."

With that, Peyton spins on her heels and tosses her empty cup into the trash, making a beeline for the church. I follow behind her quietly the last few blocks, coming to a stop across from the church. As I stride across the street, it's as if the crowds part, revealing the object of my affection. She turns toward us, her arms waving wildly above her head before locking eyes with me.

I love you, I mouth, blowing her a kiss.

She jumps in the air, pretending to catch it before bringing it to her lips and heading for the stairs.

"Could you two be any more disgusting?" Peyton whispers as Marissa strides toward us.

"You're just jealous," I respond, not taking my eyes off Marissa as she makes her way toward me, coming to a stop right in front of us.

"Hey, you. I missed you." Marissa bites her bottom lip, stifling a giggle. Unable to resist, I lean down and brush a kiss on her luscious lips, nibbling on her bottom lip before pulling it between my own. I lose myself in this kiss. Nothing else in the world matters as I pull her body against mine, my need for her rising with every passing moment.

She moans softly as I bring my other hand up to cradle her cheek, and someone clears their throat loudly, breaking the spell.

"Get a room, you two." Peyton giggles as I drop to one knee, pulling her promise ring out of my pocket, the diamonds sparkling in the light.

"You found it!" she shouts, reaching to pluck it out of my hand, but I pull it back, shaking my head no. "Why can't I have my ring?"

"I gave this ring to you to signify my promise to you when I came back to Magnolia, but now, I want it to symbolize a new chapter in our lives. Marissa, will you marry me today?"

"Yes," she whispers, plucking the ring from between my fingers and sliding it onto her finger. "Wait. Did you say *today*?"

"Yeah, about that. I didn't want to wait too long after you agreed to marry me. So, I arranged our wedding for today in the church."

"Is that why Campbell told me to stay here? And Sutton and my mom appeared out of nowhere while I was waiting?"

"Yup. And I brought Peyton with me because she can't keep a secret, so I didn't tell her till the last minute. Everyone is inside, waiting for us to come in and get ready. The rest of our guests should be here in a couple of hours to celebrate with us."

"I can, too, keep a secret. I didn't tell you about the baby," Peyton says, but quickly clasps her hands over her mouth.

"Baby?" I lean back, pulling Marissa's body away from mine and checking her stomach before my eyes flick back to hers.

"I took a test this morning." She narrows her eyes at Peyton over my shoulder before continuing. "I was going to tell you when we were alone, but now is as good a time as any."

"I told you that you couldn't keep a secret," I say to Peyton as we all laugh.

"Thank you, Finn. For loving me so much."

Tears stream down her cheeks as she cups my face in her small hands and brushes her lips against mine.

"The pleasure is all mine."

the end

Want to know what happened between Sutton, Colt, and Maxwell (never Max)? Turn the page to read *The One I Couldn't Forget*!

the one I couldn't forget

usa today bestselling author

aj alexander

one

Sutton

How the fuck did this happen? I swipe at the tears streaming down my cheeks for the millionth time since I left Knoxville. I always thought that when I returned home to Magnolia, it'd be different from when I left. I was the overweight bookworm, the butt of everyone's jokes, and the last person anyone believed would amount to anything. But the joke was on them. I left Magnolia with nothing but two suitcases and big dreams, swearing to anyone who would listen that when I returned, I'd be famous. How very *Sweet Home Alabama* of me, right? The whole idea was laughable, but I was naïve and truly believed that someone would eventually reward my hard work, and mostly, it has been rewarding, but then there are times like this when I question everything.

While I was in school, I became more confident in my appearance and in myself. It was there that I learned everyone isn't the same and that it's the people who stand out that are memorable. I learned to love myself and became even more comfortable in my skin. After graduating from The Art Institute in Nashville, my newfound confidence helped me create a clothing brand instead of joining a larger company. I'd be lying if I said it was easy. I worked long days and even longer nights, but by chance, Nicole Kidman's stylist fell in love with a dress that I made and took it to her, and the rest was history. My small brand became a household name, launching my career to the next level.

It was around that time when I met Maxwell—never Max, always Maxwell. Red flag number one. He was charismatic and drop-dead gorgeous, and his smile made my heart skip a beat. A man like Maxwell had never given me the time of day when I was younger. Red flag number two. I fell instantly and hard for him. Hell, what woman wouldn't? We spent every day for the next year and a half together before he proposed to me at his parents' beach house in the Hamptons a few months ago. Red flag number three. My life was perfect, everything I could've wished for. I had a gorgeous fiancé and an amazing job, and we had plans to build a home together. He even let me purchase the expensive 800-thread-count Egyptian cotton sheets I've been eyeing for years. It was more than I ever could've imagined for myself, and I was right.

A strangled sob bubbles out of my throat as images of my fiancé and his secretary in the throes of passion on my brand-new sheets filter through my mind. I should've said something, given him a piece of my mind. Ripped her fake blonde extensions out of her head for ruining the perfect life I'd built for myself, but I did nothing. Instead,

I turned tail and ran right to my car and pointed it toward the last place he'd come looking for me, Magnolia. That's even if he comes looking for me at all.

Fuck, what am I going to tell my parents?

I should pull over to the side of the road and call them, especially since I haven't seen them in years. I've offered to have them come to Nashville to see me, to be a part of the life I built for myself and what I thought I was building with Maxwell, but they refused. My parents have always lived a simple life. They both grew up in Magnolia, only leaving once for an overnight trip to attend my graduation, and they're happy. They've never once pressured me to be anything other than happy, which I thought I was... until this morning.

Suddenly, my car sputters loudly as all the lights on the dashboard light up. The steering wheel shudders as I try to guide my car toward the right side of the road, my muscles straining at the effort it takes for me to move the wheel. I slam my foot down, alternating between the brake and the gas, but it is no use. The car basically has a mind of its own, and right now, it wants to do anything but drift to the side of the road.

"Great, this is the last thing I need right now!" My voice echoes around the interior as I continue to struggle with the car before it finally comes to a stop with one wheel hanging off the road, hovering over a ditch, and the entire car teetering on the edge.

Fuck. Shit. God damn it. How in the hell am I going to get out of this?

The entire dashboard lights up like a Christmas tree as I frantically turn the key, the engine sputtering loudly but never coming to life. A fresh wave of tears streams down my cheeks as I frantically try to get my car going. Wanting nothing more than to have my mother's arms wrapped around me, telling me everything is going to be okay.

Why me? Why can't I catch a break?

I take a deep breath, trying to calm my emotions so I can think of what to do next. Scanning my surroundings, I notice a few key landmarks from my childhood. I'm a few miles from my parents' house—not an insane distance to walk, but I'm wearing nothing but a thin tank top, black yoga pants, and the first pair of shoes I could grab on my way out the door. I look down, sending up a silent prayer of thanks that I at least match before looking at the seat beside me.

Where the fuck is my bag?

Unbuckling my seatbelt, I lean to the right and search the floor with my hand. I pat around on the floor, looking for any sign of my things but come up empty. I left my dream home with nothing but the clothes on my back, shoes, and my keys. I don't have my wallet or even my cellphone to call for help.

I drop my head onto the steering wheel as all the emotions I've been trying desperately to keep in check come bubbling to the surface. "What the hell do I do now?" I ask no one as my heart constricts.

All I wanted was to get away from everything going

on with Maxwell, to have time to think through what I saw in our bed. To process all these feelings running through my body in peace, surrounded by people that love me, before deciding what my future was going to look like. But instead, I'm stuck here on the side of the road. Alone.

Tears pour down my cheeks as the weight of my feelings hits me. My heart feels as if it's breaking in two. I want nothing more than to go back to the way things were this morning. When my life was perfect. Instead of leaving, I'd demand answers from Maxwell. He'd explain everything was just a simple misunderstanding. He'd tell me how he loved me more than his own life and would never do anything like this again if I forgave him. But this is the real world. Maxwell cheated on me. His fiancée. The woman he declared to the world was the other half of his soul. And there's no doubt in my mind he'd do it again.

My only saving grace is that we aren't married yet. We've just begun combining our lives, so it won't take long to separate the few things we purchased together. He can keep the sheets, that's for damn sure. I'd like to say that there were signs that Maxwell was cheating on me, but that'd be a lie. I was blissfully unaware of his wandering eye until I walked in on him fucking some other woman on my dream sheets.

Searing pain flows through my entire body as waves of agony try to pull me under. I'm being torn into two different pieces, my soul breaking into two separate halves. One half is indescribably happy to have escaped a life with a lying, cheating sack of shit like Maxwell, and maybe still a little bit in disbelief that this happened at all. The other half is a writhing mass of pain, stealing my ability to take a breath at the loss of the life I'd planned for myself, yearning for the numbness to cut me off from all these feelings that I'm so desperate to forget.

My eyes fly open as red-and-blue light shines in my rearview mirror. No. No. No. My hands grip the steering wheel tightly. This could be one of two people, neither of whom I want to deal with right now.

Living in a small town like Magnolia has its perks. Lower crime rates and little to no traffic, but it also has its downfalls. Like the strong possibility that the person you spent most of your childhood wishing would give you the time of day will show up when you're at your lowest.

"Please. Anyone but him, please," I whisper, praying that anyone but him is coming to my rescue.

My heart rate picks up as tiny droplets of sweat form on my forehead. Damn, I'm getting flustered just thinking about him. You'd think after all these years, I'd have gotten over my childhood crush, but there has always been something about Colt that called to me. Whenever I talked to my parents, I found some way to ask about what he was doing or who he was dating. It's how I found out he was elected the town sheriff earlier this year.

Hell, at this point, I'd rather it be my sister, Marissa, coming to my rescue. Anyone else but Colt. But I soon realized I had no such luck. Colt Butler has always been, and probably always will be, my own personal Adonis. His large frame unfolds itself from inside the dark-colored SUV as he comes strolling toward me, with his chiseled jawline and his hair with that just-got-out-of-bed look. A leather jacket zipped halfway, accentuating his bulging muscles, and a shiny gold badge attached to his chest was a dead giveaway.

"Is everything alright?"

two

cott

I'm heading toward the edge of town when I notice a car pulled over on the side of the road. Nothing too out of the ordinary for this stretch of road, but this is the last thing I want to deal with after the last few days—hell, the last few months.

Reaching down, I flick on my lights as I spin my cruiser around and pull up behind a late-2000s pale-blue Volkswagen with a few worn-out bumper stickers on the back. A sense of déjà vu settles over me, causing me to pause.

Where have I seen this car before?

Magnolia is a small town, so it isn't unlikely that I've seen the car at some point, but it's not ringing any bells. With a shake of my head, I push those thoughts to the back of my mind and climb out of the car.

"Is everything alright?" I mumble, scanning the surroundings for any reason this car may be sitting on the side of the road.

"About that..."

My eyes snap towards the voice, coming face to face

with a pair of tear-filled, sultry brown eyes I'd thought I'd never see again.

Sutton Flores. The one that got away. The woman I've never been able to forget about, even after all these years. She's owned my heart ever since the first time I saw her across the room. I remember that day as if it were yesterday. Her long, dark hair was pulled up into a bun at the top of her head, black-rimmed glasses resting on the bridge of her nose, which was stuck in a book, the same way she was almost every day. Alone, hiding out in her world of make-believe, and the opposite of how I was in high school.

Ever since I laid eyes on her, I've wanted her. No, want isn't a strong enough word to describe the way I feel about Sutton. I want to claim her, possess her, in a way that's unhealthy. But most of all, I want to call her mine.

"Is everything alright?" I repeat, my mind working on autopilot as I attempt to process the fact that Sutton is sitting in front of me.

"Nope. Not even a little bit." She sobs, her head dropping into her hands as her shoulders shake.

"I'll be right back." I turn on my heels and storm back toward my SUV.

I've never been able to deal with a woman in tears, but hearing Sutton's sobs sends a rage, unlike anything I've ever felt before, coursing through me. I want to find whoever did this and make them pay for hurting her. But I have to find out what happened first.

I should call this in and bring Sutton to the station,

but that's the last thing I want to do. Going to the station means more questions that I'm not sure I want the answer to. But also, a sick part of me can't stop thinking about what she'd look like handcuffed and completely at my mercy.

Reaching into the window of the cruiser, I grab the radio and call the only person who may have answers for me. My grip tightens as Sutton climbs out of her car and leans against the driver's side door. Our eyes lock as a soft smile spreads across her face. She's just as gorgeous as ever—curves in all the right places, chocolate-colored hair I can't stop imagining wrapped tightly around my hand as I pound into her from behind. The soft glow of the setting sun accentuates her beauty as my eyes make their way down her body, cataloging every detail and filing it away for later use. She may belong to someone else, but Sutton will always be the star of all my fantasies.

"Good evening to you too, Sheriff Grumpy Pants." Marissa's voice tinkles across the line, raising my annoyance to a new level.

Marissa and a few of the other deputies have taken to calling me that ridiculous name since she announced Sutton was getting married to some tool bag a few months ago. Everyone in town has known my feelings for Sutton since we were kids—well, everyone except Sutton. I had finally gotten the nerve to ask her out the day she announced she was heading to Nashville to pursue a career in fashion, taking my heart right along with her.

"How many times have I told you to stop calling me

that?" I growl, reaching down to adjust my cock in my pants.

"Probably a million, but you know I'm never going to stop." Marissa giggles, no doubt with a bright smile plastered across her face.

Marissa and I have known each other most of our lives, but never really spent time together until she became a deputy a few years ago. The two of us are like two peas in a pod, but we've never been anything more than friends. Her petite frame, dirty blonde hair, and bubbly personality would bring most men to their knees, but there was never any spark between us. Probably because my heart belonged to her sister.

"Why is your sister sitting on the side of the road crying?"

"My sister? Sutton?"

"Unless you have another sister I wasn't aware of?"

"How the hell should I know, Colt? Here's a thought. How about you ask her?" she snaps.

"I should bring her into the station for you to deal with."

"Are you going to cuff her?" she laughs loudly, "I don't want to know about your kinky fantasies about my sister, Sheriff."

I groan internally, regretting the day I told her about my obsession with Sutton. Teach me to go drinking when I'm feeling sorry for myself. Surprisingly, she didn't have an issue with it. It seems the Flores family is not too fond of Maxwell Stanton, the soon-to-be newest member of their family tree. Marissa always said there was something about him that rubbed her the wrong way, setting her nerves on edge, but Sutton seemed happy. To their family, that was the most important thing, and if she stayed that way, everything was right as rain.

"If I had to guess, it must have something to do with the douche canoe she plans to marry," she grumbles before sighing loudly. "Just talk to her, Colt. I'll have one of the guys man the switchboard for calls, and I'll figure out what she's doing back in town."

I grunt in response before taking a deep breath, needing to regain some control before opening my mouth. There is no telling what filthy things may come tumbling out if I don't. Unable to stay away any longer, I get out and step around to the front.

"Hello, Colt." Her breathy voice caresses my skin, pulling me closer to her.

I take a step forward, but she holds up her hand, halting my movements.

"How have you been?" I question.

"Fine," she responds as she twirls her keys around her finger, a telltale sign of her nerves.

I reach up and rub the back of my neck. "Can I get at least something more than a one-word answer from you?"

"Yes," she responds as her cheeks pink in embarrassment. "I'm sorry. This is a lot harder than I imagined it'd be."

I smirk and take a step toward her. To my surprise,

she steps toward me, wrapping her arms around my waist and burying her face into my chest.

"Was it Maxwell?" I growl, sounding harsher than intended, but I need to know. "I promise, whatever he did, I'll make him pay."

"It's not your job to protect me, Colt." Sutton pulls away, wrapping her arms tightly around her waist as she stares off into the woods beside the road. "Maxwell cheated on me, so here I am."

The sorrow in her voice breaks my heart but is quickly replaced by a burning desire to destroy Maxwell Stanton.

"He did what?!" I shout, spinning her toward me.

Her eyes widen in surprise as I grip her chin, forcing her to look directly into my eyes. Her body recoils away from me, which is only natural. We haven't seen each other in years, and she has no idea of the hold she's had over me since high school.

"Tell me everything," I demand.

"I don't think that's any of your business," Sutton mumbles nervously as I hear another car coming to a stop beside us.

Fuck, of course Marissa chooses right now to show up.

"Hey sis, you alright?" Marisa eyes the two of us skeptically as I release Sutton, putting some much-needed space between us.

"Perfect." She plasters a fake smile on her face.

Marissa's head swivels back and forth between the two of us, trying to make sense of what's going on.

"How about we go home and talk?" Marissa asks her sister, pinning me in place with a stare and letting me know in no uncertain terms that I'm not invited.

"That sounds like a good idea," Sutton whispers as she strides past me.

Our shoulders brush slightly, and an electric current runs up my arm and directly to my heart, igniting the love I once had for her all over again. It's been years since we've seen each other, but in some way, it feels like Sutton never left. She may have a life hours away from here, but there has always been something between the two of us. This is my chance to tell Sutton how I feel before it's too late.

"It was nice seeing you," Sutton calls over her shoulder before climbing into the passenger seat of her sister's car.

"I'll call a tow truck and have someone at the garage take a look at her car."

"Thanks Sheriff." Marissa winks before ducking back into her car.

Standing as still as a statue, I watch as they pull back onto the road and drive off toward their parents' house without a second glance.

I tried to move on, to be with someone, anyone else, before admitting to myself: There's no one else on the planet that I'll ever love more than Sutton Flores.

"You got away from me once, Sutton. I'm not about

to let it happen again," I whisper into the wind as I stride toward my SUV.

She may have another man's ring on her finger, but he was dumb enough to let her slip through his. Now's my chance to let her know that I've loved her for years, and I'll do everything in my power to make sure Sutton doesn't leave Magnolia again without being mine.

By any means necessary.

three

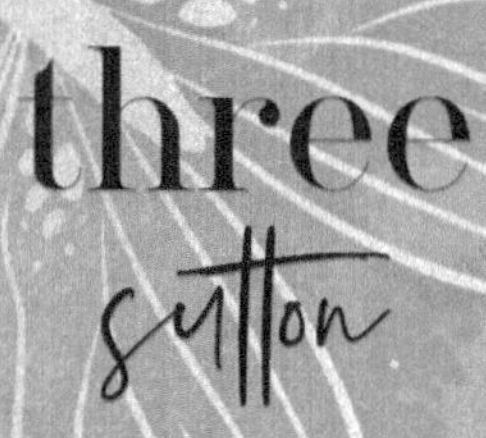

"I thought we were going home," I mumble, my eyes cast out the window. "That suspiciously looks like Tallywackers."

Marissa hasn't said one word to me since I got into the car, which is both a blessing and a curse. The last thing I want to do is explain to her why I was sitting on the side of the road with nothing but my car keys. More importantly, I don't know how to explain whatever that was between Colt and me. Just being near him for a few minutes and I'm back to the nerdy, overweight girl, hiding out in the library, wishing her crush would ask her to prom. In case it wasn't clear, Colt Butler was that for me.

"You and I both know if we went to Mom and Dad's right now, you'd get the third degree." Marissa reaches over, giving my shoulder a squeeze. "A few drinks are in order before we open that can of worms."

"Aren't you on duty? I'm sure there's a rule somewhere about not drinking while on the job."

"Who said anything about me drinking?" She pulls

the car to a stop in front of the only bar in town before turning it off and giving me her undivided attention.

"You should be ashamed to be seen with me." I chuckle humorously. "The first time anyone in town is seeing me in years and I look like this?"

I motion my hands down my body before checking my reflection in the visor mirror. There are streaks of black down my cheeks from crying almost the entire drive. My hair is a mess, and I'm not even 100 percent sure I have a bra on. Definitely not how I expected to see everyone for the first time.

"Whose fault is that?" she scoffs before throwing open the door. "If you came home more often, people would be used to you looking like a hot mess."

"Bitch," I grumble under my breath before pulling the collar of my shirt out to confirm the fact I am wearing a bra and climbing out of the car.

Tallywackers has been in Magnolia since before my parents were married, and it still looks the same. Housed in an old brothel, it lives up to its name, hosting burlesque and drag shows whenever possible. It's a place to see and be seen in Magnolia, making it the last place I want to walk into right now.

"As I live and breathe. Sutton Flores," someone shouts through the bar, alerting everyone to Marissa's and my entrance.

"Asshole," I mumble under my breath before plastering a fake smile on my face as my eyes widen in surprise. "Finn?"

Gone is the shy, skinny boy I sat next to in math class, replaced by a man who has the attention of every woman in here. His once-shaggy dark-brown hair is now cut stylishly, making him look even more handsome. A muscular frame fills out his tightly fitted black shirt, completely different from the boy who could barely do pull-ups in gym class.

"Oh my God, how have you been?" I smile before reaching over the bar and pulling him in for a tight hug. "I didn't even recognize you."

"I get that a lot." He chuckles, returning my hug before taking a step back, and his eyes immediately focus on Marissa. "And I've been all right. How's the city treating you?"

"Not as well as I'd expected." I sniffle as Marissa and I slide onto two empty bar stools.

"What can I getcha?" he asks, quickly changing the subject.

"Bottle of Jack. One glass." Marissa answers without hesitation, pinning Finn in place with her stare. "I don't have the patience for your crap today, Buckley."

"Did someone get up on the wrong side of the bed?" Finn responds in a sing-song voice before leaning forward and whispering something into her ear.

Her entire face pinks as she leans back, her hand going directly toward her gun. "I will fucking shoot you, Finn."

He raises his hands in the air before giving her a quick

wink and heading toward the other end of the bar to get our order.

"When did you become such a sourpuss, Marissa?" I giggle, turning toward her and resting my chin on my hand.

She's probably one of the most easygoing people I've ever met. When we were kids, she wouldn't hurt a fly and never had a bad thing to say to anyone. A typical ray of sunshine is what my dad used to call her, so seeing her acting like this with Finn... there has to be more to the story.

"The same time I slept with Finn Buckley."

"You did what?!" I screech as Finn places a glass and a rather large bottle of Jack Daniels down in front of us before leaving to take care of another customer.

Marissa's eyes track his movements, watching everything he's doing as he speaks to someone at the other end of the bar. I highly doubt anyone would watch someone they hate as much as she pretends to hate Finn.

"You drink. I'll talk," Marissa grumbles, filling the small glass to the brim and shoving it in my direction.

I throw the glass back, welcoming the burn of the amber-colored liquid as it settles in my stomach. "Spill."

Marissa sighs loudly before refilling my glass. "Let's call it a moment of drunken weakness. I felt sorry for myself one night and came to the bar to drown my sorrows. Finn and I got to talking, and one thing led to another..."

"And?"

Marissa nods her head toward the full glass. "Drink."

Rolling my eyes, I grab it and take a large gulp, almost finishing it before placing it on the bar in front of me. "And?"

"And nothing. I woke up the next morning and high-tailed it out of his place like my ass was on fire."

Marissa and I haven't been close since I left for college. Unlike me, she stayed close to home, going to the state college a few hours outside of our little town before joining the sheriff's department. But this is next level. The last thing I expected to hear was that she had a one-night stand, let alone with Finn.

Marissa and Finn are like oil and water. The last two people I thought would get together. I always believed he had a thing for her—the way he'd look at her, practically hanging on every word out of her mouth—but he never said a word. Marissa was the queen of the roost, the popular girl everyone wanted to be, the exact opposite of Finn and me. When I went off to college, I always wondered if he'd make his move and let her know how he felt about her.

"And now, he won't leave me alone," Marissa growls, filling my glass to the brim once again.

"Was it at least good?"

Of course, this is the first question I ask when I find out my sister and one of my old friends slept together, but it's an important one. Not that I don't already know the answer. There's no way she'd be putting up with any of this if it wasn't good. For some strange reason, she's fighting it.

"The best." Her cheeks pink, and a soft smile crosses her face. "Too bad every time we run into each other, I can't decide if I want to shoot him, arrest him, or fuck him again."

"I'm game. Just not in that order. There are laws against that type of thing," Finn says over his shoulder, winking at us before disappearing into the back.

"You're in so much trouble." I giggle, a warm tingle settling over my entire body as I grab my glass and take another healthy pull.

Marissa snickers softly. "Why are you here?"

Damn, she doesn't waste any time getting to the heart of the matter. I throw back the rest of my glass before slamming it down on the bar. "Maxwell cheated on me."

"Okay," Marissa deadpans, and my mouth drops.

"Okay? Okay. Okay!" My voice continues to get louder and louder as I repeat my sister's response.

"He cheated on me with some bimbo on my 800-thread count sheets!" I screech, grabbing the Jack Daniels bottle and throwing it back like I don't have a care in the world.

"So, what now?"

"I don't know," I cry as the dam breaks. Burying my face in my hands, I drop my head onto the bar and sob loudly, all the fight leaving my body.

I've known things have been off with Maxwell and me since before we even got engaged. If I'm being honest,

I was planning to break up with him when he proposed. But I never thought he'd do something like this. He used to look at me like I hung the moon, but something must have changed. Maybe we grew apart. I've been working a lot on trying to get my new line up and running and have been a little distant, but I never expected this to happen.

"Do you even love him or just the idea of him?"

The fuck did she just say?

"Of course, I promised to marry him."

"That's not the same thing, Sutton. I hate to break it to you..." Marissa wraps her arm over my shoulder, pulling me tightly to her side. "At no point in time have you said anything about loving him or not knowing how to live without him. The only thing you've been wailing about is your sheets."

I cock my head to the side and really think about what Marissa said. Maybe at one time, I was in love with Maxwell, but if I'm being completely honest with myself, over the last few months, things have changed. We used to spend every waking minute together. I couldn't wait to finish up in my studio for the day, wanting to get home to spend time with him. But now, I spend more hours away from Maxwell than I do with him, and deep down, I'm okay with that.

"Is everything okay here?" Finn's voice jars me out of my thoughts.

I turn toward him and frown. "No. Not at all."

"And why's that?" He chuckles.

"Her fiancé cheated on her."

"On my 800-thread count sheets!" I wail, causing my sister to laugh loudly.

"Is that the only thing you care about?" she responds before shaking her head at me. "Face it, you don't love him. Maybe you never did. You just loved the idea of being with him."

Shit. I'll never admit it to her, but she's right. At some point, the idea of having the life I always dreamed of for myself became enough. I stopped caring that Maxwell no longer made my heart skip a beat or gave me butterflies in the pit of my stomach. He became a box to check off my list. One more thing people made me believe I'd never have.

"I don't understand why you're so upset. He sounds like a piece of shit for cheating on you." The deep timbre of Finn's voice brings me back to the present.

"You wouldn't understand, Finn. You think with the brain between your legs and not the one between your ears."

Finn chuckles humorously. "Trust me, if I thought with that brain all the time, I'd have your sister bent over the bar right now instead of helping you with your life problems."

"Finn!" Marissa and I shout at the same time before I break out into a fit of loud laughter.

"I really am tempted to shoot you," Marissa grumbles before grabbing my glass and throwing back the last little bit.

"Tease." Finn winks at her, his attention focused on

something over our heads. "I've always had a thing for handcuffs."

"Oh my God! Do you ever quit?" I cackle loudly, my current troubles almost forgotten.

"Not when it comes to your sister." Finn leans forward, resting his elbows on the bar. His eyes remain focused on Marissa the entire time. "Now that you're home, how about putting in a good word for me with this one? I need all the help I can get."

"I got your back!" I shout, meaning to whisper. "Finn's a good guy, sister. Besides, you already know he's good in bed. Why not go another round?"

"She said I'm good in bed?" Finn perks up, a sly smile crossing his face.

"I said no such thing," Marissa growls before slamming something onto the bar. "I need to get back to work."

"On the house. Consider them a welcome home present for little Ms. Sutton." Finn gives her a mock salute. "I'm sure I'll be seeing you ladies around."

"You need to be nicer to him."

"You need to mind your business."

"You need to..." my voice trails off as I try to think of another witty comeback, but my mind goes blank.

Marissa and I stare at each other for a few minutes before she sighs loudly. "Look, Sutton. I have to go back to work, and I can't leave you here like this."

"Like what? I've only had a few drinks."

"You're three sheets to the wind, sweetheart."

Suddenly, I'm picked up from behind and enveloped in the most mouth-watering scent I've ever encountered. I want to get naked and bathe in it. Let it soak into my skin so I can smell it for all eternity. Turning my head to the side, I bury my nose into the soft flesh, running my tongue along it before humming deep in the back of my throat.

"You taste good." I lean back with a smile. "I've always wanted to know what you tasted like, Sheriff."

"Good lord above." Someone groans beside me as the room spins, causing me to stumble forward.

A pair of strong arms wrap around me, before lifting me into the air and throwing me over his shoulder like a sack of potatoes. My eyes focus on the sight before me, two perfectly shaped ass cheeks pulled taut as he says something.

"I got her, Marissa. You need to head back to the station and finish your shift."

"Don't do anything I wouldn't do." She giggles before the world spins again, and I clamp my eyes tightly shut.

"Traitor," I grumble, releasing one hand and throwing the bird in the direction I believe my sister is in as Colt strides out the door.

"Now behave, Sutton, or I'm going to have to make you."

The rumble of his voice vibrates through my entire body, moisture pooling between my legs as I bring both my arms up and squeeze his ass cheeks.

"Looks just like an apple," I whisper before opening my mouth wide and taking a bite.

"Behave." He groans loudly, his entire body stiffening beneath me. "You just need to sober up, and then we can talk."

"About what?"

"About your punishment for being intoxicated in public."

"Are you going to handcuff me, Sheriff?"

I want his words to mean something different. I want him to want me. To want to punish me. Wishing that, instead of him taking me home and tucking me in, he'd take me to his place, demanding to know why I was back in town before taking me over his knee and ripping my panties from my body before smacking me hard on the ass.

I bite my lip as I imagine the mixture of pain and pleasure that would course through my body every time his large palm connects with my bare skin. My pussy would be dripping, and I'd be begging him to take me hard.

"Definitely." He nips at my lips before sliding me into the passenger seat and buckling me in.

I've completely lost my freaking mind. There's no way this is going to end well for me. Not only am I still engaged to that piece of shit, Maxwell Stanton, but Colt has never looked at me twice. The last thing on his mind is spending the night with me and living out every one of my fantasies. This isn't a fucking fairy tale.

"You let me know if you're going to be sick, and I'll pull over."

I nod my head in response, clenching my legs tightly together, attempting to cool my raging libido. Fuck, it's like I have no control over my body with him around, shifting from perfectly fine to nymphomaniac in no time. I've never had this reaction to any man, not even Maxwell, but I can't deny that there is something about Colt that feeds a part of me I didn't know existed until right this moment. A piece of me I thought I'd long buried in my past, just like Magnolia.

It's insane how badly I want this man, even though he probably isn't interested in me. I wish my libido would get the memo because the last thing I need to do is make a fool of myself after everything that's happened, even though that's exactly what I'm thinking about doing.

Maybe throwing myself at Colt isn't that bad of an idea after all. I can save myself from the embarrassment of his rejection and can claim temporary insanity. Sounds like the perfect plan.

"Time to go, Trouble." Colt winks at me before gently pulling away from the curb.

four

"Why are we here?" Sutton slaps a hand on my shoulder before pointing out the front windshield. "This isn't my parents' house."

"No. It's my place," I deadpan, turning off my truck and climbing out.

I know damn well I should've taken her back to her parents' house and let her sleep it off, but I have ulterior motives. I never made my move all those years ago because I didn't want to get in the way of her dreams, but this is my chance, and I'm going to take it. There's no way Sutton and I can have any kind of serious conversation right now, but I couldn't take the chance that she'd disappear again before we talked.

With her at my house, I can keep an eye on her. Make sure she stays hydrated and can gets some rest, while hopefully, not getting a wicked hangover. Then I can make her breakfast, and we can talk. I can tell her how much I've loved her and want her to give us a chance. If she turns me down, I can finally let her go and move on.

Who the fuck am I kidding? I've been pining after Sutton since high school. Even if she rejects me, nothing will change. I decided a long time ago there was no one else in this world for me but Sutton, and I refused to settle for anyone else but her. I had every intention of spending the rest of my life in Magnolia, content with watching over the town and making it safe for people to raise their families. But the moment Sutton said her fiancé was dumb enough to cheat on her, all bets were off.

"Nice place," she muses as I open the car door and offer her my arm. "I can do it myself."

"I'm sure you can, Trouble. But it's okay to let someone help you occasionally," I grumble, threading my arms beneath her knees and lifting her in the air. I pull her body tight against my chest and bury my nose in her hair.

"My knight in shining armor." She giggles, wrapping her arms around my neck as I stride toward the front door.

"Back right pocket." My jaw clenches tightly, the muscles twitching as I fight to maintain control.

I want to mold my body with hers, grinding my cock into her pussy lips and pressing her flush against my front door, letting every fucker who walks by know who she belongs to, but I can't. Not like this.

"What?"

"The keys to the door are in my back right pocket. If you don't want to sleep in my truck, you need to get the key."

She pulls herself tighter to my chest, and we both moan loudly; the swell of her ass meets my rock-hard cock.

"I'm sorry," I growl, trying as hard as I can to keep myself still, not wanting to torture either of us as she squirms in my arms.

"Nothing to be sorry about." She whimpers. "I need you to put me down so I can reach."

Lowering her feet to the floor, I try to take a step back, but she follows me. Her tiny arms slide around my waist, and her hand goes right into my back pocket and grips the keys.

"I could've gotten them myself."

"I know," she whispers, gripping my ass tightly in her hands before pulling the keys free from my pocket and dangling them in the air between us.

"Unlock the door."

Sutton giggles softly before spinning around and unlocking the door quickly and striding inside.

"Jesus H. Christ," I mumble, grabbing my dick through my pants, trying to relieve some of the pressure.

Taking a deep breath, I try thinking of anything and everything I can to get rid of the images of Sutton on her knees as I fuck her mouth. After a few minutes of disturbing images filtering through my mind, I feel comfortable walking into the house.

My eyes widen in surprise as I take in what's happening in front of me. Instead of walking in and passing out on the couch like I assumed she would,

Sutton poured herself a large glass of Jack, throwing it back quickly, before turning her attention to me.

"You've got to be fucking kidding me," I growl, storming towards her.

I can't explain why there is still this magnetic pull I feel toward Sutton, and if I'm being honest, I don't want to. Marissa has driven me to the point of madness with all the stories about the amazing time Sutton was having with her fiancé and how she was living her life to the fullest in the city. And now, with her behaving so recklessly, it makes my blood boil, and all I want to do is put her over my knee and turn her ass red.

"Do you want one?" Sutton says, crossing her arms under her chest and lifting her tits slightly.

My mouth waters as the thought of taking one in my mouth fills my mind.

Get it together, Colt. She's drunk and not thinking clearly.

"No, and I don't think you need any more, either." I smirk, grabbing the glass from her hand. "I think it's time for you to get some rest."

"I'm not a child, you know," she says under her breath.

"Then stop acting like one, or I'll take you over my knee and show you what happens to little girls who don't listen," I growl without a second thought, my cock hardening further behind the zipper of my uniform pants.

I'm trying desperately to fight this pull I feel toward Sutton, but she isn't making it easy. The more she pushes me to the edge, the harder it is to resist her. She's like a siren, calling me to my destruction, pushing me to the limits of my control, and I have no choice but to go tumbling over the edge.

"You wouldn't dare." She tilts her chin up in defiance, and her breathing increases as she backs away from me.

"Try me." I chuckle as I stride toward her, matching each one of her steps with my own as we inch closer to the wall.

"You can't be serious." Her eyes widen in surprise as her back hits the wall, halting her movements.

"I'm very serious, Trouble." I pin her in place with my body and grind my cock into her belly as I lean down, whispering in her ear. "Bad girls need to be punished."

"What do good girls get?" Sutton's entire body locks up as bone-chilling fear rushes through my body. I should tone this down, but I don't know if I can. My need for her goes beyond something physical. It's as if my soul is calling out to her, begging her to be mine and only mine.

I bury my nose in her hair, committing her scent to memory as I send up a silent prayer that this isn't the last time I'll be this close to her.

"I'm sorry. I shouldn't have said any of those things." I pull back and look her in the eye.

"Colt," she whispers, molding her body to mine as she wraps her arms around my neck.

Her eyes never leave mine as she presses her lips gently to mine. Pleasure shoots through my veins as I wrap my hand around her waist, pulling her closer. I pull back, looking directly into her eyes, searching for permission before crushing my lips to hers again. She gasps in shock as I slide my tongue into her mouth, massaging it with mine. Sutton sighs softly, melting into my arms as she surrenders to me, giving me the only thing I've wanted since I watched her drive out of town all those years ago.

We break apart, gasping for air, and I take a step back. "I'm sorry. I shouldn't have done..."

"Don't you fucking dare," Sutton growls, pulling my head down to meet her lips again.

I clench my lips tight, not wanting to give in to my desire for a second time.

"Sutton, we can't," I whisper as she nibbles along my bottom lip and pulls it between her lips.

"Yes, we can." She groans as she leans back, indecision swirling in her eyes. "Unless you don't want me."

"Don't be ridiculous." I step backward, dropping my arms to my sides.

How do I explain to the most beautiful woman I've ever encountered that there's nothing I'd love more than burying my dick inside her, claiming her as my own? But I want her to remember what happens between us. For her to be 100 percent certain this is what she wants. Besides, she just found out her fiancé cheated on her. I want more from Sutton than a rebound fuck. I want forever.

"It's not that." I rub the back of my neck, leaning against the bar.

"Then what is it, Colt?" Sutton steps closer, threading her hand through the tiny hairs at the base of my neck. "I know what I want, and that's you."

"You're drunk."

I'm grasping at straws, searching for any excuse my body will accept, when all I want to do is fuck her right here against the wall.

"I may have been drinking, but I'm not drunk. I know what I'm doing, Colt. I just needed a bit of liquid courage." Her hand slides between us, gripping my shaft tightly through my pants. "You want me. I can feel it."

I lean my head back, sending up a silent prayer for strength as her other hand slides down my chest, pinching my nipple. Hard.

"Please, Colt." She straddles my leg, grinding her pussy down on my knee as she rocks back and forth. My resolve crumbles. I won't fuck her, but I'm going to make sure she gets exactly what she wants.

I lean down and capture her mouth with mine, pouring all my want and desire into this kiss, giving into that part of myself that I've kept locked away for so long. Reality and deep-buried desires collide in my head, making the world spin. I want everything right this second, to show her what my world can give her, but I know I have to take my time and introduce her to it one step at a time.

I thread my fingers through her hair, gripping it tightly in my hand and pulling her head back, deepening the kiss. I sweep the inside of her mouth with my tongue before sucking hers deep into my mouth with a groan.

We break apart with a gasp, both of our chests heaving at the lack of oxygen.

"So, about that spanking?" Her eyes sparkle with mirth.

Sutton Flores is fucking trouble, and apparently, she wants to play. I slide my hand between our bodies, pinching her hardened nipple through her shirt.

"I warned you not to test me, and now I'm going to teach you a lesson."

Her pupils dilate, and her breathing increases as I brush my lips against the side of her face, nibbling and sucking down her throat.

"Are we going to do this the easy way or the hard way, Sutton?"

She moans loudly, threading her fingers in my hair and yanking my head back.

"The hard way." She smirks, daring me to change my mind.

But I'm not backing down. Sutton needs to know that I'm a man of my word. If she wants to misbehave, then she's going to suffer the consequences.

"I warned you," I growl as I step away from her, grabbing her arm and hoisting her over my shoulder.

"If you wanted to be rough with me, Colt, all you had to do was say so." She giggles.

I storm toward the couch, place her feet on the

ground, and spin her around so she is facing away from me.

"Bend over," I command, placing my hand on the back of her head and forcing it forward.

Her entire body stiffens as her arms fly forward, bracing herself on the back of the couch.

I raise my eyebrow, waiting for her to move, but when she doesn't, I lean in closer, pulling her earlobe into my mouth and nibbling lightly on it. "I said, bend over."

A soft moan escapes her lips as I trail light kisses down her neck, wrapping her hair around my hand and tugging slightly. Sutton drops her head back, her breasts rising and falling as her breathing comes in short gasps. We moan as the swell of her ass meets my rock-hard cock.

"I don't want a spanking," she whines as her hand slides around the base of my neck, her fingers tightening in my hair while she grinds her ass hard on my cock, rocking from side to side.

"I think you do, Trouble." I bite down on the juncture between her neck and shoulder, unable to suppress the groan bubbling from my lips, and slide my hands down her hips and beneath the waistband of her pants.

Sutton gasps as I slide my hand into her panties, circling her clit with two of my fingers. "Your cunt is dripping wet for me."

Slipping my fingers between her lower lips, I ease them in slowly before dragging them out.

"Please," she begs, widening her stance so I can slide deeper into her channel.

Instead of giving her what she wants, I pull my hand free and shove my fingers into my mouth, licking them both clean. "Bend over."

She whimpers, trying to step away from me, but I grip her hips, holding her in place.

"You have two choices, Trouble. Either bend over and take your punishment like a good girl or you can head up the stairs to bed, and I won't lay a finger on you again."

"Are you kidding me?!" she shouts before slapping both of her hands over her mouth.

"No, I'm not." I tug her hips slightly, causing her to lose her balance and fall forward.

"Will it hurt?" she whispers over her shoulder, her hands gripping the pillows on the back of the couch tightly.

"Yes," I say as her entire body tenses. "That's the only way you'll ever learn your lesson."

My heart pounds out of my chest, waiting for her to respond. I told Sutton I'd put her to bed and never touch her again, but I know in my heart that's a lie. Now that I've tasted her, there is no going back.

"Okay," she whispers before bending over the back of the couch, sticking her ass up in the air.

I bite back a groan as I run my hand over her luscious round ass before giving it two quick but sharp blows. My cock hardens at just the thought of turning her bottom red.

"Someone is excited." Sutton pushes her ass into my growing bulge to distract me.

"Teasing me will only mean more punishment for you." I punctuate my statement with another smack.

"Fuck, that hurt," she groans, bucking off the back of the couch.

"That's the point of the punishment. To remind you I'm the one in charge." I use my other hand to hold her in place as my hand comes down on her ass in quick succession.

Smack. Smack. Smack.

"You should thank me, Trouble. Usually, I'd have you bare, and I'd be turning your ass red with each smack."

Smack.

Sutton wiggles in place, lifting her ass to meet my hand. "You like that, don't you, Trouble? Your cunt is begging for me to fuck you while bent over this couch."

"I need more, Colt. I need you. All of you," she moans as she looks over her shoulder, her eyes begging me to help her go over the edge.

"Lift your hips."

She wastes no time following my instruction as I pull her pants down to her knees and slide her panties to the side.

"So fucking wet," I whisper as her juices drip from inside her.

I quickly plunge one finger in and out, and each time, her pussy grips my finger tighter.

"Oh, God. I need more," she moans loudly, pushing up toward my hand to get more friction, but I pull back.

"You want that, don't you, baby?"

She moans loudly as I slide my fingers between her folds, slipping just the tip inside before thrusting two fingers into her, curling them slightly and finding that tiny bundle of nerves.

"I'm gonna come!" she screams, her voice echoing off the walls as I pump faster. Her walls tighten around my fingers as she tumbles over the edge.

I pull my fingers from her pussy and shove them into my mouth, licking them clean.

"Time for Princess Sophia to come out and play," she grumbles as her entire body sags into the couch.

"Not exactly what I expected you to call my penis." I chuckle, striding toward the kitchen for a clean towel and two bottles of water.

She doesn't move a muscle as I gently wipe her clean, tossing the cloth onto the floor beside us and striding around the couch. I can't help but chuckle at the sight before me. Her ass is still straight up in the air over the couch, turned a delicious shade of pink from her punishment, but she is fast asleep.

"This is going to be awkward," I say into the empty room as I get to work, maneuvering her body into position so I can lift her into my arms and carry her to bed. It takes a few minutes, but I get her tucked safely in my arms before heading upstairs.

"I can walk," she mumbles as her eyes shoot open and her arms tighten around my neck.

"But you don't have to." I plant a kiss on her forehead and carry her into my bedroom, pulling back the covers and laying her gently on the bed. "Rest, Trouble. Let's just hope you remember this in the morning."

"Oh, there's no way I'm going to forget the best orgasm of my life," she whispers, licking her lips as she rubs her hand along my hardened length. "What about you?"

I grab her hand, squeezing it gently before placing it back on the bed.

"You've had a long day and need your rest." I kiss her forehead for the second time before pulling the covers over her.

"Is it because I'm still engaged?" She rolls over, putting her back toward me.

I walk around the bed, kneeling at eye level with her. "As far as I'm concerned, you're not engaged, but you have drunk your weight in Jack Daniels. When I finally make you mine, I want to make sure you remember it."

"Promise?" she whispers as I brush a few strands of hair from her face, tucking it behind her ear.

"Promise. Now go to sleep before I change my mind."

"Thank you, Colt."

"Anything for you, Trouble. Anything," I whisper into the darkened room as I pull the door shut behind me.

Now that I've had a taste of Sutton, there is no going back. I've tried to keep my distance, admiring her from afar, but no more. Now that I know she feels something for me, I'm never letting her go.

I make quick work of locking up the house before grabbing an extra blanket out of the closet and slipping back into the bedroom, then quickly strip down to my boxers and climb into bed. As I wrap my arms around Sutton and pull her close to me, my eyes close and I release a contented sigh. It feels like I can finally breathe for the first time in years, and it's all because of Sutton sleeping peacefully in my arms.

five

I'm a chickenshit. I've been hiding in Colt's bedroom for the last couple of hours, trying to make sense of everything that has happened over the last twenty-four hours.

I'm engaged to a lying, cheating sack of shit, then realized I don't love him anymore, and I am now sleeping in the bed of my high school crush after he gave me a mind-blowing orgasm and I passed out. How in the hell did I get here? Jack Daniels and my sister, Marissa, that's how. Although I'd love nothing more than to blame her for the predicament I currently find myself in, this is all on me.

Ever since Colt pulled up behind my car on the side of the road, nothing has been the same. Until that moment, I hadn't thought about Colt or my feelings for him since high school. I was engaged to someone I believed was the perfect man, but the moment I walked in on Maxwell going at with that hussy on my brand new 800-thread count sheets, everything changed.

Fuck! I really can't let go of those fucking sheets, can I?

It should've been a dead giveaway that I was more upset about my sheets than I was about him cheating on me. Deep down, I know the reason I got upset wasn't because I was in love with him, but because I was mourning the perfect life I thought we'd have together. Checking off a box on a long list of items I wanted to have in my life. And now, this thing with Colt is insane and overwhelming, but I really think I found the other half of my soul.

The only problem is, I need to talk to Maxwell and tell him it's over. I never planned on stirring up all these old feelings for Colt that I was too afraid to act on in high school. I planned to figure out what I wanted to do with the rest of my life and where I was going to go from here. I had planned on being married in a few months, not finding myself head over heels in love with my high school crush.

The worst part is, I spent so much time checking my phone, hoping for a call from Maxwell. I wanted him to call with his excuses, begging me to forgive him for what he'd done, making him the bad guy in this situation, not me, but nothing. It's been almost twenty-four hours since I went running from the house, and he hasn't even sent so much as a text asking where I was. Nothing.

"Everything is going to be okay," I whisper into the empty room, knowing the statement to be true. "I just need to put on my big girl panties and go downstairs."

"Are you planning on hiding up here all day, Trouble?"

Colt's voice brings me back to the present, and I jump slightly.

"I didn't mean to scare you." He chuckles softly as he leans forward, brushing a strand of hair from my face.

I lick my lips, my eyes flicking toward his lips before moving back up his face and meeting his gaze. I want him to kiss me, to quench the burning desire coursing through my entire body.

Every touch of his hand against me drives me closer and closer to the edge. Every nerve ending in my body is on fire, waiting for the next caress or the feel of his breath as it washes over my skin. I want him—no, I need him. Right at this moment, I know that if I can't get control over my libido, I could ruin everything, but I don't think I care.

It's crazy to say, but I'm falling in love with Colt. I know I have another man's ring on my finger, but these feelings coursing through me can't be wrong. Colt is the person I was meant to be with, and my need to escape this small town and find something more to life got in the way. But I made that mistake once, and I don't plan on making it again. The more time I spend with Colt Butler, the more I want him to be mine.

"Just hung over," I whisper as I shift slightly, trying to calm the ache between my legs. "I'm really sorry that I took over your bed last night."

"You didn't." Colt grasps my chin between his fingers and turns me toward him, his eyes focusing on my lips before meeting mine. "I spent the entire night wrapped around your body, fighting the urge to strip you bare and bury my cock in your pussy."

"You did?" I lick my lips in anticipation, wanting him to lean in closer and claim my lips for his own.

My eyes slide shut as his lips brush against mine, but the moment is ruined as an image of Maxwell flashes in my mind.

"We can't," I gasp, both of my hands coming between us and pushing against his chest. "Not yet."

I feel like shit for doing the same thing to Maxwell as he did to me, but there's nothing left between us. But I need to at officially end things with him before going any further with Colt.

I throw my legs over the side of the bed and push to my feet, attempting to put some space between us, but he grips my elbow tightly, pulling me back on the bed and into his arms.

"Please let me go!" I protest as I try to stand up again, but he wraps his arm around my waist.

"No, I won't let you go," he growls into my ear as he nips at my earlobe, caressing the edge with the tip of his tongue.

I shiver slightly as I feel his cock harden beneath me, showing his desire for me in a very physical way.

"I don't care about the ring on your finger. You're mine."

My heart races—no, gallops—in my chest, yearning to feel his calloused fingers against my skin as he claims me as his own, ruining me for any other man who dares to lay his hands on me.

"But Maxwell…" I mumble, dropping my head onto his shoulder and squeezing my eyes shut.

"Is the dumb motherfucker that cheated on you. He didn't realize you're the most precious thing in the world. You're meant to be loved, cherished, and pampered. Not thrown to the wayside for some piece of ass."

His thumb swipes across my cheeks as I stare into his eyes, committing this moment to memory.

"I want you. I always have," he whispers against my lips before pulling back slightly.

My mind and body are at war with each other as the magnitude of his words sink in.

"Forget about everything but right now." He presses his lips against mine more forcefully. "You deserve to be happy just like everyone else in this world, Sutton."

"Colt," I groan, clinging to my last thread of control.

He leans forward, nibbling on my earlobe before whispering into my ear. "Let me love you, Sutton. Please."

Unable to find words to respond, I nod before our lips connect. My entire body tingles as he presses his lips against mine, timidly at first, increasing the pressure with each pass. I've been kissed before, but it never felt like this. It feels as if my body is on fire, and the need to be closer to Colt is almost too much to bear.

"More," I moan as I sweep my tongue against his bottom lip.

He groans, pulling me tighter into him as he takes control and claims my mouth again with a hungry and intense need that I've never felt before. I slide my hands into his hair, tugging gently on the silky strands to ground myself.

I feel the fabric of my shirt against my skin as he untucks it from my waistband, his fingers gliding across my skin. I gasp as a combination of pain and pleasure ignites through my veins when Colt rubs my hardened nipple through my bra, pinching it between two fingers.

I want—no, I need—more. I need to feel his lips caressing every part of me, claiming me in a way that only he can.

The shrill ring of a phone from across the room breaks the spell. My cheeks flush from embarrassment as we break apart, our chests rising and falling rapidly as we fight to regain our composure.

"I should probably get that..." Colt brushes his lips against my forehead before resting his head against mine. "I've wanted to make you mine since the moment you told me Maxwell cheated on you. If I'm being honest, I've wanted you since high school." He pulls back slightly before leaning down and staring into my eyes. "It's always been you. I knew it then, and I can tell you now. You, Sutton Flores, are the only woman I have ever and will ever love. You're it for me."

My entire body recoils from his embrace, pushing back against his arms, but he pulls me toward him, unwilling to let me escape. I never imagined that Colt

Butler, one of the most popular boys in high school, captain of the football team, and my high school crush, had spent years pining for me.

The phone rings loudly for a second time, making us both laugh.

"I'm going to find out who that is, and then we can pick things up where we left off." Colt groans as I slide out of his lap.

"I'll be here." I give him a mock salute as he strides out the door before collapsing onto the bed.

My cheeks are flushed, and my lips are swollen. My fingers brush against them as I remember the feel of his lips against mine. I pull my bottom lip into my mouth, trying to make sense of everything. Colt promised me forever. I can see all of it in my mind. Getting married right here in town, both our families and everyone we care about waiting for me to walk down the aisle and pledge my life to him.

Hold the fucking train... marriage? I giggle slightly but know deep in my heart that is the exact future I want with Colt. I thought I knew what love was, but the feelings I once had for Maxwell pale in comparison to the pain ripping through my body at the thought of living the rest of my life without Colt.

"Now, where were we?" Colt growls as his lips crash into my mine, nibbling on my bottom lip until I open slightly, giving him entrance.

"Who was on the phone?" I moan without thinking

as he nips at the flesh below my ear and steps away, leaving me aching with need.

"Your sister." He looks so calm as he leans back, my fingers playing with the hairs at the base of his neck. "She's on her way over here with Maxwell."

"She what?!" I screech, both of my hands coming between us and pushing against his chest. "They're both coming here?"

Before I can even process all the information, the doorbell rings. Looks like I don't have to wait any longer to give Maxwell a piece of my mind. I scurry down the stairs, trying to think of exactly what I want to say, letting my anger fester even further before unlocking the door and flinging it open.

"Morning, sister of mine," Marissa chirps, a shit-eating grin plastered across her face. "You have exactly five seconds to tell me everything that happened last night."

"And you have exactly three to tell me why Maxwell is here." I cross my arms over my chest as Colt steps up behind me, wrapping his arms tightly around my waist.

"He came to the police station looking for you. It seems you never told him anything about your family other than you lived in Magnolia."

"I was getting to it..." My voice trails off as I duck my head in embarrassment.

Add this to the long list of signs that things were not as good as I thought they were between Maxwell and me. Other than meeting my parents once after we got engaged, I never shared information about my past with him besides the fact that I had two parents who loved me and a younger sister who was a deputy in my hometown. That's probably the reason he went to the station, hoping Marissa would have news of my whereabouts.

"No matter. He also hasn't said one word about why you came back home with nothing but your car keys."

"Obviously." I roll my eyes as Colt leans down and plants a kiss on the top of my head.

"I can arrest him if you want." He growls as the sound of someone coming up the driveway reaches our ears.

"No, I have to do this on my own." I step out of his embrace before turning around and brushing my lips against his. "Then we can live happily ever after."

Marissa makes a loud gagging noise "You two are disgusting. PS I brought your car from the garage. Next time you plan on running away from home, check to make sure you have a full tank of gas."

"I'm an idiot."

"Among other things," Marissa giggles before pulling me in for a big hug. "I'll keep Colt inside with me while you talk to Max."

Marissa gives me a sympathetic smile before hooking her arm through Colt's and pulling him toward the couch. Pulling the door shut behind me, I focus my attention on Maxwell as he climbs out of the car, and I see nothing of the man I fell in love with. All I see now is a cheating asshole who has come back here to save face, wanting to keep his little indiscretion hidden from the world, which I'd be happy to do if he leaves me alone.

"We're through!" I shout as he comes to a stop right in front of me.

"I came to bring you home," he states as if it's already a done deal. I'm beyond livid but for an entirely different reason.

"Home? You mean the home I saw you fucking that bimbo in?" I ball my hands into fists by my sides. My nails dig into my hands to the point I'm sure they will bleed at any moment. "No wonder you pushed me to keep my apartment."

"What do you want? An apology? I'm sorry. You were supposed to be in the studio until dinner. How was I supposed to know you'd show up randomly?" Maxwell reaches out to grab my hand, but I snatch it back before he can touch me. Without a second thought, I pull my arm back and send it flying. A loud smack rings out across the lawn.

"Who the hell do you think you are?" I growl, pulling my hand back to smack him a second time, but he catches it. His large hands squeeze so hard I'm sure I'll have a bruise.

"Little girl, I did not waste almost two years of my life with you to lose out on what I want now. You can either get your things willingly or I can drag you, your choice."

I pull my arm from his grasp, rubbing the skin on my wrist as pain radiates up my arm. "What is it you want?"

"I want a wife that looks good on paper. I can't marry

just anyone, or my parents would have a fit. They've been nagging me for years to settle down and give them grandchildren. Who better to do that with than a small town nobody like you." He sneers before adjusting the lapels of his jacket. "It's not my fault you opened your legs for the first person who wanted you. What did you expect? You should be thanking me for pretending to love you when no one else would."

I sink down onto the ground, tears suddenly falling down my face. I hear the door fling open and know that Colt is rushing to my side. He scoops me up, cradling me in his arms as he mumbles soothing words while stroking his hand up and down my back.

colt

"I don't know who you think you are, but don't you dare put your hand on what's mine. The next time you try, you'll be leaving here in a body bag,"

The minute I saw Sutton crumble to the ground, I saw red, flying out the door and to her side.

"Don't you dare speak about her that way again," I growl through clenched teeth. "If you were half the man you think you are, she'd never have come looking for me."

"Go home, Maxwell. We're done." Sutton's voice breaks me from my rage-filled haze as she shimmies out of my lap.

Maxwell sneers at her as she climbs to her feet,

brushing herself off, and I quickly follow. "I see you went looking for the first man who'd want your fat ass."

"I'm going to end you," I growl, storming toward him.

Sutton grabs my arm, halting me in my tracks.

"Please," she begs. "He isn't worth the prison sentence."

"I doubt orange is either of your colors," Maxwell sneers.

Sutton's eyes widen slightly before she releases my arm and steps around me. She strides directly toward him, pulling her arm back and socking him in the face.

"You fucking bitch!" he screams as blood begins pouring from his nose. "You broke my nose."

Damn. Remind me never to piss her off.

"Good, but I can't say it's an improvement. You aren't worthy enough to breathe the same air as Colt, let alone utter his name!" Sutton screeches as she lunges toward him again.

This time, it's my turn to stop her.

"Calm down, Trouble," I whisper into her ear before kissing the side of her head. "I really don't want to have to arrest you. Although, seeing you in handcuffs does sound rather kinky."

She sags in my arms, all the fight draining out of her as Marissa comes strolling out my front door without a care in the world.

"Should we take a trip down to the station, Maxwell? Though I'm sure you would prefer not to have to explain to your family lawyer why you're in need of his services."

"Fuck you, bitch," he spits at Marissa as she comes to a stop directly in front of him, her cuffs twirling around her fingers.

"Do us all a favor and leave. You got whatever it is you came for," she spits at him.

"You were one good doormat." Maxwell pulls a hand-kerchief from his pocket and brushes it across his bloody nose before standing up straight and adjusting his suit jacket.

I step around Sutton, ready to tear him limb from limb, consequences be damned. He is not going to get away with treating her like that. Not on my watch. Maxwell steps back, tripping over his own two feet before landing flat on his ass.

"I'll end you," I growl as I continue to prowl toward him like a lion ready to devour its prey.

Sutton slides between us again, cupping my cheeks in her hands. "I'd really like for you to take me inside and bend me over the back of the couch again."

The rage that was coursing through my veins is replaced with a burning desire. The strength that Sutton has shown in the last few moments is astounding. Without breaking contact with me, she addresses Maxwell.

"You wanted to save face, right? I'm sure that's why you came here in the first place."

"Of course I did. No one leaves a Stanton."

A sinister smile crosses Sutton's face as she puts the final nail in Maxwell's coffin. "And if you keep running your mouth, my sister will make sure everyone in the world hears what a piece of shit you are."

The smug look on Maxwell's face disappears as we all turn our attention toward Marissa, her cell phone pointed in our direction "Surprise! You're on candid camera."

"I wish I'd never met you," he snarls.

"The feeling is mutual. Now, please leave before I let the sheriff arrest you for assault and trespassing."

I wrap my arms around her waist, pulling her close, letting her know that I'm with her 100 percent. Maxwell turns and storms toward his car. Our eyes follow him as he speeds down my driveway.

"That was sexy as fuck," I growl as I nibble my way down her neck.

"I'm not engaged anymore," she moans as her head tips back giving me access to the sensitive skin below her ear.

"You're not." I pull back, seeing nothing but adoration—and, dare I say, love—shining in her eyes.

"Nope." Sutton giggles softly.

I nuzzle my nose into her hair and kiss the top of her head. "Move in with me?" I ask, picking her up and spinning around.

I don't give a shit how quickly this seems to anyone; Sutton means everything to me.

"That can be arranged. My parents have been begging

me to come home and visit more. Besides, I can design clothing anywhere."

Deciding to push my luck, I ask for one more thing. "Marry me?"

Sutton raises her eyebrow at me. "I just got unengaged a few minutes ago. Let's start with living together first. Then we can see what else happens."

"For now," I respond before leaning down and capturing her mouth in a searing kiss.

"And that's my cue to get the hell out of here." Marissa shoves her phone into her pocket as she strides toward Sutton's car. "I'm taking your shift at the station today, Colt. You both owe me big time."

I don't even bother to respond before lifting Sutton in the air, opening the door, and striding through.

six

"You didn't have to be so rude," I say as the door slams shut behind us. "She saved both our asses with Maxwell."

"I've waited years for this moment, so sue me if I'm a little impatient. I'm never letting you go," Colt growls as he pins me to the front door with his body, nibbling on my bottom lip until I open slightly, giving him entrance. "Are you ready?"

Not entirely sure what he's asking if I'm ready for, I nod. Colt's lips crash to mine, nipping and sucking on my bottom lip, demanding entrance. I quickly grant him access as our tongues intertwine.

The world around me ceases to exist. The only thing that registers is his body pressed against mine, his hard cock pulsing into the flesh of my stomach, and the delicious ache in my core. I need Colt in a way I've never needed another man in my life, not even Maxwell. He's ignited a fire in my soul that can only be quenched by him.

"Please," I whisper as he releases my mouth and trails kisses down my neck.

"You never need to beg me for anything. Just ask, and it's yours," Colt murmurs as he quickly grips the hem of my shirt, sliding it up my stomach. "Off."

I quickly pull it over my head and toss it to the side. My chest rises and falls as I pant, waiting for him to make his next move, but he continues to stare, his once-vibrant green eyes as black as night.

"Beautiful," he whispers.

He palms my left breast, brushing his thumb over my pebbled nipple through my lacy bra.

"So soft," he says reverently as he meets my eyes, silently asking permission to remove my bra.

I give him a small nod, arching my back. Colt makes quick work of the clasp, sliding it down my arms, and it joins my shirt on the floor. With a groan, he lowers his mouth to my chest, pulling my right nipple into his mouth and swirling his tongue around it before releasing it with a pop and moving to the other one.

I feel vulnerable and inadequate, so I attempt to cover myself, but he grabs my arms. "Never hide from me. You are perfection. There's no one else on this planet who compares to you."

He scoops me up into his arms and bounds up the stairs toward his bedroom, dropping me down onto the bed with a bounce. I stare in awe as he pops the button on his pants and slides them down his thick thighs, his gaze never leaving mine, nothing but pure desire shining through.

"Let me," I murmur.

I crawl on my hands and knees toward him like a cat in heat before reaching forward and sliding my hand inside his boxers, gripping his hard cock in my hand.

"Don't tease me," Colt growls, clutching my hair in his hand and pulling, forcing my neck up so I look directly at him.

"Off," I whisper as I rub my legs together, trying to relieve some of the ache between them, and I tug on the waist of his boxers.

He helps me ease them down his legs before he takes over, pulling them down the rest of the way and stepping out of them. I lick my lips as I collect the precum leaking from the tip and make languid strokes up and down his length. I can see Colt fighting to maintain his control, but he's losing.

I torture him for a few more minutes before rising to my knees, leaning forward and licking the bead of precum off the head, and moaning. "So delicious."

In one swift motion, I take him all the way into my mouth, hitting the back of my throat as I hear a guttural moan spring free from his lips. He uses his hand on the back of my head to guide me as he fucks my mouth. I can't resist the urge to reach down and rub the bundle of nerves between my legs through my panties, humming in pleasure as I finally get a little relief.

"Hmm, your lips look so good wrapped around my

cock," he growls as his hips rock back and forth, forcing himself deeper and deeper down my throat. "I can't wait to get between those legs and taste your pussy." He suddenly picks up the pace, pumping his hips faster. "You need to stop, baby. I'm going to come."

I refuse to release him, tightening the suction of my mouth around his cock.

"Fuuuuuuccckkkkk!" he shouts, drawing out each letter.

Hot streams of cum shoot into my mouth, and I swallow them down with pleasure. After a few languid pumps of his hips, I release him and lick him clean before leaning back on my heels with a satisfied smile on my face.

Without hesitation, Colt leans toward me, capturing my mouth with his own.

"I need you. Now," he growls against my lips as he presses my body into the mattress.

"I love you," he whispers.

I freeze. A million different feelings are running through my mind, but the most prominent one is fear. I just got out of a relationship not even ten minutes ago. Colt and I barely know anything about each other besides what we've heard from other people. It's insane how quickly things are moving between us, but deep down, it feels right.

"I'm scared," I mumble.

He takes my breast into his mouth, massaging my nipple with his tongue before releasing it with a pop.

"So am I. But isn't that only natural? I've loved you

since I was seventeen years old, but you were engaged to someone else until a few minutes ago." He looks at me reverently for a few moments before leaning down and kissing me once again.

This kiss feels different. It feels like he's trying to pour all his feelings into this connection, as if he is willing my heart to open up to him.

"You don't need to say it back, but promise me you won't run from me," he pleads. "I know, in time, you'll love me just as much as I love you."

"I love you," is the only response I can give him.

I gasp in surprise as he thrusts his tongue into my mouth, groaning loudly. I wrap my arms around his neck and pull him closer to me. Nothing but pure, unadulterated desire courses through my veins as we break apart with a gasp.

"Thank fuck," he breathes as crawls backward down the bed, shoving my pants down my hips and tossing them to the floor before gripping the waistband of my panties.

"Last chance, Trouble. If you want me to stop, tell me now."

When I don't respond, he grasps the tiny scrap of fabric and pulls, ripping my panties free. He buries his nose between my folds before shoving his tongue into my pussy. My back bows off the mattress as he takes long, languid licks, bringing me to the edge, but just when I'm about to come, he stops. I mew in protest, and he chuckles darkly.

"Such a greedy pussy. I would love nothing more than to make you come all over me, covering my face in your juices, but I need inside you as soon as possible."

He uses his hips to spread my legs wider, making room for his large form. As he brushes his cock between my lower lips, we both moan.

"I'm clean. I haven't been with anyone in years." He slowly strokes back and forth, torturing both of us with each pass.

"I haven't been with anyone but Maxwell, and it's been a while," I tell him as I wrap my legs around his waist and pull him toward me.

"I don't know how that asshole kept his hands off you." The tip of his cock slides inside me, and he grips my legs tightly, halting my movements. "Are you ready for me to make you mine?"

"Yes," I moan, no longer wanting to fight the connection between the two of us.

Colt moves slowly, increasing his pace with each thrust forward. "You're so fucking tight."

"Harder," I beg, lifting my hips in time with his thrusts. "So close."

"Give it to me, Trouble." Colt bites down on the juncture between my neck and shoulder, throwing me over the edge into oblivion.

"Fuck!" I scream, my voice cracking slightly as fireworks go off behind my eyes.

"You're so beautiful when you come." He continues to thrust harder into me, and the sounds of my juices squishing as our skin slaps together fill the room. "I can feel your pussy tightening around my cock. I want one more before I give you my cum."

"I can't."

"You will."

He pulls me up and rests me in his lap. The change in position allows him to sink deeper inside me.

"Ride me, Sutton. Take everything I have to give you," he mumbles, biting down hard on my nipple and giving me another earth-shattering orgasm.

"Fuck, yes." Colt thrusts into me a few more times before I feel him shoot his load deep inside me.

We sit there for a few moments, our breathing evening out as we come down from our orgasms. He rolls over to his side, bringing me along with him, not bothering to pull out of me.

"I love you," he whispers one more time before he drifts off to sleep.

As exhaustion takes hold, I send up a silent prayer, thanking the powers that be for everything that's happened over the last twenty-four hours. To some, being cheated on is the end of the world, but for me, it was only the beginning. Now I have found my way back to the only man who has ever truly loved me.

Thank you for reading *The One Who Changed Me*!
I hope you loved Finn and Marissa's story. If you did, or even if your didn't, I would be so grateful if you could please leave a review.

Want to know what's coming next from AJ?
Scan the QR code before to sign up for her newsletter and get exclusive content, new release and sale information.

USA Today Bestselling Author AJ Alexander has been writing romance since 2018. She loves writing small town romances with found families and all the nosey nellies that help her characters find their happily ever afters! She lives in Arizona, otherwise known as the surface of the sun, with her husband, two daughters, two cats, and a lovable golden retriever.

When she isn't writing you can find AJ reading, binging the latest true crime documentary on Netflix, or binging the latest Korean Drama or Anime that's released. AJ is a cynical hopeless romantic that believes in love at first sight, that bigger is always better, and everything should be put off for a nap.

Come find her in the wild! There's nothing she loves more than connecting with my readers.